Far
Rockaway

Far
Rockaway
CHARLIE FLETCHER

*Hodder
Children's
Books*

A division of Hachette Children's Books

For Jack and Ariadne

'...no matter where I wandered
off the chart

I still would love to find again
that lost locality

Where I might catch once more
a Sunday subway for
some Far Rockaway
of the heart.'

–Laurence Ferlinghetti, 1998
A Far Rockaway of the Heart

'There's more than one way to get to Far Rockaway: stay on the A train until it runs out of track, or change at Penn Station and go via Jamaica.'

Victor Manno, to his granddaughter.

Bad Step

1 'What we call the beginning is often the end.
And to make an end is to make a beginning.
The end is where we start from.'
T.S.Eliot, *Little Gidding*

Inwood

2 'Let your soul stand
cool and composed before a million universes.'
Walt Whitman, *Song of Myself*

Jamaica

3 'The schooners and
the merry crews are laid away to rest,
A little south of sunset in
the islands of the blest.'

John Masefield,
The Ballad of Long John Silver

Broad Channel

4 'Twilight and evening bell,
And after that the dark!
And may there be no sadness or farewell,
When I embark.'

Alfred, Lord Tennyson, *Crossing the Bar*

1

Merry Christmas

Cat Manno was crossing 55th Street head down, hoodie up and earphones cranked to 11, when the speeding fire-truck hit her.

Her parents were already on the other side of the intersection putting loose change in the charity bucket of the cheery Santa Claus on the corner. They were close enough to see it happen but too far away to have any chance of saving her. Her grandfather Victor was closer, but though they all saw the danger and yelled a warning, the music in Cat's ears was so loud that their shouts didn't do any good. Neither did the fire-truck's siren or the air horn that the driver pumped an instant before impact.

Blinkered by her hoodie and deaf to any world beyond the pounding bass in her ears, Cat stepped off the kerb with her eyes locked down on the smart-phone through whose small, bright screen she was urgently scrolling. She had her hood up

3

because she was sulking and her head low because she was feeling bad about it – but not yet quite bad enough to know how to stop, suck it up and plug back into her family's annual trip back East from California to New York to visit Victor for the holidays.

All she knew was that she didn't want to go to Far Rockaway.

She was too old for that stuff.

She had better things to do.

The fire-truck that hit her was Ladder Two from Midtown, on the way to deal with a small inferno in the back of a large sweatshop in the garment district. The blaze had been started by someone drying a wet dress too close to an old three-bar electric heater and leaving the room for a quick smoke on the fire escape.

Because of that fire escape all the people in the building got lucky and made it out safely when the alarm sounded, though the sprinkler system failed so spectacularly that the entire workshop and the two floors above it burned out before the three trucks that did make it to the scene knocked the resulting firestorm down.

Ladder Two never got there.

But no one died at the fire.

Back at the collision on 55th Street there was no fire escape, no luck, no happy ending.

All there was was Cat's grandfather.

Victor Manno was close enough to see what was about to

4

happen and, at a spry 75, still sharp and agile enough to launch himself back across the street to try and save Cat by shoving her out of the way of the truck.

If he'd succeeded the story would have been a different one, maybe about a miracle, but on any given day very few miracles happen deep in the gridded canyons of Manhattan, and this one – even with Christmas three days out and closing fast – was no exception.

Victor sprang in front of the massive chrome grille on the front of Ladder Two, his long tweed coat flapping behind him as he stabbed at it with his cane and hit Cat in a full-body tackle.

He was fast, but not quite fast enough.

Instead of just Cat being hit by the truck, they both were.

But Victor did succeed in knocking his granddaughter three crucial feet backwards before Ladder Two slammed into them, and that yard made all the difference.

Instead of the fire-truck pounding an immediate full stop to the too-short story of her life, it hit her a glancing blow. It was Victor who went under the fire-truck instead of Cat, who bounced into the cars at the kerb, smacking her head with an ugly crack against the aggressively flared wheel-arch of a parked Dodge Ram.

It wasn't a happy ending.

But it was a beginning.

2

First aid

When Cat came out of unconsciousness all she could see was a world on its side, full of boots, knees and tarmac.

She tried to get up, but strong hands held her shoulders to the ground, and a stubbled face she didn't know dropped into view and told her she'd had an accident and that she should keep still and that an ambulance was inbound.

The intense professional calm in the fireman's voice terrified her and she tried again to buck upwards against the restraining hands of other firemen huddled round her.

'Cat. Stay still, darling. You're—'

Her mother's voice choked into her consciousness. She rolled her eyes and found her, kneeling at her side, winter hat askew, face white and ticking with tension.

'You're going to be fine. Just stay still.'

She tried to tell her that she wasn't fine, she was being held down on the pavement by unyielding hands when she urgently wanted to get up, but her voice seemed to have gone wrong, and all she heard herself rasp was: 'Grandpa . . . ?'

Her mother's eyes flicked left for an instant and, despite firm hands holding Cat's head still, she managed to follow the direction of her glance along the road surface, just far enough to see another huddle of backs and boot-soles kneeling around something trapped under the rear wheel of the fire-rig. Her eyes treacherously slid away from the second group of firemen so as not to linger on what exactly that something was, and travelled back along the side of the truck until they were stopped by the sight of her grandfather's cane sticking out at right angles from the radiator grille, as if Victor had stabbed the great metal beast a mortal blow and stopped it in its tracks.

It was such an incongruous and terrible sight that she choked out a defensive gout of laughter.

'Grandpa killed the truck!'

And then she started giggling, and once she'd started it seemed to build and build with no hope of stopping. The more she giggled the more she wanted to get on her feet, because the giggling wasn't a good sort of laughter, but a series of judders that seemed to get more and more intense and be shaking something loose inside. She just couldn't stop. She knew she needed to get to her feet and get her breath, but the strong hands held her down. She began to twitch and flip in her struggle to free herself, and then her mother's face dropped into view again, hat gone, eyes wet, and she held her face and spoke calmly.

'Cat. Stop moving. You need to stay still until that ambulance gets here.'

She jerked her head back towards the approaching blip-and-wail of a siren cutting its way out of the background growl of the city.

'You *really* need to be still, Cat. You hit your head.'

It was the rawness in the way her mother's voice nearly broke on the 'really' that stopped her.

The giggling dwindled and the shudders eased off and she went slack beneath the hands of the firemen.

'Stay with us, kid,' grunted the stubbled face, 'everything's gonna be cool, but you need to stay awake for me.'

The approaching siren was interrupted by two loud blasts from an air horn.

'Ambulance is nearly here. You're gonna be comfortable any minute now, OK, champ?'

Cat felt her vision begin to twitch and she realized she felt very cold.

'That's just shock, OK? It's the adrenaline flushing out of your body. You take a knock like you just took, the system piles on the adrenaline to cushion you from the immediate effects, keep you going 'til you're out of immediate trouble – like the body's got its own First Aid mode, right?' The fireman's voice was calm and reasonable. Somewhere in her head – which was beginning to throb now – Cat knew he was talking like this to keep her from giving in to the undertow of sleep pulling her away from the rising pain behind her eye. The fireman carried on. 'Tell you what, kiddo, you're going to have a hell of a black eye and a real bad headache when that adrenaline does go, but stay cool, stay awake, look at me, you're going to be fine, right? Right, Cat?'

Cat knew he wanted an answer, but she was shivering too much to get the words out. She closed her eyes for a moment.

'Cat! Look at me. Look at me . . .'

A thumb gently opened her eye and she saw the stubbly fireman smiling in at her.

'Attagirl. Stay awake now, you hear?'

Cat heard the double thump of car doors closing, and realized the ambulance siren had got really loud and then just stopped. Two figures in green paramedic coveralls jogged into view.

'What have we got?' said the closer of the two, a tall high-cheekboned woman with thick black hair braided into two long plaits.

'It's a twofer,' said the fireman, hawking a thumb towards the other group at the rear of the truck. The other paramedic guy evaporated in that direction. The dark eyes and the plaits swung into the place in Cat's vision where the stubbly fireman had just been.

'What's her name?' the paramedic woman said. Cat heard her mother's voice answer.

'Catriona. Cat . . .'

'Hey, Cat. I'm Natalie. Looks like you took a hard shot to the head here . . .' She produced a penlight from the pocket on her sleeve and shone it into her eyes, one by one.

'Can you talk, Cat? Can you tell me what happened?'

Cat tried to nod. But no words came out. She heard an urgent voice call from the direction of the other huddle of firemen.

'Natty? You OK to give me a hand here for a minute?'

Natalie's eyes didn't break contact with Cat's, although the distance between them seemed to be slowly receding, as if she was gently falling away from her and everything else.

'Cat. Can you talk? I need to be somewhere else for a moment, but I need to know you can hear me before I go?'

She tried to speak. It hurt, so she stopped trying and concentrated on breathing instead.

'Do you know what happened here?'

She got her breathing sorted out. Then she heard her own voice coming from an increasingly distant world that was already telescoping away from her, as the walls on the edge of her vision began to close in and she started to search wildly for her mother's face. It sounded like her throat was packed with gravel.

'We should have gone to Far Rockaway . . .'

3

The bad step

They should have gone to Far Rockaway.

Despite all the calculations that followed, working out the angles, measuring the marks on the road, estimating the velocities – and above all weighing the blame – that's what everything came down to. That and the fact Cat had her earphones in.

Stepping somewhere just beyond the safety of the kerb on the corner of 3rd Avenue and 55th Street the thin line between life and death came down to that one decision: Cat cranked up her tunes, stuck her 'phones in, dropped her head, started Googling something and just plain didn't hear it coming.

That explained it.

That's how it happened.

That's where the journey began. That's when that line – thin and final as a razor – got crossed.

'Why' is a whole other thing.

11

'Why', as Victor often said, is life itself. He meant figuring out the 'why' of things was what living was for. And since he was a professor – of Literature, at NYU, no less – Cat always felt there was a chance her grandfather knew what he was talking about.

Cat's father Sam used to react to this saying of Victor's by observing that 'why' buttered no parsnips (which confused people who didn't know what parsnips were or whether buttering them was a good – or even perhaps a dangerous – thing). Sam – the middle-aged, practical son of a mercurial, whim-driven father – meant that wasting time worrying about 'why' didn't make sense or pay any bills, and he said it with the righteousness of a man who paid his own family's way by spending long hours at the office organizing other people's untidy finances into neat columns that did make sense. Sam was an accountant.

Cat was always struck by how unlike each other Sam and Victor sounded when they talked: it wasn't just the obvious difference in their voices: Victor had never lost the soft contours of the Scottish accent he'd brought to America nearly fifty years ago, while Sam's speech had retained the hard edges that were his own New York birthright despite the years spent living in Southern California. It was the fact they seemed to see the world in two completely different ways.

Victor – who had never even considered filling in a stub on his cheque-book – would needle Sam about how he should get his head out of the numbers and smell the roses every now and then, and Sam would needle back by pointing out that there wouldn't be any roses to smell if someone didn't pay for the fertilizer or the gardener in the first place. In fact they had done exactly this earlier that day, in the back room at PJ Clarke's, sitting against the brick wall covered in old black and white photographs of once-young boxers as the waiter slid a platter of freshly shucked cherrystone oysters on to the red-check cloth between them.

Lunch at PJ Clarke's was an unchanging part of their annual ritual. Except this year it had changed, because, for the very first time, Cat's older brother Joe was not with them, despite the fact that he had known about it and was expected. Joe had left home in LA and come East to New York to study music. Seeing him again was something Cat had been looking forward to since September. The fact he was a no-show for the lunch was somehow making everyone irritable, she thought, like dogs circling for a fight, their low growls only registering on a subsonic level.

'Why Sam,' Victor had said, picking a half lemon out of the hillock of shaved ice between the half shells, 'the next thing you're going to tell me is that roses don't grow on trees!'

'They don't,' Cat had interrupted, trying to dilute the ribbing before it got an edge and someone took an eye out. 'They grow on bushes . . .'

'Not in the Himalayas,' smiled Victor, leaning back as the waiter stretched between them to put a hamburger garnished with a single slice of raw onion and a bilious-looking pickle in front of Cat.

'In the foothills of the Karakoram the briar rose twines out of the hillside with a trunk thick as my leg. There are rose forests there where you can't see the sky for great thunderheads of pink blossom above you.'

And he slurped the oyster and smiled happily, leaning over and slapping his son amicably on the arm as he winked a sea-green eye at Cat's mother on the other side of the table.

'See, Annie girl, you should have gone to the Himalayas on your honeymoon like I said, and seen it for yourself.'

'We didn't have the money back then, Dad,' said Sam.

'I know, I know,' shrugged Victor, sizing up another oyster. 'And Annie here had a plane to build . . . there's always something.'

There was always something. And Annie did always have a plane to build. Cat was used to people looking surprised when they were first told her mother, still delicately beautiful in an unusual blue-eyed, black-haired way, was an engineer. Cat knew she'd inherited Victor's green eyes and her mother's hair, but was pretty sure she'd missed out on the delicate beauty thing. Where they lived most mothers either didn't work, or were high-powered 'somethings' in the entertainment industry. There wasn't much in between. Annie, however, worked in aeronautical design and it was that job that had taken her and Sam to Southern California in the first place: Mom built the planes; Dad helped people pay their taxes on time. They were always busy, but they were also both good parents.

And Victor was a good grandfather. There wasn't another one like him. Cat was pretty sure of that, because he just didn't do things like other people: in a world where some follow the crowd and others take the road less travelled, Victor ignored crowds and never met a less-travelled road off which he couldn't find an even more interesting detour. He cut his own trail, tearing through life with the velocity of a downbound train that had had nearly eighty years to build up a head of steam, and showed few signs of slowing down.

And Cat loved him too.

There was no question about that.

But she was also getting to a time in her life where she felt both embarrassed by being with Victor, and ashamed of that embarrassment. Sometimes you can have too much eccentricity. Sometimes you don't want everyone turning round and looking at you. And walking in Victor's slipstream got you noticed, by association. It wasn't just the long tweed coat that flapped behind him in the wind, wasn't his loud laugh or even the walking stick he used to point and slash at the world with – the one that was really a swordstick that he said he carried in case he was ambushed by the forces of darkness which he collectively called 'the Magua', in honour of a particularly nasty villain in one of his favourite adventure stories.

It wasn't that.

It was the simpler fact that Victor swept you up like a force of nature. Cat's brother Joe once said that being with Victor and trying to be unnoticeable was like trying to surf an avalanche: you got points for trying, but in the end you just fell in and got swept away.

The whole 'going to Far Rockaway' thing was one of Victor's avalanches in the making. It had begun one Christmas trip a long time ago, when they had been on the subway, heading to 81st Street and the Museum of Natural History. They were going because Victor had decided it was ridiculous that Cat and Joe should get any older without seeing The Great Canoe, a sixty-foot-long war craft carved from a single cedar trunk.

Cat – the younger Cat – had been excited by the noise and the smell and the whole sensation of travelling through the subterranean tunnel system beneath the city. She'd loved the rattling trains and the pressing hurry of the crowd and the variety of people – people up close and personal, in all shapes and sizes and ages in a way people never seemed to be in California, where there was less variety, more space and zero urgency. She had even been fascinated by the maps on the carriage walls, tracing the city's arteries with her finger, following the A line from its origin at Inwood and 207th Street in the North all the way through the tangled web of the city's subway system to the very end of the line in the East.

Cat had let the name of the terminal station roll round her mouth.

'Far Rockaway . . .'

Victor had heard the dreamy tone in her voice and understood immediately.

'Sounds like there should be a castle there, right? Windswept and lashed by the waves, perched on a rocky crag at the end of the world . . . kind of place where it's always sunrise or sunset, and adventures are always ending or beginning . . .'

'Like a place in a story,' nodded Cat.

'That's my girl – just like a place in a story. Somewhere you'd have to escape from. Like the Count of Monte Cristo . . .'

'More like somewhere you'd have to rescue someone from . . .' Cat said after a moment's thought.

'Like the Prisoner of Zenda. Yes. Better,' smiled Victor, who unlike most other adults never seemed to mind being wrong and who could always pull a book out of his head to illustrate a point. 'Much better. She's right, Joe. "Far" is where you go, not where you start. Far Rockaway's the end of the adventure. Has to be . . .'

'Is there a castle there?' Joe had asked. Cat was already seeing it in her mind's eye. 'A real one?'

Victor shrugged. 'I shouldn't be at all surprised.'

'But is there?' Cat had persisted, wanting there to be. 'With towers and turrets and stuff?'

'I don't know, Cat. I'm told there's a clock on the beach because it feels like the end of the world and they wanted to show time didn't stop there. Maybe we should go and see some day. Stay on the train until it runs out of track. Just for the hell of it.'

17

'Just for the hell of it,' echoed Cat, returning his smile and leaning back against Joe, who still let her do things like that in those days. She was happy to be there on a trip, with her older brother and grandfather, and everything had felt exciting and special, yet safe.

When she thought back on the times when Joe had been around, when Joe had just been her Joe, the big brother who was gentle and kind and funny instead of the Joe who grew up and left, this was one of her favourite memories. Her Joe could always make her laugh more than any other person she knew. Her Joe was the musician who had sat at the foot of her bed when he was ten and she was seven and gently played his violin to her when she was sick and couldn't get to sleep. Her Joe had the best smile in the world and though they fought sometimes, when it mattered her Joe always had her back at home or in the hallways at school. Her Joe understood that she wanted to surf because though she swam well in the school pool, what she really loved was wild swimming in the ocean and trying to ride the power of the waves, not because she was some surfer-chick wannabe hanging out at the beach and getting into trouble. Her Joe had argued her case with her parents who worried about things like that, and not only got them to spring for her first proper board but used to drive her out to Zuma after school and sit in the sand doing his music theory homework while she worked out how not to eat more ocean than she rode.

That was her Joe.

The Joe who left home came back in vacation times (usually) but when he returned he was not quite her Joe any more. Each time he returned the wider world seemed to have changed him, literally leaving its mark on his skin with a new tattoo or a piece of metal stuck through it. And though he'd gone to New York to study music with his violin neatly packed in its long shock-proof case, he'd left it undisturbed, moving on to synthesizers and drum machines and loop-boxes that produced music that was no longer soothing and melodious, but was – to Cat's ears – a harsh and angry shout from a frightening and hostile world she didn't recognize.

Anyway, that earlier day had been a good one when he was still her Joe, and the train had arrived at 81st Street and they got off and headed to the museum to see what was, indeed, a great canoe.

And though they didn't go that day or the next, or even the next year, Victor kept reminding Cat and Joe each Christmas that one day they would stay on the train and not get off until it reached the end of the line, just to see what was there. But they never had, and 'going to Far Rockaway' became a kind of family shorthand for doing something just for the hell of it.

Except today they hadn't gone, and with sirens howling and brakes screaming, a small but shockingly abrupt piece of hell had come for them instead, right there on the corner of 3rd and 55th.

And not going had been all her fault.

19

4

Ambulance

Cat's mother rode with her in the ambulance. They tried to stop her, telling her that the cops would bring her, but Annie was unbending as an axe on the matter, and Natty the street-tough paramedic took one look at her and knew enough not to waste valuable time arguing with a determined mother who looked smart enough to keep herself out of the way if things started to get hectic in the back of the truck.

Sam stayed with Victor, his face flayed white with the impossible choice he was faced with: between riding with his stricken daughter or staying while the paramedics tried to get his own father out from under the fire-engine. Even when it was all over he would never know for sure that he'd made the right call, and would lose sleep over it.

Cat saw none of this as they strapped her to a backboard and velcroed a neck brace gently beneath the hands holding her head steady. She was aware of the whip-and-whine of a second ambulance sirening up, and then she was lifted gently on to a stretcher and wheeled into the back of the ambulance. They hoisted her carefully into the interior, and all the while she felt her mother holding her hand, and though her head was throbbing quite a lot now she was able to note with pride that she wasn't frightened, although she did seem to be getting cold.

'H-h-how's G-g-grandpa?' she said, only then noticing that her teeth were chattering, which seemed somehow funny.

Natty bumped the rear doors closed with a heavy thunk which cut off the outside sound of the firemen calling to each other for equipment they needed to lift the rear of the fire-truck. Her face swung in between her and the plastic roof light in the ceiling. Cat couldn't quite focus on her eyes, but instead fixed on the bright silver eagle-feather pendant hanging off Natty's necklace as it swayed against the bronzed skin of her neck.

'You don't worry about him, Cat. He's got the best of the best on his case,' she smiled down at her. ''Cept me, of course, OK?'

She tried to nod but Natty put a fast hand on her chin.

'Rule one, we're keeping that head still. Wink once for yes, twice for no. Only don't wink any 'no's at me, because what Natty says goes, right?'

She winked once, and got a big smile in return.

'Smart young woman here, Mom. Keeps doing what I say? Everything's going to turn out real good.'

21

Cat felt something tighten round her arm.

'Just taking your blood pressure, Cat, make sure your engine's running smooth.' Natty's eyes watched a dial she couldn't see as the pressure on her arm relaxed.

'Some strong girl too. Took a licking, but keeps on ticking. Head hurt?'

She remembered to wink once and watched Natty reach out to steady herself as the ambulance lurched and the driver hit the horn. Cat hadn't realized they were moving. She'd missed that. But then time had gone funny for her, gappy and irregular. She was sure there was something else she was remembering. She closed her eyes.

'Cat. Open your eyes.'

She heard the words and knew what they meant, but she stayed in the dark red cave behind her eyelids. Her head hurt less when she wasn't looking at the plastic light in the roof.

She felt a thumb open an eyelid firmly but gently, and saw a penlight shining in.

'There you go. You can sleep later, Cat, but right now, stay awake. Docs will want you alert because when you take a hit to the head it's safer that way. If I wheel you in and you're snoring, they're going to get all up in my face and Natalie doesn't like it when the docs get in her face, not one shiny bit. OK? Once for yes, twice for—'

Cat winked once. Or at least she winked down, but couldn't seem to get the eye back open. After a moment of surprise her other eye gave up holding the weight of the conscious world all by itself and dropped her into a cavern that was no longer a comforting and familiar red, but a deep and nauseous darkness.

5

Betrayals

The trip to Far Rockaway had come up in PJ Clarke's as the waitress was bringing dessert, and Sam had snorted.

'Far Rockaway? Have you ever actually been to Far Rockaway?'

'No, son,' replied Victor. 'That's the point.'

'Yeah. Well, Joe went.'

Cat's head came up, despite herself. Her Joe would not have gone to Far Rockaway, not without telling her.

'He went to Far Rockaway?'

Sam nodded. Cat exchanged a look with Victor.

'Wow,' said Victor. 'He never said. You never said . . .'

Sam's shoulders rose and fell and his eyes rolled to the ceiling.

'Dad. I've been to the bathroom too, but I don't tell you about that either. Which is what Far Rockaway kinda looks like: a toilet . . .'

'You've been to the toilet, Sam?' said Victor. 'Good for you. I thought you might have got terminally constipated out there in LA . . .'

'Victor,' interrupted Annie. 'Reel it in a little?'

Her eyes indicated the next table, all of whom were not talking and definitely earwigging.

'But . . . how do you know what Far Rockaway looks like?' said Cat, still shocked by the casual revelation of Joe's betrayal.

'He sent pictures he took with his phone,' said Sam. 'It's kind of a nowhere place, like the end of the world, you know? I mean there's a clock on a lamp-stand on the beach and apart from that, you know, a lot of chain-link fence and garbage . . .'

Annie saw the hurt in Cat's eyes. She leant over and squeezed her hand.

'Joe didn't go there on purpose, Cat. He had a gig with his "band" in some kind of bar near the racetrack out there . . .'

Annie managed to put quotation marks round the word 'band' by her tone alone, which was her way of dealing with her disappointment that Joe had given up classical music and headed down a darker alley into which his parents clearly weren't invited.

'Why didn't you tell me?' said Cat. Meaning: why did Joe do this? She kicked at the table leg with the heavy army boots she was wearing, boots Annie disapproved of for being too grungy. Which was, of course, one reason why she wore them.

Sam's eyes slid off her and when he answered he spoke to Victor.

'Because you were . . . because it was your thing, Cat. You and Grandpa. You know . . .'

'Not really,' said Victor, not helping a bit.

'. . . Well she's not little now,' explained Sam with the air of a man who knows he's actually just digging himself deeper in the hole. He glanced at Annie, looking for a lifeline.

'I thought it was *our* thing. All of us,' said Victor.

'Well, yeah, Dad, I guess it was . . .' said Sam.

'That's why they didn't tell you, Dad and Joe,' finished Annie, finally throwing the line. 'To keep the magic.'

'It's not magic,' Victor cut in. 'And Joe missed the point, just like he missed lunch here today: he didn't see the real Far Rockaway. It's not a place you go to by accident and take a snap with your camera. It's a place you make a journey to. Getting there's half the point. That's the adventure. He didn't spoil anything, except for himself.'

He said this last to Cat.

'Come on, kiddo. We'll go this afternoon. And then you'll see!'

Cat knew he was trying to salvage something. His eyes were bright, but he looked tired, like his skin was pulled tighter than normal. She saw he was trying to make up for a day of betrayals, first Joe not showing up for lunch, then the revelation that he had gone to Far Rockaway without her. Without telling her. Treating her like Far Rockaway was just Santa Claus and she was a little kid who needed protecting from the fact he didn't really exist.

'I can't go to Far Rockaway. Not this afternoon.'

As she said it her mind was racing for an excuse. She remembered it was a Saturday.

'There's a thing I have to do. Secret shopping for Christmas. The shop's closed tomorrow.'

She'd looked down at the red and white checks on the tablecloth and tasted the raw onion on her breath; it too tasted like betrayal.

She knew if she looked up Victor would start to cajole her into the adventure and she might end up going and even have a good time, but the truth is Victor suggesting that this was the time they should make the fabled trip to nowhere just for the hell of it was dangerous to her.

She knew the long journey would have involved a lot of talking, and there were things she didn't want to talk to Victor about, not just about Joe and how she felt about him leaving her behind, but something else, something that definitely would have come up.

It was her own little act of treachery.

Cat hadn't meant to betray Victor. That's what she told herself. She hadn't lied to him before. In fact she didn't lie, period. If anything she told too much truth, which she knew gave her a rep as something of a hard-ass at school, something she was working on when she remembered to.

Except this time she had lied, kind of, and the song she

sang herself about why this one lie was a white lie and OK was that she had only done it to protect his feelings. Which was partly true, though the truth-teller in her head knew fine well that this was no excuse.

The lie she had told him was that she'd read a book he'd sent her, when the truth was that she hadn't.

Every year since Cat had been born Victor had sent her a book at Christmas and on her birthday, always a hardback with an interesting binding, always with good illustrations seeded in amongst the pages of otherwise uninterrupted print. They looked great on the shelf in her bedroom, where their gilt lettering and decoration caught the evening sun as it went down.

At two books per year the little library was creeping along the shelf and beginning to look like it needed more space. But though Cat's parents had read to her when she was too young to read, somehow it had never been those books that they chose, and when Cat got to enjoy reading on her own, the old-fashioned-looking books never caught her eye as much as the bright covers on the latest ones in the bookstore. So the 'library' had remained on its shelf, undisturbed and decorative, the books winking at her each night in the reflected sunset like jewel boxes that were somehow too precious to open.

And then one summer Victor had come to stay and had yanked one of them out at random and started reading it to Cat and Joe in the evenings on the back porch, and the jewel boxes came to life and poured out their stories like old treasure.

Victor had the magic trick of being able to make the long-winded and old-fashioned writing style seem fresh and modern, the same way a gifted actor can read Shakespeare and make it sound clear and easy to understand. Cat and Joe may have stuck close to home that vacation because of their parent's busy schedules, but in their heads, thanks to Victor, they travelled the globe even though they never got more than a handful of miles from the Pacific Coast Highway. They plunged into the deep woods of Colonial America following the treacherous twists and turns of a tale that told, amidst the fights and the chases, the fate of the last two warriors of a noble and now long-gone tribe of Mohicans. The villain of this story was the very Magua whose name Victor – and now the whole family – had used as shorthand for anything bad, from lost spectacles to root-canals. Once that story had reached its sad ending Victor picked up a book called *Kidnapped* and took them on another swashbuckling chase across the Highlands and islands of Scotland in the company of a kidnapped boy and Alan Breck Stewart, the swordsman and adventurer who rescues him.

It was while recreating a sword fight in that book that Victor had slashed so wildly with his cane that something flew off and clattered into the froth of purple and white bougainvillea tumbling off the side of the house. The cane had come apart revealing a flashing length of steel where the stick usually was. Cat and Joe had stared at him. Or more specifically at the blade.

'What?' asked Victor.

Cat pointed.

'Wow! That really IS a swordstick!'

Victor looked up at the steel in his hand as if he was seeing it for the first time.

'Ah,' he said peering guiltily around until he saw the cane that had flown off the handle. He picked it up and hurriedly resheathed the blade. 'It might be . . .'

'Cool,' breathed Cat.

'Maybe,' said Victor. 'But your mother might not think so, yes?'

And Cat had to agree.

The swordstick was a thing of wonder to Cat as she grew up. It looked like a normal mottled-brown Malacca cane with a curved walking-stick handle made of ivory. The handle was joined to the ridged shaft with a gold band, on which was carved a buckle. Cat discovered that if you pressed the centre of the buckle you found it was a square button that released a catch that enabled you – if you were very quiet and only did it when no adults were in the room to stop you – to unsheathe the blade and look at the light play along its edges and very sharp point. It also had a small gold charm that hung off the gold band by a single link, which also sparkled in the sun and was, on closer inspection, a small working compass.

'It's a walking stick, Cat girl,' explained Victor that night on the porch as they examined the stick, keeping an eye out for Cat's parents. 'And if you're going on a walk, it's always good to know where you're heading.'

He took the stick back and laid it on the bench next to her.

'So which way's north?'

Cat shrugged and reached for the compass. Victor batted her hand away and stood up.

'Don't need a compass!' He stepped out from under the porch roof and looked up. 'We got the stars. Come on out here. Time you learned to find true north . . .'

And by the time Cat's mother called them in to supper he had shown them how to always find north in the night sky using the outer rim of the Big Dipper as a pointer, and had moved on to tell them why the Ancient Greeks called the constellation the Great Bear, which led to a story, this time about the god Zeus and how his wife disguised herself as a bear to spy on him.

With Victor, almost everything came with a story.

They finished the story about the Jacobite and the kidnapped boy a week before Victor had to head back to New York. He said he'd saved the best 'til last, and as the late August swells crashed into the beaches beneath the bluffs on which Cat and Joe's parents lived, their grandfather sailed them off on the high seas in search of the pirate gold buried on *Treasure Island*. When they finished it they agreed it was an excellent tale to end the summer on.

'Got to love Long John Silver,' said Victor as he closed the book. 'Even though you can't trust him. The world would be a duller place without pirates.'

'Or stories,' Cat said sleepily. She closed her eyes, and so never saw how Victor smiled at that. She did however feel him clap her gently on the shoulder.

'You know, kid? I think you're going to grow up to be just fine. You get the joke?'

But Cat had fallen asleep. It was a moment Victor wrote down in his notebook that night before going to sleep, and one that he remembered with great happiness for the rest of his life. It was the moment he thought his granddaughter really shared his deep love of Story.

This year Victor had sent her a book for her birthday in October like he always did. It was *The Three Musketeers*. And she had said she had read it on a brief phone conversation in November, secure in the knowledge that she had plenty of time to do so before seeing him at Christmas. Except somehow she'd been doing more interesting things and the book remained unopened. And one reason was that she liked the books he sent well enough, but was beginning to notice that they were always about boys having adventures and doing the swashbuckling stuff.

Not girls.

Girls seemed to be there, when they were there, to be rescued.

So she'd put it aside. And then she'd thought she could

speed-read it on the plane . . . but she had forgotten to pack it.

Victor would want to talk over the book. He'd already asked if she'd liked a character called 'Milady' and she'd said yes, faking it. A trip on the train would give time for her lie to be exposed.

'So let's go tomorrow,' Victor had said when they hit the sidewalk outside PJ Clarke's after lunch.

Cat had shrugged. Victor looked at her as her parents walked ahead. He reached over and ruffled her hair with a sad half grin.

'See, this is your mistake: you think you're too old for this stuff. Too grown up to go haring off with your crazy old grandpa—'

'It's not that—' Cat interrupted.

'Maybe not, but don't interrupt. You think Joe spoiled something. He didn't. What's meant for you won't go by you. It's all still out there. He just decided not to have an adventure. His choice. Not ours.'

'I don't—' began Cat. He rolled right over her.

'Thing is, sweet girl, at your age there's an unending supply of Christmases lined up ahead of you. Me? Not so unending. So let's do it before you have to push me there in a wheelchair. We'll go tomorrow.'

Here came the avalanche.

'OK?'

Cat could only see one way round this awkward moment.

'Sure,' she lied. 'Sure. Tomorrow will be good.'

And as he strode ahead of her towards her parents at the intersection, she thumbed her smart-phone and tried to call Joe and see why he hadn't showed and if he would come and run interference with Victor tomorrow.

One river and two boroughs away a phone resting on top of a speaker cabinet kicked into life flashing a caller-ID picture of Cat making a goofy face in a wetsuit.

Nobody heard the specially selected ringtone playing *Surfer Girl* because the basement room in which the speaker stood was already under attack from a screaming guitar played at full distort, backed by a loop-machine playing a machine-gun burst of deep grunts as a bass line.

The guitarist did however have sharp eyes, and he saw the phone light up and stopped playing. All the other members of the band looked at him for an explanation, except the tallest one who sat over a portable mixing desk with a set of cans on his ears. His arms writhed with coloured ink and, though his face was shrouded by a fall of long hair like a raven's wing, the stud through his eyebrow was just visible.

'Joe,' said the guitarist, holding up the phone. 'Your sister.'

The guy at the mixing deck looked up and lifted a can off his ear.

'Your sister, dude,' repeated the guitarist.

Joe paused, grimaced, and then cut his hand across his neck. He knew what the question was going to be on the end of that call, and right now he didn't want to get into it.

He'd call her later.

There was plenty of time.

'Kill it,' he said. 'We're working.'

Cat could tell Joe had dinked the call because there weren't the usual number of rings before she got sent to voicemail.

That was cold.

She added it to the day's betrayals, and switched screens to try Googling 'Three Musketeers' instead. She needed to find something to say about this Milady character that she was sure Victor was going to ask her more dangerous questions about.

She'd just selected a web page that looked like it might get her out of trouble when she stepped off the kerb.

6

ER

Victor didn't remember saving Cat, nor did he remember going under the fire-truck. He remembered seeing Cat stepping off the kerb and seeing the accident about to happen, and remembered leaping back across the street knowing he wasn't going to be fast enough to get Cat out of the way – but then his memory stopped. He never saw he'd been wrong and that his headlong dive pushed Cat clear of the massive sledgehammer grille and the hungry wheels beneath. He never knew that he had, on reflex, stabbed at the truck with his cane as he dived for his granddaughter, as if that slender stick could halt the tons of steel with one magic thrust.

Most of all he was saved the memory of the fire-truck catching him and running over his legs as the driver jacked every pound of his bodyweight down on the air-brakes, as if willpower and brute force might somehow buy a precious inch or two of braking distance.

And maybe it did, because a half second later and the impact itself would have snuffed Victor's flame out on the spot. His head hit the ground a fraction after the front wheels caught him, and he lost consciousness before any pain signals reached his brain. He was spared awareness of the rear wheels getting him, and he never saw the paramedics arrive or the speed and efficiency with which the shocked firemen got him free of the truck and into the ambulance that sped off after Cat's vehicle, five minutes behind.

He didn't have to listen to the paramedics coldly relay details of the injuries to his legs, or tally his flickering vital signs as they hiccupped and dwindled across their read-outs, and he never saw his son stay with him until the doors closed and he was left to follow in an accompanying police car.

He was unconscious throughout the journey and missed the increasingly tense exchanges between the paramedic hunched over him and the one driving the vehicle. He didn't hear the clack of the stretcher wheels unfolding as they lifted him out of the vehicle, nor the snap of the wheels locking into place, nor did he feel the vibrations and the rush of air as they jogged him over the tarmac and into the ER. He was spared the rapid-fire briefing to the doctors as the paramedics handed him over, and so never knew the extent of his injuries. He was unaware of the great care taken as they transferred him to a table in one of the receiving bays, put an IV in his hand and prepared to intubate and ventilate him.

But then, as they were about to put a tube down his throat

to assure his airway stayed open while they tried to figure out exactly how bad the damage to his body was, Victor opened his eyes.

He woke to a bright urgency of electric light and shiny metal surfaces, surrounded by serious-looking men and women in scrubs. He heard an alarm shrieking insistently somewhere in the near distance, and all around him the short intense exchanges of doctors and nurses working against time. He saw heart monitors and IV tubes and crash carts and plasma bags and blinking screens and bright lights . . . and Cat.

He saw it all, and knew instantly that something very bad had happened to his own body, but he paid none of it the least attention. All he noticed was Cat, lying on the table in the bay next door to his, seen through the bodies of the medics clustering around him.

They already had a tube in her mouth and two surgeons in blue scrubs were examining her head while the rest of the team, in the same green as the ones surrounding Victor, were working on her ankle. Cat looked very small on the table, as if the accident had not only brought injury but had also taken away several years of growth at the same time.

She seemed defenceless and very alone despite all the activity focused on her.

Victor's reaction was outrage.

'Cat!' he shouted, though it came out like a hoarse croak.

'Heart rate's overclocking,' said a nurse.

A doctor put her hand on his chest as he convulsed with the pain his movements triggered.

'It's OK,' she said as she signalled urgently to another nurse on the other side of him. '150 mikes of Atenol and 2mg of Midazolam, IV, *stat*!'

'I'm fine! Help her!' Victor rasped, trying to wave the doctor out of his face. 'That's my granddaughter!'

'She's being helped Mr . . .' she looked a question across his body.

'Manno,' finished the nurse, handing the doctor two syringes which she checked, plugged into the IV line and then emptied.

'She's just a kid . . . help her first!' Victor insisted.

'We've got plenty of doctors to go round, Mr Manno. The Neurosurgery team is already on the case . . .'

'Magua,' breathed Victor as he laid his head back down, straining to keep Cat in his field of vision.

'Mary, you want to close that door,' said the doctor calmly, as she kept her hand firmly on his chest. 'We don't want Mr Manno getting excited again before the Midazolam kicks in . . .'

Victor bucked against her hand as a nurse stepped across to the door and pushed it shut.

'Cat!' he shouted, somehow finding a strong and un-ragged voice. 'Don't let it get you, Cat! Don't you let the god-damn Magua get you!'

Then the door swung shut, cutting off his view into

the next bay, and as he lost sight of his granddaughter the opiate finally kicked in, flooding up his body and hitting the shores of his brain in a gentle but unstoppable tsunami of unconsciousness; he was swept under and the world went away.

Bad Step

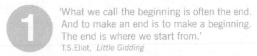

1 'What we call the beginning is often the end.
And to make an end is to make a beginning.
The end is where we start from.'
T.S.Eliot, *Little Gidding*

Inwood

2 'Let your soul stand
cool and composed before a million universes.'
Walt Whitman, *Song of Myself*

Jamaica

3 'The schooners and
the merry crews are laid away to rest,
A little south of sunset in
the islands of the blest.'

John Masefield,
The Ballad of Long John Silver

Broad Channel

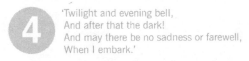

4 'Twilight and evening bell,
And after that the dark!
And may there be no sadness or farewell,
When I embark.'

Alfred, Lord Tennyson, *Crossing the Bar*

7

A deep green world

Cat Manno did not regain consciousness in the ER. She *didn't* wake to electric light and shiny metal surfaces and the intense hustle of doctors and nurses trying to cope with the everyday mayhem of a midtown emergency centre.

Cat woke somewhere else entirely.

She opened her eyes to find she was in a deep green world, flat on her back, looking straight up.

Her first thought was that her head should be hurting but wasn't, so she decided not to move it in case it did.

Her second thought was that the jagged rip of sky she could see through the trees towering around her was very, very blue.

Her third thought was that the music in her ears was too loud. She found her hands were both thrust deep in the pockets of her hoodie, and one was already clutching the smart-phone, so she killed it.

Her fourth thought was: 'Trees . . . ?'

That's when she sat up.

The last thing she remembered seeing was the plastic ceiling light in the ambulance, and the swaying silver feather round the neck of the paramedic looking down at her. She remembered Natty's hands resting firmly on her shoulder. She remembered the restraining bands across her chest, holding her down on the stretcher. She remembered the noise of the siren and the crackle of the two-way radio and the driver swearing at the cross-town gridlock blocking the street ahead.

She didn't remember *trees*.

Or sunlight.

Or a sky *that* blue.

Or a smell like the one she was surrounded by, the heady green smell of a forest in spring, warmed by the afternoon sun. She certainly did not remember this clean air, air so clean that each deep breath she took felt as refreshing and invigorating as the cold, clear water from a well.

She looked around her. No walls. No paramedics. No machines. Nothing she expected. Nothing she recognized. Just trees.

This wasn't an ambulance. This wasn't a hospital. This was the woods. The old woods.

The deepwoods.

The ground on which she sat was cushioned with the dry leaves of the previous fall, through which a bright carpet of pink ladyslipper orchids was pushing. The cliffs of foliage vaulting skywards on either side of her were a mix of bright sugar maples and yellow birch, interspersed with darker stands of eastern hemlock. The hemlocks were thick and widely enough spaced for her to realize that this was a very, very old forest.

The bit of her that stood outside herself knew she should be scared and disoriented. What kept her anchored and stopped her ballooning off into the gusts of panic swirling in from the back of her mind was the fact that this forest-that-was-not-the-hospital was not merely any forest; it was *just* familiar enough to hold on to. But at the same time that in itself was utterly weird, and not because of her inexplicable presence in the middle of it. It was weird because she knew two things at once about it that were definitely true and yet most definitely contradictory: she knew she'd been in these woods before, smelled this smell, seen this green and heard this silence; and she also knew for certain that it was a forest in which she had never, ever set foot.

Trying to balance these two mutually opposed certainties as they seesawed back and forth in her head made her feel a little sick.

And then she saw the eyes watching her and froze.

Ten feet away there was a large whitetail buck with a huge rack of antlers cutting slashes of shadow through the shaft of sunlight it stood in. It looked just as surprised to see her as she was to see it.

And since she had killed the music in her earphones, she

now realized that she was also surrounded by a profound and unbroken silence.

For a long minute, girl and deer remained perfectly still, locked in the tractor-beams of each other's eyes. Nothing moved except the pollen drifting through the sunlight between them. Cat didn't breathe. Meeting the deer's gaze was like looking into the depths of something ancient and mysterious and unspoiled, something that was looking right back into her and judging what it saw there. It also felt dangerous, and one reason she didn't move was because she wasn't sure whether the stag would spook and run, or just charge her if she did. There were a lot of points on those antlers, and they were all sharp.

The moment shattered with the flat crack of a rifle shot.

One second the deer was there. The next it twisted and leapt into the screen of leaves, a flash of white tail bobbing against the dark green – and then it was gone.

Cat dropped to the ground on instinct, unnerved and disoriented again. She pulled out her left earphone and strained to hear the next noise, and where it was coming from.

Then she heard a voice yell hoarsely from the woods at her back.

'Cat! Run!!'

It was Victor's voice. Unmistakable and urgent, and some way off.

Cat bounced to her feet.

She heard the guttural sound of other men shouting in

anger, in a language she didn't recognize – then she heard a shriek of pain.

She didn't think twice.

She ran.

But not away.

Cat didn't run to save herself. Without a thought, without hesitation, fuelled by nothing but blind instinct she ran towards the one thing she did know in the perplexingly strange-yet-familiar world she had woken up in.

She ran towards the sound of her grandfather.

And she dug in and ran fast, because it sounded like he was in deep trouble.

When Cat wanted to move, she could really shift. In the years since Victor had sat on the back porch reading to her and Joe she had grown into the flat, lean build of a swimmer, and countless evenings and weekends paddling out for catchable waves amongst the sandbars at the south end of Zuma Beach had hardened her muscles beyond her years.

She ran blind through the undergrowth, her heavy boots crashing through clumps of lowbush blueberry that scratched and ripped at the knees of her jeans as she went. She ducked a thick branch as instinctively as a running-back slipping a tackle, but then she lost her footing and went sprawling face-first down a hidden slope that ended in a marshy splash of bog. She barely had time to spit mud from her mouth before she heard another scream, and was up on her feet again, cutting wildly through a thick stand of tamarack that slashed

47

her face and tore the remaining earphone out of her ear. The cable got snagged, and the speed of her forward momentum combined with the whippiness of the conifer to rip the smartphone out of her pocket and catapult it back into one of the water-filled footprints behind her.

She burst out of the tamarack and was aware of a river whitewatering past on her left. She heard another shout, coming from further up the bank, beyond a wall of beech. She hurdled the mossy trunk of a fallen tree and sprinted for it.

She had just enough time to think that she was running into what sounded like a fight with no weapon, and without slowing much she swooped low and grabbed a fallen branch from the smashed debris beyond the upended tree. It was too long to be a club, and too short to be a spear, but having something in her hand made her feel better. It was something she could swing like a bat, at least.

She hit the wall of beech and sidestepped a trunk that seemed to leap out of the green dimness within. Her right foot snarled in a treacherously upcurved root, and she started to fall, bracing herself against another trunk with her free hand.

If she hadn't had to stop to keep on her feet she would have blundered right out of the other side of the beeches into a riverside meadow about seventy yards across.

As it was, the root that tripped her probably saved her life. The hood of her sweatshirt had jerked forward when she stumbled, and as she pushed it back out of her eyes the breath caught in her throat at the sight in front of her.

On the other side of the meadow was a majestic white pine, soaring one hundred and eighty feet above the scrubby grass. At the base of it smouldered the remnants of a small campfire, and behind it Victor Manno stood at bay, his back to the massive trunk. His gritted teeth flashed with startling brightness through a red flag of blood that streaked from his snowy hairline down one side of his face and across his chin.

He had his tweed coat wrapped around one arm like a shield and, in his other hand, his sword-cane slashed a yard-wide arc of bright steel in front of him, keeping his six attackers at bay. The pocket of the coat was ripped open and flapped as he moved it, showing it had already blocked at least one blow from his circling assailants.

It wasn't just the overwhelming number of them that stopped Cat.

It was who they were, and what they looked like.

They were Indians.

Victor hadn't lost the habit of his own childhood in calling them that. Cat's generation had been better schooled to call them Native Americans, but seeing them stripped to the waist, heads shaved into bristling mohawks bushed up with porcupine quills, their faces and shoulders darkened with black warpaint, she knew even more precisely what they were, and that was the shocking thought that paralysed her.

They were Huron.

Cat had never seen a live Huron in her life, any more than she had been in this forest that she recognized so keenly, but she knew with mortal certainty that what Victor held dancing and feinting with their clubs and tomahawks just beyond the reach of his blade was nothing more or less than a Huron war party.

Victor's yell jerked her out of her momentary daze.

'Cat, get the hell out of here!'

Victor was not looking at her. He was just shouting in all directions at once, as if he somehow knew Cat was in the woods close by.

Cat watched as her grandfather thrust, slashed and withdrew again and again, always keeping the sharp point of his blade in motion, never predictable, keeping the attackers away from him. One Huron wielded a strange broken-backed kind of war club, and as Cat watched the murderous dance at the base of the tree she saw a pattern emerging, as the other Huron coordinated their own dodging and half attacks to bring him closer to Victor.

He was taller than the other warriors, and had red paint-streaks curving back from his soot-blackened face, up and over his eyebrows and across his temples, as if his eyes were on fire. The club was an ugly thing, crooked like a gunstock, its full length patterned with brass nails and a brutal shank of metal sticking out where the rear sight on a rifle would be.

Stopping had made Cat one notch smarter than the Cat who had run blindly to the rescue with nothing but a stick in her hand. She had time to count the number of enemies and see the sharp edges of their tomahawks.

Running in with her stick wasn't an option. They were bigger than her and there were more of them. So her options were no options really, because it just wasn't in Cat to run away and leave Victor in trouble: all she could do was shout to try and get their attention – and then run. That way some would probably break off and come after her, leaving Victor to fight against better odds.

Cat dropped the stick and checked the way she would decoy them, back along the river, slanting uphill after the fallen tree, back into the stand of sugar maple, avoiding the soggy bottom, which would slow her up.

She couldn't outfight them.

Maybe she could outrun them.

Running and swimming were things she was good at.

It was a plan.

At that moment Fire-Eyes made his move and jumped forward, kicking the burning embers of the campfire at Victor to distract him as he swung the vicious club at his head. Cat didn't even have time to do more than gasp in horror, before she realized that Victor's head wasn't there any more.

He ducked and twisted and simultaneously stepped towards the attack instead of trying to avoid it. His wrist flicked with eye-bending speed as he brought the sharp end of his blade into the path of Fire-Eyes. There was a shriek of pain and anger. The Huron dropped his club and staggered back through the fire-ash, redness welling from his shoulder.

Victor stepped forward, claiming territory a half pace out

51

from the mossy trunk of the tree, and kept the tip of his sword moving as before. Only now it wasn't so bright, having bitten into the largest of his attackers.

Cat knew if her plan was to have a chance of success, now was the moment to run. She took a deep breath and prepared to step out of cover and shout.

The breath stayed in her as a hand clamped over her mouth and an arm went round her neck, tightening like an iron band.

Cat's instinct was to struggle. The arms holding her were knotted hard as an old hickory stump, without an inch of give in them. The air came out of her nose and as she breathed in again she smelled wood ash on the hand gagging her.

She redoubled her effort to escape. She felt the throttle tighten and her attacker's mouth jam in close to her hooded head, then she heard seven calm words whispered into her ear.

'Not that way, boy. He kill you.'

It wasn't an order or a threat.

It was advice.

Cat felt the whisperer turn her to look again at the safe route along which she had planned to decoy the attackers.

This wasn't the moment to tell him she was a girl.

There was a shimmer in the sugar maples topping the slope above the bog, and then another Huron came down the slope at a steady, unhurried run.

The whisperer edged back an inch and held Cat and himself in the shadow of the trees. The new Huron did not see them and did not vary his measured haste even as he crossed her tracks and scooped low, snatching something out of a puddle and pocketing it as he ran on into the meadow, unmistakably heading for the fight at the base of the great white pine.

Cat had a sense that the world slowed slightly as this new Huron ran past them, and in that extra, enhanced moment her guts turned to ice water.

The Huron ran with a grim, cold look in his eyes. An unbuttoned red coat jacket flapped behind him, revealing a naked, tattooed torso above a buckskin breechclout and leggings. A feather fluttered from the long rifle he held low and parallel with the ground as he ran, and a powder horn bumped his hip every other step. His other hand held a long-handled tomahawk with a small, brutal hatchet-head. But it wasn't the long rifle or the war axe that chilled Cat's guts. It was the 'thing', the unfamiliar/familiar thing that was now happening for the third time since she'd woken up and looked at the chasm of green and the jagged sky beyond: she had never seen the Huron before in her life, but she knew him. She knew him intimately. She knew what he was capable of.

He was a dark, revengeful and vicious opponent.

He was as cunning and subtle as a fox.

He would never stop.

He ran steadily without urgency because he didn't need to run fast.

Everyone ran from him, but he always caught them in time, and that time would always be the worst.

He was the nightmare made flesh.

Cat knew his name, but could not quite summon it to the tip of her tongue. It lurked threateningly on the edge of conscious thought, like a thundercloud about to burst . . .

The hand at her mouth relaxed and let her breathe.

She stared at the back of the running nightmare and finally whispered its name in horror.

'Magua.'

As she said it the hands holding her flinched slightly, as if her captor had got an electric shock. Cat twisted and looked up at him. He was staring at the running Huron. He had a strong face, with high cheekbones and a head shaved into a mohawk of his own. He was also without any colour at all, a uniform ash grey that covered all she could see of his torso and arms.

'Who are you?' she breathed.

'I am a dead man,' grunted her captor with complete conviction, eyes still locked on the Huron in the red coat. 'And that is the devil who killed me.'

Cat, in that moment, believed him.

She was in the presence of a nightmare, trapped in the arms of a ghost.

Her eyes were drawn away from the grey face to the true terror in the meadow, to the red coat running towards her grandfather, the grim Huron with the war axe in his hand

and cold death in his eyes.

Cat breathed his name a second time, with even more horror in her voice.

'Magua. Magua in a red coat—'

8

Intubate

'What did she say?' said the doctor.

'Mag-wah? I think she said Mag-wah,' replied a nurse, 'Mag-wah and a red coat? But she might just have been moaning . . .'

A machine beeped a warning behind her. She turned and read the lines on the screen.

'Pulse just went up too.'

Cat was still unconscious. The doctor leant in to push back an eyelid and shine a penlight into her pupil. The team of nurses around her watched and waited as she moved it from side to side, looking for some reaction from the staring eye. She clicked off the light and shook her head.

'I want a preliminary X-ray of her skull now,' she said. 'Let's get moving.'

The waiting team erupted into controlled mayhem, as machines were wheeled aside allowing others to be swung into place and aimed at Cat's head. The doctor stepped out of the bay and looked at the nurse beside her.

'Who's Mag-wah?'

The nurse shrugged and nodded towards the waiting area.

'Her mother rode in with her. You want me to ask?'

'Later. Smart money says the X-ray's just going to tell us what we know from the external signs anyway. Page the Nutcrackers and tell them they've got a customer for the donut.'

The nurse headed for the phone. The doctor peered back into the bay. It was now empty as everyone had cleared out to avoid the short burst of radiation about to be pulsed through Cat's head by the radiology nurse, who carefully positioned the apparatus on the end of a gantry arm and then retreated behind a lead screen to take the X-ray.

The doctor sucked her teeth as she peered in at Cat, alone in the middle of the bay, her body shrouded by an anti-radiation bib. She was the stillest thing in the room as her vital signs bounced and bleeped across the screens of the machines crowded around her.

As the radiation warning light flicked from green to red, stayed red, and then clicked back to green, she turned and looked towards the narrow waiting area, known as Misery Alley to all who worked the ER. It was where the walking wounded waited while the serious cases were wheeled past them, next to the tight faces of relatives and friends who could not tear their eyes from the bays where their loved ones were being worked on. You could always tell who was a waiting patient and who was a relative. The walking wounded slowly became irritated as the time ticked past, while the healthy family members just looked sicker and sicker as they stared with increasing dread towards the doors through which the next news of their loved ones would come.

The doctor hated Misery Alley, but she had children of her own, and where other colleagues would let nurses handle the interaction with parents, she always butched up and did it herself. Somewhere in the back of her otherwise impeccably scientific mind she believed that it was a karma thing, that she owed it, parent to parent. She knew that she would expect a doctor to give her the news, good or bad, if fate or accident ever consigned her to a hard plastic chair in Misery Alley and, by refusing to delegate the tough talks, she somehow believed she was preventing that ever happening to her or hers.

As soon as she had seen the X-rays and confirmed her suspicions, she took a deep breath and headed for the Alley.

As it happened Annie was easy to spot, as the only other woman in the Alley was an ancient Chinese lady with her hand wrapped in a bloodstained tea towel. The doctor checked Cat's notes as she walked over, making sure of the surname, her face – to Annie – distressingly unreadable.

'Mrs Manno? I'm Doctor Stevens . . .'

Annie came out of her seat fast, her face apprehensive and her body tensed to receive a blow.

'How is she?'

'She's had a bad bang on the head, which you know, but she's in the right place; she's doing as well as can be expected given what happened to her, and everything that can and should be done will be . . .'

The doctor heard her own words as she spoke them and knew how flat and unhelpful they were. As she tried to think of an easy way to say it, Annie cut in.

'But she's OK, right? I mean she was talking in the ambulance, she was asking after her grandfather . . .'

The doctor had looked into a lot of eyes like Annie's, eyes that were all different but which screamed the same silent, desperate 'Please!' as they searched for a lifeline to cling to. She could have told Annie that talking was not as good a sign as she was hoping. She could have told her about Talk and Die injuries, the cruel joke played by subdural haematoma, where the injured walked and talked perfectly normally and coherently until the build-up of blood silently seeping into the gap between the skull and the brain suddenly killed them. She could indeed have explained that the Nutcrackers were what the team in ER called the Neurosurgical team on the fourth floor, who regularly opened skulls in order to try and heal injuries that threatened the brain.

She could have told her all these things, but she saw Annie's eyes flick over her shoulder and widen as a very still body was moved out of the bay behind her and pushed urgently towards the lift.

'We're just going to move her to the fourth floor—'
she began.

'Neurosurgery,' finished Annie. 'OK. How bad is it?'

The doctor looked at her, wrong-footed by the way she had
leapt ahead. Annie pointed at the Hospital Directory screwed
to the wall on the pillar in the centre of Misery Alley.

'Fourth floor: Neurosurgery and Spinal unit. Please don't
treat me like a fool Doctor Stevens.'

Doctor Stevens looked at her and realized she no longer
looked like she was preparing to receive a blow. She
seemed to have grown, and her eyes were clear. She didn't
look cowed. She looked like a lioness preparing to fight for
one of her cubs.

'There's a danger of a haematoma. They will put her in a
CT scan and then we'll know more. If she IS suffering a
haematoma—'

'What is the X-ray telling you?' Annie was walking towards
the lift. 'Come on, Doctor: you all left the room, you must
have been taking an X-ray. What's it telling you?'

'It's telling us she may have, as I said, a haematoma.'

'Subdural or epidural?' snapped Annie, breaking into a jog
as the lift doors began to close. The doctor hurried after her.

Annie didn't get to the lift in time. The door closed and so
the last sight she had of Cat before she was lifted up to the
Nutcrackers was through the scratched and gridded safety-
glass window in the door.

Maybe Cat, in her unconsciousness, had heard her voice.

Or, thought the doctor as she looked in over Annie's shoulder and saw Cat's body suddenly twitch and strain upwards against the restraints holding her securely down on to the stretcher, maybe she was having a fit.

If it was the latter she hoped the lift got to the fourth floor without stopping at any of the three other floors it had to pass through to get there. Head injuries were of their nature mercurial things, and if Cat's body battling against her restraints was in fact a sign that she was having a fit, she might not come out of the elevator alive.

9

Ghost warrior

Cat struggled to free herself from the grip of the ghost, her eyes locked on her grandfather as Magua ran up to the group at the bottom of the tree.

'Let me go,' she hissed.

The arms just held her even tighter. Her captor spoke low into her ear.

'You cannot save him now. You must wait.'

Cat hacked her boot-heels back into the shins of the man holding her, trying to twist loose. The grip remained as it was. The man didn't even flinch, as if he was made of the same hard wood as the tree beneath which they were hidden.

'If I don't save him now, that's it! I mean there is only now!' Cat groaned, bucking even more futilely against the restraining arms.

'Be still . . . there is only now until now is over. Then there is then.'

Out in the open Magua came to a halt. The other Huron saw him and stepped aside. He looked at Victor. Without breaking eye contact he primed his long rifle with gunpowder from the horn at his side and ratcheted back the hammer as he aimed it at Victor's head.

Cat squirmed her head round and pleaded with the ghost.

'Please . . . they're going to kill him!'

The grey head stayed in profile, eyes burning across the meadow.

'No. If they wanted to kill him they would have done so. They are trying to capture him.'

Magua barked one word at Victor.

'Enough!'

Victor held his ground.

'Do your worst.'

Magua repeated what Victor had said to the other Huron in their own language. They laughed.

'Why do they want to capture him?' asked Cat, still trying to find a way to make this tall Indian release her.

She got the hint of a shrug for an answer.

'Who knows? But he would be dead if they did not want him alive. That I do know. Maybe it's the book . . .'

'What book?'

'The one the old warrior is standing on.'

And then Cat saw it. And as she did she realized the significance of the ripped pocket. One of the small oilskin notebooks he always carried had been torn from his coat, perhaps by a near miss from one of the tomahawks, perhaps by the blow that had bloodied his head. It lay on the ground on the edge of the small campfire mark, with Victor's foot placed firmly on it.

'Step back, old man,' barked Magua.

Cat saw that her captor was right, but it didn't make sense to her.

'Why do they want his notebook?'

Another shrug.

'Power.'

Victor was dangerously still, his sword-point now aimed right back at Magua, but his eyes were busy. He was measuring distances, looking at the river, at the trees, at the wide meadow ahead of him. There was nowhere to run.

'I do not ask again!' Magua took a half step forward. 'Give me the book.'

Victor swallowed. He suddenly looked smaller and older. He dropped the point of the sword a couple of inches.

It wasn't much, but it pierced Cat's heart to see it. It meant he'd given up. Cat had never seen him do that before. Victor cut a wide swathe through life as if the very concept of submitting to anything was alien to him.

It just looked wrong.

'OK,' Victor growled. 'It's nothing but a damn book. If that's what all this is about, hell, have it . . .'

He dropped the sword-point even further, spinning it in his hand so that the sharp end pointed behind him and the handle faced the Huron. He offered it to Magua, managing to make the gesture of surrender look, despite everything else that was wrong with it, strangely graceful. Cat saw the compass dangling off the handle glint in the afternoon sun. Magua just grunted low and deep in his chest, and shook his head. He jutted his chin at the small oilskin-covered rectangle beneath Victor's boot-heel.

'Give that.'

Victor grimaced as he creakily bent to pick up the book. Cat had never seen him look so frail and shaky. His hand closed over the scuffed covers and he looked up into Magua's eyes. They were as hard and unyielding as the gun barrel aimed right at him.

'Give!'

Victor nodded. And then his eyes slid left.

Cat's mouth must have realized what her grandfather was going to do an instant before her brain did, because it opened to yell a warning to tell him not to put himself in more danger, but before the shout got out the ghost clamped a hand over it and stifled the noise.

Victor kept his head down and spoke as if to the ground in front of him.

''Course you should have said please. Good manners cost nothing, after all . . .'

And then he moved very fast, spinning up to his full height so quickly that Cat had to put together everything he did in that one smooth but complicated movement later, when she had time to replay the moment in her memory.

The hand holding the book cocked and then snapped forward, swift and abrupt as a whiplash as he fast-balled it up and over the heads of the Huron, sending it whirring through the air, pages riffling with the sound of a startled partridge. It arced far up and over the fast-moving river and then dropped into a foamy birl of whitewater just ahead of the rocks in the middle of the rapids.

Magua did not fire the long rifle as Victor made his move. Instead his eyes followed the flying book as if they were stuck to it.

Victor – no longer pretending to be old and frail and beaten – balanced the forward-throwing motion of one arm by swinging the other one backwards, stabbing the blade of his sword-cane deep into the trunk of the ancient pine tree behind him.

He grinned and looked round at the shocked Huron.

'You may take me, boys . . .' he said, '. . . but you shan't have my sword, and that's for damn sure.'

He spat on his fists, thumbed a trickle of blood out of his eye, and took up a boxer's stance, beckoning once with his leading hand.

'Now come away with you, and have at it . . .' he winked at the giant with the gunstock war club, '. . . if you think you're men enough.'

He turned to look at Magua. But Magua wasn't there. He was sprinting towards the water, shouting urgently over his shoulder. He ripped off his powder horn and dropped his rifle into the grass as he jumped down on to the hard scrabble of pebbles shelving the riverbank. Only then did Cat see the two birch-bark canoes pulled up on the beach as Magua hurdled them and sprinted into the torrent without breaking step. The low afternoon sun sent rainbows through the spray he kicked up, and then he dived beneath the surface.

For a long beat all was calm and the river seemed to have swallowed him without trace – and then he reappeared mid-stream, his scarlet-jacketed arm breaking the surface first as he pulled himself up into the air and then swam furiously downstream, heading for the snarl of rocks in the whitewater in the middle of the river.

The Huron around Victor bunched and moved in on him. Cat couldn't see what happened, but she heard shouts and saw one stagger backwards holding a bloodied nose, and then she saw the flash of a war club and heard an impact that sickened her; they stepped back, revealing Victor lying on the ground, face startlingly white, his legs at an odd angle. His eyes blazed for a moment as he looked at them, at their fierce warpaint and cruel weapons.

When he spoke he sounded tired and a little disappointed.

'Well, you're just cowards is what you are, that's what we found out today. Cowards not men. Men would have fought fair, one by one and with their fists. So you can be damned, for all I care—'

And he slumped forward and passed out, half lying, half

sitting on the tangled pine roots at the base of the tree.

The giant leant in and jabbed at him with the war axe.

He was lifeless.

The giant said something. The others laughed, and two of them stepped up and hunkered down over Victor, flipping him on to his front and swiftly and efficiently tying his hands behind him with a strip of rawhide.

The giant stepped over him and gripped the handle of the blade sticking out of the tree. He pulled it, first with one hand, then the other. Then he put down the war club and pulled it with both hands.

It wouldn't move.

He grunted in surprise. He braced one foot against the tree trunk and tried again. This time he got nothing but laughter from the other Huron who had finished tying Victor up, and were now watching him.

He snarled and stood back. Another one tried, but he too failed to move the blade. Then the two of them tried at the same time.

The blade was stuck fast.

There was a triumphant shout from the river. Their heads turned as if they were puppets pulled by the same harsh string.

Cat felt the arm holding her give a little, as if slumping in disappointment.

'Oh no,' she breathed.

There in the middle of the river sat Magua, balanced on the

top of a slippery rock in the fiercest part of the rapids, his face split with a grin, teeth flashing white and triumphant against the warpaint streaking down his cheeks. The sodden scarlet coat and the bristling porcupine quills tufting up from his mohawk made him look like some terrible exotic bird as he laughed and shifted his weight from one foot to the other on his precarious perch.

'Crowing like a rooster on his dunghill,' gritted the voice at Cat's ear.

You only had to look at what Magua held gripped in his right hand held high above his head to know what he was crowing about.

The shiny black oilskin covers of Victor's book flashed unmistakably in the lowering sun.

The other Huron shouted their approval, and then Magua yelled what were obviously instructions. Three of them had one last attempt to pull Victor's sword from the tree, but another shout from the river stopped them and with a swiftness and efficiency that was shocking after the drama of the stand-off and fight they lifted Victor and jogged to the canoes, retrieving Magua's weapons as they did so.

In a short moment the two boats were launched. Victor's angular frame was tumbled into one like a bag of spanners, and without any more ceremony they paddled out into the river and were off downstream. The Huron handled the canoes with a fluid skill that made little of the seemingly treacherous rapids, moving through them with fish-like ease.

Magua leapt sure-footedly from rock to rock across the boiling waters until he came to a higher outcrop on the edge of the whitewater where a clear and dark side-channel swirled beneath him.

A canoe swung in under the overhang and the Huron steering it back-paddled in and found enough of a handhold to keep the boat static for a moment. Magua gripped the book between his teeth and lowered himself feet first into the boat.

Then he sat and looked back with a look so sharp and unexpected that Cat flinched back into the shadows of her hood, sure not only that she had been seen, but that Magua was staring right into her soul. And then the moment passed as the Huron turned his eye away, pointed downriver, barked a command – and was gone.

Nothing remained but the roar of the rapids and the empty meadow.

Only the dead campfire and the sword in the tree gave a clue that man had ever set foot on this virgin piece of riverbank.

The hands that held her relaxed and let her go. Cat stumbled out of cover and looked around feeling lonelier and more abandoned than she had ever felt in her whole life.

10

A name returned

Cat stood on the edge of the meadow looking downriver for a long time, feeling the loss of Victor as a physical blow that left her shaken and winded. The speed at which events had taken place since she woke up in the woods hadn't given her any chance to think about the 'thing' itself, the strangeness of her situation; the fact that she had been catapulted into this other, older world, the weirdness of which was only increased by the fact that it was – impossibly – familiar to her.

She should be panicking. She should be screaming, 'Where am I? What happened to the city? Where are the skyscrapers and the yellow cabs and the ambulances and my mom and dad?' but she didn't. She just shelved all of that and decided to deal with it later because, even though that was a huge pile of what, why and where, there was one much bigger thing that dwarfed it: her rock solid conviction that Victor was in trouble, and it was because of her, and so she had to save him.

Cat saw things very fast, very clearly and acted on them immediately: that was her blessing and her curse because sometimes she knew she jumped when she should have looked a second time. Her mother called it 'bullheaded impulsiveness', but most of the time it worked for her. In that respect she was her grandfather's granddaughter. 'Make a decision and stick to it until you're proved wrong, then 'fess up to it and adjust gracefully' was one of his sayings, usually followed by: 'The one stone truth about being indecisive is you end up somewhere you never chose to be, and who wants to be there?'

Surfing played to her decisiveness – choosing which wave to wait for in a set, when to drop in and when to bail – and she liked the clarity and mental discipline of it as much as the physical sensation of riding the ocean's raw power. If she wiped out it was her fault and no one else's, and if she didn't wipe out every now and then, she knew it was a sign she wasn't pushing it hard enough.

The ocean didn't care about it either way, but it also didn't suffer indecision and neither did Cat. She knew for certain that she'd never been in these woods in the flesh, but she now knew she'd been here in her head, and how. It hadn't made sense when she woke, but now she had seen the virgin forest peopled – now she had seen Magua and the Huron – she recognized it for what it was: it was one of the imaginary worlds Victor's voice had taken her to on the long summer days when he'd taken the gilt-bound books from her shelf and read their stories to her, one by one.

As she absorbed all this, thinking that it should feel like a dream but didn't, the river surged on past her without pause. As she stared at it she knew she could very easily give in to the tug of panic pulling at her and get swept away and drown in it. Cat didn't think of herself as a particularly brave girl, but she did know she had a brain and that things went better when she used it. Panic would lead to thrashing around blindly, and thrashing always got you in trouble, whether you were out on the ocean amongst the waves or stuck inside playing a video game in the dark.

She took a deep breath and let it out slowly, allowing the river to calm her as she figured out what to do next. Beyond the chop of whitewater in the middle distance she saw it regain its twining green smoothness until a kink in the landscape took it out of sight behind a sheer cliff of dark pine.

She heard a twig snap behind her.

She turned to see the grey Indian had begun to walk away without a word of parting.

'Hey!' said Cat. 'Where are you going?'

'I travel my own path. Go in peace,' said the Indian over his shoulder.

'Wait up,' said Cat.

The Indian kept walking. Cat knew she had to prevent him disappearing, or she would never put the puzzle of what was happening together.

'Then why did you stop me?' she shouted. 'If you travel your own path, why did you step out and stop me?'

She saw the Indian sigh and shake his head before turning. He'd walked out of the sunlight and into the shadows, and when he looked back at Cat he seemed older and weaker than the man who had gripped her so tightly and saved her life. His shoulders were slumped and every movement seemed like it was too much effort.

'Why did you stop me?' repeated Cat, gripped with the conviction that if the ash-covered warrior walked further into the shadows she would be left alone, and that that would be a Very Bad Thing.

The Indian lifted his head and met Cat's eyes.

'Because they would have killed you, and there is too much death here already.'

He said it flat, like it was an answer that made sense.

'Wait. Where is "here"?' Cat said, catching up with him. 'I don't know where "here" is.'

'Here is where you find yourself when you open your eyes.' The Indian grunted as if this was self-evident.

'That's not an answer,' Cat shot back, trying to stare the man down, thinking she had never seen such sad eyes, and that she had to provoke him into staying until he at least gave her enough information with which to get to grips with her new reality.

She was surprised when the Indian blinked first, and then hunkered down in the grass next to the fire scrape. He spoke to the ground, sifting the cold cinders through his fingers as he did so.

'Death is no great thing in the other world, but in this one? I do not know . . .' He paused, and when he looked up Cat was shocked to see the ash on his cheek cut with the track of a single tear. '. . . In this world I think it could be bad to die.'

'Wait a minute,' said Cat, a little freaked by the tear. 'What other world?'

'The "here" before this. The "here" of life.'

Cat's head spun.

'This isn't the "here" of life?'

'No. This is the "here" after.'

Cat was gripped by a cold panic that he was right.

'You mean this is heaven?'

Her voice was suddenly raw because she was of course asking if she was dead.

'With the Great Spirit, the Manitou, there is no "heaven",' shrugged the Indian. 'There is just this. The happy hunting ground.'

The catch in his throat as he said it made it clear it wasn't a bit happy for him.

'Then why are you sad,' asked Cat, 'if it's so happy?'

'Because the face of the Manitou is behind a cloud. His eye is turned from me. His ears are shut. His tongue gives no answer. I see him not. Here I have no power, no strength. Here I am nothing. The trees have no colour, the sky no light and the wind makes no music in the grass. I smell nothing, not the woodsmoke or the musk of the deer or the freshness of the dawn breeze . . .'

He took a handful of wood ash and held it to his nose, inhaled and shook his head.

'All is ashes, in my eyes, in my nose, in my mouth. I have no name. I do not even know my own name. And a man who does not know his own true name has no power in this or any world!'

Then he scrubbed the ash on his face and shoulders, repairing the damage done by the tracks of his tears and his struggle with Cat.

'This is why you cover yourself in ash? To look like a ghost?'

'Here I *am* a ghost,' gritted the Indian. 'Here I am less than a shadow. I do not know the name of my ancestors, so they do not know me. This is why I am alone. This is why I cannot find my son in these woods, who went before me, who Magua killed, my boy whom I hoped to meet in this great hereafter. For how could I, who do not even remember my own name? I am a ghost, and my fear is that if I kill I shall become worse than a ghost.'

'What's worse than a ghost?'

'A windigo. A windigo is a spirit.'

'I know what a windigo is,' Cat snapped, surprised at the strength in her voice. 'A windigo is a boogie-man, a kind of Native American werewolf, that kills people and eats them and is always hungry . . . and goes on killing and stalking people in the wild. I get it.'

'How do you know this?'

'I read about it. And I saw it in a movie . . .'

'Where is ah-move-ee?'

'A movie's a . . . it's not a place, forget about it, I just know what it is. And you're NOT a windigo . . .'

The man shook his head angrily.

'You do not understand, boy.'

Maybe it was the clear air, maybe it was the adrenaline, maybe it was irritation at being called 'boy' again, but Cat felt stronger and healthier than she'd ever felt. She certainly had lost the headache, and losing it made her realize her head had been hurting for a long, long time. Maybe she was just angry with the Indian.

Whatever the cause, something made her stride over to the sword in the tree and grip the handle. She looked down at the small compass hanging off it, sparkling in the last of the sunlight.

She grasped the sword handle tighter and pulled.

It came out of the tree with no resistance at all.

The Indian's jaw dropped.

'But they could not free it! The Huron dogs could not . . .'

'I know,' said Cat. 'I mean there's lots I don't know, but this I do know. It wasn't for him or them. It was for me . . .'

'It's magic . . .'

The Indian stepped back, alarmed, instantly tense, like an animal poised for flight. He spoke slowly, his eyes reappraising Cat.

'Maybe bad magic. Maybe it is *you* who are windigo.'

'It's not magic, and I'm not a windigo, and the sword thing . . . ?' She chopped out a short burst of laughter, half bitter, half just marvelling at the abrupt obviousness of it all as things began to connect at speed.

'It's just a story.'

'A story?'

'Of course it's a story. It's Victor. Of course it's all Victor. He says everything's a story. Guess he's right.'

The Indian stared at her. Cat put the brakes on her mind, which was racing so fast it was threatening to run away with itself, and reversed a little so he could catch up. 'It's one of Victor – that was Victor who Magua took – he's my grandfather – it's one of his stories. He read it me. And it's been a movie too . . . only the true king of England can pull this sword out of this stone and all the knights and nobles try and then this young kid who's basically a servant comes along and he tries and . . . bingo.'

She pulled the sword free again without any visible effort. The Indian raised his eyebrows, impressed despite himself.

'You are the king of Eng-Land?'

Cat shook her head with a grin.

'No. I'm not the king of anything. I'm just me but this is my sword, and I guess that means this is my thing to do . . .'

'What thing?'

She walked into the undergrowth beside the tree, picked up the length of Malacca cane that the sword was usually

78

scabbarded in, and slid the blade home until the small holding latch clicked shut.

'I'm going to find my grandfather.'

The sun was dipping behind the high ridge above them. In a minute or two Cat knew it would be gone. She swallowed.

'Will you help me? Will you guide me through the woods?'

The fire in the Indian's eyes dimmed. Or maybe it was the sun dwindling.

'I am no guide worth having. I am no warrior in this world. And being broken, I am no man to defeat Magua.'

Cat shook her head. Everything was too fast and too strange, but something that had been said earlier was itching the back of her brain.

'Wait up. You said Magua had killed you. Earlier, when you were holding me . . .'

'Yes.'

'And you just said he killed your son.'

'There are more ways to die than under a hatchet blow, boy. Magua killed me when he killed my son because when he did so he took the fire of life from my heart. After that, all was ash. A man should not see his children die.'

A second tear cut a copper-coloured runnel through the grey ash masking his face. 'I had hoped to find him waiting here for me when my time came, but he is not to be found. His name was Uncas.'

Cat's heart lurched because she now knew why she

recognized this man, and knowing him she realized why his defeated posture was so very wrong.

'But then why did you let him go? Magua. He was here. You could have . . . avenged your son. You could . . .'

She saw the shame in his face. It was so strong that it shut her up and she twisted her head to look off down the course of the river. In her mind's eye she saw Magua crouched on the rock in mid-stream, waving the book above his head, crowing like a cockerel.

'I told you, boy: I am a broken reed who walks as a ghost—'

Cat had had enough, all of a sudden. She lunged forward and smacked the heel of her hand into the man's chest, knocking him backwards. The Indian didn't resist, and this made Cat angrier, so she hit him in the same place a second time. The Indian's heel caught a root, and he stumbled backwards on to the ground. Before he could roll to his feet Cat was right up in his face.

'My name is not "Boy". It's Cat. Cat Manno. And for the record: I'm a girl.'

She pushed her hoodie right back off her head and shook her hair loose. He looked at her as if she'd hit him again. Then he shook his head and stared as if seeing her for the first time.

'You are a girl?!'

He pointed at her skinny jeans.

'But you wear a man's clothes . . . !'

'Yes. Sorry. Get over it. You are not a ghost.' She rode the burst of impatience like a wave, letting it carry her away from the dark reef of panic and uncertainty below. 'I know who you are. You are a mighty warrior. Your enemies call you the Great Snake because you are powerful and swift and deadly and you can follow the twists of other men's minds. Your friends call you by your real name.'

Cat took a breath and for a moment the forest was unnaturally quiet, as if even the trees were listening. She took a breath and spoke quietly and deliberately.

'Your name is Chingachgook.'

The Indian's head snapped back as if Cat had hit him again.

He sat there stunned, eyes open but turning in on himself as he took in the words and weighed them.

Cat spoke softly and urgently.

'If you are father of Uncas, then you are Chingachgook. And I need you to wake up and help me. Please.'

'Uncas who Magua slew,' whispered Chingachgook.

'Uncas who Magua slew,' Cat agreed carefully.

Chingachgook stood in one fast move, not looking at Cat anymore, staring at the river. He seemed to grow in front of her. The sun had reddened to a deep orange, and the ripples on the water were tipped in gold. Chingachgook's eyes flashed as he turned and looked right into Cat's face, and the fire that had flickered there earlier rekindled and blazed out from the ash-grey face.

'And you give me this freely and with no claim on me?'

'It's your name,' said Cat, suddenly wishing she'd made a deal before she'd told him.

Chingachgook's eyes gave nothing away as he nodded curtly, and then twisted on his heel and loped off towards the water.

He didn't break stride as he crunched across the shingle, and then the water sprayed around him in a burnished halo as he hit the river in a running dive.

Cat stood alone in the glowing dusk, her eyes straining up and down the bank, looking for the point where he would break surface, but he didn't. After a minute she stumbled down to the water and looked more desperately. She began to worry that he had hit his head on a rock and had been dragged down into the rapids. She could feel her heart beginning to race as a new panic began to grip her.

'Hey,' she shouted, holding her hands like a megaphone. 'HEY!'

The only answer she got was her own echo bouncing off the rocky scarp soaring above her.

She couldn't believe it was ending like this.

'Damn,' she swore, kicking at the pebbles.

At that moment the water in front of her erupted, and Chingachgook launched himself up and out of the water. Not a streak of grey remained on his face or body. In place of the broken man who had painted himself with ash to resemble the ghost he felt himself to be stood a warrior, his body washed clean by the river, its taut muscles bronzed by the gold of the evening sun and his eyes bright as his fiercely grinning teeth as he swept the water off his face and over the shaven head on each side of his black mohawk. He shook himself like a dog coming out of the water, and then pointed at Cat.

'You are Cat Man-No.'

Cat could only nod. The man in front of her was now everything she'd imagined in her mind's eye as Victor had read the story of his adventures many long summers ago.

'Then where you would go, Cat Man-No, I go too.'

His voice had strengthened. Some broken part of it had been mended.

'As you have given me back my name of life, I give you my word of death. And that word is strong, Cat Man-No, for I am Chingachgook, father of Uncas . . .'

He paused and looked up at the blood-red sun dropping into the granite ridge beyond the pine tops.

'. . . I am the Last of the Mohicans.'

11

Upside

Chingachgook stood stone still looking at the sun dropping behind the steep granite ridge line beyond the treetops. Though he didn't move, the dying light was catching in his eyes. When the red ball was half sunk below the mountain he stretched out the kinks in his neck and then turned and studied Cat for a long minute. Then he spoke.

'Can you run?'

'Sure,' said Cat, her voice level, to match Chingachgook's seriousness. 'I can run.'

He gripped her arm hard and pulled her close, his eyes searching her face for any sign of weakness or untruth.

'Yes, you can run as all girls can run. But can you run like a warrior, like a hunter? Can you run long after your body tells you to stop, after your muscles scream for rest, after your lungs burn raw, like a fire-devil has kindled in your chest?'

Cat nodded again.

'If I'm running towards my grandfather, yes.'

The serious face cracked in a smile as Chingachgook slapped her on the arm and jerked his head towards the forest beyond the meadow.

'Then come, Cat Man-No. We have a mountain to climb before dawn.'

He pointed at the rugged upsweep of the slope above the distant tree line as he strode towards it.

'Why are we climbing a mountain?' said Cat, jogging to keep up.

Chingachgook stopped by the fire scrape and squatted over it, taking a charred stick and drawing quickly in the ash. He made a mark like a long thin 'V' and pointed at the river behind Cat.

'The river flows round the arm of the mountain. It goes to sunrise and then turns a corner rushing back on itself towards sunset. You understand?'

'You mean it goes east and then cuts back west,' said Cat, looking at the small compass on the handle of the swordstick gripped in her hand, trying to make sense of the directions.

'They must follow the river. They will not reach the turn before dark then they must make camp and wait for the dawn to bring light again – for running the river at night as it quickens towards the great thunder in the west is too dangerous even for Magua.'

Chingachgook pointed at the gap in the middle of the 'V'.

'This is the arm of the mountain rising above us.'

He slashed a short line across the 'V', turning it into a long upside-down 'A'.

'We go up over the ridge and lie in wait for them downriver.'

He watched Cat who was looking from the scratched diagram in the ashes to her compass and back.

'Do you understand, Cat Man-No? If your legs are strong as your words we can cut them off and ambush them.'

Cat held out the compass and pointed at the river.

'But that's not east . . . look.'

Chingachgook peered at the small brass case and lined the wobbling pointer up with north. True enough, by the compass the direction of the river was not east, but more like south west. He grunted and returned the sword-cane to Cat.

'Compass is broken.'

'Can't be broken!' said Cat.

Chingachgook pointed to the distant rock-line beneath which the sun had just set.

'Either it is broken, or the sun is broken. And you cannot break the sun.'

'The sun goes down in the west,' said Cat, trying to square that with the fact that according to the tiny compass the sun had just set in the north east. 'Damn. It doesn't look broken.'

'Maybe it's not,' said the Indian rising and striding into

the trees. 'Maybe it's just not pointing at north.'

Chingachgook had found his way back to the tree where he had held Cat out of sight. He reached into the splay of young growth fringing its trunk and retrieved a long rifle, a cruel-looking tomahawk, a powder horn and a scarred doe-skin satchel that had a thin blanket roll lashed to the shoulder strap.

'Come,' he said as he ducked his head into the bag strap. 'We will get you a better weapon than that stick-sword.'

He set off at the same slow lope Magua had used, heading back in the direction Magua had come from, as if retracing his steps.

'Where are we going?' panted Cat, trying not to trip over anything in the growing dimness of the evening closing in around them as she slotted in behind.

'You heard the shots?' said Chingachgook, without looking back.

Cat had forgotten the crackle of gunfire that had spooked the deer and got her to her feet what now seemed like an age ago.

'Magua and his dogs lie in ambush up ahead. There will be no survivors. You saw the red coat the devil Magua had taken from the dead.'

Cat remembered the scarlet flash that she had seen an instant before Magua had burst through the screen of pale green leaves in the officer's jacket.

'Your grandfather distracted them. They did not strip the

dead of their weapons. See . . .'

He stopped so quickly that Cat ran into the back of him. It was like hitting a wall. Chingachgook pointed at a pair of horses standing uncertainly in the centre of a small open dell. At their feet lay three unmoving bodies, one in a red coat, one in a white shirt, and one in buckskin leggings and a deerskin shirt.

The red-coated body still had a rifle strapped to his back and, on the horse above the white-shirted body, two horse-pistols could be seen still in their scabbards.

'See? They never had a chance to fight. Magua back-shot them,' snorted Chingachgook. 'Let us see what pickings the Huron buzzards left, and then be gone.'

The horses, a bay roan and a grey, stood eerily still as they approached them, as if beyond fear. Cat felt a nauseous emptiness opening up inside her as they walked closer to the dead bodies. She'd never seen death on anything other than a screen or a page, and even then it had mostly been pretend death.

She kept her attention on the horses, trying not to focus on what she might see of the men's bodies and their wounds. With the tail of her eye she saw but did not focus on Chingachgook bending over each body, checking and tugging them this way and that as he relieved them of what they carried. Cat found that she had come to a halt next to the grey and had her hand on the warm slab of its cheek.

She didn't want to see the dead bodies.

She could feel the absence of life like a deep dark suck at her feet, as if she was standing on the edge of a hole. She tried to figure out if she was scared of the bodies because they were corpses and might be gruesome, or if she was scared of it being bad luck to look at them.

She decided she was just scared, period.

The roan nickered quietly and shuffled forward to nudge at her. She stood with a hand on both horses, and it calmed her enough to look at the dead without feeling the vertiginous pull quite so strongly.

They weren't gruesome. They were just inexpressibly sad as they lay there, legs sprawled across the grass, mouths hung open, eyes slack and utterly, irrevocably empty of anything. She watched Chingachgook straighten their legs and cross their arms over their chests. She saw him close their eyes and pause over the one Indian body to say something quiet in its ear.

Then he stood, picking up the dead Indian's long rifle and powder horn and thrust it at Cat.

'You take.'

Cat's hands closed on the maple-wood gunstock. It wasn't as heavy as she had imagined it would be, but it had the sober heft of a tool made for serious business. She looked at the dead Indian whose gun it had been.

'Should we bury them?' she asked.

Chingachgook peeled the deerskin shirt from the dead body and took care to lay it back straight, crossing the arms across its chest before he answered.

'They are better resting beneath the open sky where the Manitou can look down and see them than hidden in the ground with a mouth full of dirt.'

He threw the shirt at Cat.

'Take off your red jacket and put this on.'

Cat looked down at her hoodie.

'A blind man could see you coming like that. And we want to surprise Magua.'

Cat hefted the shirt in her hand. It was beaded across the chest with tiny cowrie shells, and small buckskin fringes hung off the back and sleeves. It felt soft and greasy at the same time. And now it was close to her, it had an undeniable presence all of its own.

'I don't think . . .'

'Put it on. He won't mind. I asked his spirit's permission. Told him you needed it and we were going to revenge his death by killing Magua . . .'

'It smells . . .'

Chingachgook's eyes were flat, black and unblinking. Cat put the gun down and unzipped her hoodie and stripped down to the long-sleeved waffle-knit Tee she wore beneath it. She pulled the buckskin shirt over her head and tried not to gag at the body odour left inside by its previous owner. She took a deep grateful breath as her head got back out into the open air.

Chingachgook had a knife in his hand and had grabbed the grey's bridle. Before Cat could say anything he had cut through the girth and let the saddle fall to the ground. Then he cut the bridle off its head, gently removed the bit from its mouth and moved to the roan, where he equally swiftly cut off all the harness.

The horses stood looking at them, until he took his tomahawk and slapped the grey's rump with the flat of the blade, at which point they jumped away and trotted off into the darkness at the foot of the trees.

'We could have ridden them,' said Cat.

Chingachgook was cutting a length of narrow rein and didn't bother to look at her as he replied. Cat was already getting used to the fact that he seemed to move purposefully and swiftly, without ever looking hurried.

'We're going higher than horses, higher than bears or cougars even. We're going where only the eagle lives.'

Cat looked down at her boots and decided that the half-laced look wasn't going to cut it if they were going to do some serious hiking, so she bent and cinched up the speed-laces and tied them off with a double bow, something she'd learned from Victor.

Chingachgook stood and took the swordstick from Cat. His hands moved fast, slitting the rein into two loops that he then knotted at each end, making a sling for the stick and hanging it across Cat's back. Then he did the same for the long rifle, and made a third sling from the other bridle for his own gun.

'We will need both hands to climb,' he explained, bending

over the saddlebags and rooting through their contents.

Cat reached back and raked her fingers through her hair, scraping it back out of her face as she swiftly plaited it into a single braid and tied it off with the one elastic band she carried in her jeans.

Chingachgook transferred food into his bag, and then threw Cat a water-skin that hit her in the chest like a heavy pillow.

'Drink,' he ordered. 'Two mouthfuls and then we go.'

As Cat drank Chingachgook stripped a blanket roll off one of the saddles, and picked another tomahawk out of the grass. It was studded with brass nailheads along its haft and had a small, vicious little hatchet-head. It might have been an ugly thing, but it made him smile.

'Take this,' he said, jabbing it into Cat's hands. He handed her the blanket roll too. 'Now we run.'

He set off so fast that Cat had to run hard to keep up, and every step she took made the rifle bang into her shoulders and the back of her head.

Cat swore under her breath. Chingachgook didn't slow down or look round.

'Carry the gun until we need to climb or it will knock you senseless,' he said as he ducked a low branch and cut back across the rising slope.

Cat shucked the gun from her shoulder and, mimicking the man, found the point of balance that allowed her to carry it one-handed after a couple of clumsy tries. She followed him into the gathering gloom on the cold face of the mountain, trying not to think of the last vision of Victor being tumbled lifelessly into the canoe that had swept him so far away from her.

12

Flail section

Victor was in a bad way.

Going under a fire-truck isn't a good idea at any age, but at over seventy the possibilities for complication had really stacked up against him. That's the gist of what Sam was getting from the young male nurse in ER whose name he had failed to catch. Sam had got there too late to hook up with his wife, but had been told that she had followed Cat upstairs to Neurosurgery. The split focus of worrying about his daughter and father at the same time really did feel like it was slowly tearing his brain in two, producing a low-level ripping noise in his head that only after a while did he realize was in fact the sound of a malfunctioning neon tube in the ceiling panel above him. Worrying on two fronts was stopping him from being able to concentrate on anything, even the clinical reality of his father's injuries. He had to hold up a hand and stop the nurse for a moment while he tried to figure out what exactly he was being told.

'A flail segment?' he repeated, not even sure if that's what he'd heard, let alone understanding what it meant. 'Can you run all that past me again. I think, I mean I know I'm a little punch-drunk right now . . .'

The nurse, busy, made a conscious effort neither to sigh audibly nor be seen to check his watch to see exactly how much of the time he didn't have enough of he now had to waste by repeating himself.

'Your father survived being run over by a pretty big chunk of Detroit steel, Mr Manno – which is a miracle. His legs are fractured, not to say crushed – not good. But also not at the moment as great a concern as the thoracic injuries, which are less visually distressing, but more dangerous.'

'Thoracic is the chest, right?' asked Sam, squinting with the effort of staying focused and not allowing the powerful undertow of terror about Cat to take him under and drown him in panic.

The nurse nodded.

'He's had a crushing injury to the chest. In a younger man this is less likely to happen, but with age come brittler bones, and I'm afraid that his ribcage is stove in, creating what we call a flail segment . . .'

Sam held up his hand.

'That's where you lost me.'

'When a section of ribs is broken together, it interferes with the biomechanics of breathing,' explained the nurse. 'Kind of like a trap door that sucks in and out as the lungs contract and expand. The lungs are powerful things, you see, which means that you get a strong chance of further pulmonary contusion.'

Sam sat down. The nurse allowed himself to look at his watch.

'Is he going to make it?' Sam asked.

The nurse looked around, silently cursing doctors who were quick enough to take the glory on the happy calls, but who were even faster when it came to sloping their shoulders and delegating nurses to go and drop the bad bombs in Misery Alley.

'What you should do,' he said, 'is go up to Neurosurgery reception and be with your wife. Your dad's out, and we'll keep him that way while the orthopaedic team try and stabilize the broken section in his thorax. Then they'll get to work on his legs . . . that kind of surgery sounds tough, but it's really just carpentry, you know.'

Sam saw the stutter-step in the nurse's eyes as he stopped himself from checking his watch again.

'You're telling me my daughter's in greater danger than my dad, right?' he said, trying to get things clear in his head.

'I can't make that call, Mr Manno. But I can tell you that right now your father's injuries are something we can fix, with luck. Stabilize the thorax, pin his legs. After we fix it, different story. A man his age? No guarantees, because co-morbidities like infection prey worse on the elderly. My guess is that later will be the telling time for your dad. Your girl—'

'. . . is in trouble now,' finished Sam.

The nurse shrugged. The bit he hated about carrying the doctor's water into Misery Alley was this part exactly: all people wanted was for you to tell them things were going to be OK, that there was hope. And the truth of the thing, the Law of Misery Alley was that there is no law except hope for the best and prepare for the worst. The nurse had pulled the sheets over too many faces that had come in looking like they might walk out to have any joy in giving people false hope.

'Yes,' he said. 'She's having a CT scan. She may be looking at the other kind of surgery.'

'Not the carpentry kind?' said Sam.

'No. The complicated kind. But don't worry too much, Mr Manno. Our Neuro team is the best of the best . . .'

Sam ran for the elevator.

13

Eagle feather

It seemed like they scrambled upwards forever.

Chingachgook would stop every time he got too far ahead of Cat and wait for her to catch up, gruffly ask if she was still strong and then, after Cat had nodded, unable to speak as she got her breath back, he would head off again.

This seemed unfair to Cat until the fifth or sixth time it happened and she was allowed five minutes' rest and a swig of water. The water was welcome, but stopping made it harder to start again, and then she understood there was a method behind the Indian's reluctance to pause all the time. Instead she found herself trying to match Chingachgook's steady pace and find a rhythm of breathing and climbing that became a kind of beat she could keep moving to. It took her a while, but eventually she got the hang of it, at least for most of the time.

Her legs didn't really start to hurt until they had hiked high enough to look down on to the tops of the trees below. They didn't even hurt too badly, not then, just a nagging acid ache in the muscles that she could ride out and ignore.

By the time they had climbed as high again, so high that the wide river by which they had once stood became a thin gleaming streak more lost than found in the dark cloud of forest beneath them, her legs hurt really badly.

Chingachgook still flowed upwards over the rocks like a smooth and unstoppable machine. Cat just kept pace as best she could, making her legs keep pistoning upwards, one step at a time. She felt sweat running down her back, and had to wipe it out of her eyes every minute or so.

The worst thing was that at this height the final ridge line kept teasing with a series of false horizons that only revealed themselves as deceptive once they crested them and saw the heartbreaking sight of the next ridge beckoning beyond.

It seemed like many hours passed.

Cat pushed through a wall of exhaustion and muscle pain without actually realizing she'd done it. There was something hypnotic in the relentlessness of the ascent that made it feel as if she'd always been climbing, as if the sounds of her heart thudding and her breath sucking and blowing had been the soundtrack to her whole life.

It stopped feeling bad and started feeling normal at about the time they had emerged from the tree line to face the more challenging upsweep of the high flank of the mountain. She even had time to look beyond the few feet of rock in front of her every now and then without stumbling.

The moon was rising on her left shoulder and silvering the granite scree on the slopes around them. The angle of the moonlight was such that every time they got to the top of one of the false ridges they were lit, and every time they proceeded into the shallow bowl towards the next one they fell back into the moon-shadow.

By this time they had each slung their rifles back over their shoulders, as they needed both hands to scramble up gradients that seemed to tilt a degree closer to vertical with each step forward.

Cat's stomach lurched as a rocky handhold came away in her grasp and went skittering and banging down the slope behind her. She knew enough not to look back and down. The length of time it took for the rock to stop bouncing told her that she was higher and steeper than she'd realized. Chingachgook grunted and stopped. Cat's nose was level with his heel as the calm question came from above.

'Still strong?'

Cat grunted her own 'Uh-huh' back and tried to slow the drum-machine jackhammering in the centre of her chest.

'You keep your body close to the mountain and she will hold you, Cat Man-No,' said Chingachgook. 'And you keep a grip on her too. Only move one foot or one hand at a time.'

Hiking uphill had morphed from scrambling to real climbing, and Cat felt the suck of gravity coming out of the gulf of moon-shadow behind her as they slowly pulled their way towards the startlingly clear splash of stars scattergunned across the night sky above them.

And then Chingachgook disappeared, and for a moment Cat couldn't think what had happened, and then the Indian's face loomed above her and a strong arm reached back down and pulled her the last couple of feet up and over to bestride the last ridge line. And though Cat's lungs were screaming for oxygen, she stopped breathing at the sight laid out around them.

They crouched straddling the knife-edge of the ridge, the world tumbling away on either side: to the left the dark gulf of moon-shadow they had just climbed out of, to the right a newly revealed treescape washed silver clear in the full brightness of the moon.

Cat held on to the rock between her knees and remembered to breathe as she scanned the expanse of virgin forest stretching to the horizon, unbroken by anything except the rugged chain of peaks jagging skyward through the limitless grey swell of trees like mountainous islands in a frozen ocean.

'Wow . . .' Cat said.

Chingachgook nodded, his hand sweeping out over the view as if bestowing a gift. Indeed the view, now Cat was getting her breath back to normal, did feel like a prize she'd gained for her efforts in climbing this high.

'This is what the eagle sees.'

'Great to be an eagle,' panted Cat, craning her neck and marvelling at the unending deepwood all around them.

101

'Greatest of all,' said Chingachgook, raising his voice a little against the light breeze that worried its way across the ridge, plucking gently at their clothes and riffling their hair as it passed. 'Feel what it would be to be king of all birds.'

And he stood and stretched his arms wide against the night sky, holding them like wings, as the wind seemed to rise a little and lift the three feathers tied to the hair at the back of his head. His eyes were closed and his face was turned blindly to the moon as if enjoying the warmth of the sun. For the first time since Cat had bumped into him he looked happy. He looked younger too, somehow.

He also, Cat noticed, looked extraordinarily precarious, one foot on each side of the crumbly blade of rock that formed the ridge line, with nothing to hold on to but what seemed to be a mile or so of straight-down on either side. The wind blowing his hair sideways behind him didn't add much to the sense of stability either.

Cat remained crouched where she was, gripping the ridge with her knees and hands as if she expected it to buck and throw her off.

Chingachgook opened one eye and looked at her.

'Feel it, Cat Man-No. You climbed high and hard enough to earn one moment as an eagle.'

There was something in the way he looked at Cat, something perhaps in the way the moonlight caught the planes of his face, making him look for a moment like someone else, someone Cat knew well but couldn't quite remember

102

until much later, that made her do it.

She unclenched her hand from the rock and stood up. As she did so she must have risen into the full strength of the breeze, because she felt lighter and buoyed up by it, and though she still felt the ungainly weight of the rifle slung across her back threatening to unbalance her, she took a deep breath and stretched her arms wide on either side.

'You cannot receive a gift with a fist. Close your eyes and open your hands,' said Chingachgook with what sounded suspiciously like a chuckle that was wholly uncharacteristic (for him) but strangely familiar (to Cat).

Cat unclenched her fists and relaxed her hands and, as she closed her eyes and turned her face to the moon, it felt as if her fingertips were fluttering like pinion feathers in the breeze that flowed through them. For a long beat she stood there as something swelled in her chest and the freshness of the air in her face seemed to lift her further until she stopped thinking about how precariously she was perched and just enjoyed the feeling of lightness, realizing that just as this had been the first time she'd seen Chingachgook smile, it was the first time she herself had felt nearly happy since . . . but before she could put a time on when she'd last felt happy, the Indian's voice broke in on her.

'And now open your eyes.'

Cat did as she was told, and though the world lurched she felt her face relax into a wider smile. She didn't feel foolish, she didn't feel scared of the drop on either side of her. She

103

seemed to see the moon-silvered world below better than she had done when viewing it from a protective ridge-hugging crouch, and she felt exhilarated.

She knew she wasn't flying, because she felt her feet firmly planted on the mountain, but she also felt like her head was part of the sky.

'How does it feel?' said Chingachgook.

'Like I'm between things,' said Cat, without thinking.

She heard Chingachgook grunt with approval.

'Good. Brother Eagle too lives between things, because he is the messenger who can visit the world of men on earth and take word and prayers back to the Great Spirit in the sky.'

Cat felt the pressure of wind on her palms rise and pushed back a little, almost like a wing flap. She unbalanced and a small piece of ridge shaled off beneath her right foot and skittered down the slope below. She felt Chingachgook's hand steady her as she dropped into a crouch and gripped the ridge again. She felt the comforting roughness of the rock beneath her left hand, but her right fingertips brushed something soft, caught in a fissure in the granite.

She heard a low laugh from the Indian.

'Don't try to fly before you can walk, Cat Man-No. The gift was just to feel like an eagle. Not to be one . . .'

Cat shrugged off the hand on her shoulder, suddenly stung by the words, and raised herself slightly off the ridge as she pulled the soft thing from the crack in the rock. As she did so, something caught her eye in the sea of silvered treetops far below, and it was so stark and jarring that she forgot to look and see what she had in her hand. What she had seen, far away on the edge of a razor-thin slash of silver that must be the distant river, was a tiny glow of colour: a red pinprick in the monochrome landscape, smaller than a firefly.

'What?' said Chingachgook.

Cat pointed straight down the ridge line at the red speck.

Chingachgook scrambled up behind her and squinted down her arm.

'Huh. Maybe Brother Eagle lent you his eyes, Cat Man-No. You know what that is?'

'A light?'

'Magua. His campfire.'

Cat shivered, and not just because the rising wind was leeching heat from them as they cooled down from their climb. Chingachgook sucked his teeth with a disappointed snap.

'What?' asked Cat.

'He does not hide his firelight because he thinks he is the most dangerous thing in the forest. But he has come further than I thought he could. Come. We must move fast and we will not sleep much if at—'

His voice cut off like a guillotine. The abrupt silence was shocking. He reached forward and turned Cat's hand, staring at the thing she had pulled from the crack in the ridge.

'What is that?'

'A feather,' said Cat, noticing it for the first time.

'Not just any feather. It's an eagle feather. Where did you

get it?' said Chingachgook sharply as his hands went to the back of his head, unconsciously sorting and counting the feathers tied there. He seemed relieved to find them all present and correct.

'It was just here. Stuck in the rock,' said Cat.

Chingachgook stared at Cat as if he were seeing her in a new light.

'Then it is a gift. Keep it safe.'

'OK,' said Cat.

Chingachgook looked at the mountain peak above them, and then down at the slope below. He swung his leg over the ridge and found the first foothold on the down-side. He paused and spoke to the sky as much as to Cat.

'I am the last sachem of the Mohican, Cat Man-No. I carry the sum total of all my tribe's knowledge, all the ancestors. And we know only a real human being is given an eagle feather to carry, and carrying it you must honour it. So whatever the hurt is that brings you here, take comfort in the fact that you are a real human being. Not all men are. Now take care. Any fool can come down a mountain. The great trick is to do it in your own time, on your own two feet . . .'

Cat stashed the feather inside her shirt, took a last glance at the almost invisible red spark at the end of the ridge line, and carefully followed him into the silvered world below.

14

Downside

Scrambling down the mountain was almost as tiring as the climb up to the ridge, but once they got off the steepest pitch at the top it got easier, especially as they could now see where they were going in the moonlight. Each time Cat looked up she marvelled at the fact that there were more stars than she had ever imagined were possible. It was such a clear night that she could see much deeper into the sky than she ever had before, and she saw extra clouds of new stars stacked up layer on layer behind the more familiar constellations whose names Victor had once taught her.

Then they entered the tree line and the darkness closed in again as the branches overhead blocked out the moon, and for a long time it was just about not losing sight of Chingachgook, who had the knack of not bumping into unseen tree trunks and branches – a skill Cat realized she really didn't have at all after she stepped out of his footsteps and painfully into a tree for the third time.

Her knees now ached with the pounding they were getting as they jolted downhill. She began to resent the way Chingachgook still flowed over the terrain, never getting his rifle snarled up in unseen bushes or tripping over roots that seemed to rear out of the ground and clip her ankles in the most painful way. He stopped less now and, when he did, he no longer asked if Cat was strong.

'Stay awake,' was all he said, which just reminded Cat how tired she was and made her want to stop and sleep. What kept her going was the image that kept repeating in her head of Victor being clubbed to the ground, and his limp body being tumbled into a canoe and rowed away.

Pine eventually gave way to mixed stands of scarlet oak and moose maple as the gradient flattened out, and more moonlight made its way down to the forest floor making it easier to see their way again. But even though she could see where they were going she kept dropping her head, and stumbling with exhaustion.

'Stay awake, Cat Man-No!'

They'd walked over a mountain into the early hours of the morning. She was tired to the point where she couldn't think beyond the next footstep, and she was beginning to shiver with a cold that seemed to be rising off the water they could now hear roaring through unseen rapids ahead of them.

Chingachgook dropped back and put his hand on Cat's

back. It felt like he might be holding on to her shirt, keeping her upright.

'I'm fine,' Cat mumbled, her voice groggy and flat.

The hand stayed there. Cat saw something move through the screen of leaves ahead of them.

It was whitewater.

She hoped she was going to be able to sleep now, even for five minutes. His hand stayed on her back, moving her forward until they came out on to a small crescent of grass on the edge of the water. They had hit the river just below the stretch of boulder-strewn rapids that Cat had heard through the trees. Downstream the river broadened further still, its surface smoother and rock-free.

In the moonlit distance Cat could see a big rock, almost a small island that the river forked round. On one side of the rock was another broken section of whitewater, on the other narrower side, closer to the bank, the river looked like it ran clearer, though it was hard to see for sure because a tree had fallen, making a kind of bridge that overhung but also obscured the water beyond. Chingachgook grunted in satisfaction and pointed.

'We go where the river forks.'

'Can we rest?' said Cat.

Chingachgook shook his head and pushed her into a reluctant stumble along the edge of the river.

'You have walked with a great heart, Cat Man-No. Just a little further now and then maybe a short time to rest before they get here.'

Though Cat was exhausted at the thought of even half a mile's more walking, Chingachgook's voice seemed to have found a renewed energy.

'That was a man's journey, coming over the mountain by moonlight. And I have been alone in this hunting ground too long. It is a good thing, too, to walk the woods with another.'

He clapped Cat on the shoulder and stopped pushing her, but stayed at her elbow, catching her when she stumbled and twice helping her unsnarl her rifle from the low bushes along the river's edge.

A thought that had been swimming along below the surface of Cat's mind as she sleepwalked through the second half of their night floundered to the surface as they got closer to the rock island.

'What?' said Chingachgook.

Cat was pretty sure she hadn't said anything.

'On the ridge, up there, you said a hurt had brought me here.'

'Yes,' said the Indian, pushing past a springy tamarack that seemed to want to crowd them off the lip of the riverbank into the quickening waters below.

'What did you mean?'

'You mean how did I know?'

'Yes,' Cat said. 'How did you know what I did?'

'I don't,' said Chingachgook. 'I just see in your eyes that you are sad and you want things to be better. And like calls to like. I too am sad because I came to this forest believing it to be the happy hunting ground, knowing I would see my son, even though I could not say my own name until you gave it back to me. But he was not here and all was ashes in my mouth and heart and eyes. I did not know what hurt I had done to be punished so by the Manitou, but it must have been a grievous sin.'

The unasked question lay between them as they crunched forwards along a shallow scrape of gravel towards the rock island.

'I lied,' said Cat.

'You lied?' repeated the Indian. 'You said the thing that was not?'

'I said the thing that was not,' agreed Cat. 'And because of that all this happened.'

'What was the lie?'

Cat's head spun with the impossibility of explaining to this man, in this place what had happened in a world that even now was beginning to feel like a dream.

She just shook her head and kept on walking.

Chingachgook did not ask again, accepting her silence. Cat followed him through the final couple of hundred yards until they came to the roots of the tree that had fallen across the river and bridged over to the big rock. The rapids boiled past on the far side of the rock, but did – as Cat had thought – run smooth beneath the tree-bridge.

Chingachgook stepped down into the crater that the roots

of the falling tree had ripped out of the forest floor. They had torn a rough semicircle out of the earth that stood at right angles to the ground, forming a kind of mud wall, and he sat Cat with her back against it. Now all forward movement had stopped, Cat felt like an automaton. Chingachgook wrapped her in a blanket and stacked her rifle and tomahawk and sword against the root-wall beside her.

He rummaged in his pouch and cut off a splinter of dried meat, which he put in Cat's mouth. It was hard as bark, but he prevented her from spitting it out and handed her the waterskin.

'Eat. Drink. Stay,' he said, and disappeared into the undergrowth.

Cat chewed mechanically, softening the meat, and drinking small sips. She didn't know how long Chingachgook was gone, and she must have dozed off, because suddenly her head jerked up and her nose caught the smell of smoke before she realized there was now a small fire at her side, and the Indian was crouched by it, feeding it kindling.

'These roots will hide the fire-glow from those coming downstream, and the wind is carrying the smell of the smoke away from them into the Wolf Jaw.'

'OK,' said Cat.

'Give me your eagle feather.'

'OK,' said Cat, fumbling inside her shirt. 'Wolf Jaw?'

Chingachgook didn't answer until she put the feather in his hand, and then he pointed to the river and the rock island.

'The river plays a trick here. The rapids look dangerous and they are, so the careful man steers on this side of the big rock where the water is smooth and safe, but if he does not paddle back across as soon as he passes the rock, and join the rapids lower down where the danger is less, then the smooth water on this side will sweep him to his doom over the falls beyond.'

'Waterfalls?' said Cat.

'Can't you hear?' said Chingachgook.

And Cat realized that beyond the rushing noise of the rapids there was a much deeper bass note, like the sound of the earth itself rumbling. Chingachgook saw her notice it and nodded.

'That's the sound of the Wolf's belly rumbling in hunger. The falls are called the Jaw because of the rocks that stand in the river at the very edge of the drop as the water thunders past on either side, like the hook-teeth of a wolf. The thunder comes from the waters far below which are hungry for anyone who takes the wrong turn. Now sleep for an hour, and then we must prepare, for Magua will come with the dawn.'

Cat closed her eyes and tried to get comfortable against the wall of earth and roots. The warmth of the fire felt good. She opened her eyes and saw Chingachgook passing her eagle feather back and forward through the smoke, mumbling under his breath.

Chingachgook answered her question before she asked it.

'I am telling the fire your name, Cat Man-No. The smoke

will take it to the sky and the Manitou will know it is you who bears this eagle feather, and that you are a human being. And when you or any human being wish to speak to another human being, or send a prayer to the Great Spirit, smoke and feather will take it for you.'

He began binding something round the base of the feather. Cat watched him, eyes heavy, but knowing she had to answer a question before she slept.

'I told him I had read a book.'

Chingachgook kept working on the feather, tying it to a buckskin thong.

'And you had not?'

'It was a present.'

'It was a good present. A book can be a powerful thing.'

'It was just a story book.'

'And story makes the world.'

It sounded like a reproof. Cat swallowed and went on, knowing she had to finish the confession before she could sleep.

'He always gives me books. And then he likes to talk about them. And I said I had read it because I didn't want him to think I didn't like his present, because I didn't want to hurt his feelings. So it was a white lie I guess, except then he wanted to go on this trip we always talk about on the . . .'

She realized she couldn't explain the subway to Chingachgook without a lot of other explaining, so she swerved a bit.

'He wanted to go on this journey and I said no, because that's when there would have been more time to talk and he would have asked details about the book and I'd have had to, I'd have been forced . . .'

'To tell your grandfather you had said the thing that is not.'

'Yeah. So I was, I guess, walking with my head down and hanging back and that's when there was this accident, and I think he saved me and got hurt, in the place we were before this place, and I think if I don't save him in this place, which might be like a dream place, he'll die back in the other, real place.'

'This is a real place, Cat Man-No. The heat on your legs and the ache in your muscles tell you that. It is just another place.'

'OK,' Cat said. 'I just want to see him again . . .'

'As I would see my boy—'

'Uncas.'

'Uncas,' he agreed, and though he was looking up at the moon he was clearly seeing something other than the night sky as his voice thickened with pride and sadness. 'He was a brave warrior, and his time was like that of the sun when in the trees. And I would give anything to walk these woods with him again.'

He leant forward to tuck the blanket round the girl who had fallen straight to sleep.

'Dream safely, Cat Man-No, for tomorrow we feed the Wolf.'

15

In the donut

Sam came of the elevator and began to jog, following the signs to Neurosurgery. He saw Annie alone in the hallway before she saw him. There was a bank of empty seats behind her, but she wasn't sitting. There was a screen of glass between them, and he paused, suddenly still, wanting to stretch this moment, suddenly scared.

Her body was taut as a violin string, her winter boots planted on the slick lino, braced like a gunfighter with her thumbs tucked into the waistband at the back of her jeans. Sam saw the long muscles of her legs flex and stretch as she shifted her weight from foot to foot. He knew this posture. It meant her back was hurting.

Any other day, any other circumstance he'd have strolled over and rubbed it for her.

As it was he stayed still, watching. He was stretching the moment because when he broke it she would turn and tell him something. Her face was tight. But even though he could only see a side view and the wing of hair hanging forward hid her eyes, he could see her jaw clenching and unclenching in a tiny counterpoint to the swaying she was doing with her body.

When he broke this moment she would tell him what had frozen her and why she was alone and rocking from foot to foot in the middle of this featureless corridor.

What she told him would change everything.

Every hope, every plan, every atom of their lives would change when she opened her mouth and pulled him out of his reality and into hers.

So just for another second he wanted to stay in his reality, the one where there was hope and his daughter was alive and there was no abyss to fall into. He didn't want to know what was making her jaw muscles clench like that. In another second he would have to step out of one world and into a storm, unprotected from the strong winds that seemed to be blowing through her hair. So he stayed paused on one foot.

'She's in the donut,' she said, without moving her head.

Annie missed nothing. She must have heard him coming, recognized his footfall.

'OK,' he said, stepping gently into this new world, as if a longer sentence might spook her and send those long legs running deer-like for the hills. 'OK. Donut?'

'It's what they call the scanner. Have you called Joe about this?'

'No,' he said.

'We should call him. Wherever he is,' she said, making no move to get her phone out.

He felt a flicker of anger about Joe and his not showing at the lunch, which came with a swift chaser of guilt as he realized he was really thinking that if Joe had been there then things would have panned out differently; he might have been walking with Cat and they wouldn't have been stepping off that particular kerb at exactly that wrong moment. He knew there was no sense or fairness in thinking like that. So he felt ashamed at himself for the thought and when he reached for Annie, he was looking for some comfort as much as giving it.

Her shoulders didn't give or relax when he put his arm round them. She didn't collapse and bury her face in his chest. She stood her ground, on mission, undeflectable.

He knew Annie was keeping the world spinning by willpower alone, throwing the force of her will through the glass wall she was facing, making Cat's heart keep pumping beat by beat. This was the same Annie who had sat vigil through the night on the kids when they were small and had – despite the vaccinations – got measles. She would stand guard on Cat until she felt safe to rest, which meant she would forget to eat or drink or sleep, and she would resent anyone who tried to make her do any of those things. It was part of her magical thinking, that it would be bad for her to take any comfort while Cat was in danger, that whatever ancient Gods caused these dark things to happen would only be appeased by her own sacrifice of comfort and health.

'What do they say?' he asked.

'Haematoma. A bleed in the head.'

Silence said all that was needed.

'She's a tough kid,' he said.

'OK.'

She unhooked a thumb and looked away, wiping something from her eye.

'It was a pretty tough truck,' she said.

He pulled her to him. She resisted, as he knew she would, and he continued to fold her in his arms, as she in her turn, knew he would.

He stared over her head, seeing through the glass the strange futuristic tableau she had been watching.

Cat was on a narrow stretcher, covered in a pale blue sheet, her head invisible inside a shoulder-width donut-hole in the centre of a huge white plastic machine. The circumference of the donut-hole was lit by blue light that made the little he could see of Cat, which was the underside of her chin, look like she was carved from white marble.

Three technicians or doctors hunched round a bank of screens that showed slices of the maps of Cat's head, and one was pointing, suddenly urgent, at a smaller bank of LED numbers that were cycling upwards. A nurse hurried into the room and he heard a snatch of voice say,

'Pulse rate's going through the roof again—!'

He felt Annie flinch in his arms as she heard it and turned

to see what was happening, and he too now felt the strong wind in his hair.

16

Lying in wait

Cat woke to the sound of metal against metal. The fire was out and the pre-dawn had begun to lighten the sky and leach colour back into the forest. Chingachgook sat next to her, loading his long rifle.

'Hi,' said Cat.

'A new day, Cat Man-No. Are you ready to feed the Wolf?'

Cat didn't feel ready for anything. She was cold and uncomfortable and her muscles had stiffened up during the night. She unfolded herself creakily and tried to stand upright.

'Don't worry about the cold. We have work to do that will warm you. You know how to load a rifle?'

Cat shook her head.

'Then watch. If I die you may have to do this.'

He was smiling, but his voice was matter-of-fact.

'Give me the gun you carried.'

Cat handed the rifle over. Chingachgook thumbed back the hammer on the side and then squeezed the trigger and let it go halfway back.

'Put the hammer here, half-cocked. That way if you catch the trigger it can't go off by mistake.'

He demonstrated.

'Now you take your powder and fill the barrel.'

He took his powder horn and upended it over the end of the barrel, emptying in a measure of black powder. His hands moved fast and efficiently without him needing to look at what they were doing. He took a lead bullet from the satchel at his side and snapped open a brass door in the side of the gunstock. He took a small cloth patch and snapped it closed. As Cat watched he placed the patch over the mouth of the barrel and pressed the bullet down into it. He shucked out the ramrod from under the barrel, held it close to the bottom to force the bullet about six inches into the bore, and then held it at the top, forcing the bullet all the way to the bottom of the barrel.

'Make sure the bullet and the patch are sitting on the gunpowder,' he said, tamping it down one last time and then replacing the rod. He opened the flash-pan in front of the flintlock and filled the shallow depression with a thumbnail's worth of powder, before letting the spring on the flash-pan down to cover it.

'And that's it. You understand?'

Cat nodded.

'Hammer to half-cock, patch, ball, ram them home, powder in the flash-pan – good to go.'

Chingachgook shook his head.

'Not good to go until you put the hammer back to full cock.'

His face was suddenly serious.

'OK,' said Cat. 'Hammer to full cock – then good to go.'

'Good,' smiled the Indian. 'Now come. Bring the axe.'

Chingachgook took his own war axe and walked into the forest a few paces, until he came to a small tree whose trunk was about as thick as his thigh and three times his height.

'This one,' he said.

'This one what?' said Cat.

Chingachgook began chunking small wedge-shaped chips from the base of the tree with speed and determination. Within a few minutes his back was slick with sweat and he stepped back, breathing hard.

'Now you, Cat Man-No.'

Cat took his place. On her first hit the tomahawk turned in her hand.

'Hold it tight, and when you strike, aim for a place a hand's breadth beyond where the axe will hit the tree.'

Cat's second hit did better, and soon she was chopping the small steel axe-head into the tree in a good imitation of Chingachgook's strokes, alternating high and low angles that sent wedges of wood flying across the forest floor. When the axe next turned in her hand and bounced off the wood instead of biting into it, Chingachgook instantly put a hand on her back to stop her.

'You rest now.'

They took it in turns, and as Chingachgook moved the cuts round the tree he kept looking upstream. It was getting lighter all the time.

'Stand back,' he said, and after three hard cuts he stood up and toppled the tree on to its side.

'Now what?' said Cat.

Chingachgook pointed at the larger tree that had fallen across the river.

'Put your axe in your belt. We take this tree up there and lay it on the trunk. It is the same kind of tree. They will never notice until it's too late.'

Cat helped him manhandle the smaller tree along the trunk until they were halfway between the bank and the big boulder-island that stood midstream. She could hear the rush of the rapids beyond. Below their feet the water ran smooth and deep.

'Hold the tree here. Don't let it fall in the water. Not yet,' said Chingachgook and disappeared back on to the riverbank.

Cat watched the river upstream, through the branches of the felled tree, which sat on the much bigger tree trunk like a leafy barricade. Behind her she was conscious of the bass thunder of the unseen waterfall.

'Hear the Wolf?' asked Chingachgook. He had returned carrying both rifles and Cat's swordstick. Cat slung it across her back and reached for a rifle.

'Can you shoot?' asked the Indian.

'I know how,' said Cat.

'But can you hit what you aim at?'

Cat shrugged.

'Maybe.'

'Better I shoot and you load.'

Chingachgook outlined the plan, his eyes now never leaving the distant bend in the river where Magua and his war party would first appear.

It was simple: the Huron would not want to go to the left of the boulder-island, because the entry to the rapids was too dangerous. So they would paddle to the right, where the smooth water ran under the fallen tree. They would know about the dangers of staying too long in the deceptively calm right-hand channel that led to the booming falls, so they would cut left as soon as they passed the boulder and re-enter the other fork below the dangerous whitewater.

Chingachgook would let the first canoe go past, and then drop the tree they had just felled on to the second canoe, at which point he would shoot the Huron in the last canoe. The first canoe would be being sucked downstream away from them, and its occupants too busy paddling hard left to be much immediate trouble.

'What if Victor is in the front canoe?' asked Cat.

'He won't be. Safest canoe is the middle one. He'll be in the middle.'

'What if they don't come one after another? What if they come three abreast?'

'Then we drop the tree on all of them and hope for the best.'

'But . . .'

'No buts, Cat Man-No. You have one job, and it's the same whatever happens. You must get to your grandfather and drag him to the shore. If his arms or legs are tied he will drown without you.'

'And that's the plan?' said Cat. She wasn't convinced.

Chingachgook shrugged.

'It's a shape of things as they may be. As they will no doubt be different, I intend to make my two bullets count. Add those two to the two or three Huron who will be past us heading downstream towards the rapids, that means we only have two or three to deal with if the tree we drop has not done our work for us. At worst they will be wet, stunned and surprised. And then we will go amongst them and see who the Manitou favours.'

And at that he grinned and tapped his tomahawk.

'I've never k—' began Cat, and swallowed. 'I mean I've never been in a fight.'

'There's no secret, Cat Man-No. Only fight when it's right, and if it's right and you have to fight, then the Great Spirit understands that you will spill blood. And if the fight gets hard, get angry. And if it gets harder, get angrier still. I have seen men less skilled in battle soar over greater warriors on the wings of a truly righteous anger.'

Cat thought of the giant Huron callously stepping in to club Victor to the ground.

'I can do angry,' she said. But the butterfly in her stomach told her she could do fear too.

Chingachgook unhooked something from his own neck and held it out to Cat. It was her eagle feather, bound with buckskin on to a couple of green glass beads and a thong.

'All we can do is our best. And if we die like human beings, then we will maybe meet again in another happier hunting ground, Cat Man-No.'

Cat put the thong over her neck and tucked the feather inside her leather shirt. She'd got used to the smell by now, she realized. Or maybe it just now smelled of her after all the sweating she'd done coming over the mountain. She looked up and saw the lofty granite ridge far above them. She couldn't believe they'd climbed that high. She was about to say thank you when three canoes slid sideways into view around the distant bend in the river.

Her guts felt like water again.

Chingachgook moved very slowly, looping the strap of one rifle over his shoulder, and picking up the other. They were hidden from an upstream view by the screen of leaves from the small tree laid in front of them.

The canoes were getting bigger very quickly. Too quickly.

'All you have to do is get your grandfather out of the water,' said Chingachgook. 'You can swim, can't you?'

'Now you ask!' said Cat.

Chingachgook looked at her in alarm.

Cat smiled tightly.

'Yes I can swim. Swimming's the one thing I can do well.'

Chingachgook returned her smile.

'Good. Then all you need do is push when I say push and then dive in and get him.'

'That's all,' said Cat. She wanted to be sick.

'That and one thing more,' said Chingachgook, eyes now locked on the approaching canoes. 'If this goes badly and you meet my son Uncas in another place, tell him I remember his name. And tell him one day I *will* find him.'

There was a shout from the river. Magua steered the front canoe and was gesturing with his hand. He was pointing out the direction they should take, and it was, as Chingachgook had said it would be, underneath their hiding place. Cat saw a familiar flash of green in the second canoe. It was Victor's coat.

'He's in the second boat,' she whispered, but Chingachgook didn't reply, his face tight with concentration as he sighted down the long unwavering barrel of his rifle, watching Magua steer his canoe towards them with long, lazily confident strokes of his paddle.

'I could kill him now,' he breathed.

Cat felt her heart banging in her chest and her throat tightening.

'But then we might not get your grandfather. And I gave you my word,' said Chingachgook, so quietly that his words were almost lost in the sound of the waters rushing below. 'Be very still—'

Magua's canoe led the other two by no more than thirty feet. Victor sat in the next one, head erect and grey hair sifting back in the morning breeze. An ugly bruise purpled the side of his head from hairline to eyebrow, but below it his eyes were surprisingly bright as he watched the forest slide by with something Cat recognized as wonder and delight. Cat felt a surge of relief, though she also noticed Victor's hands were bound in front of him. Three Huron sat in the final canoe, two paddling and one carrying his rifle ready as he too watched the forest, his eyes bright, not with delight, but with suspicion.

And then, much too soon for Cat to have composed herself and be ready for what followed, Magua adjusted the steering on his canoe with a neat fishtailing action that first fought and then used the swirl of the waters as they divided on either side of the giant boulder-island. And he was there, right up on them.

Cat saw the corded muscles on Magua's neck flex as he dug the blade of his paddle into the river, already adjusting his course to hug the smooth sides of the boulder-island, and he never looked up as he passed directly below Cat's feet. The

Huron in the canoe with him, however, did look up, at the very last possible minute, and even as his eyes widened and he opened his mouth to shout something, Chingachgook yelled.

'Now!'

Cat used every ounce of strength to help push the smaller tree off the bridge into the water below. It hit the river in a confused splash, dropping on to the nose of the second canoe before the paddlers had any chance to avoid the sudden chaos of branches falling out of the sky above them.

Time jerked and went strange for Cat as things happened both very quickly and painfully slowly, as if some of what happened was on fast-forward, whilst simultaneously being in a kind of horrific slow motion that allowed her to see what needed to be done or what was going to happen whilst herself being unable to move quite fast enough to do it or avoid it.

She saw the canoe below driven down into the water as the Huron in the front was hit by a thick branch and went under . . .

But Victor looked up at the moment of impact, saw Cat and threw himself sideways into the water . . .

The Huron in the rear of the canoe leapt the other way and grabbed at a branch to save himself . . .

BANG!

Chingachgook fired next to Cat's ear and she looked up in time to see one of the Indians in the third canoe clutch his head and tumble back into the rifleman in the middle of the canoe who was – terrifyingly – already aiming his gun at them as the rear paddler slewed their canoe sideways in the flow, like a skier trying to stop dead.

There was a distant crack and a flat smack overhead as the shot went high but way too close.

Green tweed swirled past in the water below her . . .

Chingachgook tossed one rifle to the riverbank as he shrugged the other off his back, cocked and aimed it in one fluid movement . . .

BANG!

Flint sparked powder and the gun fired a gout of flame from the barrel, immediately followed by a bright white cloud of powder smoke that the breeze blew back over him.

And then Cat was in the water without remembering jumping . . .

And her hands were flailing and grabbing . . .

And only when they clutched the rough tweed of her grandfather's coat did her brain let her feel the bone-crack cold of the river with a shock that stopped her breathing—

And then she was choking lumps of whitewater out of her throat and kicking for the shore ten unreachable feet ahead of her.

She saw Magua look back and shout as his canoe disappeared round the boulder-island.

Victor's head broke surface as Cat scrabbled for a handhold amongst the rocks and roots of the bank on the other side.

Chingachgook stood silhouetted against the sky on

the bridge above as he plunged the ramrod in and out of his rifle.

The tree they had dropped on the canoe was being slowly swept beneath the bridge, the current pulling the trunk downstream. As it moved it revealed the third canoe beaching upstream and the two Huron leaping into the forest, one minute a blur of skin and metal, then just leaves . . .

BANG!

A bullet smacked into the undergrowth where they had disappeared, dropping a small branch and then – a beat of calm –

And then the tree swung more in the current revealing the surviving Huron from Victor's canoe scrambling through the branches and up on to the log behind Chingachgook.

It was the giant Huron with the war club.

Cat shouted.

The giant charged Chingachgook, scything the club at his head.

Chingachgook threw himself backwards like a limbo dancer and the club slashed the air millimetres above his chest as he corkscrewed,

impossibly agile,

clubbing his own rifle round at ankle level and

taking the giant's feet from under him in an ugly crack,

toppling the Huron into the waterlogged trunk below,

bouncing him into the river,

sinking like a bag of rocks.

Victor grabbed Cat's arm, staring at the Indian on the bridge above them, his eyes shining in wonder.

'Chingachgook!'

Cat smiled.

'Yes.'

Victor's face cracked in an answering grin of his own.

'It had to be.'

He gripped her arm in excitement, waving at the panorama around them, the water, the trees and the thundering falls beyond.

'You know where we are, Cat?'

He looked at her, willing her to remember.

'The deepwoods. *Last of the Mohicans.*'

He nodded and shook his head at the same time, laughing as he did so at the wonder of it all.

'It exists! And there he is. In the flesh! Chingachgook!'

Cat dragged him further up the bank.

'We came to rescue you,' she panted.

'Me?'

Victor looked suddenly confused, the smile dying on his lips.

'Of course . . .'

Victor gripped Cat's arm even more tightly and shook her.

'But it's not me that's important! It's you! All I have to do is get to Far Rockaway. You're in trouble—'

Cat squirmed and found that the thing that had been jagging into her back was the tomahawk in her belt.

'I'm fine.'

Victor's hands gouged painful welts into her arm.

'No. No. You're not fine. Cat! You must get it!'

He pointed at the tree working loose below the trunk Chingachgook was kneeling on as he scanned the riverbank and reloaded his rifle. The canoe was caught in its branches.

'The canoe?' asked Cat.

Victor's voice scraped raw with urgency.

'The book. The book is in the canoe. All is lost, you are lost without it! Magua must not have it at any cost. Cat, if you believe anything I have ever said to you believe this: the book is everything and EVERYTHING IS LOST WITHOUT IT!'

The tree shivered as if responding to the physical force of his words and finally broke free. Victor reared up off the bank, staring at it, panic in his eyes as it gathered a jerky forward momentum, the branches below the water catching on the riverbed and then bending or snapping free.

'Free my hands, I must . . .'

'I've got it,' said Cat, pushing him back and diving into the water as the canoe drifted past ten feet away

In five freezing strokes she was at the tree and scrambling round to get at the canoe. Her hand closed on the birchbark-wrapped gunwales and peered in.

The book was visible inside a leather satchel. She pulled herself higher and reached in, grabbing it just as the tree lurched and twisted, lifting the canoe right out of the water and submerging her in the same movement. She kept hold of the book and booted her way to the surface, finding air amongst the scrabble of leaves and twigs at the edge of the tree's canopy.

The canoe tore loose and almost immediately snagged on a bush on the riverbank. Cat was stuck on the wrong side of the tree trunk and was being pulled away into midstream.

She felt the undertow quicken and drag her and the tree in a dangerous lurch to the right, and she realized that she was being dragged down the fork in the river towards the waterfall.

'Swim, Cat Man-No! SWIM!'

Chingachgook's voice carried over the hundred yards of water that had suddenly opened up between them. Cat knew she didn't have time to think. She jammed the book between her teeth and let go of the tree.

She ducked her head into the water and swam with all her strength.

She swam as she always did, breathing every third stroke, made harder by having to exhale and suck air round the sides of the book.

She knew she had to swim sideways, not against the current. She was a Southern California girl. She surfed. She knew about getting out of rip tides.

Only no riptide had ever had a booming waterfall sucking it back, and no California beach had water so cold that within three breaths her head was splitting in a colossal brain-freeze that made her want to sob with pain.

She knew if she thrashed she was dead, so she kept concentrating on long strokes, swimming in the water not on it, corkscrewing her body as her hands reached far ahead and then deep, while her legs churned like a machine behind her. She barked her knuckles on passing boulders a couple of times, but she kept her rhythm, and hauled herself through the water in what seemed like a long and silent scream.

Her hand found the bank and latched on instinctively, and then she kicked and scrambled half upright, hauling herself up on a tree root that had been exposed through the overhanging cornice of a hollow bank on the very end of a spit of land pointing at the falls behind.

She had hit the final place that could have saved her, because the curve beyond the spit was too far, and she would have been pulled inexorably to her death if she had missed this last desperate landfall.

She was shaking with cold and the brain-freeze was more painful than anything she could have imagined, but she was exultant. She tore the book from her mouth, which immediately allowed her teeth to chatter uncontrollably, and waved it back up the river at the tiny figures of Chingachgook and Victor.

'H-h-hey! I g-g-got it!' she yelled.

She couldn't hear what they shouted back, or work out what they were waving at. Her brain was in a kind of self-inflicted hibernation because of the insult the freezing water had inflicted on it.

She just felt happy.

It was going to be OK. She'd saved Victor, and she'd got the book.

She clung on to the root and smiled.

The bullet came across the water with a flat crack, and she heard it an instant after she saw it sever the root an inch above her hand.

By that time she was falling backwards into the water.

As she spun in the air she saw a puff of powder smoke on the opposite bank below the boulder-island, where the river forked. She saw a red coat too, but before she could think 'Magua' she had hit the water and was being sucked back towards the falls.

And this time there was no bank she could possibly reach in time.

17

Nutcracker suite

The door to the CT scan crashed open and Cat was wheeled out and down the corridor at a fast jog. The surgeon jogged alongside and beckoned Sam and Annie.

'Please come with me. I need to tell you this but can't waste time standing round doing it . . .'

He smiled apologetically but didn't break step. They caught up and kept pace, Annie's hand now clenched on Sam's arm. Her eyes were locked on the stretcher turning the corner ahead of them.

'Cat has a haematoma – that's blood pooling between the skull and the brain and building pressure. We're going to have to open her skull and try to relieve that pressure and find the source of the bleed and close it. Do you understand?'

His eyes said please do, I have to get to work.

'Yes,' they replied as one.

He paused in the double doors beneath a sign that said

NEUROSURGERY O.R.

'It sounds gruesome, but if it goes well, it gets us to a good place. You look after each other, anything you need ask the nurses; I'll look after Cat. And Mr Manno, Mrs Manno?'

Their heads came up.

'I do this every day. I will put every ounce of that experience to work to help your girl, but I'm not going to lie to you. Your daughter has a fight on her hands . . .'

18

Feeding the Wolf

The rocks that jagged skyward from the lip of the waterfall were like irregularly spaced teeth. Water thundered past them in an unending torrent, dropping off the edge of the world into a deep mist-bank far below.

Cat could only see the too-short horizon approaching at fatal speed. She knew she was too close to the edge to out-swim the current, which had her firmly in its grip now. The banks on either side were too far to reach.

She was inevitably going to be shot over the falls and plummet to her death on the unseen rocks far below.

The tree they had thrown in the river was bobbing ahead of her, close to the left hand of the falls, approaching the terminal drop at speed. And then an underwater rock caught a dragging branch just long enough for the whole trunk to yaw sideways before tearing free, so that it hit the lip side-on and stopped dead, jammed between two rock teeth on the very edge of the abyss.

Cat didn't have the time or the geometry to fight the implacable hydrology hurtling her towards the falls. But she did think if she swam sideways with all her strength she could maximize the slender chance that when she hit the edge it might be in the space between the teeth that was now blocked by the tree.

She ducked her head and swam so hard it felt like she was tearing muscle off bone with the sheer effort. She raised her head and saw she was going to miss it by inches.

She tore at the water and flung her shoulder blade so far forward it ripped pain through her body, but her outflung hand caught a branch and she held on as the force of the water spun her body round and tried to send her feet first over the edge.

She fought the pounding current that was trying to wrap her round the jutting rock tooth and hauled herself on to the tree trunk, which was juddering like a runaway locomotive between her legs.

One look to her side showed her a gulf of sheer nothing that she didn't want to see again or think about, so she looked straight ahead. The other end of the tree was being drummed against the first rock from the bank, and the gap between it and safe ground looked almost jumpable.

Almost.

She bit down on the book between her teeth and inched along the tree trunk, very carefully, trying not to unbalance things. There was a lone pine on the riverbank, right up on the cliff edge. She focused on that and tried not to think of the drop. Her hands were numb with cold.

And then she saw help coming and she almost dropped the book yelling in relief, and then her eyes twisted into focus and she saw that help wore a red coat and was not Chingachgook but Magua and the other Huron from the first boat, and was not help at all.

She risked a fast look upstream, and her heart fell further. She couldn't see Victor any more.

'The book.'

Magua stood twelve feet away across the water with his tomahawk pointed at Cat, while his companion knelt by the lone pine, looping something round it.

Magua shouted again.

'The book!'

Cat looked back upriver. Victor was gone. But his words of warning remained in Cat's head. She shook it.

No.

Magua took a few steps back and took the rawhide rope that the other Huron had cinched round the tree, wound it round his wrist three times and tied it off.

Then without warning he ran forward and leapt.

One minute Magua was on the riverbank.

Then he was in mid-air, legs bicycling.

And then Cat felt the lurching bounce as he landed on the tree trunk ahead of her.

He slipped, but chunked the tomahawk into the wood like a climber using an ice axe, and held on, letting his legs dangle on either side of the trunk.

He gave Cat a nasty smile.

'Now give me the book.'

Cat shook her head.

'Give me the book, and I will save you.'

He sounded like he almost meant it.

Cat shook her head a third time. Magua pulled his axe free and pointed it at Cat.

'Shake that head again and I will open it and wash my hands in your brains. Now give me the book.'

Cat had nowhere to go. She had no control over anything now. Her way to safety was blocked and probably fatal even if it wasn't and she had tried to jump the gap. Magua was safe, tied to a lifeline that would save him if the tree went over the edge.

And over her shoulder Cat saw the other Huron aiming a rifle at her, unsmiling, waiting for the command.

Strike that, she thought. She did control one thing. She slowly raised her hand to her face and took the book out from between her teeth.

'Good girl,' smiled Magua. 'Give me the book and all will be well.'

'Yeah well,' said Cat, noticing the shake in her voice and hating it. 'That's not what I heard.'

And she threw the book high and far – out over the gulf of

air beyond the waterfall. Its pages were too wet to riffle as it flew, but the covers snapped back like broken wings, giving it the look of a shot bird as it plummeted into the rolling mist at the foot of the falls.

The trunk between her knees bobbled and she grabbed at it with both hands, and looked up just in time to see Magua chopping the axe sideways at her head, his teeth bared in a shriek of pure malice.

Cat snapped her head back as the tip of the blade brushed the skin on the side of her jaw. She dodged the axe, but her movement and that of Magua rolled the trunk and she felt herself sliding and dropping. As she went over the edge she snatched wildly for a handhold and felt the sickening pain in her shoulder again as her hand snagged a branch and suddenly all her bodyweight was hanging from that one hand and she was nose to nose with the downbound wall of water on the wrong side of the falls.

She flailed for a second handhold but couldn't find it. She scrabbled her tomahawk loose from her belt and chopped it into the trunk overhead. She pulled up but the axe came loose. She felt the waterfall clutching at her boots and made another desperate effort, this time pulling up with her hand as she swung the hatchet. The blade went in higher and held as she lifted herself a couple of feet.

A face came over the top and looked down. Magua loomed over her, balanced cat-like on his feet on the trunk, the rawhide safety rope tethering him to the bank pulling taut as he leant down and spat in Cat's face.

Cat just held on. She really was now out of ideas, energy and luck.

'I told you I would split your skull, girl. Now your bones will bleach in a broken tangle at the foot of the Wolf Jaw.'

He flexed upright as he drew back the axe for the killing blow.

Cat flinched her eyes shut on reflex, and then hated herself for it and opened them, defiantly trying not to blink at what was coming, staring hate at the Huron.

She was out of luck, but not letting Magua see her fear was the one final thing she could still take from him, and she was surprised to find that that mattered.

Magua spat in her eyes again. She blinked fast and continued to stare,

'Fine. Drink in the last of the light, for I am sending you into the dark forever, girl.'

Cat didn't close her eyes, but she did change their angle as something grabbed their attention across the top of the vibrating tree trunk between Magua's feet.

'Wait,' she gasped.

Chingachgook was paddling at full speed, straight for them, his own tomahawk held between his teeth. He must have run to the canoe that had snagged on the bush upstream and tried to come to the rescue.

Except he'd left it too late, and the only thing in his eyes now was revenge.

The Huron on the bank must have turned and seen the Mohican at the same time Cat did, because there was a warning shout and the crack of a rifle at the very moment Chingachgook rammed the tree, T-boning the trunk at such velocity that the front of the canoe went down, flipping the back straight upwards, catapulting Chingachgook forward through the air like an avenging angel.

Again time went funny for Cat, a series of slo-mo jerks and freeze-frames:

Magua twisting too late.

Chingachgook ripping the axe out of his mouth.

Then slashing at Magua as he slipped on the trunk and struck back at him.

Chingachgook's stroke was wide, too wide.

And then Cat saw he was not aiming at Magua at all.

He was cutting his safety rope.

His blade passed through the taut buckskin and it snapped apart with a whipcrack at the same moment he caught Magua by the throat. He was not fast enough to stop the Huron's axe from biting into his side, but Cat later realized that was not what he was trying to do.

What he was trying to do was take Magua over the falls with him.

Magua shrieked in anger and terror as the two of them went out over the void beyond Cat, and it seemed that Chingachgook's exultant eyes found Cat for a frozen instant, and though it cannot have been real, Cat heard his voice in her head laughing.

'Fly like the eagle, Cat Man-No.'

What Cat definitely DID hear, until they disappeared into the mist below, was Chingachgook laughing.

And then that abruptly stopped dead.

And all there was was the burning of her muscles and the pain in her fingers as they tried to keep a grip, and the relentless roar of the water plucking at her dangling legs. She was starting to shiver badly. She had no pull left in her. She couldn't get up on to the tree again.

But she was never ever going to let go.

She'd just hold on until the river dried up or something. No way, no damn way was she ever letting go of the tree, because the tree was life and the falls were something else entirely. So she locked her hands on their holds and tried to think of what to do.

Cat wasn't a quitter.

She held on for dear life.

She held on through the pain and into the next one.

She never let go.

She held on until the tree let go.

A branch snapped and the world tilted and she was suddenly, sickeningly and terminally downbound.

And something snapped out from her shirt and slapped her in the eye and, held there by its buckskin thong, the whiffling feather in her face reminded her of Chingachgook's last words and being on the ridge line at night, and without

147

thought, as in a dream, she let go of the useless branch and put her arms wide like an eagle or maybe a crucifix.

But girls do not of course fly.

She still fell.

But she fell like an eagle.

Head up.

Eyes front.

Nowhere to go but down as she depth charged through the mist and then hit something feet first with such a colossal impact that the breath left her body so fast that when she reflexively breathed in the air was gone; everything was river and the fall was over, but now she was being tumbled and pounded to the rocks on the riverbed with a force of water that held her fathoms-deep as the falls sledge-hammered down, and her head hit a rock and the lights went mercifully out as her lungs filled with more river and she never got to watch herself go about the serious business of drowning.

Bad Step

1 'What we call the beginning is often the end.
And to make an end is to make a beginning.
The end is where we start from.'
T.S.Eliot, *Little Gidding*

Inwood

2 'Let your soul stand
cool and composed before a million universes.'
Walt Whitman, *Song of Myself*

Jamaica

3 'The schooners and
the merry crews are laid away to rest,
A little south of sunset in
the islands of the blest.'

John Masefield,
The Ballad of Long John Silver

Broad Channel

4 'Twilight and evening bell,
And after that the dark!
And may there be no sadness or farewell,
When I embark.'

Alfred, Lord Tennyson, *Crossing the Bar*

19

Castaway

Even before she opened her eyes Cat could smell the sea.

She woke with a mouth full of sand and the lazy thump of distant surf in her ears. She was spreadeagled face down, hammered flat by the blast-furnace heat of a midday sun beating down on her back.

She scrabbled her scattered limbs together and sucked up just enough strength to peel her face off the ground and spit.

Her throat was raw.

Her mouth tasted of salt and dead things.

She cranked an eyelid and flinched at the harsh smack of sunlight slamming back off the sea beyond the dark sand beach she was lying on. She spat again and choked herself round on to her back in a series of uncoordinated jerks and sputters. Then she just lay there exhausted and coughing for a while, working at the other eye that had got itself gummed shut with a dried strip of seaweed.

Having got both her eyes open she stared up into the deep blue of the sky wondering where the clouds were and why – if she had just drowned – she felt so incredibly thirsty.

It didn't seem right at all.

And something was digging into her spine.

She felt backwards and realized it was Victor's swordstick still looped over her shoulder on the leather thong.

She wedged herself up on to her elbows and hung there like a broken deckchair, staring beyond the familiar terrain of her knees at an unknown sea stretching off into the horizon of what seemed like a whole new world.

She squinted at the intense sparkle flashing off the blue-green water. She pushed herself further upright into a full sit and looked to right and left. A black sand beach curved gently away on either side in an arc that disappeared into symmetrical vanishing points lost in distant heat shimmers.

There was sand, there was sky, there was sea.

She scooted round and checked behind her.

There was no deepwood. There was no mountain.

There were palm trees.

And more sky.

And that was it.

Wherever she was, it was a long, long way from the forest she had been in.

There was a submerged reef about two hundred yards in front of her where white-capped waves curled and thumped on the shelf of coral below. Their mirror-green faces were carved perfectly by a light offshore wind blowing in over her shoulder from the rattle of stubby palmettos and towering thatch palms behind her.

Even though she was disoriented she found herself smiling at the natural perfection of the long glassy curl as wave after wave toppled in on itself in a perfect left-break right in front of her.

They looked like eight-footers, and for a moment she wanted nothing more than a surfboard and to be out there, on one of them.

And then she remembered Victor and the accident and the ambulance and Chingachgook and Magua and the waterfall and drowning – and she wondered if she was now dead, really dead, not stuck in some limbo peopled by characters from a book Victor had once read her, but in some kind of personal paradise.

That would explain the perfect reef break.

Cat had never been unhappy on a beach, not once. She'd been unhappy *leaving* a beach, sure, but that was a whole other ball of wax. Beaches she loved. All through her growing up she had heard her mother say:

'You never see an unhappy kid at the beach.'

And mostly, for nine out of ten kids, that was true. And for Cat, always.

She heard her dry mouth smacking and choking out something before she knew she was trying to speak.

She realized she was trying to say: 'It's heaven', but she

was too parched and her throat was too raw from retching sea water to get anything other than a muted snarl of consonants out.

Which probably meant that this wasn't heaven at all, since if it were she wouldn't be feeling quite so bad.

Her front was still itchy and damp from where she had been lying on it, but the back of the buckskin shirt had been dried stiff by the sun. She could feel bad sunburn kicking in on her neck and the backs of her ears. She must have been splayed out on the black beach for quite a while before she woke. But though she could feel various other aches and pains from bruises and salt-scoured cuts and grazes, the worst thing was the thirst.

Her tongue felt like an old dried-out insole that had swollen and got too big for her mouth. She decided to get to her feet and start looking for fresh water. She lurched upright and took a step towards the band of palm trees at the top of the shore.

The world lurched and she ate more beach as her legs buckled beneath her.

She tried to spit the new sand out, but there wasn't enough moisture left in her to do it effectively. She got to her feet slower this time and didn't try walking for a good two minutes as she got her balance back, watching the perfect left-break out on the reef curl in again and again.

Then she unlooped the swordstick from her back, took the thong off and wound it carefully round her fist and then thought of something. Victor had taught her to take care of things, and the sword had been as wet as her. So she unclicked the blade and wiped it down with the sleeve of her shirt. She was surprised and a little disappointed to see it was already tarnished where once it had been shiny, and a kind of rust was already beginning to pit it quite deeply. She slid it back into the cane and leant on it for support as she turned and crunched slowly through the dry sand towards the palms and the welcoming shade beneath them.

Out of the sun she stumbled through a tangle of creeping beggarweed and passionflower littered with dried fronds that had shaled off the thatch palms above, looking for a stream or a pool. There was none that she could see, and once she had gone a hundred feet into the trees she stopped and looked around.

The relief from the sun was good. There was a rank smell from the passionflower foliage she had damaged as she crashed through it. It was an unlucky, carrion smell.

She tried to ignore it and figure out how to find water.

She looked up at the palms, thinking of splitting a coconut and drinking from it, but as far as she could see they weren't those kind of palms. Certainly no shells were visible amongst the desiccated bark-peel and fallen debris on the ground around her.

She knew the next step was to find the high ground and look for any freshwater run-off in streams or trickles – or even a spring if fate was smiling. Even the thought of clear water bubbling out of the rock made her thirstier and she ploughed on into the interior as the ground continued its gentle rise above sea level.

She caught a flash of red in the vegetation and dog-legged off course towards a scraggly manchineel tree with silvery bark and shiny green leaves which had sprouted some small fruits like miniature apples.

She was hungry and picked several before noticing her hand was coming out in a rash where she touched the tree. She stopped and thought. Then she put a couple of apples in her pocket but didn't eat them.

She wasn't so hungry that she was going to flirt with a possible poisoning right now. She'd keep a couple for later, she decided, and only eat them as a last resort. The rash itched badly and she tried not to scratch at it as she walked on.

After another hundred yards she stopped again and turned round. This deep into the palms everywhere looked like everywhere else in the dappled shadows, but she was pretty sure she had not walked far enough to get turned around. And yet the rising ground was now no longer rising. It was falling gently downwards again.

She stumbled onwards, and soon the shade began to lighten ahead of her and she saw the sparkle of the sea, and then she had walked out through another band of palmettos and beggarweed and on to the beach again. For a moment she definitely thought she had walked back on herself but then she looked at the sea and the waves and there was no perfect left curl, no reef break or any kind of real waves at all, just broken wind-chop from a breeze that was still blowing into her face as it had been when she entered the palm grove.

She lurched down to the water's edge and looked back. It was almost a mirror image of the beach she had woken on, except the other way round. She had just walked across a sand spit and come out on the other side. If it was connected to a mainland it was a very long spit, because no bigger mass was visible at either end of the beach.

The world started to spin a little as dehydration and dizziness mixed with disappointment, making her realize how hot she was.

'Great,' she sighed. 'Just great.'

She stuck the cane in the sand and peeled off the buckskin shirt. She took off the T-shirt she wore beneath it and walked into the sea. It was tempting to take just one mouthful, but she knew it would make her sick as a dog. Her throat and the inside of her mouth were still raw and salt-numb enough for her to know that she'd had too much seawater in her recently anyway. She felt the sun's rays hammering her bare shoulder blades, and put the buckskin shirt back on to protect them. Then she dunked the T-shirt, soaking it, before putting her head back through the neck hole, just far enough to wear it like a headdress as she fanned the body of the shirt back over her shoulders and tied it in place by knotting the sleeves behind her head.

The water evaporating would keep her cool, she hoped, and the shirt itself would keep the sun off the back of her neck as she walked, though she wasn't going to walk very far unless she found something to slake her raging thirst.

She was in trouble here, alone on a beautiful but desolate shore, and her body was beginning to pack in. Walking in this heat without water was like running a car on no oil; sooner or later she was just going to seize up and stop working. She needed to think straight.

'Need to find water,' she mumbled.

Great, she thought, now I'm talking to myself.

'Give me a break . . .' she muttered and kicked the beach in frustration.

Something spun out of the spray of sand and landed six feet ahead of her.

It was a battered rectangle of scuffed oilskin and well-thumbed cream pages.

She recognized it immediately.

It was Victor's notebook.

20

Something in the water

In two paces Cat had fallen on the book and she held it tightly in her hand. It was warm and dry, which was almost as unbelievable as the fact she had just kicked it out of the sand, since the last time she had seen it, it was plummeting into the waterfall.

As she tried to figure out how it could have got there, or who might have dropped it, she spun and looked first at the palm grove and then out to sea.

Her hands paused in the act of opening the notebook.

There was something large in the water, close to shore. Something that had not been there last time she'd looked. She was sure of that. She wasn't light-headed enough to have missed something that big.

It was a boat, or what looked like a boat, fifty, maybe sixty feet long, and it was capsized, rolling sluggishly hull-up in the light chop raised by the onshore breeze.

She slipped the notebook safely into the pocket of her jeans and quickly took off her boots. She stepped into the water, wading gingerly towards the upturned hull. By the time she was knee-deep, she realized there was something familiar about it.

As it moved heavily in the water the bow lapped to the surface and revealed a great painted eye that stared at her. And then she stopped dead because there was a small man on the bow, and she leapt back with a great splash, fumbling the sword out of the cane before she realized it was just a carving of a monkey or perhaps a bear, stylized and grimacing a mouthful of red tongue and white teeth at her.

She exhaled in relief and lowered the tip of the sword.

'Getting jumpy,' she said, trying to stop the shaking that had taken over her body.

She knew this boat. Though it was not really a boat. It was a canoe, not the fragile birch-bark canoes of the Huron but a solid dugout carved from a single massive cedar trunk.

It was the Great Canoe that Victor had taken her to see many Christmases ago, the one that hung in the Grand Gallery of the Museum of Natural History in New York.

Her smile strengthened. She had no idea why it was here, but the association with a happy memory relaxed her. She waded up to mid-thigh, and the next time the grimacing figurehead lolled up out of the shallows she caught the v-shaped notch in the wood above it and pulled, trying to right the boat.

It rolled surprisingly easily, buoyed up by the salt water, and as it did so some things that had been hidden inside it flopped over the side and slid lifelessly into the water. Her first thought was that they were sacks or bags, but then she saw feet and elbows and stopped breathing for an instant as she realized they were bodies.

She stared at them as they floated face-down for long enough to know that they must be dead.

One of them still gripped a gunstock war club in his hand, and Cat recognized the giant Huron whom she'd seen die at the falls. She had no idea how he came to be here with her, on a tropical island half a world away from the deepwoods of *The Last of the Mohicans*, any more than she knew why Victor's book was here.

She stood staring at the lifeless bodies bobbing alongside the Grand Canoe and decided she would just leave them to the tide. Especially the one furthest from the shore.

The one in the red coat.

There was a bag of something cinched to a peg on the inside of the canoe, and she wondered if it was, as it appeared to be, a fresh waterskin. She walked gingerly closer to it, as she did so approaching the bodies that floated alongside.

She couldn't quite reach it without touching one of the corpses, and so she tried pulling the boat closer. It wouldn't come, grounding itself on the rising shelf of sand below with an audible crunch.

She still didn't want to touch the dead Indians, so she tried to reach it with the hooked handle of her swordstick and then drag it towards herself.

That's what saved her.

As she leant in her hip accidentally bumped the head of the corpse and it rolled in the water.

It was very dead, already puffy from the time in the ocean, ocean that filled its gaping mouth.

The eyes appeared shut.

But then they didn't.

The giant seemed to stare at Cat without blinking.

It must have been a trick of the light.

Which was a good enough explanation. Only it didn't explain how the other two dead Indians were slowly uncurling and standing up in the water behind her.

The giant blinked again and his war club sucked free of the waves.

And as he snarled in rage Cat's hand was moving without thought, slashing the sharp blade in a whip-fast slash across his face.

She saw red blood and heard the rage turn to pain; and then she was in the air as her body took over and leapt her out of the water so fast that her feet were spitting sand behind her before she even knew that she had decided to run for the cover of the palms and try and lose them.

She heard splashing and sharp hisses of anger behind her and only risked a fast look back once she was fifty feet past the stubby palmettos fringing the grove and running in under the tall cover of the overarching thatch palms.

It wasn't a heartening sight.

Four water-slick pursuers were silhouetted against the sea behind her, already on her trail as they crashed into the grove in a maelstrom of pumping knees, bared teeth and glinting tomahawks.

Worst of all the last of the Huron was Magua, red coat flapping as he caught up with his warriors and began to overhaul them, face stretched so taut it looked flayed, teeth clenched and bared in a furious rictus of concentrated malice.

Cat ran for her life, and as she ran deeper into the trees she saw a flash of colour ahead of her as a parrot exploded off a bush and flew ahead of her.

At least they didn't have guns.

That was about all Cat's head had room to think as her body jinked and hurtled its way through the palm grove, following the parrot through the gaps in the trees.

If they'd had guns her back would have made a broad and unmissable target, no matter how fast she ran. As it was she could feel a kind of naked itch between her shoulder blades, tingling in anticipation of a crippling blow from the giant's war club.

She wondered if she was far enough ahead to start thinking about doubling back or ducking and hiding while they crashed past in the undergrowth. A fast twist of her head put paid to that wildly optimistic hope.

The Huron were now only about ten paces behind her and,

far from crashing through any undergrowth, clearly had the disturbing ability to move at speed in a dangerously silent manner. Magua's swiftness had enabled him to overtake one of his warriors and he was now only two men behind her, and gaining with every step. The grim determination etched into all their faces was unnerving, especially because those faces were not the faces of living men but, in some way she had no time to analyse but was absolutely sure of, death masks.

Which begged the question of whether there was any point, when she hit the wall of exhaustion that was approaching at heart-stopping speed, of turning to fight them.

She was sure she wouldn't be able to defeat even just one of these warriors in a fair fight on a good day. On a bad day like this her only hope was that the end would come quickly. And yet her body wasn't giving up. Whatever reserve of adrenaline it had stored up for any fight-or-flight emergency was still pumping hard.

Once more, as she body-swerved a thin palm trunk she saw the parrot's wings whir explosively, and then it accelerated out of the tree cover towards the bright blink of water ahead. Cat jinked and followed the bird, and as she did a tomahawk whirred in over her shoulder, so close that it grazed her cheekbone with a small sharp bite as it spun past, surgically severing a palm frond from a tree right next to her and burying itself in the trunk of the next tree on from it.

She batted away the falling palm leaves without slowing,

and as she passed the tree her free hand snaked out and snatched the tomahawk out of the trunk.

Clearly her body was still thinking for itself, because she felt the strangely comforting heft of the weapon in her fist without knowing that she had decided to grab it. In fact she knew if she had had time to think about doing so, she would undoubtedly have muffed the catch. Whether it was fight or flight that was in the driving seat, it was obviously best to leave them alone and avoid any kind of second-guessing or back-seat driving that might trip them up.

She careered out of the palm grove and stutter-stepped left along the beach, finding a hard-packed strip of sand as fast as she could and digging in, lungs screaming for oxygen and leg muscles twitching with the searing burn of lactic acid that she knew was a warning sign of the wall she was about to hit, a wall made of muscle cramp and dehydration.

Even thinking the word 'cramp' bunched her thigh muscle in a warning spasm.

She stumbled and as she did so saw how close the giant was. She needed to slow him up right now because he was only a couple of paces behind – and one pace closer would bring her within the fatal arc of the war club he carried.

Cat didn't have a fraction of any second to turn and throw the tomahawk. Instead she raised it above her shoulder as she dropped her head and dug in for a final burst, swinging it down in a desperate underarm throw, releasing it as it swung past her thigh and spinning it straight backwards with every last ounce of strength she could muster.

The giant was so close that she couldn't miss.

There was an ugly noise like an axe chunking into wood, and a roar of anger that cut off in a loud thump as something hit the beach behind her.

Another fast look back revealed the giant tumbling forward in the sand, his momentum rolling him onwards as he curved around the axe handle buried somewhere in his mid-section.

Sadly what she also saw was the next Huron hurdling his stricken comrade without dropping a beat in his relentless pursuit, and then Magua behind him did the same also without breaking cadence, and the chase continued.

If anything Magua and the two remaining Huron were faster than the giant who had led the pursuit, and the unintended side effect of felling him was that the gap seemed to be closing faster now.

Cat heard her heart pounding, her feet hitting sand and the T-shirt headdress riffling and snapping in the slipstream behind her as she ran. She couldn't hear their feet, so had to judge their closeness by the noise of their breathing. It wasn't a normal human noise. They punched out exhales in short angry bursts and sucked air in immediately, seeming to hold a full lung for an unnaturally long time, until they had used every bit of oxygen, before spitting it out explosively and grabbing the next lung-full. It had an angry, venomous rhythm to it.

And then she saw the dark scarecrow figure on the beach ahead of her.

Her vision was jerking too much as her feet thumped the hard sand to have more than a jarringly blurred impression of a figure next to a beached rowing boat about one hundred and fifty yards ahead of her. Silhouetted against a sky beginning to bruise into an ominously red and purple sunset he looked disturbingly like a human thundercloud bestriding the dark sand, his long sea cloak billowing sideways behind him in the quickening offshore breeze.

Cat, who had been expecting the worst for what seemed like forever, now knew she was running pell-mell right into it, caught in a pincer between the dead Huron behind her, and Doom itself straight ahead.

Her legs were too gone to even consider trying to dog-leg back up the shallow slope of the beach through the soft sand she'd have cross to get back into the illusory cover of the palm trees, so she decided to cut right and try and make it into the ocean before the Huron could switch direction and cut her off. Once in the water she hoped her arms could take the strain as she struck out for the reef.

It wasn't much of a plan, and certainly had no phase two if she did manage to reach the wave-crests beyond the lagoon, but it was a plan, and as with all plans, best laid or otherwise, it might have worked—

But at the very moment she bunched muscle to screw sideways the next time her left foot slapped into the sand,

Magua, who had now overtaken the front most Huron, got a hand on her head.

Cat ducked instinctively, feeling the grasping talon rake her scalp as the T-shirt headdress ripped free.

Before she could switch directions the hand was back, digging into her shoulder and twisting her round, and then she saw Magua's exultant death mask and the tomahawk raised above it for the killing blow, and though she tried to rip free and dodge she couldn't—

And the next thing she felt was something bite her ear as a bullet ripped over her shoulder and snapped Magua's head back, pinwheeling him off her as if he was being hurled aside by an invisible hand.

Cat heard the shot after she saw its effect, which tumbled him into the two following him so quickly that even their fast reflexes were unable to adjust speedily enough to dodge the red-coated body taking them down in an untidy tackle of tangled limbs.

Cat bounced off her knee and didn't waste time looking at the remaining Huron trying to regain their own feet. She dug in and sprinted towards the Scarecrow of Death who she could see now was a sailor wreathed in powder smoke from a musket that he was busily trying to reload with a kind of fumbling ineptitude that was unangelic and distressing – given the fact that the two Huron were now back on their feet and closing in on Cat's tail again.

It was hope, and Cat ran to it.

It was also a dynamic equation, and as she ran she was very aware that it was unlikely to solve itself in a way that she came well out of: one sailor, plus gun (unloaded) against two Huron (dead, vengeful, armed), the likelihood of him being able to reload in time to fire another shot decreasing with each pace they took towards him. So the gap closing between them was not Cat running to safety: it was Cat and the sailor – who had now of all things DROPPED the ramrod – running out of time.

She saw the sailor pick up the ramrod and then – and this was the last straw of hope blowing away in the wind – SPILL the bullets from his pouch.

The Huron saw it too and greeted the sight of the fumbling nemesis-revealed-as-fumble-fingered buffoon with a brutal shout of laughter.

They too had done the maths on the dynamic equation Cat was on the wrong side of.

With an exultant whoop they both sped up and actually ran past Cat, having worked out that they needed to dispose of the sailor with the gun first, before turning back to deal with her.

As if to emphasize the contemptuous ease with which they knew they would be able to do this, one of them just shoved Cat as he passed, knocking her off her feet with such a sharp blow that she had time only to claw helplessly at the passing air for support before she hit the sand with her ribcage and knocked all the air out of her lungs.

She lay there on the damp sand, fish-mouthing for breath that wouldn't come, watching the victorious Huron close down the remaining distance between themselves and her cack-handed would-be rescuer.

They split right and left, planning to attack him from both sides at once, which meant Cat had a clear sight of what was about to happen to the sailor.

Except the Huron's plan went just as well as Cat's had.

The sailor, as if aware that his end was nigh, threw the unloaded rifle to one side, and for a moment faced his attackers unarmed, leaning against the side of the boat that now blocked his chance of an easy retreat.

They whooped and raised their axes.

At which point the sailor did something that Cat's eyes had to twist to make sense of: he grabbed his own leg and raised it to his shoulder.

It wasn't a leg at all, but a second musket that had been leaning against him where his left leg should have been, but now evidently wasn't.

There was another explosion and a plume of blowing smoke as the gun spat flame and folded the right-hand Huron into an untidy somersault that had not ended before the one-legged sailor threw the empty gun at the remaining Indian. The heavy musket ankled the Huron and he too tumbled into the sand, but rolled nimbly and came up with a snarl and a raised war axe.

The sailor snarled right back at him.

'Stay dead, my pretty.'

And throwing back his sea cloak he drew two horse-pistols from the thick yellow sash that he wore as a belt, and emptied them both into his attacker, who flipped and twitched and hit the sand again with an untidy thud.

Cat got her first breath, then her second, and on the third found she had got back to her feet. She stared at the one-legged sailor who was staring unblinkingly back at her as he lowered himself to the ground and retrieved a crutch that had been lying unseen at his feet. As he wedged himself back upright by jamming it under his arm, Cat was unsurprised to see a small explosion of colour as the parrot flared its wings and dropped companionably on to the pirate's shoulder.

Of course it was a pirate.

It was THE pirate.

It was—

Before Cat could name him, just at the very moment she allowed herself the treacherous thought that her troubles were at an end, the pirate reached behind himself and produced another pistol, twice as big as the other two put together and aimed it unblinkingly at Cat.

'Shut your eyes,' he barked.

'Wait,' yelled Cat.

'Sorry,' said the pirate.

And pulled the trigger.

In the splinter of time that was just enough to know she

was going to die – but too fleeting to unlatch her frozen mouth and yell for mercy – her brain went into a final high-speed sensory max-out trying to cram in as much living as possible into the final shard of existence that remained for her. Everything became hyperclear and superslow, like a movie shot with a hi-speed camera.

And unnaturally loud.

She heard the flat metallic click of the trigger as it unlatched the spring on the firing mechanism.

She saw the hammer on the side of the pistol snap down and kick a shower of sparks sideways as the flint hit the flash-pan with a sharp crack.

Her senses were so heightened that she distinctly heard the separate flare as the sparks ignited the priming powder, sending a small gout of flame into the tiny touch-hole in the side of the barrel.

And then the larger charge in the barrel detonated in a thunderous ear-burst and her head automatically jerked sideways as she tried to dodge the un-dodgeable bullet, her eyes finally scrunching shut on reflex, not quite fast enough to miss the terrible sight of the barrel jerking and spitting flame. Her whole world went searingly bright and then brutally silent as she was knocked backwards, blasted off her feet as much by the shocking noise of the explosion as the impact in her face.

Her brain scrabbled for consciousness so hard that she stayed aware all the way down until the back of her head

hit the hard sand with a sharp crunch and her own
little movie smashcut to black—

21

Cranial bolt

'And now I'm going to put a bolt in her head,' said the neurosurgeon, looking across Cat's anaesthetized body laid out beneath the bright lights of the operating theatre. 'Why?'

The trainee surgeon standing opposite him swallowed nervously. This was the first time he'd attended a real brain operation, and he was mainly concentrating on not fainting. He'd dissected cadavers in med. school and thought he was pretty well hardened to this kind of thing, but seeing the surgeon at work on this girl's head had somehow got to him on the blindside, and he was seriously reflecting on whether he'd chosen the right specialization, and wondering if it was too late to change to dermatology.

'Um,' he said.

'No um,' said the surgeon, reaching for the shiny metal bolt being held out to him in a sterile dish by the staff nurse. 'We don't have time for "um". Break it down. Where are we?'

The trainee watched him bend over Cat's head and tried to think straight.

'Patient presented with blood pooling between the skull and the dura matter on the outside of the brain, following an impact.'

'Come on,' said the surgeon, reaching a hand out without looking up. 'Spanner.'

The nurse put a small tool into his hand and he gently began to tighten the metal bolt down into a hole in the side of Cat's skull.

'You performed a small craniotomy, centred over the thickest portion of the clot, and drained the blood, relieving the pressure and decompressing the brain,' said the trainee, aware he was sounding like a textbook. 'And then you were able to isolate and repair the ruptured vein.'

'Call it a cortical vessel,' said the surgeon, tightening the bolt. 'Be specific.'

'OK,' swallowed the trainee. 'You stopped the bleed. And then you replaced the bone-flap. And now you're putting a cranial bolt in the patient's skull.'

'Why?' said the surgeon.

'To measure ICP,' said the trainee.

There was silence.

'Intracranial pressure,' he added.

'Why?' said the surgeon, checking the position of the bolt on a screen beside him.

'Um . . .' said the trainee. 'To see if pressure builds up again.'

'To see if I made a mistake,' said the surgeon. 'I do, you know. Any surgeon says he doesn't is a liar. Post-operative monitoring is as important as surgery. Your nursing staff is as crucial to the patient's wellbeing as you are, and only an arrogant idiot thinks otherwise. We'll be watching this girl like a hawk for the next few days. The bolt's a warning device. Like those buttons you put in the side of your Thanksgiving turkey, the ones that pop out and tell you it's cooked. Except this doesn't pop out. Not unless I REALLY messed up.'

He grinned mirthlessly at the nurse and took the electrodes she was holding out to him. He carefully attached them to the contact on the bolt.

'These sensors warn us if the pressure goes up again, which in turn tells us I was too confident in thinking I got the bleed stopped. The vessel could open again, or there may be other ruptures I missed. We've saved her from the initial haematoma, but she isn't out of the woods yet . . .'

22

Honest John

The world rebooted with a sickening lurch and Cat was back.

The pirate was bending over her, thumbing her eyelid open, looking into her eyes, searching for something. Whatever he found seemed unexpected, because the weather-beaten face creased into a surprised half-smile as he straightened up, pushing his hat back, revealing the flash of a blue bandanna that he wore wrapped round his head beneath it. The evening sun glinted off a gold hoop in his ear, and there was a sudden further flash of colour as the parrot sifted out of the gloaming and perched on his shoulder.

'Sorry, young lady—'

The pirate jerked his chin, pointing to something behind Cat.

'But he was right on your shoulder.'

Cat turned her head and saw a bare foot in the sand next to

her nose, toes to the sky, still twitching slightly.

She scooched up and away from it, and as she twisted she saw Magua stretched out in the sand behind her, two penny-sized holes just off-centre in his forehead, a skein of dark blood leaking out from the hidden exit wounds on the back of his head.

Cat's hands went to her own face, suddenly aware of the pain across her cheek. The pirate nodded and grimaced an apology.

'That'll smart some, I shouldn't doubt. But it's just powder-burn, and won't do you any permanent disservice. But by the powers, 'tis a lucky thing you heeded my warning and closed your peepers when you did, 'cause I've known some unlucky creatures lose a gig-lamp to muzzle-flash when fighting as close-hauled as we was.'

He reached out a hand. Cat hesitated, then let herself be pulled to her feet. The man leant on his crutch and gazed at her with a shrewd, lopsided gaze, screwing one eye half closed as the other opened wide and looked her up and down.

The only sound was the wind in the palms and the surf booming on the reef to Cat's left. Then the parrot squawked and broke the silence.

'Fiddler's Green! Fiddler's Green! All dead and gone to Fiddler's Green!'

'Stow it, Cap'n!' hissed the one-legged man. He didn't break eye contact with Cat as he brushed the parrot off his shoulder.

'Pay him no mind. That's Cap'n Flint, and he don't have the manners of the man I named him for, and he has precious few enough, you may lay to that.'

The small wooden gig pulled up in the sand behind the pirate was not very much longer than a rowing boat. A mast and sail had been lowered to lie along the length of the craft, jutting forward of the bows by about three feet. The parrot flared its wings and landed on its tip, peering at Cat with an unfriendly eye like a tiny bead of tar.

'First I took you for a boy, running straight and strong as you was down the beach, blood on your cheekbone and all sunburned like, but close up I sees that though dressed boyish-like, you're of the gentle sex – though I'd wager that heathen you chopped down so handy with his own war axe wouldn't think you so. That was close work and bravely done.'

'Thanks,' said Cat.

'And what would your name be, if I might make so bold?' said the pirate, who now leant down and picked the musket out of the sand with a nimbleness that was surprising, given that he was operating one leg short of normal.

'Cat. Cat Manno.'

The pirate nodded as if Cat had just confirmed something he already half knew. His face was tanned to a deep mahogany, out of which his sea-green eyes sparked like cut stones. His hands were reloading the gun with a brisk efficiency that was nothing like the pantomime of bumbling clumsiness he had fooled the Huron with.

'Cat? Well that's as plain and honest a name as you could want, and a fine one too for a roaring girl such as yourself, and there's the truth of it. Would you condescend to do me the great favour of picking my pistols out of the sand, Cat Manno? You'll have noticed I voyage through life with a spar shot away, like, and you'll be a sight nimbler than I.'

And here he nodded at his one leg. Up close you could see the other had been taken off close to the hip.

Cat crouched and picked up the two discarded pistols, blowing the sand from their triggers and side-locks as she did so. She looked up to find the man had finished loading the musket and was again drilling her with his eye.

'Though a young lady, Cat, you've the look of a boy of my acquaintance called Jim, and a world of trouble he was under his fair-weather face. You'll not be a world of trouble, I'll be bound.'

'No,' said Cat, wondering if she was lying, and if the pirate would know if she did. He had the kind of sharpness to his eye that made you think he would. Cat had been mad-dogged a few times on Zuma beach when other surfers had thought she was dropping in their wave, so she knew not to look away. She stared right back and fired a question of her own.

'And your name?'

The head split in a broad white smile as the pirate propped his musket on the keg and reached a hand out to Cat, gripping it firmly.

'Split me if I ain't forgotten my manners! My name's John,

Honest John to my friends and I ain't got no enemies living to call me different, though there's some I've sailed with knows me as Barbecue, or . . .'

'Silver,' breathed Cat. It wasn't a question. 'Long John Silver.'

The lines radiating from the edges of Silver's eyes lengthened and deepened. The smile was like the contrasting dazzle of sunlight suddenly flashing out from behind a stormcloud.

'Sharp girl! Smart as paint. Knew you were soon as I clapped eyes on you. You'll have heard of me then?'

Cat nodded. Silver was reloading his pistols with as much speed and efficiency as he had loaded the musket, sliding them inside the sash he wore as a belt once they were finished. There was an urgency to the way he was working that was at odds with the bluff cheerfulness of his voice. Cat wondered who he was preparing to defend himself from, and as she did so she felt a colder breeze blow across the beach to match the darkening sky.

'Well, Cat, there's those as sits about telling tall tales, and those as gets about the world a-doing of deeds and a-getting told of. And of them as sits safe and snug in port telling tales, the half of them is liars and the other half is envious of those enterprising gentlemen who take the early tide and head out for the clear water beyond the horizon. Which is to say: don't believe the one half of what you may have heard tell of me, and take the other half with a puncheon of salt!'

He bent to lift a small barrel from the boat and pulled the

bung: she watched him tip it to his lips and drink. Just watching made Cat realize her mouth was dry as sandpaper.

Silver finished and held out the barrel.

'Wet your pipe, young Mistress Manno. You've a sun-parched look to you.'

Cat took the barrel, surprised at the weight of it, and drank. Silver watched her glug it down.

'Easy, girl. There's plenty more and you'll bloat your gut and spew it up if you take in too much in one go.'

Cat handed it back and watched Silver smack the bung back in.

'Now I've a question for you. I don't suppose, as enterprising a young lady as you seem to be, that you know how to pull a rope and keep your head down when you're told to?'

'I guess,' said Cat. 'Why?'

'Why indeed?' said Silver. 'I likes a person that asks questions, by the powers so I do. "Why?" she says . . .'

He took a step forward and loomed over Cat, again dark and ominous as a thunderhead.

'Because if you can help sail this gig, and shift sharp beneath the boom as we come about and clear the reef, we might have a way to get off this island. And though I ain't a superstitious man, getting off this island afore it gets too dark might be a healthy thing to do.'

He looked at the bodies of the Huron splayed untidily down the beach where he had shot them down.

'I shot that savage in the red coat clean through the head once, and he got up. Now you saw I put another ball through his brain, but I don't know how long—'

'SILVER!!'

The shout came from the trees. They both spun round in time to see a blood-streaked sailor charge barefoot out of the palm grove. He was stripped to the waist and carried a cutlass in one hand and what looked like a blunderbuss in the other. His teeth were bared in a red-toothed snarl and his one good eye was blazing with fury.

The fury and the weapons weren't the most frightening thing about him: nor was it that he was still running and shouting despite the fact his other eye was not, strictly speaking, there (the side of his head having been blown away by a gun held close enough to have set his hair on fire when he'd been shot).

It wasn't even the fact that his hair was still smouldering that was the most frightening thing.

What was most frightening was the fact that he didn't seem to mind.

'SILVER, YOU TREACHEROUS SCURVY BASTARD!'

Silver was off-balance and leaning on his crutch as he swept his sea cloak back and reached for one of the pistols at his waist.

The attacker levelled his blunderbuss and fired as he ran.

If he'd stopped he would probably have done a better job of aiming, but in its way the shot did half the job he needed.

There was a BOOM and an explosion of wood and sand sent shards and grit left and right as the shot powdered the crutch about a foot and a half from the ground. Cat felt a small sharp pain as a splinter of wood-shrapnel jagged into her calf.

Silver lurched sideways and went down like a felled tree, snarled in his cloak, smacking his head on the side of the boat as he went down.

The attacker flung the empty gun away and leapt towards him with a wordless shout of victory, raising his cutlass high above his head as he sprang through the air.

Cat heard herself shout 'NO!' and felt the handle of the swordstick in her hand before she realized she'd grabbed for it. She must have accidentally hit the release-catch with her thumb, because as she jumped between the stricken Silver and the incoming attacker and instinctively swung the stick towards him, the centrifugal force shucked the stick off the blade and sent it clattering against the side of the gig.

Cat didn't know that she'd done what she'd done, let alone why she'd done it, because it was all reflex, but there was a shockingly solid impact as the sky-borne assailant thunked into her fist which was braced at the end of her straight arm, and though she stumbled back with the force of the collision, she kept her footing.

It was only when she looked up and saw the snarling face now inches from her own that she realized the handle had smacked home to the hilt, right over the attacker's heart,

184

which explained why nearly a yard of cold steel was now sticking out of his back like a gruesome car aerial.

Close up the face was worse.

Blood had streaked across the cheek and into the mouth, and the red teeth gnashed in frustration. The eye was looking down at the stick-handle attached to its chest. The smell of sweat and burning hair was bad.

Cat thought 'I've just killed him'. Which would have upset her more if the one-eyed sailor wasn't looking so horribly alive. He dropped his cutlass and grasped Cat's wrist, trying to heave himself off the blade.

The lone eye swivelled up and looked her in the face. For an instant, despite the fact half of his head was shot away and his hair was smoking, he looked strangely human and surprised.

'What have you done?' he faltered.

Cat swallowed.

'I'm sorry?' she tried.

The man's head jerked back as if Cat had hit him and all the humanity drained from his eye and then he jerked his head forward as if trying to bite her.

'SORRY?' he snarled, blood and spittle spraying into Cat's face.

She pushed him back with another thrust of the sword handle. The eye looked down and up again quickly – then began to flutter, like a candle guttering out.

'This ain't over, girlie,' said the man. 'I'll see you in Fiddler's

Green. And then you'll dance to MY tune . . .'

And with that his eye rolled back in its socket, filling it with white, the hands flexing once and then letting go as his hair, perhaps kindled by a stronger gust of the evening breeze, burst into flame and he fell back off Cat's sword and sprawled unmoving on the sand.

Cat stood there, sword-blade beginning to tremor in her hand as her mind caught up with her body and she had the unpleasant luxury of thinking about what had just happened as she looked at the flames dwindling back to a smoulder around the head of the dead man.

23

A nasty discovery

'Billy Bones was always a hothead,' said a voice from the ground behind her. 'But that's egging the pudding a bit, by the powers.'

Cat looked round and saw Silver was lying on the ground holding out his hand, the side of his face covered in a thin layer of beach that had stuck to it when he had fallen. She gripped it and helped him back to his feet. Silver tossed the sawn-off crutch into the boat and balanced himself against the side, looking at the smoking head of the dead sailor.

'I killed him,' said Cat.

'Join the club,' said Silver, spitting sand sideways with a grimace. 'Least I thought I had.'

He bent and picked up the hollow cane and handed it back to Cat. Cat looked at the blade.

'Wipe it on his shirt,' said Silver. 'He won't mind.'

Cat didn't want to get too close to the terrible head, so she squatted and wiped the blood off on the ragged cuff of the dead man's trousers, trying not to look at the bare feet sticking out of them.

The blood came off, but the blade was no longer shiny at all. It had begun to rust badly, and looked worse than when she'd wiped it earlier. She scrubbed at it with the hem of her shirt, but it wouldn't get any cleaner. She wondered how it could be corroding so fast, then decided that working that out was the least of her problems.

She straightened and sheathed the pitted blade as Silver put a hand on her shoulder.

'I'd say as you just saved my bacon there, Miss Cat. I'm obliged, and in your debt.'

And he swept off his hat and bowed with surprising gracefulness.

'It just happened,' said Cat, who had never been bowed to before and was not quite sure how to respond.

'Well I'm powerful grateful that it did,' said Silver, jamming his hat back on with a grin. 'I shall die one day, more's the pity, same as any man, but I wouldn't choose to do it here, not on this cursed island of all the places in the world. Let's make shift and put a few leagues of clean blue water between it and us before the shadows lengthen and more dark comes.'

He paused and peered at Cat.

'That is assuming you wouldn't a-rather peg on under solitary colours, like?' he said.

'No,' said Cat. It was an easy call. 'I'll come with you.'

She knew she maybe shouldn't trust Silver in the long run. The man was a pirate after all. But in the flesh he was like two people anyway: on the one hand he was the bluff and cheerful figure smiling clear-eyed at her, and on the other, well, the other Silver was calm and lethal enough to face down three armed men rushing down on him and coolly drop them one by one, without wavering or worrying about the consequences – even perhaps the possibility – of one missed bullet. But her problem was not a long-run one anyway. It was very short run: she felt the hairs on her neck begin to prickle at the thought of what it would be to sleep a night on the island with these corpses that had already come back from the dead once. What had happened once could happen again, she imagined.

'Shake a leg then, and let's get this barky back in the briny,' said Silver, leaning over the gig and putting the musket inside. 'Time and tide wait for no man. Or girl.'

Cat joined him in pushing the boat into the water. As they shoved and heaved, the water suddenly took the weight of the boat and Silver tumbled himself aboard in a lunge and a twist that was both well practised and an extraordinary combination of great strength and unusual agility. In an instant he had yanked the mast upright and secured it with a backstay, and the wind bellied the sail and began to push the boat towards the green curl of the reef break a hundred yards ahead.

Cat was left waist-deep in the sea, watching the gap lengthen between her and the boat, and then she knew that Silver had tricked her and had only wanted her help to get the boat off the beach and back afloat.

Then she heard hard feet slapping wet sand, and spun to see Magua running for her, hands stretched in front of him like talons, the two bullet-holes still leaking blood from his forehead.

He shrieked in rage as he came.

The noise froze her in her tracks for an instant.

But in the time it took for her stomach to drop at the unkillable horror running after her, Silver had turned and reached out a large hand from the back of the boat.

'Come on, Cat! Lively now or the crabs'll be picking at your bones before the tide turns!'

And Cat plunged chest-deep after the boat, too slow to make contact, and missed the hand. But Silver was fast, and snatched the broken crutch and thrust it desperately back across the widening gap between them.

'Clap on, girl, clap on like a limpet!'

Cat grabbed the T-section at the top of the crutch and felt a blow on her foot as Magua threw himself in a final leap and caught her heel and held her for a moment – until Silver's great strength ripped her free as he dragged her through the water, and then grabbed the sword-cane still looped over her back and hoisted her bodily inboard, dropping her into the scuppers at his foot.

He busied himself with the rudder and the sail which was beginning to flap as the boat yawed with no one steering. The parrot flapped up behind him and landed on the bench at his side, and then hopped beneath it, disappearing behind his sea cloak.

'Up the bow, girl, and keep a weather eye on the water ahead. Sing out if you see coral, for we shall rip the bottom out of this gig if we hit the reef at this speed.'

Cat scrambled to the sharp end of the boat and hung over the edge, her eyes scanning the water ahead.

'What do you see?' shouted Silver.

'Sand!' she shouted back.

She snatched a glance backwards to where he'd wedged himself with the tiller under one armpit, steering with it whilst using one hand to tighten the backstay and the other to hold on to the rope controlling the boom. He was grinning, as if delighting in his power at doing three things at once, but his face blackened as he saw Cat turn to look at him.

'Keep your eyes forrard, ye swab,' he roared, 'or we're shark-bait.'

The small boat was now ripping through the light chop of the inner lagoon, continuing to accelerate as it ran straight before the wind that was now gaining in strength with every yard forward, as they came out of the wind-shadow of the retreating island.

The bottom ahead was still sandy, and the water clear

enough for Cat to see pilot fish streaking just ahead of the growing bow wave.

A sudden dark shadow-wall lurched into view on her left, like an underwater hedge rushing at them.

'Rocks!' she yelled, pointing.

'That ain't rocks,' shouted Silver, calmly adjusting the tiller and making the now speeding sailboat carve strongly to the left. 'That's the reef!'

Cat couldn't believe they were there already, but the boat was flying now.

'Clap hold now, and hope I've a-timed this right. This will be touch and go, my beauty!'

Cat suddenly saw jagged coral right below and had no time to shout a second warning, but then there was a sickening slow lurch as the whole sea suddenly lifted in a green slope and the coral disappeared as it sank into the deeper green of a rising wave.

She looked ahead and stopped breathing.

They were climbing the forward face of a huge wave, and she could see the furious white curl of the crest falling in on itself racing towards them like an express train.

Behind her she heard the inexplicable noise of laughter as Silver stared down the inevitable disaster that was inbound. It was simple physics: the wave got steeper as they neared the crest, and so they slowed down. If they slowed down too much – as they appeared to be doing – then they would not make it over the crest and into the open sea beyond before the curl took them and tumbled the boat backwards end-over-end, back down on to the coral teeth waiting at their back. Cat knew enough about waves to be certain they weren't going to make it.

'If you know a prayer, Cat Manno, now's the time!' roared Silver as she looked right down the tube of the curl ripping in from the left. For an instant she thought about diving off the boat and taking her chances by trying to swim below the break, but it was too late, and as the whitewater hit—

The gig breasted the top of the wave at the last possible moment and then, in the sudden and merciful smoothness that opened up on the other side of the crest, they were accelerating along the downslope, free of the lagoon and clear of the reef.

She looked back at Silver and saw him calmly shake the water off his hat from where the leading edge of the curl had caught the tail of the boat, and then he grinned and adjusted the tiller.

'Hold on now,' he laughed. 'We'll have an easier passage over these growlers now the reef's behind us.'

Cat watched him take the boat off the wind and steer a less aggressive angle across the following wave sets, waves that eased in intensity and height as the gig fought clear of the grip of the island. In a few minutes they were in calmer water, making good speed towards the sunset.

After the narrowness of their escape from the clutches of the fatal reef break it was like being able to breathe again.

'Nicely done,' said Silver. 'Sharp eyes you had, keeping us off the coral at the last minute. You hadn't have sung out as you did, I'd have missed my mark and we'd have been pounded to kindling, and you may lay to that.'

Cat looked back. The island was already getting smaller as it receded in the distance, but it was still close enough that she could see something that made her catch her breath: beyond the wind-blown plumes of spray coming off the waves, beyond the back of the reef break she saw the figures now standing knee-deep in the water at the edge of the beach watching them head out to sea. She swallowed.

'Those men you killed . . .'

'Savage redskin devils all, no doubt,' said Silver. 'Gone to a happier place, or not, as providence disposes. We got one like them back on the ship, picked him up out of a canoe drifting off the Grand Banks last September, and a surly dangerous bastard he is and all. Give him a wide berth when we get aboard and you shan't go far wrong, and give 'em as is dead no more thought . . .'

Cat shook her head and just pointed back at the beach.

Silver's Adam's apple bobbed as he swallowed and then shook himself as if throwing off an unpleasant thought.

'Well. I told you it was an unchancy island. Even the dead don't stay dead there.' He grimaced. 'But they do *stay* there. Which is a consolation, I'll be bound.'

He dragged his eyes away, pulling a compass from his pocket and checking it against the sun.

Cat couldn't take her eyes off the five dead men standing at the water's edge, and so she watched them until they were impossible to make out and lost to sight in the distance.

She shivered. The wind was cold this far out on the open water and she stuck her hands in her pockets. It took her a moment or two to realize what was wrong. When she did so, it felt like another kick in the stomach.

'What's wrong?' said Silver.

'It's nothing. Just cold,' said Cat.

'Well, sit down, out of the wind. And wrap yourself in that coat.'

There was a seaman's canvas jacket balled under the thwart at her side. It was a weather-beaten navy blue, with white patches where salt water had dried on it. She held it up. It looked as if it was her size, more or less. It was certainly too small for the large man steering the boat.

'Go on,' said Silver with a dry chuckle. Jerking his head very slightly back towards the island. 'Billy ain't going to need it any more. Where he's going'll be hot enough, and he ain't going to be worrying himself about keeping any warmer, you may lay to that.'

Cat understood how Silver had got the boat out of the water in the first place, and why he'd needed her help to refloat it. He'd come with Billy Bones as a partner and left him on the island. Killed him, perhaps. But that wasn't what made Cat sick in her gut. What did that to her was what she had found when she put her hands in her jeans pocket.

In the right-hand pocket there was nothing.

And it was in the right-hand pocket where she had put Victor's notebook.

It had gone.

24

Post-op

'She looks so alone,' said Annie. 'So trapped and lost.'

Cat lay unmoving on the bed. Her head was bandaged, but not enough to hide the fact that one side of her long hair had been shorn away above the ear in preparation for the surgery she'd just emerged from. Wires looped from it to overhanging monitors, while tubes and catheters connected her arm to small boxy machines and ominous drip-bags.

Her skin, normally healthy and tan, was pale and waxy and appeared to have collapsed on to the underlying contours of her skull.

Sam and Annie sat by the bed, sandwiching Cat's free hand between their own.

'Joe should be here,' said Annie. She opened her mouth to say more, but choked on a half sob instead. Sam put his other arm round her shoulders.

'She's not going to die,' he said.

Annie shook her head angrily.

'Why didn't he come to lunch? He should have come to lunch.'

He squeezed her.

'Annie. She's going to get through this.'

Her eyes turned to him and he saw ragged holes of pain.

'How do you know? How the—?'

He squeezed her tighter, burying those eyes in the crook between his neck and his shoulder.

'Because she's tough. She's tough like you.'

He held her like that until she stopped shaking, his eyes locked on Cat's face over the top of her head. She took a deep breath and sat back and wiped her eyes. She nodded once, tightly. Thanks. Took another breath and looked at their daughter.

'I'm going to sit with her.'

'I know. I should go see my dad . . .' he said.

'I know,' she took another deep breath. 'You want me to come?'

'Yes. But not as much as I want you here, watching our girl.'

Her eyes thanked him again. Then another thought ambushed her.

'We should call Joe.'

He squeezed Annie's hand gently and stood up.

'Let me check on Dad, then I'll step out the building and try him.'

'I . . .'

He leant down and kissed the top of her head.

'I know. Me too.'

The nurse who Sam had spoken with on the first floor had gone off shift, and he had trouble finding someone who could point him at Victor, but eventually he was pointed down the hall to a room guarded by a tall nurse who looked at him with a kind of brisk suspicion.

'Are you Joe?' she said.

'*Joe?* No. Joe's my son. His grandson . . .'

She let him through the door. Victor looked as lonely and helpless as Cat had, but somehow brittler. His skin looked almost see-through and stretched to breaking point.

'They're figuring out whether to operate on his legs now or wait,' she said. 'His breathing's better so they might go for it.'

'OK,' said Sam, unsure if that was good or bad news. 'Why did you think I was Joe?'

'He was awake a while back. Kinda confused, but adamant about one thing. He wanted Joe. Wanted to warn him about something called Maggie or Magger . . . ?'

Sam looked at Victor's hand, clenched like a liver-spotted chicken's talon on the flat white sheet.

'Magua,' he said. 'It's a someone, not a something.'

'Well he was pretty bent out of shape about it,' she said. 'He said it'd got his cat.'

'He hasn't got a . . .' began Sam.

Then he caught up.

'Oh,' he said. 'Cat.'

'I guess,' she said. 'You can sit with him if you like? I can page a doctor?'

'In a minute, yes please,' he said. 'But I need to make a call. Our son doesn't know about any of this. Our daughter was in the same accident . . .'

'I heard,' she said, with the professional sympathetic smile of one who's heard worse. 'The payphone's in the lobby. If you use your cell, you need to step outside,' she said. 'Sorry.'

Night was coming down as he stepped out of the hospital into the no-man's land of stress-smokers and pacing phone-users on the covered area beyond the sidewalk.

Joe's face smiled at him from the smart-phone screen as he punched up his name, and hit dial. But his voice when he picked up was wary and apologetic, without a trace of that other-day smile. Thumping drum-and-bass in the background made him almost inaudible.

'Dad,' he said. 'Look. I'm sorry about lunch. It was just . . .'

'Joe,' Sam said. 'I've got bad news. So I'm just going to give it to you straight: Cat and Victor are in hospital. They got hit by a truck.'

Sam felt Joe's silence on the line, felt it as badly as if he'd just sucker-punched his son. All he could hear was the pounding music. And then that stopped abruptly. He heard some other voice complain and heard Joe chop that voice off with a muffled swear word. Then he came back on the line, his voice changed.

'Cat . . . ?' he said, and in that one shocked syllable Sam heard the years drop off Joe, heard a fear and a vulnerability he barely remembered.

'Joe. They're stable for the moment. But you need to get down here fast . . .'

25

A broken night

'Are you all right, girl?' asked Silver, peering at Cat in the gathering dark.

Cat wondered if the large man had seen the colour drain from her face with the shock of finding that she had lost Victor's notebook so soon after stumbling across it. She had known finding it was a big thing according to whatever cock-eyed rules the game she had woken up in was being played by, and that meant losing it was doubly bad.

'I'm fine,' she replied. She took her hands out of her horribly empty pockets and steadied herself against the side of the boat as she slid down to sit out of the gathering wind. As if to distract attention from what her hand had discovered she trailed it over the edge, fingertips skimming the waves as the boat cut across them.

She was lying. She was anything but all right. She was at sea in more ways than one and she was sure it was written all over her face where Silver could read it plainly so she turned away and looked ahead. The reddening sun was drowning itself amongst dark streaks of cloudbank lying along the distant horizon. It wasn't a cheerful sight. She wondered whether—

'Look out!' yelled Silver.

Cat spun just in time to see him move with blinding speed for such a big man, snatching up a pistol and cocking it and firing it in her direction.

Cat's head snapped sideways, as if it could move fast enough to follow the track of the bullet, and saw a flash of white belly and a hideous crescent mouth crammed with row on row of triangular teeth as a shark rolled up just where her hand had been trailing in the water an instant before. In the second before the boat's speed took them past the attacker she saw blood feathering out of a pale belly where Silver's bullet had found its mark.

'Lord hates a shark,' said Silver, looking back. 'That's why he never gave them the blessing of sleep. Why even the lowest serpent dozes in the sun. But a shark?' he spat after it. 'The devil's pet, and you may lay to that.'

Cat could see the dorsal fin of the wounded shark rolling slowly in their wake, and then there were suddenly more fins and other sharks and the white water boiled red as they tugged and tore the injured shark to pieces.

'Now that's a happier sight,' Silver laughed. 'See that, Cat? It's a dog eat dogfish world and no mistake.'

Cat just shivered. The furiously silent carnage behind them

was as shocking as the fact she'd been within an inch of losing her hand to a shark bite. The sea had always been a place of escape for her, somewhere calm and powerful and challenging. She knew enough about rip tides and currents and undertow to gauge its dangers and, by respecting them, act accordingly. She'd been tumbled and held to the bottom by breaking waves enough times to know it could kill you if you were unlucky or stupid. If you surfed, the possibility of drowning was always there, a tiny possibility in the distant recesses of your mind, a tiny whine that was pitched so high and at such a low volume as to be almost unnoticeable. It was like living in California and knowing about earthquakes: sure, you *could* die in one, the possibility was real. It simply wasn't the first thing you thought about every day. It was just part of the background noise, familiar and ignorable. And drowning was one thing: it was solitary and somehow self-inflicted, something you did because you went too far out or got too tired in the wrong current at the wrong time of day.

The killing frenzy of the sharks was different. It was brutal and unnerving in the speed and the silence with which it took place. One minute open sea, the next sharp fins and wild threshing and gore staining the clean water as the ocean revealed its hidden teeth.

'Here, girl, put that coat on before you catch a chill.'

Cat shrugged into the heavy canvas jacket. It was double breasted, reaching halfway down her thigh, with a high collar that you could button up to keep the wind and rain off your neck and face in a storm.

'Like I said, Billy won't be needing it,' Silver said, as if he could read Cat's thoughts. 'He come the high hand with me back on that island, more's the pity because we were once fast friends. Which is how come he isn't making the return voyage, and that's the truth on it.'

'You killed him,' said Cat.

A spark flashed in Silver's eye and then disappeared just as quickly as he damped it down with a smile.

'Let's see that leg, for you seem to be bleeding,' he said.

She let him look at her calf, and winced as he quickly pulled out the shard of crutch that Billy Bones's blunderbuss had lodged there. He pulled a bandanna out of his pocket and swiftly bandaged her leg with it.

'You're a plain speaker, to be sure, and I like that in a girl,' he said as he cinched the knot tight. 'He was an old friend who tried to play me false. I took no pleasure in killing him, being a Christian man, but as a Christian I've always favoured smiting them as cross me, smiting them hip and thigh, rather than turning the other cheek, and them as knows Honest John knows that, you may be sure.'

Cat looked away, forward as he sat back in the thwarts.

'That's just a flesh wound, but you must keep it clean,' he said.

She just nodded her thanks.

Darkness was moving swiftly across the water as the sun

lost itself beyond the blood-red curve of the world.

'Penny for 'em, shipmate,' said Silver. 'What thoughts have blown in and troubled you?'

'The Indians you killed. I saw them die,' said Cat. 'Twice now.'

Silver's eyes came back from that distant horizon and focused on Cat. It was a hard look.

'I'm telling the truth,' she said.

Silver held out a placating hand.

'I'm not saying as you're wrong, not a bit of it. Quite the opposite.' He gripped the tiller and settled back against the thwarts. 'Have you ever been on the island of Hispaniola, maybe come ashore on the long quay at Port-au-Prince?'

'No,' said Cat.

'Well it's not a place for a Christian lady, and there's the truth of it, but there's stories of voodoo magic and dead men walking there that'd stretch the credulity of the most gullible fool, and yet, Cat Manno, I've seen the look them savages had in their eyes as they was a-chasin' you in the eyes of other broken creatures shambling in the back alleys of Port-au-Prince, creatures you wouldn't want to look at twice in case they caught your eye and came after you . . .'

He grimaced.

'They call that island we just got away from Malos Muertos.'

Cat shivered.

'Doesn't sound good,' she said.

Silver nodded.

'Means the Bad Dead. And though I've never thought to wonder exactly how it come by that name, seeing Billy coming back from the grave and blasting away at me gives me a clue I've no wish to think on much further. I'm just glad we're safe off the damned sand spit—'

He broke off and felt the wind with his hand. He nodded in satisfaction.

'Wind'll hold now. We'll have an easy passage until dawn.'

He rummaged in an oilskin bag wedged in next to the water barrel and threw a pale square at Cat, who caught it on reflex.

'Ship's biscuit,' explained Silver. 'If you don't crack your teeth eating it, it'll stop your ribs sticking together until we gets where we're going. Unless you got food of your own?'

She reached in her pocket and pulled out the small apples she'd picked.

'Where'd you get them?' said Silver, suddenly very still.

'On the island,' she said, holding them out.

He slapped her hand and sent them spinning into the sea.

'You didn't a-try of them, that's for sure,' he said. 'Little apples of death is what they was: "Eat on Malos Muertos: stay on Malos Muertos", that's what they say, and you'd do well to remember it, girl. Stick to honest ship's biscuits and you'll not go far wrong.'

He snapped off a corner of a biscuit himself and looked at the moon rising over his shoulder. Cat swivelled her head and tried to ignore the stinging in her hand.

Apart from the tiny island dropping away behind, there was nothing but the wind riffling the top slopes of the ocean swell all about them. They were moving at a fast clip and the bow wave was boiling past on either side, but they seemed to be heading out into nothing but more sea.

'Where are we going?' she asked.

Silver settled himself on his seat, pulling the billowing sea cloak round him, so that he seemed to envelop rather than hold the tiller.

'Well, that's a question now, isn't it? I know where I'm headed, but you ain't said where it was you was in such a hurry to get to when you come bursting out of the palm breaks with them heathens on your tail like the hounds of hell themselves.'

Cat thought of saying she wasn't going anywhere, that she was just running away from them as fast as she could, but she knew that Silver was asking her a different question. She was grateful to him for saving her, but he was more than half a pirate and wholly unfit to be trusted. And yet here she was, alone with him on the high seas, again reliant on him for her survival.

So this was the thing: when Cat paused and thought about this world that she found herself in, she knew two things: firstly although it might be a dream world it was not like a dream. It hurt when you fell and you could be tired and hungry and everything was just . . . real.

The second thing she knew was that there was some logic to what was happening to her. She knew it all joined up. She knew beyond doubt that she had to get to Far Rockaway. She knew Victor was in real trouble and that the solution lay in finding him somewhere in this bewilderingly wide world. She knew that finding the book on the island of the dead was a clue or a key meant especially for her. And she was pretty sure that losing it was a huge setback, given how hard Victor had fought to keep it out of the grip of Magua. And since all she knew was his determination to get to Far Rockaway was only matched by the importance he placed in the lost notebook, it seemed she had to get the book back and take it there herself, wherever that might be. Because Victor could be anywhere, but he would, being Victor, get to his destination come hell or high water, and she was determined to meet him there with the book.

Maybe that would save them both.

She'd plunged down the waterfall and left the world of Chingachgook and *The Last of the Mohicans*, and seemed to have woken up in the world of another story. Meeting Long John Silver was no more an accident than stumbling over the book on the wide empty beach. So she decided to tell him where she needed to go. She couldn't see how she could play it any other way.

'I need to go to Far Rockaway,' she said.

'Far Rockaway?' said Silver, cocking his head.

'Do you know it?'

He shook his head.

'Can't say as I do.'

Cat knew he was lying. She knew it instantly and without a scrap of doubt. But she had no idea how she knew. Maybe it was the steady eyes or the bullet-proof smile.

'What manner of place is it?' asked Silver.

'I don't know,' Cat said. 'I think it's a castle at the end of the world.'

It sounded stupid saying it and she wished she hadn't, but Silver nodded as if such a thing might easily and reasonably exist.

'Can't say as I know where that might be, Cat Manno.'

'Fiddler's Green, Fiddler's Green!'

Captain Flint hopped out from under the bench beneath him and pecked up a shard of biscuit that Cat'd just dropped, giving her a jolt. She'd forgotten about the parrot. Silver laughed and threw the bird a bigger chunk from his own biscuit.

'Cap'n might be right and all. "Castle at the end of the world" doesn't quite sound like a real place, if you'll pardon me saying. Sounds a bit more like Fiddler's Green or Davy Jones' Locker . . .'

Here he paused, blew on his thumbnail for luck and spat into the ocean.

'Sort of a place that's got a name, but don't exist, not in the real world.'

'It exists,' said Cat.

Silver looked at her.

'Then what manner of place is it?'

'I don't know.'

'That's an honest answer. But not a very helpful one. What takes you there?'

'My grandfather.'

'Your grandfather?'

Cat pointed at the sword-cane, which Silver had stuck between the bench and the side strakes of the boat at his side.

'That's his stick,' said Cat.

Silver pulled the cane out and looked at it.

'May I have it?' asked Cat, holding out her hand.

Silver squinted as he peered at the gold band running round the cane, hiding the join where the blade was hidden.

'Gold,' he said. 'And a nice curlicued monogram, I should say.'

He pulled it in so close that it almost touched his nose.

'V P M,' he read.

'Victor Paul Manno,' said Cat. 'My grandfather.'

Silver rolled the cane back and forth between his fingers and thumb, like a man testing the quality of a cigar.

'A gold band in a Malacca cane,' he said. 'He'll be a rich old gentleman then, your grandfather?'

His face was open and without guile, and he leant forward and handed over the cane with a smile, but Cat knew in her gut that the more he smiled and the easier he seemed to be, the deeper he was thinking about how to profit from this encounter. The noise she could hear was not just the wind in the sail and the fizz of water rushing under the overlapping strakes of the hull beneath her: it was the sound of Long John Silver figuring out the angles.

Cat put the cane beside her on the bench. She felt a little happier with it close to hand. Silver rubbed his chin.

'So he will be pleased to see you, no doubt?' he said.

Cat nodded.

'Yes. I have to get to him.'

Silver looked at the moon and adjusted course with a push on the tiller.

'And he's in this Far Rockaway?'

'Yes.'

'But you, pardon me for asking, do not know how to get there. Am I right?'

'Yes.'

'No map. No chart?'

'No.'

Silver tutted. The boat sped on.

'I had a book.'

'A book?'

'It was my grandfather's book. But it must have fallen out of my pocket as I ran.'

'You lost it?'

Cat nodded.

'And there was a map in that book?' Silver cocked his head.

'No. Maybe. I don't think so, I mean I just found it, and before I could read it I was, I mean they came out of the water and I just ran.'

Silver nodded, again as if this was the most normal thing in the world.

'So the map might be in the book?'

'It's more that the book is, um . . .' Cat struggled for the right way to say what she felt without sounding too mad, 'important.'

'So the book was a thing of value?'

Cat nodded again.

'Why?'

The question hung there for a long while. It was the right question, but Cat had no idea what the matching answer might be.

'I don't know.'

Again Silver nodded as if what she'd said made sense.

'But it is a thing of value?'

'It was a thing of power,' said Cat, and wondered where that suddenly came from. It was true. But not what she'd known she was going to say.

'A thing of value and power you say, but you lost it?' Silver shook his head slowly. 'Mayhap we should lay to, and weather the night, then go back for it at first light?'

'No,' said Cat. 'No. I don't want to go back to that island.'

Silver bared his teeth in another smile, a slash of good humour in the darkness that now surrounded them.

'Well, Cat, seeing what we saw, I can't say I blame you, and I'm much of the same opinion myself, truth to tell.'

He pulled a short clay pipe from his jacket and reached under the seat, pulling out a lantern that he opened and wedged between his knees. He put the pipe between his clenched teeth and pulled a tinderbox from another pocket and started striking it to light the candle within the lantern.

'Tell you what, Cat. I shall have a pipe on it and see what my thinking can construct by way of a plan that may help you.'

He pointed with his chin.

'You stretch out over there and I'll cogitate as I take the first watch.'

Cat did feel exhausted. She pulled the coat around her and wedged herself into the side of the boat, her ear against the strakes. She heard the gurgle of the ocean passing by on the other side, which was restful in itself. But, on the other hand, she was so uncomfortable on the hard wood, which seemed to exist only to produce angles and edges that dug into her, that she knew sleep wouldn't come.

She watched Silver light the lamp, then use the flame to kindle a spill that he somehow kept alight in the wind as he lit his pipe and puffed it into a red glow at the side of his face.

'You never said where YOU were going,' Cat said sleepily.

Silver sucked a lungful of tobacco and held it in as he considered what Cat had said. Then he blew a thin stream of grey into the following breeze and settled back in his seat, pulling the cloak around him.

'No,' he said. 'Nor I did.'

He sucked on his pipe, and that seemed to end the conversation. Cat wondered what he meant by that, and if she should ask, but then before she could come to a decision, she forgot she was too uncomfortable to sleep, and did so.

She woke in the moonlight. She didn't know how long she had slept, but the moon had risen much higher in the sky. She didn't move for two reasons. Firstly she was very stiff. And secondly, Silver was hunched over something, half turned away from him, the lantern making a kind of shallow cave out of the fold of his cloak. And within the hollow of the cloak, lit by the flickering lantern, was that thing, the thing that kept Cat very, very still, even though the boat was digging into her in about thirteen uncomfortable places.

The thing was a small book. With black covers. She had no doubt as to what book it was. It was Victor's.

26

A pocket picked by moonlight

Cat didn't move. She didn't want Silver to know he was being observed. She lowered her eyelids to a slit and concentrated on breathing as if she was still asleep.

Silver was thumbing slowly through the book, nodding as he did so. Whatever he was reading or seeing was making him smile in satisfaction. The wind snapped the sail loudly and he looked up, adjusted the tiller and hauled a rope tight in one easy move, as if the boat was just an extension of his body, and then he stopped and stared towards her.

Cat's blood ran cold.

She knew in the rational part of her mind that it was too dark for Silver to make out the details of her face and see that she was spying on him through half-closed eyes as she lay where she was in the darkness of the moon-shadow, but the other part of her brain took over and she lowered her eyelids the final millimetre and lay in the dark, pretending to be asleep.

Silver must have gone through her pockets when she knocked herself out falling on the hard-packed sand and banging the back of her head. She didn't think she'd been unconscious for very long, but then again, how long would it take? She didn't know why he hadn't said he'd found the book, or why he had filched it, and she certainly didn't know why he looked so pleased. She did know that knowing Silver had it – while Silver didn't know that she knew – was about the only advantage she had going for her right now.

She must have dozed, or it might just have been a minute or so before she felt a boot nudge her ribs.

'Cat. Cat Manno. Time to shake a leg and stand your watch.'

Cat stretched and pantomimed a yawn, wondering if she was overdoing it.

'What?' she said. 'Where am I?'

She was definitely overdoing it.

'On watch is what you are, young lady, and rocked asleep on the cradle of the deep is where you've been,' Silver said with a yawn. 'Come aft and catch hold of this tiller for a spell while I rest my peepers a while.'

Cat slid in beside Silver at the back of the gig. She took hold of the smooth wood of the tiller, and was surprised to find that it was quite hard to keep steady. It had a life of its own and was always pulling to the left.

'Clap on tight, girl, put your elbow over and jam it to your side. That's it.' Silver let go, and Cat had control of the steering. Silver watched her, and after a while nodded and pointed ahead.

'Now let's get you acquainted with your course. It's a point off north, which means you should aim the barky about the width of your thumb off the North Star. Now, you lean your head in here and take a sight down my arm and you'll see which star that'll be . . .'

Cat didn't move. Instead she looked at the scatter of stars in the sky above and pointed.

'Got it.'

Silver looked at her.

'Have you now?'

He didn't sound as though he believed Cat.

'Yes,' said Cat, pointing. 'Polaris. At the end of Ursa Minor. Or the tail of the Little Bear, whatever you want to call it.'

'*Polaris* and *Ursa Minor*! Why, how fancy you are, Miss Cat. Talk like a dictionary you do, and no mistake. It's the plain old North Star and the Little Dipper as I call 'em, simple words for a simple man. But bless you for your wisdom and learning, for all that – I'll sleep sounder knowing if trouble rears its head as I rest, you'll be able to wake me with its Latin name!'

Cat saw Silver's teeth flash white in the moonlight and knew he was mocking her, but couldn't work out why.

'Don't mind me, girl, I've a rough sense of humour and

mean no harm by it. Now you hold that course and by the time the sky's lightening you should see an island ahead, an island shaped like a penny loaf and two buns side by side to its starboard side. Soon as you see them, forget the stars and steer to the outside of the buns. When they're about level with your shoulder, wake me, for we shall need to keep our eyes peeled to get back to my ship that's moored thereabouts, and that'll take more than Latin, you may lay to that.'

He sniffed the night air and held his hand up to the moon, and then nodded, as if he had confirmed something.

'This wind should hold well enough, but give me a shake if it changes direction or blows up much stronger.'

He pulled his cloak tight, stretched out and tipped his broad three-cornered hat low over his face and, for all she could tell, fell asleep instantly.

Cat held the tiller stiffly to begin with, and took some time to relax enough to breathe normally, but somewhere in the first hour she must have done, because she surprised herself by noticing that she was smiling.

After everything that had happened to her, it was an odd sensation, but there was undoubtedly something exhilarating in being young and awake and in control, all alone on the open ocean, running before a stiff breeze beneath a full moon with nothing to do but hold course and listen to the slap and hiss as the gig sped across a gently heaving sea of wind-scalloped silver.

The tiller definitely had a mind of its own, pulling and

dragging against her, but she didn't mind. It kept her sharp, and as she got used to the feel of the boat and the beauty of the night, she was even gladder not to be sleeping.

She was so engrossed in this unusual sensation of lonely power that she forgot the dark question of why 'Honest' John had not come clean about her grandfather's book.

For a long time Cat was just that most valuable and fugitive thing: simply happy.

The boat scudded on, and the rhythm as it gently and surely crested swells and slid in and out of the shallow hollows beyond was both restful and somehow gave her a sense of purpose. She had felt helpless for a long time, a victim of whatever accident had propelled her into this world, and had been either chasing or escaping something ever since she got here: this was different.

She was in charge.

It might have been a tiny boat on a vast ocean, but she was the only thing moving across it, and she was the only thing awake and seeing it. She was conscious of the tension between the wind that bellied out the sail pushing in one direction, countering the rudder pulling in the other, and realized that the power she felt was being the person controlling the push and the pull between wind and sea, balancing them so the boat would continue to travel in the direction she chose.

A small boat on an open sea with a good wind and a firm hand on the tiller is about as good an example of controlled willpower in action as you could wish for, and Cat, for an hour or so, just revelled in the feeling.

Victor had always said that most of the time happiness crept up on you when you were doing something else. He also said no happiness was ever wasted, because every happiness stays in you, and you can revisit it in your memory any time you're sad, or lonely or depressed. It was kind of corny, but like a lot of corny things, it was true. Maybe that was what made it corny in the first place.

Thinking of Victor, Cat wished he was beside her right now. He loved doing things outdoors, and night-sailing was an adventure he'd never thought of. Cat would have given anything to have him beside her instead of the sleeping cloak-wrapped hulk of Silver.

Comparing Victor to Silver broke the spell. She hadn't really forgotten the book, she had just been accidentally not thinking about it, kind of on purpose, parking that thought for later, when she would decide what to do. She looked across at Silver again. He had shifted in his sleep. His cloak hung open and the front of his jacket billowed out just enough to show the pocket in which Cat had seen him stash the book.

That thought about the book was not going to stay parked any more.

Now *was* later.

She had to decide what to do:

She could do nothing.

Or she could just gently reach across and pull the book out of the pocket.

And if it was wedged in, well then she would stop and just wouldn't do it. She didn't want to wake Silver. That didn't seem like it'd be a good thing, she thought.

So maybe she should do nothing.

She checked her course. She was good, just a sliver off true north by the Pole Star, just as Silver had ordered.

And anyway, she had never picked a pocket before. Tempting though it was, it would be crazy to try.

The boat barrelled over a swell and tried to corkscrew as it descended the other side. Cat kept the tiller tight under her arm and didn't let that happen.

So, she thought, if I'm going to slide the book out, I need to do it on the upslope of a swell, because I'll need one hand to keep the tiller straight and the boat's less squirrelly going up than when it's going down.

But why was she planning something sensible like that when she'd obviously decided NOT to do something crazy like trying to pickpocket the pirate anyway?

Because the book was important.

Why was it important?

She had no idea, other than it was. She flashed the memory of Victor fighting beneath the white oak, the constantly moving tip of his sword keeping the Huron at bay as the flag of blood coursed down the side of his face, defiantly standing with one foot on the book to stop them getting it.

No question.

The book mattered.

And anything that mattered to Victor might – must? – help her find and release them from this world and get them back to their world safely.

Because she wasn't really steering towards a loaf-shaped island with two buns alongside, an island she could now see looming out of the dawn about two miles off, she was travelling towards what lay beyond it.

She didn't know how, but getting to Silver's boat was a step towards Far Rockaway because it was positive movement forward at least, if only because staying on the island was the opposite.

She wasn't waiting for something.

She was doing something.

And that was the real underlying thrill of the power she'd been feeling.

That must explain why she was holding her breath and timing her move as the wind took the gig's sail and bellied it out of the shallow trough and up the slope of the mild swell ahead.

That must be why she kept one hand on the tiller and reached across, into the pouch created between Silver and his jacket.

That must be why she moved as carefully as a surgeon, her fingers inching into the void, keeping clear of the shirt-front and the chest beneath, favouring the coat side where the pocket lay.

The one thing she hadn't done was time the boat's progress

up and down the swells. Even as her fingertips brushed the hard edge of the book, the gig tilted and began its downward surge. The tiller bucked as the normal impulse to corkscrew made itself felt, and Cat snatched her hand back just in time to correct the pull of the rudder.

Silver slept on.

Cat's heart was firing like a trip hammer as the adrenaline rush overclocked her system. She timed the next three ups and downs by counting elephants. It was about seventeen elephants to crest the upslope of the swell, and about fifteen to shoot down the other side.

Seventeen elephants sounds like a lot, but they go past very fast when your hand is inside someone else's coat, trying to slip a small book out without waking him.

It was like trying to play that kids' game where you had to use tweezers to pick cartoony body-parts out of holes in a man without touching the sides and setting off the buzzer, but it was like playing it on a slo-mo roller coaster.

She should definitely stop trying it.

And if another memory hadn't popped into her head, of Magua crouching on the rock in midstream, holding the book he'd rescued from the boiling waters over his head, crowing like a rooster on top of his dunghill, she would have.

Instead she flexed her fingers like a concert pianist warming up and waited until the boat hit the next trough, and then she reached over once more.

It must be true that fortune favours the brave, because this time Silver had shifted and the coat gaped even more expansively. To make things better, the sky was lightening just enough for her to see the top edge of the book and the fact it was going to come free easily, with nothing to snag it as she eased it out of what was now, she felt, a particularly large and welcoming pocket.

She felt the tiller cut into her side as she leant over, but found that this was actually helpful, because she could sort of hunch her body over it and hold it on course in the L-shaped crook of her torso.

Her fingers gripped the cover of the book and pulled very gently.

It slid easily, no friction, as if it was on runners, as if it was helping her, as if it had a mind of its own, as if she wasn't stealing it at all, but merely helping it escape.

She smiled tightly. She had it within half an inch of freedom.

It was going to be easy.

She was definitely doing the right thing.

She heard the click an instant before she felt the gentle prod in her stomach that turned her to stone.

She hadn't felt Silver move, but there was a large gun poking her insistently in the sternum. She didn't even dare swallow.

The boat caromed over and down a swell and was well up the next slope before Silver cleared his throat apologetically. His face was still hidden by the hat pulled down over it.

'Now, shipmate. What would the Latin word be for . . . "thief"?'

Cat had no words.

The pressure of the barrel increased as Silver slowly rose up on his other elbow.

'While you're thinking of it, perhaps you should back oars and stand off a couple of lengths, because this gun here has a trigger that's even more sensitive than I am, and when I open my eyes, Cat Manno, when I open my eyes and see daylight I don't much want to see it through the big hole this here cannon will blow in your chest, do you catch my drift?'

Cat backed slowly off over to her side of the tiller.

Silver's gun followed her all the way as the pirate seemed to uncoil and rise up from his sleeping position in defiance of the normal laws of gravity, looming over Cat like a dark thunderhead.

As soon as he was upright he tilted his hat back on his head, and Cat saw his eyes, glistening cold and hard like wet pebbles in the early morning light. He scowled and spat over the side of the boat.

'Didn't take you for a swab, Cat. Didn't take you for no footpad nor a thief in the night, didn't take you for a sneak of any stripe, and that's the pity of it. For here I am waking from a deep and happy dream to find light fingers trying to relieve me of cargo what's mine and no man else's.'

The gun lifted from Cat's chest. She found she was looking into a dark 'o' that didn't waver any more than did the eyes that were aiming it right at her.

'Now, Cat, there's no one to see us here, and a person might do another a terrible turn, and slip the evidence over the side quiet-like, and do it ever so private that none but him and the sharks would know what he's done, am I right?'

Cat nodded. Her heart was still hammering, and her guts seemed to be falling down a vertiginous lift shaft that had opened up inside her, creating a sickening rushing void in her stomach that was stopping her thinking straight.

Silver nodded back at her.

'No one would hear the shot. And nothing closes up faster than a hole in the ocean, that you may lay to.' His voice was flat and matter-of-fact. It would have been easier and less frightening if he was angry, but he wasn't.

He was just in control.

He had the gun.

He had the power.

Cat had nothing.

Except the tiller. The tiller that she had spent the last couple of hours or so holding on to. The tiller whose strong urge to rip free and swing towards Silver she could still feel pressing hard against her hands.

The gun barrel drifted forward and planted itself between her eyes.

Silver smiled as if he could read her thoughts.

'That's right, Cat. That's the play, if you was a gambler, the last throw of the knuckle-bones, as it were, against a man set up with a fine pistol as I am, if that man was of a mind to do murder afore he's a-breakfasted. Now Honest John may not know Latin, but he does know a "situation" and he does know gunnery. And the moment you tries it . . . ?'

He thumbed the side-lock and gently cocked the gun.

'Click. Bang—'

He smiled grimly.

'Your brains'd be feeding fishes ten yards behind your head before your body bounced off the side of the boat.'

27

Joe

Joe Manno had been hanging with members of his band in an apartment in the grey area where Brooklyn shades into Queens. He baled and ran full tilt to the subway on Euclid Avenue and jumped on the 8th Avenue Express, a subway train that betrayed the optimism of its name by clanking its way into the bowels of Manhattan with painful slowness and a series of inexplicable stops between stations.

Joe couldn't sit calmly.

He paced up and down like a trapped animal, attracting the attention of a transit cop who got into the next carriage during a long pause in the broad subterranean expanse of Hoyt-Schermerhorn station, and stood eyeballing him through the connecting doors as the train chuntered sluggishly onwards.

Just before finally entering Manhattan proper at Broadway-Nassau, the train stopped in the dark.

Joe exhaled loudly in frustration and kicked the pole in front of him. The heavy steel-toed engineer's boots he was wearing made a solid clang, and brought the transit cop into the carriage, his hand fading back to rest unobtrusively just above his holster.

'You want to tone it down a little, sir?' he asked.

Joe looked at him. He knew what the cop was seeing. He knew he looked like trouble – the heavy boots, the grimed jeans, the grimier hair, the skanky leather jacket and the metal in his ears and eyebrow. He looked like trouble on purpose, partly because of the band, partly because it was his way of coping with the beast of a city he'd chosen to live in, his way of getting his retaliation in first. At least that's what Victor had told him, and Victor had a way with words that made them stick in your brain like they had barbs.

'Sir,' said the cop. 'Plenty of free seats, no need to be kicking stuff. Ain't gonna get any of us where we need to be any faster.'

Joe stared, not defiantly, just brain-fused by worry and not knowing how to react.

The cop's hand stayed above his holster but moved a little lower.

'Sir? Are you on something?'

Joe sensed everyone in the carriage looking at him, stepping back a little.

He sat.

'No,' he said. 'No, sir. I don't do drugs and stuff. My

kid sister's in the ER, Midtown, got hit by a truck. I only just heard.'

He choked up.

'I've just got to get there.'

The cop hadn't worked eighteen years on the subway without being a good reader of people. His hand came off his hip and on to Joe's shoulder.

'Which hospital?'

'Bellevue.'

The train jerked into motion.

'OK,' said the cop. 'Change at the next station, take the 4, 5 or 6 to 28th Street and then head one block south and four east. You can't miss it.'

Joe looked up and tried to smile a thank you. It got snarled up.

'She's just a kid . . .' he explained. 'I think she's in a real bad place.'

28

False colours

Cat wasn't breathing. Her world had narrowed down to the gun-barrel and two hard eyes that didn't seem to need to blink at all.

Then, after a long, long time, they did.

Silver uncocked the firing mechanism and slowly put the gun down.

'It's lucky for you I'm not a man disposed to murder, Cat Manno. It's lucky for you I'm an Honest John and not a Billy Bones or others I could mention. Why Flint himself would have grabbed his cutlass and split you from fore-top to bilges without a by-your-leave . . .'

Cat watched a slow smile break over Silver's face. It was an engaging smile. She took a breath, then another. The relief was enormous. Her guts stopped falling down the lift shaft. The vertigo disappeared. Her mind kicked back in.

And then Silver held up a finger.

'But do tell me one thing, Cat,' he said. 'Tell me one thing and we shall be friends again. Tell me what you was a-fishing for in the depths of my sea coat?'

Cat dry-mouthed. Silver's finger cocked and pointed at her like the pistol.

'And don't play me false with your answer, mind, for I shall spy it out if you do, and though you've a-taken a notion to go a-sneak-thieving in the night, you've not got the face for cloaking crooked deeds and I shall read you like a book, so I shall, like an open book, and you may lay to that.'

Silver's eyes blinked, flat and hard as gunmetal again. But Cat had been called a thief one time too many and she answered without thinking.

'You can "lay" to whatever you like, but you were a thief before I was.'

Silver raised an eyebrow.

'Was I now?'

'Yeah,' said Cat, 'yes. You were.'

'Well, ain't you the game little bantam to be telling me that?' said Silver, blowing out his cheeks in surprise. 'Well. I likes your pluck, Cat Manno, and since there's no one else here to hear you libel me I shall leave your tongue in your mouth and not hack it out with the blunt side of my jack-knife for the villainous lies it tells.'

'I'm not the liar,' said Cat, wondering if she could get to her sword-cane before Silver picked up the gun again. 'You took Victor's book. I told you about it and you were all innocent

233

and interested, and then I woke in the night and saw you reading it. So who's the thief and who's the liar?'

Her blood was up and the words were pouring out several lengths ahead of herself. Silver glared.

'You saw me reading your grandfather's book in the night, did you?'

'Yes,' said Cat. 'And then I saw you hide it in your pocket.'

'Hide it, did I? And when did I lay my hands on it?' said Silver, dangerously calm.

'When I was knocked out on the beach,' said Cat. She was sure she could get to her sword if she let the tiller swing free and it bashed into Silver as he went for his gun.

It was Silver's laughter that stopped her. He threw back his head and roared with merriment, his shoulders shaking and his eyes watering. He gulped air and wiped his eyes and then started again.

'I stole your precious book . . . on . . . the beach? The beach where I saved you from the savages?'

He tried a deep breath and mastered the hilarity.

'And why would I save you from the savages if I meant you ill? And why bring you with me off the island if I just wanted some blessed book?'

He shook his head.

'And yet you say you saw me reading a book. And for that it's plain as a pickle-barrel that you don't trust Honest John further than you could throw this gig!'

His hand disappeared into his coat and came out with the book.

'Here, girl, and I give you joy of it. Read all you will and you shall be all the better for doing so.'

He lobbed it to Cat who caught it clumsily.

She looked down at the small black volume in her hands and turned it over.

There was a worn gilt symbol embossed on the front cover. It was a cross. She'd never seen that before.

She spun it in her hand.

There was writing on the spine.

It read 'Holy Bible'.

It wasn't Victor's book at all.

She heard a click. She looked up.

Silver had the pistol in his hand and had just cocked it.

'Something you want to say, shipmate?'

'Um,' said Cat. 'Sorry . . . ?'

Sorry didn't seem to cut it. Silver still stared at her, eyes steady and unimpressed.

'Simply said, and I'm sure you are sorry, but sorry for what? Sorry for mistrusting the man who saved you, or sorry because you don't trust him and he still has a loaded pistol and no witnesses but open sea and all the little hungry fishies below?'

It was a fair question, but the problem with the answer was that it was both things: she wanted to trust the big man, but she knew he was a buccaneer, a man capable of treachery and cunning and cold-blooded killing . . . and yet there was also something about him that appealed to Cat, something large and generous. He inspired confidence. But Cat remembered the story in *Treasure Island*, and that Silver had been most dangerous when he was most trusted.

She could smell the sea and feel the wind and the rising sun on her face. She felt tired and in need of a shower, and she felt hungry. And Silver wasn't a character that she'd imagined as Victor had read her a book. He was a large cliff of a man with a gun in his hand and an unreadable face above it, a face that was patiently waiting for an answer.

'If you can't see the angle, play it straight.'

No one had spoken. Silver still had her locked in his gaze. The voice was not in the boat, but in her head. And it was Victor's voice. It was another of the sayings that he seemed to pepper his conversation with, like he was sneaking you a candy to unwrap later. As a small kid they hadn't meant much to Cat, but they were, she realized, insidiously hard-wired into her brain now. And in the absence of a better plan, she went for it.

'Both,' she said. 'I'm sorry for both reasons.'

She watched the answer land. Silver didn't react at first. Then he tilted his head, thinking. And then he nodded.

'That's an honest answer. And I see as how you're boxed in on a lee shore with this. Trust is a hard thing, and that's another truth. Got to be earned and you're right to keep a-hold of it until you know you're giving it to the right person.'

236

He uncocked the pistol, and then spun it on his finger and held it out to Cat, handle first.

'Take her, Cat, take the gun.'

Cat didn't know what was going on. But she reached gingerly across the tiller and grasped it. It sagged in her hand as Silver let go and retreated to his end of the bench.

'Now you've the upper hand, Cat, see? Now you've no reason to be sorry that I've got you at a disadvantage. Now you can decide who to trust and not to trust, and what you feel sorry for.'

Cat looked at the gun and back at Silver. She felt the power of the weapon in her fist, but she also felt kind of stupid pointing it at the one-legged man.

'How do you know I won't shoot you?'

Silver's teeth flashed white against the windburned tan of his face.

'I don't. That's why it's an act of faith. Most friendship is a gamble against long odds, Cat, and whatever you've heard of me, whatever tales of dark deeds and double-dealing at the crossroads, tales and stories is just what they are and no more. You should chart your own course on the observations you make with your own eyes. All I'll say more is that I'm a man as would rather have friends than enemies, because enemies is hard work, and old and hacked about as I am I've a taste for ease and comfort.'

'Comfort?' said Cat. It was an odd word, given the circumstances.

'Since I started a-reading of that book you have in your hand I'm a changed man, and I make no apologies for seeking to be comfortable in this world, for it's true I've lived a life doing precious little to make me think I'll be comfortable in the next.'

Cat lowered the gun. She wasn't going to shoot someone in cold blood. And what Silver said made its own kind of sense. He shook his head.

'Keep the gun, Cat, and if I play you false, you may shoot me down like a dog, without a by-your-leave, for I give you that leave now as a marker on our friendship, for you saved my life when poor old dead Billy come a-running with his blunderbuss. You may call that marker at any time you choose, and that's my word and here's my hand on it.'

Silver stuck a ham-sized fist across the tiller and unfolded his fingers in an open gesture of friendship. Cat reached over and let her hand be enveloped in it, and they shook.

'Handsomely done. And now, before we tack round this here island and fall in sight of the ship, there's things we must do to make you safe once aboard.'

'What do you mean?' Cat asked.

'I mean it's a ship full of rough men with low morals and definite views, half of whom will be sore tempted to treat you in a most ungentlemanly fashion, and the all of which may think it bad joss to have a female aboard.'

He reached across to the thole pins set on the gunwales of

the boat to keep the oars in position when rowing, and wiped a smear of grease off them.

'You must sail under false colours, Cat Manno, and pass as a boy for safety. Take a dab of this grease and work it into your face, and by your leave I shall plait your hair into a sailor-like pigtail, and grease it down with the rest of this.'

'Grease it?' said Cat.

'Well, we don't have tar, which would be the first choice, but grease'll do I suppose,' said Silver. 'Or I could hack it off with my knife.'

'I can plait my own hair,' she said, rubbing some of the dirty grease into her face.

'Not like a sailor, so turn round and take a telling, just this once. It's a ruse, but it may save unpleasantness.'

So Cat found herself sitting still while Silver gathered her hair and pulled it tightly and with surprising dexterity into a thin queue down her back, which he then tied off and greased.

'Now let's be seeing you,' he growled.

She turned and he looked her up and down.

'Well,' he said. 'You make a sort of a boy, I suppose.'

He took off his hat and removed the red bandanna from his head.

'Tie this muffler-like round your neck, lest anyone should have a keek at your Adam's apple and see you ain't got one.'

He watched her as she did so.

'Well, Cat, we shall call you Kit from now on. With the dirt on your face and your sunburned skin which is to be sure a lot browner than is strictly ladylike, we may pass, we may pass indeed, especially if you speak little and low, and if you walk as a man not as a dainty.'

'Yeah,' she said, eyeing the masts of a tall ship that were looking over the top of the high rock they were sailing round. 'I don't really do "dainty" anyway.'

'Nor you do,' he grinned. 'And poor dead Billy would lay to that too, I'll be bound.'

He lost the smile and spoke fast and low.

'Now, "Master Kit" – as I think we shall have to call you – when we go aboard and meet the captain and all the rest of the merry crew, don't say a thing about the books, not the one in my pocket here, nor the one you've lost. It doesn't suit me for my shipmates to know I carry a pocketful of words, and it would not suit you if they was to know about your grandfather's book. For the truth of it is that treasure is treasure, and gold is gold, but books is something else and rarer than hen's teeth in this world. Books is power.'

Cat looked up at the three-masted man-o'-war now looming above them as they approached.

'She's a beauty and no mistake, but don't let her fine lines and fancy looks deceive you, she's a privateer, which is to say we sail under no flag but our own, and answer to no man but Flint himself. Choose to come aboard and you'll be under my protection and none shall harm you, be they ever so ill-disposed, and you have my word that you shall be put ashore at the first port we call at to continue your search. Or you may take the gig and sail on where you will, free and clear and on your own. I owe you that for the life you saved a-killing of Billy Bones when he was like to cut me short.'

Silver's face was as clear and fresh as the new dawn lighting up the sea and sky all around them. Everything in Cat wanted to trust him, everything except the niggling splinter of memory that told her the Silver in the story Victor had read her was most dangerous when he seemed most open and generous.

She wanted to trust Silver, she wanted, wanted more than anything, to find a way of getting to Far Rockaway and Victor. She needed a clue.

The man-o'-war creaked and wallowed in the light swell ahead of them, anchored close in against the backdrop of dense vegetation covering the bun-shaped islets behind it. The sails on the three masts were rolled, leaving the spars and rigging stark and bare, like waiting gallows. Maybe that was the sign.

But then when she looked away from the boat and the deserted islands, all there was was ocean, a vast empty wilderness of waves on which she would be lost and alone and – frankly – useless without an experienced sailor to help her navigate and handle the boat.

As Cat thought this, and quite as if he could hear her thoughts, Silver neatly tacked the gig, one hand automatically reaching out to push Cat's head down and out of the way as the boom swung from one side of the boat to the other. The change in direction took them round the back of the man-o'-war, and Cat saw the two rows of windows stepped one above the other in an overhung gallery either side of the great ironbound wooden mass of the rudder dropping into the sea below. The morning sun reflected off the many glass panes making it hard to see within, but just for a moment Cat saw – or thought she did – a grim face staring back out at her. Then the angle changed and the sun turned the glass window into a mirror and the face was gone, and Cat saw the name of the boat sweeping across the flattened curve between the topmost gallery of windows and the bow rails of the quarterdeck above. The white lettering stood stark against a band of black paint, and was, Cat realized, the very hint she had been waiting for.

She heard Victor's voice in her head saying: 'There's more than one way of getting to Far Rockaway. It's your choice: you can just stay on the A train until it runs out of track, or change at Penn Station and go via . . .'

She said the last word out loud. It was easy. It was there, spelled out in bright white paint across the back of the boat.

'Jamaica.'

29

Flint

Silver brought the gig round and steered it towards the middle of the man-o'-war where a ladder made of slats and twisted rope hung down between the closed gun ports studding the wooden cliff face of the boat's side. Two sailors stood at the railing, looking down at them, and Cat could hear shouts and running feet on the unseen deck beyond.

Silver loosened the rope twisted round a cleat at his side, and the sail dropped into the middle of the boat in an untidy collapse of salt-crusted canvas. He cursed and levered himself to the mast, beckoning Cat towards him.

'Give me a hand here, boy!' he roared.

Cat steadied herself against the uneven motion of the boat and bent forward to help gather the ballooning sail. As soon as her head was close to Silver, Silver dropped the angry face and winked at her, unseen by the sailors now beginning to line the taffrail above them, now only about fifty yards off and getting closer with every second. His voice was an urgent whisper.

'Now, Cat, we must talk quick and low, because ships have ears as well as eyes, and you must steer carefully through the rocks and shoals as lie ahead once we're on board. Two things above all: never a breath that you killed Billy Bones, not if you want to live. You just follow my lead in the tale I'll spin, for he was not only a favourite of Flint's, he was a particular friend to his messmate Pew, and murderous vengeful will he be if he catches on you had a hand in his extinction. You catch my drift?'

Cat nodded, her eyes locked on the crew assembling on the deck, now about thirty yards away.

'Good,' hissed Silver. 'The second thing is Flint himself. He's as bloody-handed a buccaneer as ever sailed beneath the black flag, but the worst thing you can do is treat him fearful. He can smell fear like a terrier scents a rat, and he gorges himself on it. 'Tis said God hates a coward, so it must be that the Devil loves them, for I never seen a man glut himself on the fear of others as greedily as Flint, and the good Lord knows he's part devil himself.'

And then there was a bump as the boat grazed in at a shallow angle against the side of the *Jamaica*, and Silver reached back without looking and caught hold of the rope ladder, stopping the gig dead in the water.

Two sailors dropped down the ladder, nimble as monkeys, and had the gig secured to the side before Cat had time to register them as anything other than a blur of sunburned muscle and patched and sea-bleached clothes. She saw Silver swarm up the rope ladder ahead of her, and she did have just enough time to marvel at the man's strength in hauling his barrel-like torso up the hull by main force alone, as if the leg he was missing was something of no account entirely. She heard Silver bellow and send someone off to fetch 'My second best crutch!' and then saw him lean back over the rail and beckon her upwards with a curt wave of the hand.

Climbing the ladder was not as easy as it looked, because the man-o'-war was wallowing queasily in the swell, and the ladder was not attached anywhere but at the top, so it swung free like a slow and erratic pendulum. She kept getting twisted and slapped against the wooden ribs and gun ports that studded the hull, and by the time strong hands reached down and pulled her on to the deck, her knuckles were grazed, her knees and shins were painfully barked, and her face was red with exertion and embarrassment at the waves of mirth her ungainly progress had sparked in the waiting crew.

She part stepped, part stumbled over the railing and looked up to find them ranged in a shallow arc around her.

They weren't friendly faces.

Nor were they particularly hostile.

They were just waiting.

And the look in their eyes made her feel that whatever it was they were waiting for was not going to be especially kind or pleasant.

No two of them wore the same type of clothes, though they

all went barefoot. They came in all shapes and sizes, and every colour under the sun, from the bluest black to the freckliest ginger-haired Celt, and everything else in between. Without trying she registered African, Scandinavian, Lascar, Malay, Arab, Turk, Slav, Chinese – and then the crowd parted and Flint stepped through.

He alone wore boots, but without them he would still have towered over all but the tallest of them, a giant frost-eyed Swede and an even taller Ethiopian pirate with a gold tooth that matched the heavy ring dangling from his ear. Flint was not as tall as either, but he carried with him a sense of size and threat that made him seem somehow much bigger than both. His face was half hidden by a great black beard that jutted down like a spade, and his nose had a big chunk cut out of it just below the bridge where an old sword cut had slashed a scar from below the left eye and up across the right eyebrow to where it disappeared into the shadows cast by his wide-brimmed hat. The way his skin had pulled as it healed and tightened up around the puckered slash mark made his face look as if it was stuck in an expression of permanent disapproving surprise.

His body had a similar feeling of being permanently under tension, like a huge steel spring that might uncoil at any minute on the slightest provocation, and the long full-skirted scarlet coat he wore did little to hide the muscle beneath. One shoulder was held higher than the other, like a fighter keeping his body cocked and ready to throw a counterpunch at the first sign of opposition, and his hands were constantly in motion, even when he himself was still, slowly and repeatedly opening and closing, as if they had a will of their own and wanted to grab or slash at anything that came within their range.

The crew, Cat noticed, stepped away from him on instinct, and once they had done so, stayed out of reach. The path he had walked through them as he approached did not close up behind him, because the sailors knew he would have to turn round and return to the quarterdeck at some stage, and no one wanted to find themselves in his way.

Everything about him said 'danger', but it was his eyes that said it loudest. They were the piercing, patient eyes of a successful predator, eyes that had been washed curiously colourless by the amount of blood and pain they had seen and been responsible for. They swept over Cat, paused for an uncomfortably long microsecond, and then came to rest on Silver, who had just been handed a crutch by a panting cabin boy who had clearly run in both directions on his errand.

When Flint spoke, his voice was curious for two reasons: firstly – given his fierce battle-scarred look – it was unexpectedly well spoken and educated. And secondly it was hoarse and full of sharp edges that slid against each other, as if he had to force his words out through a throat full of gravel.

'Well, John, I sent you out with Bones and you come back with fresh meat,' he rasped, jutting his head at Silver. 'Where's Billy?'

Silver, Cat noticed, did not step back, unlike the rest of the crew. Instead he calmly busied himself getting the new crutch comfortably situated in the crook of his arm. He looked calm and self-possessed, but it also meant, Cat noted, that he didn't have to meet Flint's eyes as he spoke.

'Oh, Billy's had his last voyage, Cap'n. He's crossed the bar and you may lay to that. We won't be seeing him no more, not till we're all a little south of sunset in the isles of the blest, as it were.'

Flint cocked his head.

'You killed him?'

Now Silver met his eyes. He looked calm.

'No, Cap'n. Not me. Billy and I was messmates.'

Flint's head ratcheted round and found Cat.

'This scrap of a boy. He kill him?'

The force of his glare was almost like a blow. Cat swallowed. Silver shook his head with a short chop of laughter.

'Scrawny little tike like that kill Bill? I seen day-old lambs with more muscle on 'em than that boy. No, Cap'n. Not him. Cannibals.'

Cat heard the crew breathe in as one.

'Cannibals you say?' creaked Flint.

'A whole crew of 'em, and fixing to feast on this here boy, clear as I could see. We comes on them in the palm grove, and "Bill," I says, "Bill, they're going to eat that boy," and Bill he looks me in the eye and says, "Yes, Barbecue, so they are, and what's that to us?"'

The crew laughed. Flint allowed the ghost of a smile to flick across his face, like the shadow of a fox passing.

'That's Billy Bones to the life, a man as could keep his mind on the job in hand, and I think well on him for it, to be sure. He was always a sound one.'

'Sound as guns,' said a voice from the crowd.

'You got it right there, shipmate. Cold as Norway steel was Billy,' agreed Silver.

'So how come Billy gets stretched and this puppy escapes, if you leave them to it?'

'The boy made a run for it, and before we knew it we had cannibals on all sides and was fighting for our lives. Billy kills five or six and then a great big one gets behind him and puts a spear through his gizzard, pinning him to a tree, and that's the last of Billy Bones.'

'Pinned to a tree?'

'Dead as a doorknob on the poorhouse privy. Mind you, he'd a liked it like that, dying standing up. Ain't no man going to be able to say he fell down on the job.'

Flint looked hard at Silver, then at Cat. His eyes were what made him so scary. They caught your own eyes and seemed to enter your skull and have a good root round, testing and looking at whatever thought was in your head.

'What do you say, boy? Is that how it happened?'

'Yes,' said Cat, immediately, keeping her voice low. She was going to give no room for Flint to get further inside her head. 'Except for what he said.'

She saw Silver's head turn and look at her in surprise. Cat felt the warning but ploughed on.

'He didn't die immediately. He had enough time to swear at the giant who killed him. He called him a scurvy bastard, and told him he'd see him again in Fiddler's Green, and that then he'd dance to HIS tune.'

Flint's eyes bored inside her head for a long beat. Cat began to think she'd overdone it, embellishing the lie like that, but she'd thought the way to keep Flint off-balance was to put as much real detail into the story as she could.

Maybe she'd said too much . . .

. . . maybe he was noticing she wasn't a boy at all.

And then she saw the ghost of the smile return to Flint's face and stay there, fleshing out into a low chuckle as the wiry man turned to clap Silver on the shoulder.

'That's Billy, calling everyone scurvy but himself, and he without half the teeth in his head because of soft gums.'

Silver nodded.

'And he always said we'd all be together in the end at Fiddler's Green. Wherever that turns out to be. And he was a great one for dancing, wasn't he, Israel Hands?'

Silver looked up and stared at a gaunt muscular pirate who was standing at Flint's shoulder, his eyes reddening as his jaw worked with some deep emotion.

'Wasn't Billy a one for the hornpipe?'

Hands took a deep breath and looked at Cat with an inexplicably intense look of deepest hatred. He nodded, as if unable to speak.

'So you didn't get my casket?' said Flint, turning his smile off like a switch. 'You didn't get my Spanish gold?'

Silver shook his head again.

'We barely got off that island without ending up on the cooking fire. We'd have stayed and tried to dig up the chest, they'd have got it and you'd have been none the wiser. Was my decision that we'd do better to live to fight another day, and go back once the flesh-eating horrors were gone.'

'Still,' said Flint, sucking at his teeth as if to get the flavour of the words he was about to share with the crew. 'Still and all, an order is an order, Barbecue, even for you, even though you be quartermaster of this ship. And I gave it you under the eyes of all the crew here. What happens if I let you . . .'

Cat could see the looks flicking back and forth between the watching pirates, as if they knew something bad was going to happen and they were just waiting to see when and how terrible it was going to be. They were looks of interest and excitement, veiled but definitely there, an excitement borne of the fact the crew were relieved the badness was not going to rain down on them this time.

Silver appeared to see none of this. He stood his ground, as if he was the equal of Flint, and in that moment Cat realized that he actually was, that half of what made Flint so terrifying was people giving him the right to make them frightened. There was something quite heroic in the way Silver breezily ignored all the danger signs and carried on regardless.

251

'You sent us to bring back a thing of value, Cap'n, you sent us for treasure. And treasure of a sort I have brought you, even though it might not be the very kind you intended. But I give you my word it's treasure of a more powerful and lasting kind. And if we might step inside – AWAY from the eyes of the crew – I'd be happy to show you what it is . . .'

Silver had Flint's attention – and from the rumble that swept round the assembled deckhands, he had the interest of the crew as well. Silver swung towards the door at the foot of the quarterdeck stairs.

'You come too, Master Manno, for this concerns you too. Israel Hands, you come and babysit the boy while we speak private like.'

Silver had shifted the balance of power on the deck. Flint was captain, but the one-legged sailor had his own kind of power that was as much to do with momentum as anything else. Flint oozed anger and threat from every pore, but Long John was a force of nature in his own right.

He stood aside and let Flint lead the way into the doorway beside the steps up to the quarterdeck. Cat felt a hand on her shoulder as Hands pushed her in after the others, and in seven paces Cat was in the ante-room to the captain's cabin and hearing the door latch shut behind her.

Silver and Flint passed through an inner door. Silver turned and held up a hand to stop Cat and Hands following.

'Keep an eye on him, Israel, while me and the captain speak. Don't let any others of the crew talk to him either, mind. You sit there on that barrel, boy, and do what Mr Hands here tells you. Which will be to stay put, hold your tongue and mind your manners.'

And with that he pivoted on his crutch and swept into the inner cabin, ducking his head, as did the parrot on his shoulder, to avoid the low beam crossing the doorway.

Cat had time to see the sparkle of the waves beyond the leaded lights in the gallery window, and then Flint stepped into the door, looked back at her with an unreadable face, and slammed it shut.

For a long moment there was no sound but the creak of the boat and the murmur and foot-scuff of the sailors outside going about their business. And then Hands spoke:

'I don't like you,' he said. 'Not a bit of you. You've a soft look and fine bones and the stink of a Jonah about you.'

He stared at Cat, eyes wide enough to show an unblinking ring of white all the way round the iris. Cat looked down.

'OK,' she said, as non-committally as she could manage.

She heard Hands sniff something loose at the back of his throat, and then heard the sound of him spitting an instant before she saw the phlegm starburst on the deck at her feet.

'That's Billy Bones's jacket you're a-wearing, and Billy Bones was my messmate. It sounds like if you hadn't run off and brought them heathen cannibals chasing after you, they wouldn't have seen him, nor eaten him or whatever they is a-doing right now.'

Cat said nothing. She could feel Hands coming closer.

'You should have stayed put and let yourself get ate,' he said.

Then there was a snicking noise and a foot-long knife-blade entered her field of vision and slowly lifted her chin until she was eye to eye with the pirate.

'So here's the thing. I could bury this dirk in your guts just for the pleasure of watching you squirm. I wouldn't turn a hair, not unless you got some of your blood on my nankeen britches, then I'd make you scrub it off afore you died. Because you cost me something I value. A boon companion and a righteous shipmate. How are you going to make it better, pretty boy?'

The dirk pricked the soft skin under Cat's chin.

''Course if you don't got nothing to say by way of an answer, I might as well give a little push and skewer your tongue to the roof of your mouth, mightn't I?'

'I don't know,' gulped Cat. 'I don't know how to make it better.'

'I do,' breathed Hands.

He moved in very close to Cat, so close she could feel the man's stubble against the side of her face as he whispered in her ear, and smell the rank cocktail of dirty clothes and dried sweat mixed in with equal parts of rum-breath and raw onions and a whole lifetime's absence of toothpaste. Cat felt sick, and only partly with fear of the knife under her chin.

'I know just what you can do, my pretty. Flint and Barbecue are having a little private parley-voo on the other side of that door, and I can't abide a secret. It's a failing in me, but there it is. I wants to know what it is that Barbecue thinks he's brought back from that damned island that's so valuable.'

He turned Cat's head to look at the door to the inner cabin ten feet across the floor.

'Now if Flint was to catch me eavesdropping at that there door, he'd nail my ears to a barrel of rocks and drop it over the side just to see how long I could hold my breath. So what you can do is listen for me and we'll call it quits, right?'

He waved Cat towards the doors.

'Step lightly though and mind that middle board, because it squeaks.'

'Hang on,' said Cat, imagining HER ears getting nailed to a barrel. 'What if—'

'What if Flint catches you? He'll flay you with the cat and throw you to the sharks. IF he catches you. But happen you don't do what I say, I WILL take this blade and split you from belly button to breastbone, and watch your heels dance the dead-man's hornpipe on the deck while you try to stuff your bloody entrails back into the darkness they come from, my lovely.'

Hands meant every word. Cat could see it in the mad heat round his eyes and the tight whiteness rimming his mouth.

So she stepped softly across the room and put her eye to the thin crack where the door met the jamb.

After all, she reasoned, she wasn't doing this because she was frightened of the scary pirate with the knife and the equally disturbing hygiene issues – she wanted to know what was going on in there too.

All she could see was the back of Silver's coat and the parrot. The parrot was, a little disconcertingly, sitting backwards on his shoulder, so that two beady eyes seemed to be staring right at her. But she could hear well enough, Flint was talking.

'. . . better be something that tickles me, Barbecue, because I sent you for a casket of Spanish gold—'

'Oh this is better than Spanish gold, Cap'n. Spanish gold is commonplace compared to what I got us.'

'Fine words, Barbecue, but I didn't see nothing in the gig when you come up the side—'

Silver laughed, a low rumble that Cat could feel almost vibrating the thin wood of the door at her ear.

'Oh it's not in the gig, Flint. It's right here.'

As he shifted his weight on his crutch and reached inside his coat, Cat was sure he was going to pull out a pistol, and tensed herself for the explosion that would follow.

But he didn't pull a pistol, and as he shifted and the parrot flared its wings and settled more firmly on the blue cloth stretched across his shoulders, Cat saw it.

His first thought was that it was the Bible.

Flint thought the same too, for he stared angrily at Silver.

'That damned Bible we took off the Portuguese merchantman we sunk at the Dry Tortugas? Why I thought I told you to toss it overboard . . . !'

''Tis not the bible, Cap'n. Look closer.'

Silver turned the book in his hand and Cat saw the covers. Plain black. No gilt cross embossed into the leather. In fact no leather at all, just oilskin.

It was Victor's book.

It was her book.

Silver put his finger on the cover, pinning it to the tabletop.

'Now a book like that, Cap'n, that's a thing of power in this world, in the hands of one as knows how to use it.'

Through the crack in the door Cat saw Flint's eyes get hotter as he licked his lips and reached for the book. Silver removed his finger and let him open the cover and riffle through the pages. He looked up at Silver.

'And the boy does? He knows how to use it?'

Silver shook his head.

'The boy don't have a clue.'

Flint looked at Silver and licked his lips as his eyes went distant while he thought about what he was being told.

'And we don't know either?'

'No we don't.'

Flint tossed the book back on to the table with a shrug.

'So it's useless.'

'Not to the man whose book it is, Cap'n.'

'And who is that, Barbecue?' growled Flint.

'I don't know,' shrugged Silver. 'But the boy does. It ain't none other than his grandfather.'

'And who's he?'

'That be the wrong question, begging your pardon, Cap'n. The right one is where is he . . . and the boy does have an idea about that . . .'

The chuckle in Silver's voice as he said it snapped something in Cat. She realized why Silver had saved her, in that moment, when she should have felt more scared, and when she felt the sick bitter taste of betrayal rise in her gorge like poison, she felt something else, something that had been in her a while, and now could no longer be controlled.

Her fists clenched.

Just because she'd deeply, weakly, wanted Silver to be good, she'd let herself be fooled. Just because of that she'd let Victor down. The pure rage she felt flushing white hot across her shoulder blades and clenching her hands into tight fists was not at Silver, it was at herself, because THAT was the betrayal: she had let her grandfather down.

She was so furious at herself for having let herself be fooled that she forgot Israel Hands standing behind her with his dirk. She had the pistol Silver had given her stuffed into her belt under her coat, and she felt it digging sharply into her reminding her of its presence. Her right hand found it and pulled it free at the same time her left hand twisted the door handle and flung the door open with a crash before she'd even begun to wonder what the consequences might be.

30

The empty threat

The sound of the door crashing open spun Silver and Flint towards Cat, but the sight of the large pistol in her hand stopped them dead.

Which was lucky, because Cat realized there was something she needed to do, which was cock the hammer before they noticed the gun was not ready to fire. She yanked it back and stepped further into the room.

'That's the wrong move, "Master" Manno,' Silver said with a warning glare. 'No good will come of this.'

'Give me the book,' Cat spat.

'And what will you do with it, you puppy?' said Flint. 'You got one pistol and one ball, and there's three of us.'

That's when Cat remembered Israel Hands, just before she heard his feet scuff across the floor behind her. She swung the pistol and aimed it at Flint's unblinking eye.

'Tell him to step back or you're the one I'll shoot,' she said, hoping her voice wasn't betraying the fact her brain was now catching up with what she'd done but wasn't coming up with any very good ideas about what she was going to do next.

'Step back, Israel,' said Flint, not looking away from Cat's face.

'Now give me the book,' repeated Cat.

'Give me the gun,' said Silver.

His voice was calm, but there was a hint of sadness in it, as if Cat had disappointed him.

'It ain't loaded. Pull that trigger and all you'll get is a snap of the lock and that knife Israel has there buried in your back.'

Cat swallowed. Silver was lying. That's what he did. He must be lying.

''Course now Barbecue tells us you're waving round an empty piece, Israel might as well throw the knife anyway,' said Flint.

Cat spun and aimed the gun at Hands who did indeed stand five feet behind her holding a knife by its blade, arm cocked and ready to throw.

'Easy, bucko,' said Hands, his eyes flicking to Silver. 'You telling the truth about that gun being unloaded, Silver?'

Silver snorted.

'Put the gun down, boy. Didn't think I'd give you a gun as was loaded, did you? And us on such short acquaintance.'

Cat could see Hands was still trying to make up his mind. She stepped sideways, trying to get to a position where she could see all three of them at once. Flint had not moved, but he had the stillness of a snake ready to strike.

'Give me the book,' said Cat for the third time. Silver picked it up, and then tossed it towards her. Cat reached for it and caught it cleanly, but as soon as she did so, Silver lunged, bringing his crutch scything up and across so fast and so brutally hard that Cat couldn't get her hand out of the way. The crutch tip hit with a sharp crack, sending a jolt of pain back down her arm as the gun flew out of her hand and across the room.

Flint uncoiled and lashed an arm sideways, snatching the spinning pistol out of mid-air.

Cat gasped in pain and dropped the book as her free hand folded round her damaged hand. And then it was her turn to stop dead.

Flint swung the pistol in a short arc across the room and pointed it at her face.

'Don't!' Cat gasped.

Flint pulled the trigger.

There was a snap and a spark but no explosion.

Flint looked at the pistol in disgust, and dropped it with a clatter on to the floor.

Cat breathed again.

The hot flush of immediate fear had washed through her, but left her feeling clammy and very shaky, as if her legs were made of water.

Flint looked at Hands.

'Cut his throat and put him over the side.'

'Aye aye, sir,' said Hands, his knife-blade flashing in the light as he stepped forward. 'Now come on, Jonah, time to feed the whale, so let's not have any fuss about this.'

Silver planted his crutch between him and Cat and lurched forward.

'Now lay off a moment, Israel.'

'I gave an order, you swab,' Flint flared at him.

'Indeed you did, but I'm not a great one for cutting throats, Cap'n. Especially not throats as belong to geese what lays golden eggs,' said Silver. 'I told you. We knows the value and the power of that there book, but we don't know how to work it.'

'And you already told me he doesn't, so let's do and be done with him.'

'That's one way to skin a cat, Cap'n, but when we get to his grandfather, having him alive as a bargaining token might make him more likely to use the book to our advantage, don't you think?'

Cat watched Flint's eyes retreat again. When they came back they found hers.

'Where is your grandfather then, boy?'

'Far Rockaway,' said Silver. 'Least that's what he told me.'

'And where do we find it? Place is an old sailor's tale,' said Flint.

'There's truth in most tales, Cap'n,' said Silver. 'And we ain't never tried to find it before, have we? Once we put our mind to it, who's to say what we'll learn . . .'

Flint thought and then nodded.

'No loss in looking, you're right . . . no need to be hasty. We must think on it . . .'

'But what about the Jonah?' Hands said nastily, pausing in the doorway. 'Bursting in here with guns—'

'Be on your way, Israel,' Silver said, cutting him off with a warning look. 'Cut along sharpish afore we remember you was charged with guarding him and not letting him eavesdrop in the first place.'

Flint's pale eyes found Hands, interest kindling in their depths. Hands blanched and evaporated.

Silver looked at Cat and then at the captain.

'You think he's a Jonah?' said Flint.

'I think Israel calls everyone he don't like a Jonah, Cap'n,' Silver replied. 'You know that. And Billy was his boon companion. He's out of sorts.'

Flint nodded non-committally.

'And yet he's right about one thing. The whelp must be punished and must be seen to be punished. Discipline is everything.'

Flint jerked his finger upwards.

'Masthead him.'

31

Joe and Victor

Joe ran the four blocks from the 28th Street station, his heavy boots clomping the sidewalk like a carthorse. He crashed into the ER and skated up to the desk. The receptionist waited as he got his breath back and then sent him to the first Manno on her list, which was Victor.

Sam looked up as a dark shape filled the doorway. His first thought was of a raven, but then he saw it was Joe, and rose to meet him.

'Hey,' he said. And folded him into an awkward embrace. He felt Joe stiffen and knew he was seeing Victor's unconscious body over his shoulder. 'He's just out for the moment. He's not as bad as he looks.'

'No I'm not,' a voice growled thinly from behind him.

Sam turned and he and Joe looked at Victor, who lay there with his eyes closed.

'I'm worse,' he said, opening one eye slowly, the phantom

264

of a grin twitching the side of his mouth. 'Much worse.'

His lips smacked and his tongue sounded sticky as he tried to speak. Sam took his hand.

'Dad,' he said. 'You're going to be fine—'

'You know what I've been lying here thinking?' said Victor. 'I've been thinking nobody lives for ever—'

'Dad.'

'Don't interrupt. If you believe the scientists – and I do – we are all made of stars, and everything that is was once born of stars and will die and one day be blown through another star and be reborn as something else . . .'

'Dad,' said Sam. 'This might not be the time.'

Victor gripped his hand.

'It might be the only time, so stop interrupting: I was thinking that until we get blown through that distant star, the nearest thing to living for ever is to be in a story . . .'

There was a pause as he got shaken by a sudden coughing jag. He got his breath and continued.

'See, someone makes a story and people pass it on down the generations . . . it's not living for ever, but it's the closest we get. And maybe that's OK, you know? We're human. We don't do perfect: sometimes close enough is just fine. You know what I mean?'

Joe knelt by the bed next to his father's seat and put his hand on Victor's arm.

'I get it,' he said. 'Hey.'

Victor's eyeball rolled up and took him in.

'Hey, Joe,' he said. 'Cat's in trouble. Magua got her.'

'The Magua got you both,' smiled Sam. 'But you saved her, Dad. You hadn't jumped and pushed her clear, she'd have died.'

He swallowed and turned to Joe.

'He saved her.'

'Crap,' said Victor. 'She saved me. Magua took me and she saved me, but then he got her. On the falls. We've got to help her!'

Joe and Sam exchanged a look.

'Don't look at each other like that. I don't mean a general Magua. I mean the real one. He got her. We have to get her back. She's lost out there—'

'Where is Cat lost, Dad?'

'I don't know. There. I told you. In a story. Where I've been. In the woods.'

'In a story in the woods?'

'Yes! Cat's there and she's lost and Magua has her and we have to help her find her way home.'

'OK.'

'She thinks she's rescuing me. She doesn't get it. She's on the wrong tack.'

A nurse entered the room and stopped dead. Victor looked at her.

'My granddaughter's in trouble.'

'Yes,' she said, stumbling a little. 'Er how did . . . ?'

Sam was on his feet.

'What kind of trouble?'

She's beginning to spike a fever. Your wife wants you to go and—'

She was talking to an empty door.

Victor reached for Joe's hand.

'Did you tell him?'

'No.'

'Tell him. I was wrong about that. You were right. Tell them. And tell them why you didn't come to lunch . . .' He coughed again, pink flecking his lips.

'It doesn't matter now, Grandpa,' Joe choked, looking at the door. 'Nurse!'

Victor tightened his grip on Joe's hand.

'It matters, Joe. Everything matters now.'

He batted the nurse away.

'Just a minute, Joe. This is important. Cat's lost.'

'You said—'

Joe looked anxiously at the nurse. Victor yanked his hand.

'You can save her! You always could. Just like when you were a little kid and she was ill. You were the sweetest boy. You played for her then. She's lost and alone out there, so you have to do it again: play her home, Joe. Play our girl home . . .'

The nurse looked away from the monitor and saw the big dangerous-looking guy with the long hair and the metal in his face and the ink on his arms reach gently for the old man's face and stroke it. And as he nodded she saw the tear streak down his cheek and splash on to the linoleum beside his boots. And then he too was gone, leaving nothing but the sound of his boots clomping urgently away down the hall as he ran towards the street.

32

Shackled to the sky

Cat stumbled out of the Captain's cabin with Silver close behind her. Her mouth was dry and it wasn't just her legs that felt watery now. Her whole body seemed bathed in a fever – sweat of barely controlled dread, a dread that she was determined not to show, despite the fact that just walking was a battle against knees that wanted to buckle and drop her to the deck with each step she managed to take. They emerged on to the deck to find the world of the boat had changed completely in the short time they'd been inside.

The bare tracery of masts and rigging that had stood so desolate and gallows-like against the earlier morning sky was no longer naked, but had sprouted full-bellied canvas sails, creaking and straining against the yards and shrouds overhead as the boat cut water away from the islands already dropping towards the horizon behind them.

This new world of sun-bleached canvas that had appeared

overhead as if by magic was not a deserted one: sailors swarmed up and around it, performing a complicated aerial ballet as they climbed higher and edged nimbly to the very edges of the yardarms, urgently unfurling more canvas to snap and stiffen in the following wind.

Cat felt dizzy with vertigo just watching them.

'Flint wants every scrap of canvas, so we shall have skysails and moonrakers set before they're done up there. All them sails against a clear sky. It's a sight as you could never grow tired of, is it not?' said Silver.

Cat didn't answer. Silver's tone was as friendly and conversational as it had been in the gig, as if he had not betrayed her at all, as if Cat had not pointed a gun at his head. Cat found it made her angry just listening to it. She wasn't going to talk to him ever again.

'Know the difference between a sailor and a fisherman, Cat?' he said quietly.

Cat stuck with the silence. Silver clapped her companionably on the shoulder.

'Fisherman works his nets below the waves to catch every fish in the sea. Sailor works in the air, trying to catch every scrap of wind in the sky.'

There was a shrill whistle from the foot of the mainmast. Faces looked down from above. Hands shouted to the closest sailor in the rigging above him.

'Pass the word to the main-top and tell Pew we've got a customer to be mastheaded.'

The faces turned away one by one as the message was repeated higher and higher until Cat couldn't see who they were shouting at up in the rigging at the top of the mast, far beyond the curve of the main course. As they went back to work, more sails sprouted as busy hands freed the topgallants and royals.

She felt Silver's hand on her shoulder again.

His inexplicable friendly tone was stoking the rage again building inside Cat.

'No, but mark me, Cat – from down here it does look beautiful, but from up there it'll take your breath away – permanently – if you was to miss your grip or reach for a halyard that ain't quite where you thought it was. So you just keep your eyes sharp, and don't let go of one thing afore you're laid hold of the next. Just hope I didn't hurt your hand too bad with that knock I gave it, for you'll need both of them once you get up amongst the foretops.'

That's when Cat realized what mastheading meant. And before she could get her reaction sorted in her head, a stinging pain burst on her other shoulder as something hit her.

'No call for that, Hands!' Silver barked sharply.

Israel Hands stood beside them, a short length of thick rope spliced into a tight Turk's-head knot swinging threateningly from his fist.

'Cap'n said masthead him, Barbecue, and the Jonah's still on the deck.'

He raised the rope again with a nasty smile.

'Belay that!' growled Silver. 'Cap'n said masthead him, not hit him. He's of value to Flint and I, so you go easy with that little starter of yours, Hands, or it'll be me as works the cat, and your back that bears the stripes.'

Silver pointed at the bandage round Cat's calf.

'Boy's got a bad leg, so you be sure he takes his time and don't miss a step. I know what it's like to have an oar out of the water, so to speak, and I'll take it bad if you take advantage of him for it. Here, lad,' he said to Cat, pointedly, 'you'll need your stick when you come down, because you'll be stiffer than salt-cod after your time in the air, and walking won't come easy.'

He took Victor's cane and stuck it between the main-shrouds and the rail. He spoke loudly, in a way that was to no one in particular but everyone in earshot.

'The boy's stick is put there by Silver, and if any other than Silver or the boy takes it, I'll have their hide. Taking a man's stick is like taking his crutch and leaving him helpless in the world, and it will be a personal insult to me if it happens . . .'

Cat had no idea why Silver was now acting in such a solicitous and friendly manner. And as if to confuse her even further, Silver's face when it turned back to her was hard and unreadable again.

'Mastheaded, Flint said, and mastheaded you must be. Now start climbing, boy, steady as you go and don't look down. Hands won't strike you again, unless you stop climbing, but climb you must, and be shackled to the main-top stump until the Cap'n calls you down. You'll be a night aloft, maybe more'n one, depending on his humour. So think on this: 'Kit' Manno coming home to a safe harbour depends on you persuading your grandfather to use his power for us. No help for us? No future for you. Now get aloft with you.'

Hands took her arm and roughly pushed her towards the rigging.

The first part of the climb was easy enough, despite the twinge of pain in her calf and the throb in the hand that Silver had struck. The shrouds were woven together into a giant grid, making a sloping triangular rope ladder that was widest at deck level then narrowed as it climbed higher up the mast. The ropes were tarred and stiff beneath her hands and feet, but because they were taut with the strain of bracing the mainmast they were stable which made the going easy.

She ignored Silver's warning about looking down, and was not very frightened about the distance to the deck, not until the pit of her stomach began to lurch the moment she looked away and saw the sea beyond. Where the deck was stable and fixed in its position beneath the rigging, the sea bucked and dropped away with a vertigo-inducing heave and swell. Once she realized she was not only climbing, but being waved from side to side as the boat tacked across an awkward cross-sea, she really began to feel sick. She made it to the first platform on the mast and looked up at the impossible climb still ahead of her.

She received a blow on her bad leg and looked down to see

Hands climbing behind with a set of chains jangling hanging round his neck. As she watched he overtook her and swung out and over the lip of the platform above, disappearing from view for a moment. Cat knew she could not manage such a sure-footed move, swinging against the roll of the boat, hanging eighty or so feet above the hungry sea below. Then Hands's head appeared close to the mast, where there was a small man-sized trap door.

'Come on, Jonah, through the lubber's-hole with you, for though it'd be great sport to see you take a tumble, Flint would skin me, and I values my hide.'

Cat clambered gratefully forward and up through the hole. She rose to a crouch, steadying herself against the solidity of the mast, and tried to work out where to look. Down was too gut wrenching, and straight ahead was worse as the horizon bucked and yawed from side to side with horrific severity, making it impossible to ignore the fact that the higher she got the wider were the arcs in which she was being whipped across the sky.

Hands reached over and thrust the chains at her.

'On you go, and carry your manacles with you. Pew'll know what to do.'

Cat looked up as Hands hung the rough iron shackles round her neck.

Looking up didn't help at all.

The mast narrowed and the shrouds got thinner too, and the gilded tip of the mast scribed a woozy figure of eight across

274

blueness above as it marked the hogging motion of the boat.

There was another yardarm crossing the mast above her head, and beyond that smaller sails. Just below the mast-top was a further tiny platform from which a man was watching her.

Cat was horrified to realize she had only climbed halfway up the mast. Her hands were raw, her shoulders and arms hurt, and she was beginning to shake with exhaustion. The wind here on the platform was noticeably stronger too.

'Move, Jonah, or I'll split your head!' Hands said, showing Cat the rope's end.

Cat set off up the next stage, and as she did so she saw another man, stripped to the waist in a pair of ragged blue canvas britches, moving swiftly in from the outer tip of the yardarm above. He had his back to Cat, but Cat noticed with a shiver that it was covered in tattoos of the kind, but not exactly the same as the Huron warriors she had run from. His head was shaved into a single mohawk from which a feather fluttered in the stiffening breeze as he approached. This must be the Indian Silver had warned her about, the one they'd picked up adrift off the Grand Banks.

Cat froze as he swung out over the yard and found a foothold on a cross-sheet below it, before transferring his weight on to the rigging Cat was climbing. He was on the opposite side, facing her, which meant that he was leaning back over the gulf of air as he climbed down, which didn't seem to bother him at all.

She stiffened and held on tight as the feet descended to her nose level. She tried to ignore the yaw of the ship and focus on what to do if the Huron – if he was a Huron – attacked. She wound a foot round one of the perpendicular ropes to get a better purchase, and then grabbed the manacles from round her neck, quickly winding them round her fist. They would make a good enough weapon if things got ugly, and she didn't have much choice anyway as the Indian was moving so fast and sure-footedly downwards that they were suddenly eye to eye, inches between their noses.

Cat had enough time to see the Indian's eyes take her in, and then he was gone.

She breathed a sigh of relief and put the chains back round her neck, happy she wasn't going to need a weapon after all. She was getting jumpy.

She was about to haul himself upwards again when the Indian's face jerked up and filled her field of vision again.

A hand shot through the web of rope separating them and clamped round the chain on her neck, half choking her. She tried to protest, but all that came out were consonants.

'Gggddkkk . . . !' she choked.

The Indian loosened his grip, and Cat saw he was not looking at her at all. Instead he was looking at the eagle feather round her neck. He darted a look into her face and she saw his eyes widen in surprise. He dropped the chains and hissed something at her. She didn't hear words that she could understand but she got the message loud and clear: stay still. She didn't move an inch.

The Indian took the feather in his hands and turned it gently over. He stared at the way it was lashed to the buckskin strap round Cat's neck as if he could read something in the intricate weave of the overlapping knots. He rolled the small beads between his fingertips and then dropped it, reaching behind his head and pulling round the feather hanging off his mohawk.

There was a similar bead and, to Cat's eyes, the knotting looked very like the one on her feather, but the feather itself was a sad thing, in fact hardly a feather at all anymore. It had been clipped or cut, so that only about two inches of it remained, and what did looked like it had been scrunched and crushed and then smoothed out again.

The Indian dropped it back behind the nape of his neck when he saw Cat looking at it, as though he was ashamed of it. His chin came up and he barked something at Cat.

'I don't understand,' said Cat.

The Indian pointed at Cat's feather.

'You,' he said. 'That. Not worthy.'

Their eyes locked.

'You girl, not boy.'

That's what he'd seen.

'I'm a boy,' she said, gravelling her voice.

'You liar too,' he said. 'Double not worthy.'

Hands yelled from below, breaking the spell.

'Shake a leg, you lazy heathen bastard, the captain wants you.'

The Indian looked down. Then back at Cat.

'One day I kill him,' he said quietly and matter-of-factly, and then he dropped from sight.

'And you get climbing, Jonah, or by Christ's bloody tears I'll come up there and knock your lights into the next ocean but one!' roared Hands.

Cat made it to the top by looking at nothing except the mast as she climbed. Most of the time this worked to shut off her peripheral vision and ignore the lurch and swagger of the boat, but every now and then a particular motion would jar her, and she would have to notice how savagely she was now being whipsawed through the air.

Hickory-hard hands reached down and the lookout Pew pulled her on to a tiny platform seven feet below the gilded pinnacle of the mast, and she found herself looking into a grinning windburned face that seemed to have only slightly more teeth than nostrils. The gap-toothed pirate had made up for his dental losses by adding earrings, so he jangled as he swayed his head back and forth taking Cat in.

'Mastheaded are you, boy?' Pew wheezed, taking the manacles from round Cat's neck as she stared in rising horror at the heaving seascape all around them, gripping the stays attaching the platform to what was, she now felt, a ridiculously thin mast-tip.

'Yes,' she gasped.

The sailor clicked one end of the manacle through a metal ring-bolt on the mast, and then, before Cat could really focus on what was happening, snapped the other end shut around her wrist.

'Don't look at the sea: it'll make you sick. Don't look at the sky, because the sun'll blind you. And don't close your eyes, or the horrors will come, sure as Neptune rules the seabed. Other than that?' He wheezed out a laugh and jangled as he shook his head. 'Other than that, you may do what you wish and make free of all the comforts and liberties of the main-top stump, you lucky, lucky little lad.'

And with a final jingle of his earrings Pew swung over the platform and left Cat alone, open-mouthed with exhaustion, and shackled to the sky.

33

Fever

When Sam got to Cat's room he was stopped outside by Annie who had been banished to the hallway while the Intensive Care team worked inside.

They could only watch as the nurses and a doctor held Cat's unconscious body still and quickly and firmly tied a vest across her and secured meshy straps to the rails on the side of the bed.

'What the hell are they doing tying her down like that?' said Sam, hiding how scared he was in a rush of outrage. 'That's a strait jacket!'

'It's a Posey Vest,' said one of the nurses. 'It's OK. We just don't want her thrashing around with this fever and disturbing any of the instrumentation we've got on her head. It's just preventive.'

The doctor appeared in the door.

'We've got her on antibiotics in case the fever is infection related, and we've given her something to take the temperature down. We'll monitor her. This isn't unusual at this stage.'

'Is it bad?' said Annie.

'None of this is great, but none of it is terrible,' he said, touching her arm with professional gentleness. 'It's serious but not grave. We're doing all we can. We just have to hang in there. She seems like a fighter.'

They watched him walk away.

'Serious not grave?' said Sam. 'Like that clears things up.'

Annie looked back at Cat, now lashed to the bed.

'She looks so small,' she said. 'Where's Joe?'

Sam looked round at the empty hall behind him.

'He came,' he said. 'He's with Victor.'

Annie nodded.

'OK.'

Cat twitched and her sweat-slicked cheek spasmed. It was a small movement, but it broke Annie's heart all over again.

'He should be here.'

34

The horrors

Cat lost track of time quite quickly. The sun was hot and although she could squirm round the mast so that her head was more or less in shadow most of the time, she couldn't keep anything like her whole body out of the direct heat, and with that and the windburn, she became very thirsty and then increasingly confused.

Despite, or maybe in defiance of, Pew's warning she spent what seemed like the first hour or so steeling herself to look at the heaving ocean all around without becoming nauseous or gripped with mind-numbing vertigo. It seemed like an hour; it might have been the first morning or the first ten minutes by the time she finally closed her eyes, so disoriented had she become.

When she closed her eyes, the horrors did, as advertised, arrive. And they came, as Victor would have said, not as single spies, but in battalions. From the moment her head dropped and she nodded off and then woke up for the first time, she was unsure as to whether she was jerking awake again and again, or lurching from dream to nightmare and worse.

Everything came at her in fragments, as if time had shattered, but one of the two things that underlined all she felt while shackled to the masthead was a thrumming sense of dread that crept into her consciousness like a low drone that underpinned everything and grew in intensity until it became unbearable.

The second thing was that the more unbearable and frightening things got as reality broke apart and came at her in great spinning chunks of shrapnelled time, the angrier she got. What began as fear rose and rose and then plateaued out, maybe because the mind just can't go on escalating the fear it feels forever, but reaches a point where it decides you've had your limit. But everything she experienced – dream, nightmare, delirium – needed a reaction, and since her system had maxed out its fear quota, she got angry instead.

But the more angry she got, the darker grew the clouds above and the wilder the sea below – and then, as the wind rose to a shriek, the horrors that came in on the wings of the storm were even worse.

To start with she woke parched and hungry. Her lips were stuck together and cracked as she worked them open and tried to lick them with a tongue that was bone dry. The sun was dropping into a blood-red bed of clouds that smeared the horizon, but it seemed not to get any cooler as it dropped. She saw a sailor on the mizzen-mast behind her and tried to shout for water, but the croak she managed to come out with didn't make it across the thirty feet of air between them . . .

Then she must have fallen asleep, because she woke thinking she was tumbling through space—

And then smacked her cheek on the mast as the ship hit the bottom of a wave trough and the ship's head came up again; she scrabbled for a handhold to stop herself sliding off the tiny platform her ankle was chained to . . .

She held the mast for hours that may have been minutes or several consecutive nights, and watched the huge following sea harry the *Jamaica* from wave to wave, as the wind howled with a malign intensity that blew the tops off them in smirrs of white spindrift that kept pace with the boat like phantom outriders in the moonlight.

Then there was no moonlight but clouds everywhere like a lead ceiling pressing down and splitting her head . . .

And then there was rain and soaking and then more parching and baking in the sun, and in the middle of this she mysteriously acquired a tattered oilskin jacket that had almost as many holes as it had oilskin, but it kept some of the rain off . . .

Then she had a ghost-sense of someone putting water in her mouth from a flask and she thought first it was her mother and then perhaps Chingachgook but he was dead and gone over the waterfall and when she tried to focus her eyes and see who it was they were gone too and she was alone in the sky again . . .

But she later found she was clutching a piece of the dried meat sailors call pemmican, which she may have found in the pockets of the oilskin, but when she tried to find it a while afterwards because she felt hungry it had gone . . .

Then later still, or maybe much earlier, she found a piece of meat stuck between her teeth on the right-hand side when the sun was high and she spent a day, maybe a month, perhaps a minute or so, working it free and enjoying the delicious meat juice taste for an instant before she swallowed it, so possibly she had eaten the big piece of pemmican anyway and just forgotten about it. Which made her angry . . .

And then the sea was driving the ship across more spindrift and the moon was low and casting deep dark shadows in the scallops of the waves that were sinister and pulled at the eye in an insistent way that she didn't like and then liked even less as she saw the jaws of a great red-crested sea-monster surge out of one; but then it wasn't a sea monster at all when it hit the moonlight it was wood; it was a canoe; it was the Great Canoe and all the dead Huron were paddling like the devil was on their tail except the devil was not on the canoe's tail at all, he was straddling the prow in his red coat, proud as a rooster on his dunghill, and he was Magua and he was pointing forward exultantly and what he shouted at Cat was— lost in the wind or Cat forgot it or it never happened.

When she tore her eyes away and looked up she was not

chained to a mast, not any more, not a wooden mast with a gilded top, but instead she was chained to a metal stand and an ornate pillar that disappeared into the bottom of a metal box decorated with Victorian ironwork. It hung over her like an anvil about to drop out of the sky and as she tried to scrabble away, first on this side then the other, she saw each of the four faces of the box were clock faces and the hands were whirling around at wildly different speeds and in both directions at once, wantonly both firing time into the future and dragging it into the past – and this made her very, very, VERY angry because if you don't know whether you can trust the time, you might know which way the wind blows but how do you know if you're going to be late and she must not, absolutely must NOT, be late because of something important that she couldn't remember . . .

And not being able to remember the VERY IMPORTANT THING choked her and the waves hurled the ship forward and the clocks stopped as one and turned into compasses and all of them pointed forward at the same time and stuck there and she looked ahead with a shock of cold horror as she saw a ship, another ship, except it was the *Jamaica* too and it was side on and closing, and her *Jamaica* was going to T-bone the other one and she screamed a warning and she saw herself at the masthead of the other *Jamaica* screaming another warning back at her. But as the distance closed she saw she wasn't herself not because she was thirsty and heat struck and starving and weak with exposure but because the her on the incoming

Jamaica wasn't her but was him and he was Victor and he too was chained to the mast and then her *Jamaica* hit his and the world bucked and a ship screamed and shuddered and splintered and Victor's ship was cut in half and they sailed on and over the two sinking pieces of the other *Jamaica* and as she looked left with horror she saw the mast go straight into the sea, straight down true and inexorable as a piledriver heading for the centre of the earth, and Victor was chained to it. And as it disappeared beneath the waves the last thing she saw was Victor's mouth open and shouting and then his hand clawing the last foot of air and then nothing did indeed close up faster than a hole in the ocean . . .

And Cat leapt – she jumped – she threw herself after Victor in a despairing dive but she was yanked back short-chained by the ankle and she tumbled hanging face down beneath the masthead platform swinging like a pendulum staring at the deck, the tears falling from her eyes straight down and down and down . . .

And then there was no deck; the deck was sea and the mast was dropping and it was her turn to ride the piledriver express downbound into the storm-tossed white-caps and she bit one last huge lung-popping mouthful of salt air before her face hit the water and then the mast top overtook her and she was jerked round so her head faced the roof of the sea above and she stared up with blearing eyes through the fathoms of ocean at the farewell white of the moon until it was no moon but a pearl and then a pinprick and then a memory in the cold black marble tomb of the sea . . .

And then she couldn't not breathe any more and she opened her mouth without meaning to and saw the last light in the world bubble up and away from her towards the surface as she reflexively inhaled a dark chunk of ocean and let the inkiness spread inside until she was one with the bible-black beyond her plummeting body and she was gone and she was nothing, then less than nothing, just an absence like the starless void into which she had been swallowed up.

35

Alan

Cat's eye flickered open to find herself upside down and over someone's shoulder and being carried down the last length of rigging to the deck. Rough hands took her as she was unflopped from her rescuer's shoulder and laid on the scrubbed wooden boards where she could see a sea boot, a crutch tip and a parrot standing between them eying her critically.

Her rescuer knelt and turned her face to the sky.

It was the Indian. He looked at her critically, felt her forehead and nodded at Silver.

'Too much sun. Too much rain. Not sleep enough.'

Silver turned to the watching sailors.

'What are you all standing about for flapping your traps? Captain wants the sails reefed and the ship made ready for weather, so shake a leg or I'll break out the cat o' nine tails!'

'Weather?' said Hands, spitting tobacco over the taff rail while keeping an eye on Cat. 'Worse than weather I'll warrant,

289

and the Jonah to blame for it all, mark my words.'

'I'll mark your hide if you don't get up the mizzen and take in a reef,' growled Silver.

The sailors went aloft. Silver turned back and looked at Cat and the Indian.

'Get the boy to his feet, give him his stick so's he can walk. Give him water and biscuit and then lock him in the brig. There's a storm coming.'

The brig was a small wooden cell two decks down, jammed into the narrowing space beneath the bowsprit where the ship's prow curved in to a point. To begin with that was all Cat knew, because it was also unlit and the moment she stumbled in leaning on her stick, the door slammed shut behind her, leaving her in the dark with no noise but the creak of the boat's timbers and the roar and smack of the sea against the hull at her back, a sound she could feel as much as hear as the ocean growled past only a couple of inches away on the other side of the planking she was leaning against.

She steadied herself against the sickening slo-mo see-saw of the deck, a motion all the more nausea-inducing now that she was blind, and lurched the three short steps to the door, smacking her forehead on the low roof as she did so. She banged on the rough wood hard enough to make the iron bolt on the other side bounce and rattle in its shackle, and yelled. All that achieved was to make her fist hurt as much as her head.

No one came.

'Fine!' she shouted. 'Fine. You're all thieves and cowards. I hope you all drown!'

The door yanked open and Cat stepped back despite herself. The Indian stood filling the space, his bare shoulders glistening with rain.

'No,' he said. 'Unsay it.'

'What?' said Cat.

The Indian thrust something at her. It was a tin cup with a lid on it, and from the way it sloshed Cat could tell it was water. The Indian thrust two pale discs at her.

'Biscuit. You eat.'

Cat took them. They were about the size and consistency of a pair of hockey pucks.

The Indian snapped his fingers at Cat.

'You give me my coat,' he said.

He was talking about the oilskin Cat was still wearing. As she struggled to cobble together her fragmented memory and sort out what had been real and what had been dream or delirium on the masthead, she realized that this Indian must have climbed up and given her the oilskin to protect herself from the elements. And it had been this Indian whom she had later mistaken for Chingachgook as he knelt by her and gave her water and pemmican.

She struggled out of the jacket and held it out.

'Thank you,' she mumbled.

The Indian didn't reach out.

'Unsay the curse,' he said.

'Curse?' Cat said.

'You say we must all drown. You must unsay it.'

'I was just shouting—' Cat began.

'No!' said the Indian, voice hard and final as a church door slamming. 'You carry the eagle feather. You speak, the Manitou hears your prayers.'

He snatched the stump of his own broken eagle feather from where it hung at the back of his neck and jabbed it at Cat.

'The great Spirit cannot hear me. He cannot see me. I cannot speak with him and my ancestors do not know where I am on this wide water. My father cannot find me in the dark as he swore he would. But you have the power of the eagle feather who are not even of my people, and you bore a book of power, Barbecue says. And you use those powers to curse men to die. You are the Jonah. This storm is yours!'

Cat now saw that the wetness on the Indian's face was not all from the rain lashing the decks above. She pushed the coat at him again.

'You're wrong,' she mumbled. 'I don't have any power—'

The Indian's eyes flashed.

'But I do take it back.'

She had a memory hit of Victor's hand clawing the final foot of air above the wave tops before it disappeared, and as she remembered it she tasted ink-black seawater in her own mouth, and it smacked of rank despair.

'I don't want you all to drown. I just, I just want . . .'

'If wishes was horses, beggars would ride . . . and then where would we all be in that topsy-turvy world, eh?' said a harsh and familiar voice as Flint appeared behind the Indian and flung him back towards the steps to the deck. 'Get aloft, you tattooed monkey, or I'll skin you and fly your red hide from the main-top as a warning to all lazy work-shy beggars.'

He leant into the brig, his eyes sparking with malice.

'And you shut your yap, pretty boy, and stow that mumbo jumbo, for even if you be a Jonah, Flint's the captain of this ship and Flint don't believe in gods nor monsters, no more'n they believe in Flint. No Flint don't believe in anything but Flint, and maybe that book o'power Barbecue took off of you, so you work out how we get to your grandfather and how you'll persuade him to work the book for Flint when we do!'

And he slammed the door so hard the hinges jumped, and the blackness that came after was absolute.

Cat slid down the wall and braced herself against the planks, listening to the sounds of the ship barrelling into the teeth of the storm. She gripped the eagle feather round her neck, but got no thrill of power from it. She scrabbled her hands across the floor and found her cane, which she pulled into her lap, turning the compass back and forth between her fingers.

'No way,' she said out loud. 'No way.'

Speaking into the darkness seemed to ease some of the anger and frustration building up inside her.

'You can go to hell.'

The darkness had no answer to this. She dropped her head.

'Wish I did have power.'

Something hard dug into her ribs. She shifted and felt. It was one of the biscuits. It felt more like a piece of tile than food. She tried to bite a chunk off, but it was like gnawing on a paperweight. She found the tin cup and soaked the edge of the biscuit for a few minutes, listening to the distant shouted orders on the deck above, the sudden thrum of bare feet overhead as sailors ran to and fro, and the closer creaks and knocks that told their own story about how the ship was protesting its treatment in the rough hands of the storm.

She got the edge of the biscuit soft enough to break off a chunk and chew it.

'Wishes were horses? I'd take one and ride right out of here. Wish I had light.'

She chewed off another chunk.

'Wish someone would help me get out of here so I can find Victor.'

There seemed little chance of that, though she did wonder why the Indian had been as kind to her as he evidently had been in the delirium she'd fallen into at the masthead. She bit more claggy biscuit and worked on it. It was more punishment for her teeth than it was actual nutrition, but it kept her mind off her situation and gave her something to work on.

'Wish I hadn't been bloody kidnapped.'

'Kidnapped?' said a voice out of the darkness, much too

close, from a direction where Cat was pretty sure there had been no one an instant before. 'Well, there's a pretty predicament we both find ourselves in.'

The voice was calm and even and inescapably Scottish, not the guttural urban Scots Cat's friends dropped into when they wanted to impersonate a Scot, a caricature learned from bad movies, but the gentle Highland accent that Cat recognized from Victor and the musical shadow of it that sometimes emerged in her dad's voice when you least expected it to.

There was a scraping sound, a match flare, and in the startling suddenness of light that accompanied it Cat saw a pair of eyes looking straight at her from the other side of the brig. The eyes had a kind of sparkling craziness about them that was, in the instant she saw them, both a little unnerving and wholly attractive.

The match was applied to a candle, and the candle was put inside a tin lantern that was hung on a peg on the roof-beam and Cat and the man sat facing each other.

His face was exactly what Cat realized she had been expecting from the instant she heard the voice in the dark: it had the dark weathered complexion of a man of action who lives outdoors, a soldier's face scattered with freckles and dented with pockmarks across the cheekbones and lower temples.

He was not a big man, but his frame was powerful and wiry, and even as he sprawled against the wooden bulkhead, one leg stretched across the floor, the other cocked with a hand resting lazily on it, he managed to give the impression that he could spring into furious action at any moment. He wore a dark greatcoat over his shoulders, and beneath that a blue coat with silver buttons and a buff-coloured waistcoat. The clothes looked travel-stained and dishevelled, but the set of his head was alert and he showed no sign of tiredness.

Cat had the strangest conviction that she had conjured him out of the darkness by just wanting him, but of course he was too solid and real and earthily present to have been conjured out of any ether.

He was, however, the hero Victor had most loved and, of course, Cat thought, of course he was here. And the crazy logic behind this world of adventure she had woken up in was not crazy at all. It was just Victor's logic, born of Victor's love of stories. Chingachgook and Long John Silver, and now the one true hero, the real love of Victor's boyhood tales.

Of course it was him.

How stupid Cat was.

It was always going to be him.

She felt such a thick surge of hope coursing through her that she had to clear her throat before she spoke.

'I'm Cat Manno,' she said. 'And I'm really pleased to meet you.'

The dancing eyes held hers, and then with one smooth move the man was on his feet and inclining his head in the smallest of bows.

'My name is Stewart,' he said, and then he smiled. 'Alan Breck they call me.'

Although the space was cramped and they were locked in and his clothes were weather-beaten and crumpled, he stood there as if he owned the ship and had not a care in the world.

Cat scrambled to her feet and looked at him.

'I know,' she said.

'And a pleasure it is to meet you too, Cat Manno, for though you bear a name that I do not know, and though it has a hint of the Spaniard—'

'Italian,' said Cat.

'Spaniard, Italian, there is very little difference between the two when viewed from the perspective of a son of the North,' Alan continued blithely. 'And as I was saying, though you are, as you tell me, of Mediterranean origins, I have met several people of good family from Southern climes, and I do not share the common prejudice for I can see you, despite the dire straits you find yourself in, are a gentleman.'

And he stuck his hand out.

Cat grinned. This was the prickly, proud Alan Breck whose swagger and vanity had enthralled and irritated Victor and herself when Victor had read her the story a lifetime ago. He wasn't a perfect hero and might even have been a murderer, but as ruthless and implacable an enemy as he was, he was the best of all friends in a tight spot, and his friendship, once given, was unbreakable.

'I'm no gentleman,' she said, reaching out and gripping the offered hand. 'Cat is short for Catriona.'

He dropped her hand instantly and took a step back in surprise. Then he leant in and peered at her closely.

'Well by the saints, lassie, so you are not . . .'

Cat was amused to see how much his mistake put him off his stride. He seemed offended at himself somehow, embarrassed even.

'I mean to say, you'll forgive my making sae bold with your hand, Miss Catriona, I should never have mistook—'

'You were half right,' she grinned. 'I'm definitely in dire straits. And please: I go by Cat, and I have no problem shaking hands with people.'

She watched while he swallowed this and recalibrated.

'Well, a trouble shared is a trouble halved – just as a meal is,' said Alan after a pause, eyeing the biscuits in Cat's hand. 'I have not filled my belly for several days, and while I would be delighted to be advised of your predicament, I'm sure I should make a better audience were my hearing not drowned out by the grumblings and eructations consequent to the nagging void in my belly.'

'Sorry, what?' said Cat, floundering in the backwash of Alan's language.

Alan grinned and pointed at her hand.

'Gie's a wee bit biscuit, Cat girl, and I'm all ears.'

So Cat did. And as they took turns dunking and gnawing on their biscuits she told him of her quest. As the ship rolled and tossed in the gathering storm outside, and they watched the lantern cast wildly swinging shadows across their small wooden box, she told everything about the deepwoods and the mountain climb and the fight at the waterfall. As they heard the wind rise to such a high-pitched shriek that she had to half shout the story, she told him about the island of the dead and the Huron chasing her again and how Honest John had saved her and their voyage and the book and the betrayal and Flint and the mastheading.

She told him she must get to Far Rockaway and rescue her grandfather. She didn't tell him about New York or LA or sirening ambulances or screeching fire-trucks because she didn't think it was necessary and as she spoke into the night that distant world and that other life seemed insubstantial and blurry and like a dream anyway. And she really had no idea how to speak of it without sounding way crazier than anything else in this mad world she'd found herself in.

Alan listened well and asked questions when Cat stumbled or wasn't clear, and seemed to understand and believe in her quest without questioning it. And when she was done he sat there, his eyes distant, watching the candle flame rock to and fro for a long while. And then he sighed, got to his feet and began pacing the two steps to the door and back.

'I am pleased to have been right, Cat, I am pleased that you are indeed a person of parts, for the story you have told me tells more of you than you know. You have undergone great dangers and privations, and all for love and loyalty to your kin. Gentlefolk do not come from fine houses and fancy manners, Cat, and I speak as one who has lived in palaces and peat bogs. Gentlemen and gentlewomen come from the heart, and they come from all stations in life. And I have met more gentlefolk beneath the peat-smoked blackened rafters of a lowly Highland croft than I have in the gilded salons of Paris or London.'

He banged on the door in frustration.

'Why, Cat, to be shut up here powerless and without a weapon as the world turns on its head all around us? It's a cruel turn fate has played us, and no mistake. Why, if I had but a sword in my hand I would pledge my arm to your quest, Cat, for there is no cause that thrills the heart of Alan Breck as much as one that lesser men think lost and hopeless.'

He banged and shook the door again, and then sank back to his haunches, sighing in a way that Cat, although moved by his performance, couldn't help but notice was more than a little theatrical.

Alan shook his head and stared at the floor.

'If I had but a short yard of good steel, Cat, we should see what we should see and deliver a great surprise to this crew of false fleeching beggars! And now would be the time for it, when they think they have nothing to fight but a tempest! Why a mere tempest is nothing compared with the blade-storm that Alan Breck would unleash on them. And yet more's the pity, for the time is right, but alas . . . if we only had a sword!'

'Just a sword?' said Cat.

'A sword in my hand and I can make the world anew, Cat girl,' he rallied with a bright smile and a flash of his eyes, but then he smiled sadly again. 'But it's no' to be.'

'Oh. I wouldn't say that,' said Cat, and she clicked the stud on Victor's cane. 'Would this do?'

Alan's eyes had sparkled as he strutted and talked and listened to his own words, but the true flame, the real Alan Breck blazed forth like wildfire as he watched Cat slowly unsheathe the sword from the cane. He reached over without a word and took the blade.

'Why, Mistress Manno. 'Tis a pretty trick and a blade to match. You fair take my breath away . . .'

He looked closer at the blade. Cat was shocked to see the rust had got even worse, browning the steel from hilt almost to the tip. It was an unnaturally – even supernaturally – fast kind of corrosion, she thought. And at the back of her mind she wondered if the rust was getting worse because she was doing such a bad job of getting the blade back to its owner.

'Though you might have kept it in better condition, for it will soon be useless, so rusted have you allowed it to become – still . . .'

He slashed the sword right and left and stamped forward into a couple of practice lunges, then he straightened and smiled dangerously.

'Still, the point is sharp enough and that is the very thing.

301

And why did they let you in here with such a fine piece of metal?'

'They didn't know, said Cat. 'Not any of them. Except Silver . . .'

She realized Silver both knew and had made sure she was given the sword to lean on as she made her way from the mast to the brig. It made little sense, now she focused on it.

Alan was balancing the blade on one finger and tossing it up and catching it by the handle with rising glee.

'Silver knew, did he? The one-legged man? Why did he do that I wonder? I had him marked for as sharp a customer as that murderous captain of his . . .'

'Why indeed, shipmate?' growled a voice at the jailer's slit in the door. 'That's the conundrum, you may lay to that.'

But it wasn't just a voice. It was the flared barrel of an ugly-looking blunderbuss. And the face behind it was Silver's.

36

Surprised below decks

'Now you'd oblige me, my Highland friend, by putting your sword on the floor and stepping back,' said Silver, his voice as steady and unwavering as the gun he held pointed at Alan through the slit in the door.

Alan stood tensed like a spring, ready to leap, his teeth gritted.

'He can't miss,' said Cat. 'At this range with that thing, he'll probably hit both of us without trying.'

'And be picking bits of you out of the hull from here until Christmas,' agreed Silver. 'Pay her mind, Scotsman. And don't you try a-leaping at me or a-throwing of that sword, because I got three solid inches of English oak between me and you and when this blunderbuss goes off, well, a feisty bantam you may be, but that cause is so lost even you shouldn't sign up for it.'

Cat realized Silver must have been listening at the door for a long time. Alan put the sword on the floor and leant nonchalantly against the wall as if so doing was his idea entirely.

The bolt clanked and screeched, and then the door was open and Silver stood braced in it against the swing of the boat, looking at them both.

For a moment all was quiet, except for the rising growl of the storm building outside the ship.

'Well, Cat Manno. Sounds like I had more faith in you than you had in me.'

And before Cat could speak, Silver reached behind him, took out a pistol and tossed it to her. As she caught it Silver tossed her another small leather pouch.

'Load it yourself this time, girl, and be sharp about it, for there's dark deeds to be done before this storm blows out.'

He stepped into the room and looked at Alan.

'Now you're a dangerous man to be sure, and I'm a-thinking a sensible captain might think it better to be shot of you than keep feeding you in the vain hope some Highland chieftain might pay a ransom one day. Highlanders, and I mean no offence by this, is not always keen to open their purses and we might be feeding you a long, long time, not to mention the mischief you might cause.'

A spot of colour pinked Alan's cheeks, though he kept his voice calm and eyed the sword on the floor.

'If a Highland gentleman keeps his purse strings cinched tight, is only so as not to shame the English king who has stripped him of its contents,' he said with a cheerfulness that didn't match the look in his eyes.

'No doubt, and I mean no harm by what I said. Kings of all stripes is worse thieves than any who sail beneath the black flag, to my way of looking at it. Now . . .'

And here he gave Alan a look that was just as hard as the one Alan was giving him, so like it that for a moment Cat's eyes seemed to blur and she thought she was looking at the same man staring out of two different faces.

'. . . if I was to give you your sword, would you give me your word not to hack at me 'til we have spoke further on a matter of mutual advantage?'

He pointed at his stump with his chin. After a beat Alan relaxed and nodded.

'You have my parole, if only to see what you will say next, Silver, for you talk straight but seem to play a devilish crooked game.'

'Yes,' said Cat. 'You betrayed me!'

'Did I now?' said Silver, flicking the sword across the floor to Alan with a sweep of his crutch tip. 'Or did I get you safe on board and far away from that damned island of the dead. And did I not keep you safe by making Flint, a man with no love for passengers, or young ladies for that matter, think you was a valuable prisoner? And did he not keep you safe and away from the prying questions of the rest of the crew by mastheading you, out in plain sight where none of them might ask you about their late lamented shipmate, Mr William Bones or look too close and see you are, as Mr Stewart here has noticed, a roaring girl? I'd say I played a canny game and kept you safe as if you was tucked up in a featherbed . . .'

A shrill yell came from close behind Silver

'Silver, you treacherous bastard!'

He spun in time to see Pew lunge at him with a cutlass. He parried the blow with his crutch, but the force of the attack and the lurch of the ship took his one leg out from under him and he went down hard. Pew drew back his arm for another blow screaming.

'Flint shall make me quartermaster in your place for this, you one-legged devil!'

As the blade swung down Cat felt rather than saw Alan leap forward, but he was going to be too late, and she had already launched herself at Pew, spilling the bullets from the bag in her hand as she cocked the half-loaded pistol.

'No!'

She pulled the trigger and there was a snap and a crack and a sharp bang and a scream as Pew staggered back out of the white muzzle-smoke, dropping his sword as he clutched at his powder-burned face. He jerked round and ran terror-struck towards the companionway leading to the upper deck.

'My eyes! MY EYES!! You've blinded me, you little—'

Cat never knew what he was going to call her because the blinded Pew ran slap bang into a wooden cross brace with a sound like an axe biting into a tree trunk and dropped to the deck, knocked out cold. As he fell he revealed two sailors coming down the companionway. As soon as they saw Silver and Cat they turned and ran for the pitching deck above, yelling for help.

'Now we shall have trouble,' said Silver, hauling himself to his feet. 'Thankee, Cat Manno, 'tis the second time you've pulled me off a lee shore, and I'll not forget that neither.'

Alan was at their side, shaking like a terrier with the tension of wanting to chase down the sailors but knowing it was the wrong thing to do. He clapped Cat on the back.

'That was bravely done, lass, bravely done, but make haste to reload your piece for we shall have need of it soon enough now.'

'Aye, and this time put a lead ball in for luck, because it'll take more than bangs and flashes to stop this lot once Flint puts the scourge to them,' said Silver.

'Show us the way, man,' said Alan. 'For you know the terrain.'

Silver swayed ahead of them, bypassing the companionway and heading down the length of the ship. From where Cat was it looked like he was heading into a world of shadows and hiding places where they could be ambushed at any point.

'My plan was to go up the forrard companionway there and work aft along the deck fast and so be at the captain's cabin before any had the wits to notice,' said Silver over his shoulder. 'But now we shall have to move fast and quiet below decks and get to the aft companionway, hoping they'll still be waiting for us at the top of that ladder instead,' he gestured at the companionway up which the two sailors had fled. 'For they'll be laying for us now, make no mistake.'

Cat felt Alan slip past her and take the lead with Silver as they crept fast and low through the long dark maze of the gun deck. There were cannons lashed to ringbolts into the floor in front of closed gun ports every ten feet or so, and the storm could be heard howling through the gaps where the ports didn't fit tight.

The motion of the boat made the rolled hammocks strung from the ceiling sway back and forth like pale horizontal wraiths, and beyond the thick trunk of the mainmast lay a zigzag of bulkheads where temporary walls had been erected.

Cat heard a noise behind her and spun, very conscious that she had not begun to reload the pistol, but there was nothing there but swinging hammocks and the crouched shape of the guns.

'Come, lass, move fast,' said Alan from up ahead. 'No time for nerves.'

They passed the mainmast as it dropped from the deck above down into its foundation on the keel far below, and they funnelled through the narrow alley between the bulkheads, before coming out into the aft end of the gun deck. Silver and Alan paused for a moment, eyes reaching into the shadows. This part of the deck was a little broader, and at the end of it Cat could see the slats of the other companionway leading up to the foot of the quarterdeck and the doors to the captain's cabin.

'Looks OK,' she whispered hopefully.

'Aye,' said Silver, too loudly. 'Looks like clear sailing.'

He turned and held out his hand and whispered, 'You loaded that pistol, girl?'

Cat looked at him, unsure what was going on. She shook her head. Silver clicked his teeth in disappointment. Alan reached across and crisply took the pistol and the powder horn from her, giving her the sword to hold. His hands moved with great speed and nimbleness charging the piece and ramming home a bullet as he pointed with his head at the companionway.

At first Cat could see nothing but a pale square patch of moonbeam swaying across the lower deck with the storm-tossed motion of the boat, but then there was a flash of lightning that cast a momentary blast of light down on to the wall behind the companionway, and in that flash Cat saw the shadows of a crowd of men and swords who were crouching in wait at the top of the steps on the deck above.

'Right, Silver,' Alan said, again loud enough to be heard at some distance away. 'We shall go up the aft ladder.'

And he handed Silver the gun with a nod. It was as if each knew what the other was thinking, and Cat felt strangely left out. They moved sideways and began to make their way along the edge of the gun deck.

And then Cat was grabbed from behind.

A hand covered her mouth and nose and a blade pressed to her neck. She didn't even have time to gurgle a warning, but

Alan must have had ears like a bat, because he turned and raised his sword before freezing.

'No,' hissed the voice at her ear. 'They wait for you at top of steps.'

Silver lurched round and stood looking over Alan's shoulder.

'We know that,' he whispered. 'What we don't bloody know, pardon my French, is why you've suddenly found your tongue to warn us.'

Cat felt the hand release her and the blade go away, and turned to look at her captor. It was the Indian, and he pointed at Cat with his knife.

'She knows,' he said. 'The feather she carries bears the knots made by a great chief. The last of a long line of chiefs. And that man was my father. And if my father gave her that feather and she did not steal it like a carrion bird, then she knows.'

His eyes were glittering bright with a kind of longing that Cat recognized.

'I don't know who your father is, I don't know who you are, but I come of kings and I bear a king's name, and I tell you now is not the time—' Alan gritted, pointing at the companionway.

'He is Uncas,' hissed Cat. Of course he was. How had she not known before? She must be getting sick or weak in the head. 'Don't piss him off. He's on our side.'

'Fine,' said Silver, turning. 'The more the merrier.'

'I was not going to urinate on him,' whispered Alan as Cat

310

came level. 'What a disgusting notion.'

They had edged almost level with the companionway and were crabbing sideways towards a solid-looking door set in the end wall of the gallery when they were discovered.

There was a warning shout from the deck above and Alan grabbed Cat and ran her towards the door, all need for stealth gone.

There was a padlock on it. Cat's heart fell. Alan and Uncas formed a wall between her and the rabble of pirates tumbling down the companionway and running towards them.

Silver aimed the pistol at the lock.

'Look away,' he said, and fired.

Hot metal spanged and spun past Cat's face, and then Silver kicked the door open and shoved her through.

'Come on, lads,' he roared. 'Fall back!'

Alan was dancing from foot to foot, a savage smile on his lips as he held his blade ready, but Uncas just looked at the overwhelming odds rushing at them and grabbed him by the collar, dragging him unceremoniously backwards through the door.

Silver had just enough time to slam it shut and Cat to smash home the bolt before the roaring horde of new attackers hit the other side and could be heard shouting and hacking at it in frustration.

Alan looked at Uncas, one hand rubbing his neck where the yanked collar had chafed him, the other twitching the sword-blade in frustration.

'Ach, laddie, I ken ye meant well, but no need to have been so precipitate, I could have . . .'

'Yes,' said Uncas. 'But not for long.'

They stood looking round them at the stacked baulks of timber neatly arranged in piles on either side of two cannons that were lashed to their ringbolts behind closely dogged hatches. There were hand tools and saws lining the walls between them, swinging on hooks against the motion of the boat.

'Carpenter's store and the aft carronades,' said Silver pointing at the wood and the cannons. 'We might like to shore up that door pretty sharpish, I'm thinking.'

Uncas and Alan worked as one, grabbing thick timbers and wood and wedging them against the door and nailing them to the deck to brace it up against the growing assault raining down on it from outside.

'Safe for now,' said Silver, looking at the roof. 'But now won't last forever.'

'It occurs to me,' said Alan, looking round, 'that your plan was to ascend the aft companionway and rush the captain's cabin. That plan has gone awry. I hope we have not just smoored our own fire and blocked ourselves in a trap of our own making.'

Uncas nodded and took a hatchet from the wall. He hefted it like a tomahawk and shrugged. 'One place is as good as another to die . . .'

'No one's going to die and no one's trapped,' said Silver,

pointing at the ceiling. 'Know what that is?'

'The ceiling,' said Cat.

'It's the floor,' smiled Silver. 'It's the floor of the fore room outside the captain's cabin. And we can go through it.'

'It'll take time to saw a hole, and they'll hear us, my friend,' said Alan.

Silver just grinned wider and bent to loosen the block shackling the nearest cannon to the floor.

'I wasn't thinking of "sawing" anything,' he said. 'Though they'll certainly hear what I have in mind.'

Cat was set to guard the door with the pistol and Silver's blunderbuss, with the instructions that as soon as the first hole was opened up by the attackers, who they could hear working on the other side of the door, she was to put a ball through it and reload, whilst keeping the trumpet-ended scattergun handy in case they looked like coming through before she got a second round primed and ready.

She faced the door, and listened to the hacking and the cursing on the other side of the planking. Behind her she could hear the three men straining and heaving at the heavy cannon.

'We can't lift it,' grunted Alan. 'And that's the truth.'

'That's a landlubber's truth,' laughed Silver. 'A sea-going man don't lift nothing, not when he has a block and tackle to do it for him. Grab hold of this rope and pass it through that ring in the ceiling . . .'

Cat risked a quick look backwards and saw that Silver and

Uncas were rigging a pair of pulleys to the cannon. Then the noise outside the door stopped suddenly and the boat seemed to pause for a moment in its tilting and yawing.

There was a polite tap-tap-tap on the door.

'That'll be Flint,' said Silver grimly.

Flint's voice came through the wood, muffled but clearly audible.

'Now, Silver, that's no way for a shipmate to treat an old companion or his crew, is it?'

Silver just carried on working, winching the cannon's mouth slowly off the horizontal towards the vertical. It was painfully slow work.

'I was going to say give me the boy and we shall be friends, but standing out here, hearing poor blind Pew demanding revenge for his lost sight, I think time for friends is gone. And you know what else?'

Flint let the silence hang there as the boat rolled onwards.

'I don't think I need the boy to persuade his grandfather to work his book for me? I think all I need is his clothes and a lock of his hair and a promise he shall be free if the old man does my bidding. That's what I thinks.'

Behind her Cat heard nothing but grunting and the sound of taut ropes being squeaked slowly through a series of wooden pulleys.

Flint's voice dropped, but the murderous intensity grew.

'So here's how it's going to be. There's no way out of there, and if you're thinking of using the gun ports, I've men posted with guns on the taff rail above. So you're rats in a trap, and I've sent men for coals from the cook's fire, and swabs and water buckets, and you know what that means, you know how you'll die now, a-choking and a-gasping and a-crying for mercy and fresh air and you shall have none and neither from Flint, and that, Silver, YOU MAY LAY TO!'

'He means to smoke us out,' said Alan.

'Aye,' agreed Silver calmly. 'He's a man as never tires of finding new ways to kill people, and that's but one of the reasons I ain't sailing with him no more, treasure or no treasure. But don't worry, shipmates, we shall be out before the smoke gets us. Now hand me that ball.'

Cat turned to see Uncas lift a heavy cannonball and pass it up to Silver who stood by the cannon that was now pointing at the ceiling, held in place by a web of ropes and pulleys, wedged solid with thick timbers from the carpenter's store.

'Right,' said Silver, as he heaved the ball into the mouth of the cannon and heard it roll down the iron tube and thump home against the wadding of the gunpowder charge. 'This will be noisy and there will be splinters, so hunker down and take cover.'

He stuck a thumb's length of fuse rope into the touch-hole of the cannon, which was now at calf level, and applied a taper that he lit from the candle-lantern in the roof.

''Course this could go badly and just send this cannon here through the keel instead. So say your prayers, my hearties, because one way or another this is going to be instructive, I say.'

The fuse began to fizz with a bright white flame, and Cat ducked and turned her back.

The cannon detonated and the shockwave and the gout of flame seemed to take all the air out of the small space, knocking Cat off her feet, blowing out her hearing entirely and splaying her on the floor.

What happened next was a series of blurred fragments, as if the explosion had smithereened time and space.

Alan's mouth was wide and shouting, his eyes almost deranged with elation, his face blackened with powder blast.

Uncas disappeared through a ragged hole in the roof.

Alan followed.

Silver grabbed her shoulder.

Hands reached down and grabbed her, yanking her up through the ceiling that became, once through it, a floor outside Flint's cabin.

Silver's crutch flew up through the hole.

Uncas opened a door and pushed Cat into the galleried cabin beyond.

The sea was heaving and billowing through the windows of the gallery, like a windblown black satin sheet.

Out of nowhere the parrot fluttered across the room and landed on Silver's shoulder.

Cat didn't know how Silver had got into the room with them, nor how they had barricaded the door.

She did know that they were, for the minute, safe.

316

37

The fight in the captain's quarters

Cat didn't know how she had ended up on the floor.

She couldn't remember what the thing was she still had clutched in her hand or why she'd brought it.

Then she thought 'blunderbuss'.

She looked up and saw the three others continuing to barricade the door, and Alan turned and flashed that exulting smile and reached a hand and pulled her to her feet, his mouth making a soundless question.

Cat shook her head and pointed to her ears.

And then they were all looking at her and they were all smiling and white teeth and her hearing came back as suddenly as it had gone and she winced because the sound of their laughter was loud and unexpected and, she realized as she joined in, very welcome.

'Right,' said Silver. 'Let's look for that blessed book.'

They split up and ransacked the room quickly, opening chests and cubbyholes and turning over the mattress on the box-bed, sweeping the tables clean and turning over the drawers, but though they made a great mess on the floor they found no book.

'Well, a book's a small thing. It's as like as not the devil has it on his person, more's the shame of it,' said Silver disappointedly.

'Then I should go and make a sortie to relieve him of it,' said Alan, picking up his sword and walking to the door. 'It will just be a matter of cutting my way through a wheen* of those toothless dogs that the cur surrounds himself with.'

Silver was opening his mouth to stop him setting off on this suicidal mission when two of the leaded windows on the rear wall of the cabin smashed and three rain-soaked sailors leapt into the light, and fell on Uncas and Silver.

Alan turned and ran back to their aid, shouting at Cat as he passed.

'Watch for more of them, lass!'

As if on cue the black socket of the window filled with another two sailors scrambling in. Cat had the blunderbuss cocked before she thought about what she was doing. She ran across the cabin and pulled the trigger.

The explosion and recoil cleared the window instantly, and blew her off her feet. She scrabbled backwards avoiding

---

* Wheen = few

the feet of the fighting men around her and reached for her cutlass.

By the time her hands had found it and closed over the handle it was all almost over. Uncas had shattered the sword of his assailant with a mighty downward blow from his hatchet, and then had knocked him flying with a savage uppercut on the back swing. He turned to help Silver, but Silver was fighting with a sword like a man with two legs, his face grim and focused as the tall Swede facing him kept trying to kick out his crutch as he lunged and swiped at him. Every time Silver parried and counter-attacked the Swede leapt out of his way and laughed at him.

'You don't have enough legs, old man,' he laughed.

Then his smile died as Silver trapped his foot under his crutch tip and bore down. The Swede tried to leap back but was stuck to the floor, and Silver ran him through cleanly.

'See that, Cat girl? He got ahead of himself. Never talk when you should be fighting,' he said. 'One thing at a time.'

The Swede fell back to the deck, surprised and dead.

Alan was well matched to his opponent, despite the fact that he was a good foot shorter than the pirate. The bigger man was surprisingly quick for someone his size, and the reach of his sword was much longer than Alan's. Nevertheless the wiry Highlander bobbed and weaved in and out of danger so fast that they cancelled each other out.

Uncas stepped forward to help, raising his axe.

'He's mine, bonny lad. Step back,' snapped Alan, his eyes remaining fixed on those of his attacker.

The big man snorted and lunged at Alan who turned the blade aside so narrowly that the point tore through the sleeve of his jacket and pinned him to the wall. Cat's heart leapt into her mouth, but Alan instantly surged forward like a terrier, ripping the sleeve and his assailant's sword free as his own blade seemed to whirr with the speed of his counter-attack. The bigger man was beaten back inch by inch, the sweat starting to drip on his forehead as Alan feinted and lunged right and left, high and low with an intensity that actually seemed to increase the closer he drove him towards the smashed window and the sea beyond it.

And then his opponent broke and flung his sword at his face, and as Alan ducked, he swung out of the smashed frame and scrambled away to safety. Alan grunted with disappointment and sprang after him. He stopped dead as he hung out of the window and looked up.

After a beat he shook himself like a dog coming out of the water and turned his smile on them.

'Now,' he smiled. 'Would I be right in saying that that is a boat swinging above this window?'

'Yes,' said Silver. 'It's the captain's jolly boat.'

'And a pretty way out of our predicament, I'm thinking,' said Alan.

'Indeed it might be,' said Silver. 'If someone can get up aloft there and cut the davits.'

320

Alan stuck the sword-cane in his belt and pointed at Cat.

'Throw me that cutlass, if you please.'

Cat did so. Silver pointed her at the door.

'Cat girl, go keep a sharp eye through that keyhole and sing out if you spy them coming.'

'And load that blunderbuss while you're at it,' said Alan from where he stood framed in the window. 'For I've a feeling that the pinch is coming.'

Cat grabbed the blunderbuss and powder horn as she scrambled to the door and bent to the keyhole.

Silver turned to Alan.

'And don't forget the oars. They'll be laid down inside the poop taff rail, so you'll have to get them into the boat before you—'

Cat's eye's widened in horror as she peered through the keyhole. Flint stood there in the outer doorway smoking like a devil fresh out of hell. The smoke came from burning lengths of slow fuse he had twisted into his beard. His eyes were red-rimmed and wild, and his mouth was twisted in a rictus of savage glee. His crew stood back in the doorway behind him, bristling with swords, pikes and boarding axes.

That wasn't the worst thing. The worst thing was the thing in front of Flint, the gaping black mouth of the cannon pointed right at Cat's head.

'SILVER!' roared Flint. 'WHAT'S GOOD FOR THE GOOSE IS GOOD FOR THE GANDER!!'

And he yanked a burning slow fuse from his beard and held it to the cannon's touch-hole.

Cat threw herself sideways, twisting and yelling, 'LOOK OUT!'

And then there was an explosion of wood and flame and something terrible flew past and the window disappeared and there was a big hole where Alan had been. Before she could get to her feet Flint had leapt into the room and dragged her up into the air by her hair, effortlessly lifting her feet off the floorboards.

She tried to raise the blunderbuss, but Flint batted it away and it clattered to the ground.

At the other end of the cabin Uncas and Silver were pulling themselves to their feet in a daze.

'Oh no, saints preserve us,' said Silver, sounding distinctly unimpressed. 'He's only gone and lit his beard. That never ends well.'

'Shut it, for I shall spit you and roast your gizzard, Barbecue!' roared Flint, shaking his cutlass at him.

Silver picked up his sword and took an unsteady step towards Flint, his lip curled in contempt.

'Drop the girl and have a go at someone your own size, you strutting play actor,' snarled Silver, 'for I've had enough of your devilry.'

'Girl is it?' snarled Flint, twisting her head and looking at her. 'Why, so she is . . .'

'Drop her I say!' gritted Silver.

'My pleasure, you peg-legged bastard, drop her I will, in

two parts,' smiled Flint. 'Body first, and then we'll see how her head bounces on the decking after my blade here has discontinued their acquaintance!'

And with that he drew back the sword, yanked Cat's hair higher, stretching her neck as her feet kicked helplessly in the air, and then he swung.

The blade moved fast but Uncas moved faster. He threw himself between the cutlass and Cat, and took the full force of the blade in his side.

He took the impact with a percussive grunt of shock and pain, but his right hand still found Flint's throat beneath the fizzing tapers and choked him in a death grip that made the pirate's eyes pop.

'Uncas!' yelled Cat.

Uncas didn't react. His eyes were locked on Flint's and all the last power in his body was focused in his bunched fist and the tendons standing out in his neck as he clamped as hard as he could.

Flint was so surprised that his legs locked, and he seemed to have forgotten he held Cat a couple of inches off the floor. For an instant the three of them made an odd statue, and then Cat moved.

She had dropped the blunderbuss but still had the leather powder horn in her hand. She thrust it right in Flint's face and squeezed as hard as she could. The powder puffed out and the lit tapers in his beard did the rest: there was an almighty WHUMP as the powder ignited and a shriek from

Flint as he dropped her and staggered backwards, his head a ball of flame.

Cat saw Victor's book poking out of the pocket of his waistcoat and she leapt forward, snatching hold of it just as Flint's heel dropped into the hole in the floor and he plummeted out of sight, leaving the crew behind him staring downwards in shock.

'Like I said,' Silver smiled grimly. 'Never ends well when he lights his beard.'

There was a crackle from below and flames began to glow through the rent in the floor.

'All that wood in the carpenter's store,' said Silver sadly.

The pirates who had been standing behind Flint began to edge forward, building the courage to rush them. The first two stepped gingerly over the hole, cutlasses and boarding axes at the ready.

There was a second much bigger WHOOF of flame as something ignited in the carpenter's store, sending a pillar of fire through the hole that made the pirates shriek and run back out on to the deck, one of them wildly patting out the flames that had caught the hem of his jerkin.

'And then there was that blessed powder keg. Powder don't explode unless it's in a narrow chamber, but it does like to burn,' said Silver.

Cat wasn't listening. She was bent over Uncas who lay on the floor, his copper skin becoming pale and dull.

'Why did you do that?' choked Cat.

'He was going to cut your head off,' Uncas breathed.

'I know. Thank you,' said Cat, aware her voice was unsteady. 'But. Why did you help me?'

Uncas's grimace shaded into a smile for a moment, and his hand twitched weakly, pointing at Cat's neck.

'Because you too are a Human Being. Because you carry the eagle feather. I thought . . .' He coughed. His spit was pink. 'I thought you might lead me back home.'

Cat saw two tears splash on to Uncas's face and realized they were her own. She wiped her hand across her cheek and when she looked down again, Uncas's eyes were screwed shut and his mouth twisted in a surprised grimace of pain as he coughed more pink on to his chin.

'Cat,' said Silver. 'We can't stay here. Ship's afire and the jig's up.'

'We can't leave him,' Cat growled, surprised by the intensity in her own voice. Silver swung over and put a hand on her shoulder. His voice, when it came, was surprisingly soft.

'We ain't leaving him, Cat girl. He's leaving us. And where he's going, we can't follow. Now come on . . .'

Cat ignored him, reached round her neck and took off the buckskin thong. She found Uncas's hand, and closed it around the feather.

For a moment nothing happened, and then the hand twitched and Uncas felt the ribbed quills between thumb and forefinger and though his eyes stayed shut his grimace once again melted into a smile, and this time it stayed there.

'Prettily done, lass,' said a voice from the window. 'For was he no' a bonny fighter?'

It was Alan.

'I have a boat here that we might avail ourselves of if we have no other plans?'

Cat looked down at Uncas.

'He's gone,' said Silver. 'And so should we be.'

Alan swung out of the window again, and Cat followed. The wind clawed at her and she held on tight, following the Highlander as he climbed up the outside of the stern gallery, taking care to avoid being crushed by the heavy jolly boat swinging to and fro in the davits below the poop rail.

Alan timed a jump and disappeared inside the boat, then reappeared and held out a hand to Cat as she climbed higher. He shouted something that the wind snatched away, and Cat leapt to the boat. Alan grappled her inboard and they got their breath for an instant, and then he looked down.

Silver stood in the lit window below, looking up.

'He'll never climb that with one leg,' shouted Alan.

Silver bellowed up at them but the only word the wind let through was '. . . sheet . . .'

'What did he say?' yelled Alan.

Cat was searching the floor of the boat and came up with a coil of line.

'He wants us to throw him a rope.'

She paid out the rope and Silver caught hold, wrapped it several times round his arm and then made a slashing motion with great urgency.

'Cut us free,' said Cat.

'But . . .' Alan began.

'Do it now,' snapped Cat, eyes on Silver's urgent gesticulating, 'I don't think we have much time.'

Alan leant over and looked at the ropes on the davit. Then he raised his arm and, without any more ado, hacked the cutlass down.

What happened next was another blur of images for Cat as the jolly boat dropped like a stone.

She passed Silver almost nose to nose and then the sea reached up and smacked the bottom of the boat with a hideous crack that must have knocked her senseless, for the next thing she knew Alan was yanking her out of the scuppers and pulling at the rope he still had wound round his arm, and then she was pulling too, and between them and the wallowing hulk of a ship now lit from within by a growing red glow was a giant fish that turned into Silver coughing and spluttering towards them.

And then they were laying hold of him and manhandling him on board, which nearly capsized the boat, and then they all lay back against the thwarts and got their breaths as the sea hummocked and dropped them in and out of sight of a stricken *Jamaica* that was now heeling into the wind with topsails flapping free.

'Well,' shouted Alan. 'Heaven smiled on us.'

'Heaven may have smiled, but Hell is about to roar and blow us all to blazes,' Silver shouted back. 'Flint's standing orders is to keep the cannons loaded and once they heat up they'll blast the sides off the ship even if the fire don't reach the powder magazine first and blow us all to Fiddler's Green! So we must row! Row for our lives.'

He lurched to his feet and looked wildly round the boat.

'Where are the oars?'

'Oars?' said Alan.

They stared at each other.

'We could swim for it?' said Alan.

Silver pointed to the immense emptiness of the sea all around them.

'Swim for what?' he said.

Cat reached out and grabbed each of them by the collar.

'For your life,' she shouted.

And dived head first into the incoming face of the next wave, dragging them with her.

Too late.

As her feet left the deck the fire got to the cannons and the dark swollen mass of the *Jamaica* was split apart as the gates of hell did open. The red-hot cannons blew the gun ports off in a rolling broadside that sounded like the crack of doom and something hit her on the head and it may have been the sea or the jolly boat or a piece of the *Jamaica* but it didn't much matter because Cat had just an instant to feel the sudden shock of pain in the side of her head before she abruptly switched off like a light switch.

Snap.

Click.

Gone.

38

The bleed

Sam and Annie jerked awake the instant the warning alarm kicked off on the monitor closest to Cat's head.

They had not meant to fall asleep, but adrenaline only carries you so far and the strain of sitting beside her watching her fever slowly tick downwards on the digital readout had been the final straw. Annie had dropped her head against Sam's shoulder, and before he was able to get more comfortable, he too fell asleep, and their systems took advantage of the downtime to start to mend and unravel the mental carnage of the past hours.

The alarm spoiled all that, cutting them out of the darkness and jerking them into a bright-lit reality as the crash team burst into the room.

'What's happening?' Annie choked as she was firmly pushed to the wall beside Sam.

The nurses kicked off the brakes on the bed and had it

moving out of the door as the surgeon arrived. He took one look at the monitor and shouted at them.

'Move it! OR 1 now! Where's the anaesthetist?'

'Here,' said a flustered-looking woman sliding into view behind his shoulder, munching on something and trying to swallow it at the same time. 'Was in the canteen.'

'Let's go,' he said. 'Cranial bleed, post op.'

He looked at Sam and Annie as if noticing them for the first time.

'I thought we'd got the tear in the meningeal artery. It may have ripped again, or there may have been a smaller tear we missed. Got to relieve the pressure or she's in real trouble. I'm going inside the skull again.'

'Is she—' began Annie.

A shout came from down the hall.

'No pulse. She's in arrest! Code Blue!'

An alarm began to wail.

'If you pray, do,' said the surgeon, running for the door. 'If you don't . . .'

He looked at Sam as he flashed past.

'Be a good time to start.'

And then he was gone.

Bad Step

1 'What we call the beginning is often the end.
And to make an end is to make a beginning.
The end is where we start from.'
T.S.Eliot, *Little Gidding*

Inwood

2 'Let your soul stand
cool and composed before a million universes.'
Walt Whitman, *Song of Myself*

Jamaica

3 'The schooners and
the merry crews are laid away to rest,
A little south of sunset in
the islands of the blest.'

John Masefield,
The Ballad of Long John Silver

Broad Channel

4 'Twilight and evening bell,
And after that the dark!
And may there be no sadness or farewell,
When I embark.'

Alfred, Lord Tennyson, *Crossing the Bar*

39

Buried in the mist

Cat was in her coffin. Two people stood beside it talking, but they were not Sam and Annie. They were gravediggers, and they were stomping their feet and blowing on their hands to keep warm.

They weren't Annie and Sam because they were both men, and they must be gravediggers because she could hear the clomp of heavy boots as they stamped the cold out of their feet, and who else wore heavy boots to a cemetery?

Her hands splayed on the wooden lid above her face. She should probably say something, shout even, but she was very tired and a little sleep would probably stop her shivering anyway, so she shut her eyes and wondered why Sam and Annie had paid for a coffin full of rocks . . .

And then she thought 'coffin?' and woke up properly and started kicking against the lid and yelling for help.

Then the roof came off and she saw Alan and Silver heaving

it up and she realized she had not been in a coffin at all, but lying under the upturned hull of the captain's jolly boat, and her parents had not put her in a casket lined with rocks, but that she was lying on a very cold and wet scrabble of stone in the middle of a fog bank.

'We turned the boat over because it was raining,' said Alan, lifting her to her feet. 'I mean no offence by it, lass, but you look pure wabbit*.'

'You do look a sight, and that's the truth of it,' agreed Silver. 'Paler than a flounder's belly and twice as cold, I'll be bound.'

'Where are we?'

'Lost in the mist, Cat Manno, is what we are, lost in the mist and no mistake.'

Silver and Alan looked just as cold and wet as she felt. She turned round and saw that what they were standing on was a shelf of black limpet-covered rock not much more than a foot above a perfectly flat sea. Visibility ended a yard or so beyond the edge of the rock.

'Why aren't we dead?' she said.

'You saved us, bonny lass, taking us into the water. The boat had its fore-end lopped by a cannonball, but had we been standing, we should no doubt have lost our own heads—'

Alan pointed at the front of the boat where the fore-post was shorter and more raggedly splintered than when Cat had last seen it. Silver clapped her on the shoulder.

---

* utterly exhausted

'Was the right thing to do, Cat Manno, and we owes you our bacon, but we had the devil of a time getting you back into the boat. You was spewing out half the ocean and raving, and then you slept like a baby, and then we bumped up here on this skerry, fathoms deep in fog.'

He looked around.

'It's clearing,' he said, sniffing the air. 'And I smell sausages.'

Alan scrambled up on to the upturned hull of the boat with his nose in the air like a hunting dog on point.

'Sausages be damned,' he said. 'That's mutton . . .'

'Mutton or sausages, that's hot food cooking somewhere close by, and hot food is what I'd give my other leg for right now, and you may lay to that,' snorted Silver. He grinned at her. 'I think we're saved, Cat girl. I think we're close to land.'

'We're between two islands,' said Alan, reaching a hand down to Cat. 'Come and see for yourself.'

Cat let Alan hoist her up on to the hull next to him. All around them the mist lay like a blanket, maybe six feet deep, but even as she looked around she saw it was thinning in the sunlight.

And though it was a low winter sun she could feel the rays heating her up.

'Well what can you see?' said Silver plaintively from below. 'Sing out and tell us what you spy!'

There were, as Alan had said, two islands on either side of the skerry which she could now see was right in the middle of

337

a broad channel of perfectly flat water, deep green and viscous, almost like a pool of oil. The islands were about the same size, but there the resemblance ended: the one on their left loomed up into the sky in a dark and unclimbable cliff face that must have been six or seven hundred brooding feet above them. There was no sign of life on it, and even the fulmars and skuas that flew round the rocks at the base of the cliffs were silent.

In contrast the island to their right was soft and green and welcoming. The grass swept gently up from a dark sand beach in a long slope that rose into a kind of half bowl as the hills and the heather beyond took over from the sea-lawn and encircled it on either side. The island was treeless, and dotted amongst the shallow swell of grass above the dunes Cat could see black and brown sheep grazing between heather-thatched croft houses whose low-rounded grey stone walls seemed to swell organically out of the landscape and be as much a part of it as the rocks on the distant slopes beyond.

Smoke was rising from the chimney of the house closest to the water's edge. Cat sniffed the air and smelled not sausages or mutton, but a mild, sweet and undeniably pleasant burning smell.

'Peat smoke,' said Alan. 'Peat smoke, Cat my girl. And is that not the smell of home to me?'

Cat saw his eyes were shining. A light breeze skirled the final shreds of mist off the skerry, and Silver pointed behind them.

'Ahoy the boat!' he roared, waving. 'Boatman ahoy!'

Cat and Alan turned to see a small rowing boat turn and make for them. The oarsman wore some kind of dark hooded oilskin cloak against the weather, and had his back to them, and it was only when she checked behind her and unshipped an oar to fend off the rocks that Cat realized she was a she and not a he at all.

She swept back the hood and said something very fast and so jumbled with soft consonants that Cat couldn't make out any of it, and it was only when she heard Alan answer that she realized they weren't speaking a language she recognized at all.

'That'll be the Gaelic,' said Silver. 'That's why he looks so happy.'

Silver was looking pretty cheerful himself.

'Thought we was marooned in the middle of an ocean, Cat Manno, but fate has smiled on us. Ask her where we be, Stewart, and if she will take us off this skerry to where them sausages is!'

Alan jumped off the boat hull and stepped across the rocks to help steady the woman's boat.

'She's the ferryman. And she will take us where we choose.' He smiled at her and said something in Gaelic. She smiled and her cheek flushed a little.

'Ferry*man*?' said Silver.

'She says her husband is drowned, and so she plies the boat across the broad channel in his place. She will take us to whichever island we will, *Achaiell am fidhleir* or *Eilean nam mairbh olc* . . .'

The Gaelic names came soft and lilting at the end of the sentence, like well-loved old friends. It was as if the Scots-English Alan normally spoke was a harsher language around whose sharp consonants and guttural vowels he had learned to steer, while the Gaelic came with the gentle ease of a tongue learned at his mother's knee.

Silver looked at the forbidding cliff face of the dark island, and then at the green slopes and welcoming chimney smoke of the other.

'I votes we go to that one, shipmates, whatever it's called!'

She smiled and said something to Alan.

'She would be happy to take you there, and has food on the fire which she would be pleased to share.'

It was the work of a minute for them all to scramble aboard the small boat and push off into deeper water.

The sun was shining with greater heat now, and their rescuer got the boat sculling towards the grassy shore and then shipped oars and took off the oilskin cloak and folded it into the bottom of the boat. Her dark hair and grey eyes contrasted with the bright red of the dress she wore beneath it, and as she smiled Cat thought she'd never seen anyone more healthy or more beautiful. The young woman said something to Alan and he laughed, obviously also captivated.

'She says we mustn't forget to pay her or it will be bad luck.'

'And how much is the fare?' laughed Silver.

'Not much. Just two pennies,' Alan replied.

'Each?' said Silver.

'Yes,' said Alan. 'Well, she actually said as many pennies as we each have eyes, but that's just her way of speaking. It's the tradition, she says . . .'

As they approached the beach Cat saw that what she had assumed was rocks or seaweed was in fact just dark sand, almost black.

The boat crunched softly ashore and their saviour leapt nimbly over the side and began heaving it energetically towards the dunes.

They tumbled out and helped her get the boat above the waterline. Then she beckoned and ran ahead, white feet flashing on the dark sand until she crested a steep dune topped with long tufts of marram grass and turned to shout something at Alan before running ahead of them towards the croft with the smoking chimney.

As she ran she whistled and waved happily at the distant crofts on the lower slopes on the hills, and received an answering wave from a figure who stood looking at them for a beat before waving again and walking back into the shade of his own building.

'She's going to stop the pot burning,' Alan explained. 'She spent too long out in the channel bringing us in. And it's mutton, not sausages.'

Silver grinned back at him.

'Meat of any kind will do me fine, shipmate. I'm just happy to be back on dry land.'

They followed the woman's footsteps. As they climbed the steep sand Cat looked sideways and noticed with a kind of pleasure that the upswept face of the dune had been sculpted by wind and water into its own perfect curl, even to the point that the grass fringing the top of the dune peeped over the lip just like a wave-crest, always about to collapse into a perfect tube, but never quite getting there. She liked the way the shape of the land mirrored the shapes of the sea it bordered.

They topped the dune and she and Alan heaved Silver up after them, and then they headed across the sheep-cropped sea-lawn, which was low soft grass sprinkled with red wildflowers that peeped out from amongst the green.

'What is this called,' said Cat

'This is the *machair*,' said Alan. 'The sea-lawn . . .'

'No,' said Cat, looking around and feeling the bright salt-tanged air moving gently across her skin, as soft as the grass at her feet. 'What is this island called?'

'Well,' said Alan.' She didn't specify, but the two islands as I told you are *Achaiell am fidhleir* and *Eilean nam mairbh olc*. And since the latter means Isle of the Evil Dead, I rather think we must be on the other one!'

Cat shivered and looked at Silver who looked across the channel at the grim cliffs of the dark island.

'Malos Muertos by another name,' he breathed.

The woman appeared in the low doorway of the croft and

shouted merrily at them.

'Food is ready,' said Alan, quickening his pace. 'And there is crowdie* to follow!'

Cat stayed a beat longer looking at the dark cliffs across the water before she tore her eyes away and followed. A sheep bleated at her and then trotted away across the grass, its clumpy black wool bouncing on its haunches as it went.

'What was this other island called again then?' she said.

Alan smiled from the dark mouth of the croft door.

'*Achaiell am fidhleir*. And is it not a lovely poetical name for a place so green and welcoming?'

'But what does it mean?' said Cat.

'The meadow of the fiddle player.'

'Fiddler's Green,' breathed Silver. 'Well, here we are after all, and lovely it looks too, I'll lay you, safe harbour and dry beds for us all.'

Cat looked at the black beach and the red flowers in the grass, and was about to say something, when the smell of the food reached her and her stomach shut her up and pulled her into the door of the black house by her nose.

---

* soft Scottish cheese

40

Play her home

The surgeon found the second tear in the meningeal artery, a tiny rift that had leaked blood back into Cat's skull, putting dangerous pressure back on her brain. He worked fast and precisely to close it up, and took great pains to ensure he had not missed anything else. Finally he reset the ICP bolt in the side of her head and monitored the readings for a good twenty minutes, and only then allowed her to be pushed back out into the Recovery Room.

Her vital signs flickered along at low level, taking forever to rally to a point where they felt able to let her be put back in her bay in the ICU proper, and in the time this took, Sam and Annie suffered and waited and tortured themselves.

Eventually Cat was gently wheeled back into her room, and they were allowed to see her. She looked smaller and paler and Annie had difficulty standing, let alone talking, so shocked was she at the sight of her girl looking so reduced.

Sam clung on to her, and she to him, and somehow they both stayed upright.

'It's touch and go,' said the surgeon. He was too tired to sugar-coat it more than that, and anyway he didn't like lying to people, especially parents. They deserved time to prepare themselves for the worst.

'What can we do?' said Annie. 'We already prayed.'

'Hope,' said the surgeon. 'Talk to her. Hold her hand.'

'Can she hear?' said Sam.

'I don't know,' said the surgeon. 'But we won't know how she's doing until she's awake. And the longer she's out . . .'

'You need her awake?' said a voice behind him.

'Joe,' said Annie. 'Where have you been?'

'I had to get something,' he said, and tossed his leather coat into the corner.

'You should have been here!' said Sam.

'Victor made me promise,' Joe said. 'Sorry. But I can get her back.'

The surgeon looked at the big young man with tattoos sleeving both arms.

'You?' he said.

'Yes,' said Joe. 'I think so.'

And he put the long case on the floor and unclipped it.

'He can't play that in here,' said the nurse. 'It'll be too loud – I've got other patients to think of—'

'Nurse . . .' said the surgeon.

'I'm sorry, doctor,' she said. 'I don't want to be a hard-ass,

345

but what happens on the Unit post-op is my responsibility. I can't have the whole unit disturbed for one patient—'

The surgeon didn't need this at the end of a double shift. But he was a good guy. He turned to Sam and Annie.

'Do what you have to do,' he said, and left.

The nurse took his place in the doorway. Joe stood with his violin and shrugged apologetically at her as he tensioned the bow.

'I'm playing. No offence and I'll play low, but I'm doing it.'

He looked dark and defiant and, frankly, threatening to her eyes. She didn't like people crossing her even on a good day, which this one wasn't anyway.

'You can't. I'm sorry. I'll have to call security.'

'OK. How long until they get here?' said Joe, putting the violin under his chin. 'How long have I got?'

'They'll be here in sixty seconds,' she said, bristling.

'Yeah,' said Sam standing up. 'But they'll take longer than that to get past me.'

'Oh they won't get past us,' said Annie, stepping in behind him. 'Not both of us.'

They blocked the door like a wall.

'Play, Joe,' said Annie.

Joe grinned at his parents for a fast beat, then turned and sat on the edge of the bed next to his sister.

He leant low and played lower still, and a gentle Celtic tune from the isle of Eriskay filled the room with its heartbreaking song of love and loss and longing and maybe there was a magic in the sound of it, because it reached out and stopped the nurse as she strode towards the phones.

She turned and tried to square the sweetness and delicacy of the tune with the heavy-metal-thrash-band look of the player, and somewhere in there she thought twice about calling security and just stepped back and quietly closed the door on them.

'Good call,' said a voice from the next-door bay.

The surgeon was lying on the empty bed, exhausted. He kept his eyes closed, but gave her a thumbs up.

In the room Sam and Annie joined Joe and stood there, each with one hand on Cat and the other on their son as he played.

And though they weren't really praying people they each, in their own way, did again.

'Come on, Cat,' whispered Sam. 'Time to come home.'

41

Black house, dark island

Cat had to squint as she ducked beneath the low door, eyes adjusting to the darkness within after the brightening sunshine of the morning outside. As she got used to the gloom – at least half of which was due to the fire that smoked badly as it glimmered beneath a hanging cauldron in the rough stone hearth – she made out some of the detail.

A small table stood in the thin light beneath one of the deep-set windows, and three stools had been pulled up round it in front of three bowls and horn spoons. In the murk at the back of the room was a wooden wall, and against it a box-bed. A chair with a woven back like a basket sat close to the fire, and on the stone lintel two thin iron lamps hung, open boat-shaped saucers with wicks made from peeled rushes whose guttering flames added as much smoke as light to the room, all of which smelled (not disagreeably) of peat, lamb fat and fish oil.

Cat wiped her eyes and looked up at the sooty rafters from which hung festoons of dried fish and baskets.

'Well you can see why they call them black houses and no mistake,' said Silver, swinging in to take a stool at the table.

The woman bunched up the skirts of her red dress and used it as a potholder to carry the small cauldron over to the table so she could ladle stew into the bowls.

She said something to Alan with a pretty smile.

'She says if we give her our gear and jackets she will dry them by the fire as we eat.'

He and Silver hung their sword belts on a hook by the door and set about taking off their outer layers, which was an awkward thing to do in a confined space. Cat saw the woman smile at her and motion that she should do the same.

She stood and, because there was no room for three people to struggle out of their coats and shirts, backed into the doorway as she peeled the buckskin shirt over her head. As she did so, she could, for an instant, see nothing, and then she had to pause and readjust her grip to get it over her head and in that instant her eye was level with a hole torn in it, and she was able to look at the young woman, unobserved: her smile had gone and she was staring with steely concentration at Cat's jeans, and specifically at the front pocket, the pocket in which she could feel the comforting square shape of Victor's book. As the woman's lively eyes noticed she had stopped moving and turned up to look at her, Cat pulled the shirt on up and off, and, not sure what she'd seen, handed it to her. The woman smiled and took it away to the fire, firing a burst of cheery Gaelic over her shoulder.

Cat stood in the door in jeans and an undershirt, between sunlight and shadow, and in the distance heard something that stilled her shivering: somewhere far away on the very limit of her consciousness she heard broken snatches of music, but when she tried to work out where they were coming from, the breeze swirled and the tune was lost.

'Did you hear that?' she said to Silver.

'Hear what?' said the pirate.

Cat listened. Maybe she had imagined it.

Cat tried to hear the violin on the breeze again, but it had gone and then she caught it once more. It sounded familiar and right in one way, and her heart had risen to it, but it also sounded wrong in a way she couldn't quite put her finger on.

She stepped out into the sun and tried to see if she could work out where it was coming from. It wasn't coming from nearby, or from the hill. It seemed, as near as she could fix it, to be coming from the sea, from the direction of the skerry, maybe even from the dark island beyond.

That was what was wrong about it.

The familiar fiddle music was coming from the *wrong* island.

She felt a tug at her arm and looked round to see the woman pulling her back inside, into the smoky gloom, and pointing at the table, where food lay waiting. She was laughing and saying something she didn't understand, but the tug on her arm was too insistent, and matched the steel that she again saw flash in the depths of the woman's eyes where the laughter didn't reach.

Behind her the breeze dropped and she heard a louder snatch of the music, and recognized the tune. She found herself unwittingly singing snatches of the song that went with it under her breath. It was a song her mother had sung her a thousand times to help her sleep as a child, a song Joe had later played her on his violin when she was ill or couldn't rest, and as she listened she happened to look at the compass on the sword-cane.

From the position of the sun, the dark island was pretty much due west of them.

But the pointer was aimed right at it, as if it was true north.

Cat had a memory-hit of the compass pointing upstream towards the approaching canoes when she and Chingachgook had set the ambush. It had pointed right at them, even though they were bringing Victor downstream from the east.

The compass didn't point at north.

But Chingachgook was right.

That didn't mean it was broken.

It meant it was pointing at something else, like he'd said.

Someone else.

The woman must have heard her singing and then suddenly stop as realization hit her, because she looked alarmed, and then smiled and said something cheery and urgent, pointing at the food on the table as she took a dark bottle from a shelf and plonked it on the table between the bowls of steaming food.

'She says we must eat up now,' said Alan. 'And what's more there is good whisky and clean water to drink, and I for one do not need a second telling—'

He lifted the spoonful of stew to his lip with a grin – a grin that died as Cat lunged across the table and knocked it spinning across the room to splat and clatter against the stone wall.

Everyone froze.

The temperature seemed to drop.

The woman stared icily Cat as if Cat had also knocked a mask off her face.

'Well! That was like a slung stane*, Cat Manno. You may not like mutton stew, but that's no reason to—'

'Ask her which island this is,' Cat said.

Silver stared at her as if she had run mad, his own spoon halfway between bowl and lips. He looked at the woman. She pasted on a smile and pointed at the food, as she bent to pick Alan's spoon from the floor and wiped it clean. She handed it back to him and said something else.

'Cat girl, you've sore offended the lassie. She thinks the stew is not to your taste and bids us try it and tell her if you or she are right.'

His spoon hovered in the air.

---

* stone

'ASK HER,' said Cat. 'What is the name of this island?'

'Now, Cat,' said Silver. 'You're tired and you've—'

'I'm not tired,' said Cat. 'I'm exhausted and I'm cold and I'm hungry. But if you eat that food, you'll never leave this island.'

Two spoons slowly sank back into their bowls. The woman was very still.

'This is the island of the bad dead, isn't it?' said Cat. 'Tell her I said that.'

'I was just giving you something to eat,' the woman said in English that had an odd French accent to it. She shrugged. 'I meant no harm. I thought it would pass the time until friends arrive.'

'Eat on Malos Muertos: stay on Malos Muertos,' Cat said, looking at Silver.

'But Cat, this is not Malos Muertos!' he cried. 'This isn't a tropical island, this—'

'This island has black sand and the only flowers are red, just like the other one,' said Cat. 'And she knows about the book. It's Malos Muertos by another name.'

It was the way the woman's smile stuttered that betrayed the truth of that, and brought Alan to his feet.

'What friends?' he said very calmly. 'Ma'am, would you do me the great favour of telling me who your friends are that we are a-waiting on?'

She met his eyes calmly, and in that calmness she seemed to stand taller, as if shrugging off the character of the simple

353

island woman and becoming something colder and prouder and much, much more deadly.

'*Mais ils ne sont pas mes amis . . .*' she said.

'Why, now she spouts like a damned Frenchy!' said Silver.

She acknowledged this with the coolest twitch of her eyebrow, and then stepped back and bent in a hint of a curtsey to Alan as she swept her hand theatrically towards the window behind them.

'. . . *ils sont à vous.*'

They all turned to look in the direction she was pointing, and in the instant their backs were turned she leapt for the door and the open air beyond.

The first they knew of it was the sound of the door slamming.

In the half second it took Alan to dive across the narrow room they heard the snick of the lock, and when his shoulder hit the solid wood all he managed to do was to bounce back off it with a grunt of pain and a muffled curse.

Cat looked at him, then at Silver.

'What did she say?' she asked. 'In French, what did she say?'

Alan took the swords from the hook on the wall by the door and threw Silver his cutlass before answering.

'She said: "But they are not *my* friends . . ."'

He handed Cat the swordstick and pointed at the back window as he drew his blade.

'She said: "They are yours."'

354

'Well,' said Silver, bending down to peer out of the small single casement at the back of the house, 'that may be the one thing she wasn't lying about . . .'

Cat followed his gaze, and the shock of what she saw hit her so hard she felt her heart stutter.

The woman was running across the broken slope, fleet-footed as a stag, towards a phalanx of men running to meet her. The men were people Cat had seen before. More exactly, they were people she had seen die before.

There was the Huron war party. There were pirates. There was Billy Bones, Israel Hands and others she recognized but whose names she did not know. And at the centre of the line there were two men in red coats, one a pirate, one a Huron.

They were unmistakably Flint and Magua, back from the dead.

And the girl turned and walked back with them, her red dress matching their coats at the centre of the line. She was talking and pointing at the black house and its captives, and though they were three very different faces, each had the same look of exultant revenge as they approached.

Alan put his hand on Cat's shoulder and looked grimly at Silver.

'Now,' he said, 'let our hands keep our heads, for the grip is coming.'

42

The grip

'The front windows,' cried Silver lurching to the other side of the house where the two small deep-set windows flanked the front door. 'If we cannot shift the door we must burst the windows and escape before they get here, or we shall be caught like rats in a—'

There was a tapping noise on the outside of the wall that stilled everyone.

It was a deliberate, precise noise, but there was something about it that was also chilling.

They listened as it moved carefully along the outside wall at the end of the building, as if someone was making their way around the croft.

'Wh—?' began Cat, and then stopped as a raised hand from Silver chopped the word off.

The tapping stopped, as if the unseen figure outside the black house was also listening back at them.

Alan looked a question at Silver, who shrugged his shoulders.

Cat remembered to breathe.

The tapping started again and moved towards the single rear window that Cat was guarding. Cat decided it was the most sinister sound she'd ever heard, and waiting for the next tap each time stretched her nerves tight as piano wire.

And then it stopped, and did not restart, and the silence that followed was if anything worse, a kind of torture as she waited for the next tap to tell her where the mysterious unseen figure was.

Alan looked at the roof and raised an eyebrow in question.

Silver cleared his throat quietly and shook his head.

'Is that you, Barbecue?' said a whining voice with shocking abruptness, leaping on the tiny noise as if it had been waiting for it.

A dark silhouette filled the single rear window by Cat and a head leant forward against the glass, close to, as if sniffing blindly for them.

'I hears you . . .'

Two ruined eyes set in a blackened face hideously scarred with powder burn peered sightlessly in at them.

It was Pew.

'. . . I hears you, and I smell the girlie too, the girlie as took poor Blind Pew's powers o' seeing from him . . .' he simpered. 'But we shall have you both now, and all debts shall be paid in kind, Barbecue, debts shall be paid for. I'll be double-damned if she leaves this island with her eyes, by the Black Spot I swear it!'

He rubbed a finger on the powder still blackening his face, and pressed it against the window.

It left a squashed sooty circle on the glass.

'See that, girlie? 'Tis the Black Spot, and I put it on you for a curs—'

Alan sprang across the room and thrust his sword straight through the window, shattering the glass and skewering Pew to the sword hilt.

'You'll keep your damned curses to yourself, blind man,' he spat, and yanked the sword back. 'Now die quietly like a Christian and take your precious Black Spot with ye . . .'

Pew staggered back from the window, hand clenched over the wound welling in his neck, opened his mouth to speak, and then dropped from sight.

The light in the room strobed as several other figures ran past the windows on the outside, and there was the noise of someone landing on the heather roof above them.

'They're here, and the trap is shut, more's the pity,' said Silver, sweeping the food and crockery from the table and quickly laying the three pistols from his sash out on it. He uncorked a horn powder flask with his teeth and speedily began to load the first pistol.

'Then stand and fight it is,' said Alan. ''Tis all one to me, and my sword can slash the heads off these blackhearts as easily under a roof as in the open air . . .'

There was a scrabbling at the front door and the sound of the lock turning, and then the door yanked open and the silhouette of a Huron was backlit for a moment.

There was a loud detonation as Silver swung his loaded pistol and fired, and the Huron cartwheeled backwards, his tomahawk flying one way as he went the other. Then Israel Hands rushed in with an ugly hooked boarding axe raised over his head, but Alan ran straight at him and caught the axe-handle on the downstroke in one hand while he ran him through with his sword, the velocity of this counter-attack forcibly ramming Hands back out of the house, before Alan jumped back and slammed the door again.

Just as Cat heard someone try and open it again, Alan smashed the bolt on the inside shut.

'That'll nae hold for long,' he said, his sword dripping on to the earth floor as he looked up at the heather thatch, holding up a finger for silence as he listened to the muffled footsteps above them. 'By your leave . . .'

And he stepped nimbly up on to the table in front of Silver and thrust his sword through the heather three times in rapid succession. There was a shriek and the sound of someone falling off and he calmly stepped back down to guard the door.

'. . . now I suggest you and I take the front door and these pair o' windows, Silver, and you watch the smaller back window, lass, and load Silver's pistols as he needs them. These rogues are hungry for the bloodiest mischief, for that was just a dram before meat.'

'Fairly said,' said Silver, and laid a loaded pistol on the window ledge in front of Cat.

'Use your sword when you can, and only fire when you must,' he said. 'For we have precious few balls to crack at them.'

He took another pistol and put it in his sash, before drawing his cutlass and swinging over to take up a position by the front windows.

Cat loosened the sword from the cane with difficulty, and was alarmed to see it was really badly corroded now. It looked brown and rust-scarred and more like a poker than a blade. The uncannily fast decay of the blade was as frightening as any other aspect of their predicament, because it seemed like a sign, and not a good one. It seemed to be like a reminder that time was running out for her in her quest to find Victor and save him.

There was a tap-tap from the glass next to Cat. She looked back to see Blind Pew smiling grimly in at her again – as if the fatal wound in his neck, which she could see clearly had cut him to the bone, was nothing at all.

'Hello, girlie . . .' he leered, 'I can smell you there. Now you see me . . . soon you won't.'

And he brandished an ugly seaman's dirk, tapping the window with it.

'I thought he was dead,' said Alan.

Pew's smile turned to a snarl and he lunged in the window, slashing blindly at Cat's face. She didn't even have to lift the pistol off the ledge. She just found the trigger and pulled, blasting him out of the window.

'He was,' she said. 'They just don't stay dead. Not on this island.'

She was reloading fast, and as her fingers scrabbled in the bullet bag she was horrified to find only a couple more rounds.

'This island is like that bright-eyed devil in a skirt who played us false with the mutton stew,' said Alan, eyes locked on the front of the house. 'It vexes me that something seeming so fair could be so foul.'

'If we can't make them stay dead,' said Silver, with what Cat was alarmed to detect as a falter in his voice, 'maybe I should talk to them? See what their terms for a parley is?'

'If their "terms" involve blinding that lass at our backs, then my steel will do all the talking I need,' said Alan. 'And if I cannot die as an old man amongst the hills and heather of my true home, it has ever been my wish to go while my sword hand still sung, and this place is as good a place to die as any.'

More feet landed on the thatch at the far end of the black house. They looked up and listened to cautious movements on the roof above.

'That's where I fear you are wrong,' growled Silver. 'This place may be the WORST place to die as any, for I think if we die here we may become like those undead devils outside – unhealed yet unkillable.'

Cat shivered at the thought, and then all coherent thought stopped for a while as there was an urgent flurry of hacking from the thatch above and then a ragged hole opened to the sky and the attack began in earnest.

Silver pistolled the Huron outlined in the roof-hole before he could jump down, but the tall Swedish pirate leapt boots first into the room in his place.

If there hadn't been a stool underneath the hole, he would have taken Silver's head off with the cutlass he swung at him as he came, but as it was one boot landed on the stool and the other continued down to the floor, making him tilt and stumble away from his target, missing by inches.

The momentum of his swing chunked his blade into the table leg, and before he could get to his feet or yank it free, Silver had pinned him to the ground with his crutch tip and the full weight of his body, and emptied his second pistol into him.

He tugged the cutlass free from the table leg and tossed it to Cat.

'Watch him. He may not stay dead.'

Cat hoped he did. She didn't want to look twice at what the gun had done to the Swede's face, and certainly didn't want to see it come back to life.

And then the door smashed in, and someone tried to stab her through the window at her back, and she found herself blocking the blow without thinking, and then as she thrust back on reflex it all went very fast and simultaneously slow in that complicated time-choppy way again because she was fighting for her life, something she did as much on blind instinct and muscle-memory as on conscious thought.

The pirate at her window thrust at her again.

She parried his blade by clubbing it away with the heavy pistol in her left hand and stabbed back at him with the rusty sword in her right, sending him stumbling back out of the window clutching his chest.

In the doorway Alan fought two men at once, his sword a flickering zigzag of bright steel as he thrust and parried and counterthrust, moving fast and always managing to avoid the angry blades that hacked and slashed at him. He had the gift of moving so swift and light that he was never quite still in the space where they aimed their blows by the time their sword points arrived in it.

One of the pirates lunged at him with a grunt of frustration, stumbling in front of the other in his desperation to get Alan within reach of his sword and skewer him.

Alan's blade met his and slid along it until the two hilts clashed together.

He twisted his wrist so fast that the pirate's sword was ripped from his hand and flew into the air.

Without a second's hesitation Alan jumped forward and passed his own steel through the disarmed man as he snatched the tumbling blade out of the air by its handle and cut the second pirate a mortal blow through the neck and shoulder in the same savage movement.

Then he stepped back, letting the first of his attackers slide off his sword on to the floor.

He stood there with swords in both hands and looked back for an instant, catching Cat's eye, and laughed.

'Ach, Cat lass, the heather's on fire inside my wame*. Was that not a joyous thing to see?!'

The window by Silver smashed and she saw him grab the attacker's tomahawk and pull, letting his body weight drag the Huron inside over the broken glass and then impaling him with his cutlass.

In the suddenly revealed frame of the window Cat saw something beyond the dying Huron's kicking heels that sent a further chill of fear through her veins.

The woman in the scarlet dress was standing with a burning oil lamp in her hand, and as Cat saw her she seemed – impossibly – to be able to see her right back inside the darkened croft, and she smiled and tossed the lamp up and on to the thatch where it landed with a whump of flame as the oil burst and ignited the dry heather which immediately began to crackle and burn.

'That's not good,' gritted Silver, busy reloading his pistols.

And then before Cat could shout a warning two more figures crammed the door . . .

And she saw one was Flint.

And then her view was blocked as Alan darted forward,

---

* belly

fighting two-handed, driving the attackers back into the sun with the speed and ferocity of his defence, dropping the pirate beside Flint and stepping over him.

Parrying an axe blow from Magua who came at him from the side, he slashed a scarlet stripe across Flint's face – and leapt back, slamming the door on the scene beyond as he thrust his borrowed sword into the staples of the wooden bar that had been burst, bolting the door shut again.

'If they would stay dead, this would be a fair enough fight,' he said, breathing hard.

'Aye,' said Silver, 'but when fighting fair don't work, what choice have we but to parley?'

They all looked up at the thatch, which was rolling with smoke and dotted with bright points of flame.

'No,' said Alan. 'They'll not harm the girl while I breathe.'

'They don't want the girl,' said Silver, nodding at the fire above. 'And tell me how long you feel we may breathe that smoke and yet defend ourselves?'

'But parley for what?' said Alan, beginning to cough as the dark smoke dropped lower and cinders began to fall through it like red snowflakes.

'They want the book she carries . . .'

Cat opened her mouth to protest, her mind whirling, her heart breaking that he could be about to betray her after all they'd gone through . . .

But the dead Swede got off the ground at her feet, and she shot him back on to the floor on reflex.

And the window behind her darkened and something fell out of the sky and hit her hard and sharp in the side of the head.

And the last thing she heard was Alan yelling a warning to her –

too late,

too loud,

too hopeless,

to stop

the dark.

43

Honest John's treachery

Cat jolted out of the darkness and three things were wrong.

She was outside.

She was upside down.

And she was moving.

For a moment she stared at the tangle of soft green grass and blood-red wildflowers passing below her, and then she saw the handle of a sword bouncing on the hip of the man carrying her, and realized she was slung over Alan's back as he walked across the *machair*.

She arched her head and was about to tell him to put her down when she looked back and saw a sight that silenced her.

The croft house was ablaze and already nearly a hundred yards away. Between them and it was a sinister half circle of pirates and Huron keeping pace with Alan as he walked to the shore. In the middle of the threateningly curved phalanx was

Magua and Flint and the scarlet-clad woman, and in front of them was the thing that was keeping them at bay.

It took her a moment to realize that the flaming torch Silver held in one hand, a torch made from a heather broom, was not the thing stopping her enemies attacking. What held them back was the thing Silver held above his head, impaled on the tip of his sword.

It was a small black book, and it was, for reasons Cat didn't understand, dripping wet.

Then she saw the whisky jug Silver held looped casually through the forefinger of the hand that held the broom-torch, and began to understand.

She wriggled like a salmon and dropped off Alan's shoulder before he could throw an arm round her waist and hold her back. She scrabbled her hands into her jeans pocket and found exactly what she feared was there.

Nothing.

No notebook.

Just a void filled with Long John Silver's betrayal.

She kicked out, trying to get at him.

'Easy, lass!' Alan hissed into her ear, his arm as unbending as an iron band around her middle.

'What have you done?!'

Flint seemed to enjoy her squirming and his nasty laugh crossed the thirty feet of *machair* between them.

'We have had ourselves a parley, and come to an accommodation.'

'But . . . !' Cat cried.

Silver looked back at her and shook his head warningly.

'No "buts" and no raging, if you please, for the accommodation is a delicate one, seeing as trust is hard to come by amongst them as has killed one another previous, like,' he said. 'The balance is this . . .'

He pointed to the book impaled on the sword tip above his head.

'The precious book is doused in the fine whisky we never drunk inside of that house.'

He nodded at the blaze behind him, and as if to punctuate his speech the roof chose that moment to fall in with a spectacular eruption of sparks and a fire-stained mushroom cloud of smoke that rolled lazily up into the early evening sky above it.

He gestured with the flaming brand held in the hand that also gripped his crutch handle. The jug banged against the crutch pole as he did so, sounding hollow and at least half empty.

'The price of the book is that these fine gentleman and that fine lady allow you and the Scotsman to the boat down yonder.'

Cat took a moment to look behind her and realized she and Alan now stood amongst the tall marram grass on the lip of the dunes, and below them a small boat sat on the very edge of the beach, rocking slightly in the shallows.

'The guarantee of their good faith is that if they rush you

before you are clear of the island I will light the book and all shall be losers . . .'

He lowered the book towards the flame to demonstrate, and there was an angry growl from the semi-circle of pirates and Indians and they took a step forward before Magua barked something and Flint yelled 'Belay that!'

Silver hoisted the book up into the air again, away from the flame.

'And you?' choked Cat.

'I shall remain and rejoin my old shipmates, and since we have rubbed along well enough before, I don't think we shall have a problem reacquainting ourselves to our mutual satisfaction,' grinned Silver. 'Especially as I have brought them the means with which to give them some greater power over their present predicament and future destinies.'

'We must go,' whispered Alan. 'The man's right. And his torch will not stay aflame much longer, and then the bauchled* hellhounds will be around our ears.'

'I can't leave the book!' cried Cat. 'Without it all is lost!!'

'Aye,' said Alan. 'What will be, will be. You can and you must. Are we agreed?'

His arm still gripped her.

'Are we agreed?' he repeated.

After a beat she nodded and it relaxed.

'Come now,' he said, stepping off the lip of the dune.

---

* misshapen

370

Cat grabbed his sword hilt and drew the sword as she threw herself back across the grass at Silver. Her plan, inasmuch as she had one, was to tackle Silver, grab the book and outrun the Indians to the boat. Alan dived after her and caught her by the ankle. She went down hard, and before she could get her breath back he had her gripped around the waist with one arm while the other picked up his sword.

'You have a man's fire in your heart, but no sense in your head,' he said, pulling her away towards the beach.

'You may lay to that,' said Silver. 'It's a foolish girl as will not let herself be rescued . . .'

She struggled, her feet hacking at Alan's legs.

'Traitor!' she yelled at Silver.

The Indians and the Huron laughed nastily, enjoying the show.

'You're nothing but a bloody traitor!'

Silver bowed as if receiving a compliment, then swung a few paces towards her. The mob of Indians and pirates took the same number of steps as him, keeping their distance but staying as close as they could.

'Ah well, there's loyalty, and then there's loyalty,' said Silver. ' And the first loyalty I have is to my own skin.'

Her sight was blurring with the tears of frustration she was trying desperately not to let leak down her face.

'I saved your life!' she spat. He just bowed again, his smile infuriating.

'And I'm saving yours, if you look at it right . . .'

'You're not! You're killing my grandfather . . .' she pleaded.

'You I owe, Cat Manno,' said Silver, his face suddenly hard and his voice business-like. 'Him I never met. Him I am under no obligation to, whatsoever . . .'

And before she could say another word, Alan stepped back off the lip of the dunes and they stumbled down the almost sheer twenty-foot upcurve of sand that took them on to the beach.

She tried to break free and run again, but Alan yanked her back by the sword-cane that was now looped back over her shoulders. He spun her and threw her over his own shoulder and jogged to the boat as she tried to make him drop her, all to no avail.

'Traitor,' she spat. 'You're a damn traitor too.'

Magua and Flint and the woman and all their crew had advanced almost to the edge of the dune above them and all laughed at her as she shouted and struggled.

Silver stood on the very lip of the dune, outlined against the smoke-palled sky, his cloak billowing in the quickening breeze, looking every bit as much the grim scarecrow for which she had first mistaken him on the other, tropical, island.

Alan swung her into the boat and as she tried to leap back out his hand lashed forward and gripped her by the chin, stopping her in her tracks. She had no choice but to look into his eyes.

'Never a traitor,' he said. 'Alan Breck is as much a traitor as that man up there, who is trying to save your life at the peril of his own eternal spirit.'

'What?' she said. 'But . . .'

He shoved the boat loose of the sand and she felt it buoy up on the water as he pushed it out into the sea.

'As you love your grandfather, haud your wheesht* and get the oars set,' he hissed. 'For this will be a damned close-run piece of business, and we shall be rowing for our lives afore it's done . . .'

His eyes were so level and straight that it stopped her in her tracks.

He raised his hand to the watching figures.

Silver nodded and turned back to the line of waiting pirates and Indians.

'Honest John's word is good, my hearties,' he said, dropping the whisky jug on to the grass at his feet as he relaxed. 'And bad cess to them as says it ain't. Here's the book, and I give you joy of it!'

He whipped his sword arm back and then forward, casting the book high into the air above them. For a moment Cat had the wild hope that he was, at least, throwing it into the distant fire so that they should not have it either. Magua leapt high for it, but the book just clipped his outstretched fingers and Cat's spirits dropped as she saw it land safely in the grass behind him. All his men instinctively turned to watch this, and as

---

* 'be quiet' (literally: 'hold your silence')

373

they did so, Silver dropped the flaming torch on to the whisky-soaked grass at his feet.

The grass ignited and he leapt the flames at the same moment, hurling himself pell-mell down the slope to the beach in a staggering turn of speed for a man with one leg.

Alan ran to him, grabbed him and part carried, part dragged him to the boat. A Huron sprang after them vaulting the flames, but Alan just pulled a pistol out of Silver's sash and shot him in mid-air, and he hit the sand like an untidy sack of cabbages and stayed there.

Silver hoisted himself aboard and Alan pushed and got the boat launched into the surf and followed suit at the very moment that a tomahawk whirled past Cat's shoulder and buried itself in the thwart beside her.

'Pull now!' yelled Silver. 'Pull for your life!'

He and Alan bent their backs and tore the blades through the rising waves, and since there were only two oars, Cat stood looking back, and saw the line of dead spread out along the black sand, staring angrily after them.

She turned to Silver.

'But they have the book!' she choked. 'I can't save Victor without it! You had no right!'

'I had every right,' he said. 'It was my book.'

And as she caught up he nodded at Alan.

'Pick his pocket for a change, why don't you?'

Alan grinned at her.

'Left-hand front,' he said.

She reached into his coat and her fingers closed on a familiar rectangle of oilcloth binding.

Her heart soared.

She pulled out Victor's notebook.

'The Bible will save you, so they say,' said Silver. 'And so it did. All of us.'

'You tricked them,' she said. 'You used your Bible . . .'

A thought hit her like a flung brick.

'I called you a traitor,' she said. 'I called you both traitors . . .'

'Aye,' said Alan. 'And didn't that just help the devils believe the book on the end of yon man's sword was the very thing itself?'

Silver returned his grin.

Cat looked back at the island, a lump in her throat, clutching the book tightly in her hand. As the gap grew and the view began to bounce, she had time to notice that the previously flat sea had become increasingly violent. But still . . .

'Thank you,' she said. And then she said, 'Oh no.'

Silver missed a stroke and looked round.

'What?' said Alan.

'They've got boats,' said Silver. 'Row.'

The dead were running previously unseen boats from hollows in the dunes and throwing them into the water, which immediately churned with their oars as they latched on in furious pursuit.

Ahead of them, across the rising sea that was filling the broad channel, was nothing but the black cliff face of the dark island and the squadrons of fulmars and skuas that endlessly flew round it.

And now that they were heading for the cliffs, Cat could hear the violin once more, skirling into a fiddler's version of a wild and warlike pipe tune. That noise, more than anything else, lifted her heart and made her sure that heading for the dark island was the right thing to do.

44

The why

Cat stirred on the bed, and Joe paused in his playing.

'Don't stop!' said the nurse, who had been leaning in the doorway. She pointed at the screens flashing and bleeping round Cat. 'Hell. Those numbers are good and getting better. Keep on playing . . .'

Joe looked at his parents.

'Dad,' he said, 'Victor's ill.'

'Well yeah, Joe, he got hit by a truck,' Sam smiled tightly. 'Keep playing.'

Joe stuck the violin under his chin but didn't raise the bow. He grimaced. Annie saw that whatever he had to say was coming hard to him.

'No, Dad. It's why I didn't make the lunch.' He shook his head. 'We had an argument. He didn't want to tell you he was ill. I saw the letters from the hospital at his house. I said you'd want to know; he made me swear not to tell you.'

'But—' said Sam.

Joe rolled on, sure that if he stopped he wouldn't get it out right.

'He wanted one last happy visit. I didn't think I could sit there and pretend everything was great. I knew you'd want to know, want to help. And then he wanted me to witness this living will, saying he didn't want to be revived and kept alive when things got tough. And I couldn't do that and not tell you. So I kind of chickened out and stayed away.'

He shrugged, eyes wet.

'What's wrong with him?' said Sam.

'It's not good . . .' began Joe.

'It doesn't matter,' Annie said decisively. 'You need to be with him now. Go. We'll be fine here.'

And she hugged him and kissed him and shoved him out of the door. And as he hurried for the elevator he heard Joe's violin break into a tune he recognized as the boatman's song from Mingulay.

45

Fiddler's Green

Magua and his boats were gaining on them, and as they skirted the dark cliffs of the second island, Cat took over from Alan, rowing as he rested and got his strength back.

The distant sound of the lonely violin had stopped for a while but had returned, playing another tune that Cat also recognized.

'You hear that?' she shouted. 'You hear the music?'

'Only music I hear is my heart beating like Drake's Drum,' said Silver in between great heaving breaths.

'It's a rowing song!' shouted Cat. 'I know it! We're on the right track.'

A stocky puffin lofted itself off a passing rock and went over them, its short legs dangling comically behind it as it flew away seeming to defy the normal laws of gravity and flightworthiness that should have applied to its stubby and seemingly unviable shape.

Alan watched it with a smile which he lost as he stared at the narrowing strip of water between them and their pursuers and shook his head.

'The music is in your head, Cat. But this would be a fine moment to have a long rifle, for I could birl them into the water one by one from this distance—'

There was a puff of white smoke from the lead boat and something went smacking the air over their heads.

'I'm thinking they're of the same opinion,' growled Silver. 'Difference being they *do* have a gun—'

Another bullet spanged off the kelp-fringed rock face they were skirting.

'Guns,' said Alan. 'They have more than one, God rot them – but they're missing us by a lowland mile, thanks be—'

A third round whirred overhead, and then Alan fell back into the bottom of the boat with a grunt, in the same instant they heard the delayed report of a fourth shot, clutching his chest.

There was a distant shout of approval from the boats behind.

Cat missed a stroke and nearly lost the oar as she lurched forward to see where he was wounded.

Alan grinned tightly up at her, his one hand clamped over a wound that was already darkening the shoulder of his shirt.

'Row on, girl, row on with all your strength, and

dinnae fash* yoursel' – the bullet's gone clean through and no bones broken.'

Cat heaved at the oar, getting back into rhythm with Silver.

Alan ripped the sleeve off his shirt and tore it into two strips using his good hand and his teeth. Then he set about staunching the blood with a makeshift bandage.

'You all right, Scotsman?' panted Silver.

'Ach, I've had worse,' said Alan. 'They just pinked me with a lucky round. And they missed my sword arm entirely – an error they shall come to rue if they come within reach of my blade again.'

'Stewart,' laughed Silver. 'I'm coming to like the cut of your jib, so I am.'

'I'm still good for the fighting, but one-armed is no' sae canny for the rowing, so by your leaves I shall lie here and give them false hope by pretending to be dead. For if that gallus besom** with the sparkling eyes and the bewitched mutton stew can play a man false, it is only polite to play false with them,' grinned Alan. 'I have always believed turnabout is fair play.'

They rowed hard and long, and the boat surged along the curve of the island, seeming to gather speed as the cliff tops sloped lower and lower until they were less than fifty feet

---

* bother
** mischievous hussy

above them and beginning to show green grass beyond through gaps that appeared and disappeared as they passed.

Cat's arms and back were really starting to ache, but since Silver showed no sign of slowing the pace and had been rowing for twice as long as her, she didn't let herself slow down.

'Look out!' Alan cried and pointed to the cliff above them.

It was only about twenty feet high now, and as Cat snatched a quick look she saw a flash of bronzed skin and a feathered mohawk disappear, as if someone was running to keep pace with them along the upper edge of the island.

'One of the devils must have got ashore and be running us down to get a shot,' Alan scowled. 'Though how he scaled the cliff I've no idea, for I have seen no relief in the sheer rock, and it would be a pretty piece of scrambling to have done it.'

The pursuers had disappeared around the increased curve of the island, and within twenty or so strokes the hidden side of the island revealed itself fully as the cliff dwindled into low limpet-studded rocks that formed the end of a spit, and they found that they were looking into another grassy bowl that had been hidden behind the forbidding escarpment. It was exactly the same landscape, the same accident of rock, grass and sand, with one significant difference: the sand on this island was pale shell-sand, the colour of rich vanilla ice cream, curving off in a long arc of beach that extended away from them on the other side of a long sand bar that jutted out from the spit almost across the whole bay. The tide was out, and a long rippled plain of wet sand stretched towards the beach proper, where it swept up into grass-topped dunes that rolled on into another gentle *machair* landscape dotted here and there with other low croft houses.

It looked a lighter and happier island than the one they had fled from, all the more surprisingly since it had hidden its true nature behind such dark and forbidding cliffs as the ones that guarded its back.

'What do you think?' said Silver.

Alan raised his head and craned round.

'I think it is dry land, and it looks fair, and if the choice is rowing on into the open sea until our arms drop out of their very sockets, or getting ashore and finding a place where we may fight with a wall to our backs—'

The boat grounded with a decisive thump that jerked them all off their seats.

'The tide has made the decision for us, lads, so make haste along that sand bar and head for the dunes,' roared Silver, throwing his oar from him in disgust as he grabbed his crutch and levered himself swiftly up and out of the boat.

Alan and Cat disembarked on his heels and the three of them splashed and stumbled through the ankle-deep water, heading for the dry beach beyond.

As they ran in, Cat saw a strange thing on the beach ahead: her first thought was that it was a Victorian street lamp, but as they got closer she recognized it as the four-faced clock she had seen in her feverish dream when shackled to the mast top.

'This is the right place,' she panted. 'This must be Far Rockaway!'

'Far Rockaway or Fiddler's Green may be one and the same for all I know,' huffed Silver. 'It's as good a place as any to make a stand . . .'

'Watch our backs, Cat, while I cut this scoundrel out of the road,' yelled Alan, drawing his sword with his good arm and running ahead.

Sprinting towards them at equal speed was the Indian whom they had glimpsed running down the cliff tops beside them.

He carried a long rifle and a tomahawk and he ran at them full tilt, as if he was going to try and ram them back into the sea by speed alone.

Alan slashed at him as he swerved at the last minute, wrong-footing the Scotsman, who stumbled to one knee as the force of his mistimed blow hacked into nothing but air.

Silver in his turn cut savagely at him with his cutlass, but the Indian leapt over the steel, knocking him sprawling in the wet sand with a hard shove as he passed, and ran straight at Cat, who fumbled with her sword and then stopped, too late as the Indian dropped his own axe and planted the splayed fingers of his hand square on Cat's chest, winding her and stopping her dead.

'No, Cat Man-No. You must not cross the bar.'

It was Chingachgook.

She couldn't believe it.

'I met Uncas!' she blurted without thinking.

'I know,' he said. 'He came to me in a dream last night with your eagle feather. So thanks to you I know now I shall find him, no matter when or where or in what world he now is.'

Alan and Silver had turned and were running back to Cat's rescue.

'It's OK!' she stuttered. 'He's one of us.'

'No,' said the Indian with a curt shake of his head. 'You are not one of us, Cat Man-No, though you are a brave heart and a Human Being and your word is good. You must not step on to dry sand here.'

Cat's surprise and delight both died stillborn at the look in his face. It was deadly serious.

'But why?'

'Because if you cross the bar, walking from wet to dry sand, you can never go back. You can stay here, but back there, where your life is, it doesn't go well. You do not wake.'

His words hit her low in the stomach, and took the wind out of her.

'You mean I die?'

He didn't blink.

'Yes.'

'But . . .'

A voice she knew as well as any in the world cracked urgently over the sound of the distant surf.

'No "buts", Cat. Not on this. For once in your life, take a telling. The dry sand marks the bar. Don't cross it. On your life, girl, stay on the wet sand!'

She looked from Chingachgook's steady eyes to Alan and Silver as they stepped aside to reveal Victor striding towards her from the *machair*, the wind whipping at his white hair and fluttering the tails of his long tweed coat behind him. He looked strong and healthy and his eyes were shining and proud.

46

The roaring girl

Cat's heart leapt like a salmon at the sight of her grandfather swinging vigorously towards her across the beach. Her immediate unthinking impulse was to run to him, forgetting all the warnings, but Chingachgook's firm hand held her back on the wet sand.

Victor strode right up to the very edge of the dry sand and held his hand out to gently stroke her cheek.

'My girl,' he said. 'My wild girl. Nothing could stop you, could it?'

Her hand covered his and squeezed tight.

'I came to get you.' She was so happy and confused at the same time that she could barely speak. 'I came to save you.'

'I know,' he said. 'But look at me. I've never been better.'

All she seemed able to do was beam at him. So hard her face ached.

'You have something for me?' he said.

She fumbled in her jeans and held out the book.

'No,' he said, pointing at the sword in her hand. 'I meant my sword.'

'Oh,' she said, switching hands and holding it out. 'Here . . .'

He took the swordstick by the handle, and looked at the blade. What once had been straight shiny steel was now brown and blistered with rust.

'I'm sorry . . .' she began.

It looked as if it would shatter into flakes at any moment. Yet as he pulled it slowly towards him, as it crossed the invisible line between the dry and the wet sand, an extraordinary thing happened: the corrosion did indeed shale off into leaves of rust that fell on to the wet sand at Cat's feet as the blade renewed itself to its former gleaming beauty, flashing sharp and dangerous in the sun.

'Thank you,' said Victor. 'You took good care of it. You got it to me.'

Cat looked down at the rough half circle of rust flakes and the perfectly straight line that marked on the wet sand the bar she must not apparently cross.

'Fiddler's Green,' breathed Silver. 'By the powers . . .'

He pointed at the sword.

'Fiddler's Green where all is mended, the lost are found, hearts eased, and . . .'

He broke off and looked at Alan, who stood there, his shoulder red with blood.

'Step over the line, Stewart.'

Alan was looking backwards to where the pursuers' boats were disgorging their enemies on to the wet sand a hundred yards behind them. They were in no hurry to chase, it seemed, lining up along the waterline.

'What?' he said.

Silver grinned and shoved him. Alan stumbled forward on to the dry sand, already turning with a spark of anger reddening his cheek.

'Why, Silver, that was an ungentlemanly—'

Silver was laughing and pointing at his shoulder.

Alan looked down. The wound was gone. His bare, bloodied arm was no longer bare but sleeved again, and all sign of blood had disappeared. He was made new and looked fresh, vigorous and ten years younger.

'That,' he said, 'is passing strange.'

Silver lifted his crutch tip and swung it over the line, heaving himself across on to dry sand. There was silence as they all looked at him.

'No, Stewart,' he said, chuckling. 'THIS is strange. Doubly strange.'

And he stuck his crutch in the sand and walked away from it in a short circle on two good legs.

He too looked younger and stronger, the grey grizzle in his hair gone and more life in his eyes.

'Well by God that crutch served me well and true, but I shall not miss it a tittle, and you may lay to that!'

And he jumped in the air and clicked his heels.

As he landed with a double clump he looked at them all.

'Please, shipmates,' he said. 'Don't try and tell me you wouldn't do the same thing in my boots.'

And he laughed again.

'Boots! Two good boots, by the powers!'

Cat felt the book hanging heavy in her hand and held it out to Victor.

'Here. I got this back too.'

She thrust it out to him, over the invisible bar.

Victor shook his head and did not reach out for it.

'I don't want it.'

'But *they* want it,' she said urgently, gesturing over her shoulder towards the line of enemies on the waterline. 'Magua wanted it. Flint wanted it. The woman wanted it!'

'Of course they did.'

'But why?!' she said.

He reached across and stroked her hair out of her face, his eyes as gentle as his touch.

'Because it's a new book, Cat. Because that's a kind of magic, a kind of life. And with it they can make this world anew. They can control everything. They can make it *their* story. Nobody wants to be a villain, Cat. Most villains don't see themselves like that. They see themselves as heroes of their own stories. Give them a blank page and they'll rewrite this world until up is down, wrong is right and they're at the centre of it with everyone seeing them as the good guys . . .'

Cat looked from the island to the sea and the line of pirates and Huron stretched along the waterline. An autumnal sunset was beginning to gild the sky to the west, bathing everything in a golden light, somehow making it look more than just real, more than just something she was seeing with her eyes, something like a memory too.

'What is this world?'

Victor looked at the glowing sky and smiled.

'Well, I don't know. I've been thinking about that. Thinking a lot. And what I think is that just maybe we're in the space that stories come from. Or perhaps where they go . . . I don't know. We're just "here". And it's a different here from the one where you belong, Cat, the "here" you must go back to.'

'And you,' she said fiercely. She was getting very uncomfortable with how comfortable Victor seemed to be in this world. 'That's why I came. You have to come back with me!'

The wind caught a tendril of her hair and blew it across her eyes. He reached over and tucked it behind her ears.

'I think I belong here now, sweet girl.'

'NO! You come with me. That's what this was all about. You rescued me there, I rescue you here, we go home!'

Before he could answer she heard the sound of running feet and saw Chingachgook stiffen and Alan and Silver step up behind Victor, faces suddenly serious.

'Don't move, lass,' gritted Alan through clenched

teeth as he drew his sword.

She turned to see a man with half a smoking head sprinting towards her, much closer than she expected.

The mouth in the half face opened wide and the single eye flashed with malignant glee as the attacker raised his sword and shrieked.

'Prepare to die, you she-hellion! I told you we should meet again at Fiddler's Green!'

It was Billy Bones. Victor and Chingachgook both splayed their hands on Cat's back.

'Don't let him knock you over the bar,' said Victor.

Billy Bones leapt towards her, arm slicing down at her head – only to have the sword knocked out of his hand by a whirling tomahawk hurled at the last minute by Chingachgook.

He landed right in front of Cat and stopped dead, nose to nose.

'Ah.' He sighed, as if horribly disappointed. And a little hurt. 'Now that's not fair, lads. Three against one. That's not fair.'

He looked down. She followed his eyes.

Three swords – Victor's, Silver's and Alan's – had all been thrust beneath her arms, and they all skewered Billy Bones in place.

She ducked Alan's arm, careful to keep on the wet sand.

Billy Bones hung on the swords like a scarecrow.

'That's not fair at all.' He coughed and looked back. His own sword was stuck point down in the sand six feet behind him. His hand reached reflexively for it, and then gave up.

Alan and Victor removed their blades, but Silver kept his old shipmate upright with the guard of his own sword wedged against his breastbone. 'You got your leg back . . .' said Billy in wonderment, drooping a little as his own legs began to give way. 'How does that happen, John?'

Silver shook his head and smiled sadly.

'Now, Billy, this is Fiddler's Green, where all is mended, hearts shall be eased, the lost found . . . and friends turned foes are fellows again.'

'Friends, John?' choked Bones. 'As we once were?'

Silver gave him a long hard look and decided something.

'Aye. Friends as ever was, Billy.'

And he stepped back, pulling his sword out.

Billy stumbled forward, head first into the dry sand.

And then he turned and looked up at Silver, and they all looked back into his two eyes and a head that was, now that it was a whole head again, a tolerably good-looking and cheerful one.

'John,' he said in wonder, 'you were never as black as you was painted.'

'You may lay to that,' agreed Silver. 'Unlike that murderous bastard over there, I'll be bound.'

They all turned to look at the waterline. And ahead of the long and unmoving line of the dead there was just one figure walking purposefully towards them. It was Magua in his red coat, and he walked across the beach as if he owned it. He beckoned with one hand and shouted across the tide-ribbed sand.

'Give me the book!'

'He wants the power. He wants the magic,' said Silver.

Cat looked at Victor, then at the book in her hand, then jabbed it at him again.

'But if it's magic – use the book against him!'

'It's not that kind of magic.'

'Well what kind is it?' Cat was beginning to feel the familiar boil of frustration, and she knew a lot of it was to do with Victor not wanting to save himself or let her do it for him.

'It's just magic like every book is magic.'

She watched the lone figure approaching, his long shadow thrown across the sand towards them by the sun dying at his back.

'Now *every* book is magic?' she said. 'But . . .'

'That's how stories work,' said Victor calmly. 'A good story changes how we see the world, using nothing but the right words in the right order, just like a magician uses a spell – which is after all just the right words in the right order – to change things.'

'Victor,' said Cat, nodding at Magua's silhouette. 'This isn't the time for that. He's getting awful close.'

'Isn't he?' said Victor calmly. 'Anyway, more importantly, it's not my book.'

Magua stopped dead and stood looking at them.

'IT IS!' cried Cat.

Victor shook his head.

'It's *your* book. It always was. Look . . .'

He reached over and riffled the pages. Cat stared at them. They were all blank.

'But there's . . . nothing in it!'

'I know.' Victor's smile flared like autumn sun on golden leaves. 'Great, isn't it? Nothing more exciting than a blank page, Cat. I envy you. And that's just how it should be. It's yours to use.'

'But what do I do with it?!!'

'You know what to do. The book is life. That's why they want it. But it's yours. Fill it. Fill it with living. Fill it with your story. That's the real adventure, Cat. It's your journey, not mine, not your dad's, not your mum's. There's no beaten track you have to follow. Make your own road by walking. And if you're lucky, like me, it'll be a long trail and an exciting one, and you'll stay interested in it all the days of your life, and when it ends, well then . . .'

'Well then WHAT?' Cat was almost bursting with frustration. She was so aggravated that she didn't notice the familiar/unfamiliar noise coming from Magua's direction.

'Well then, you'll leave it excited about the new blank page that lies ahead. The one you know nothing about. But for now, Cat, before this gets ugly, you need to get away from Magua and find your way home.'

She set her jaw firmly and shook her head.

'I'm not leaving you.'

'You have to.'

'And I don't know how to get home anyway,' she said, as if that trumped anything he might say.

'I do,' said Magua.

And though he spoke calm and low they all heard him and stared across the fifty feet of wet sand between them.

'I know how you get home.'

As she tried to make out what he was holding above his head, her eyes seemed to twist, or looking into the sunset made things go skew for a moment as he seemed to split into three, as if Flint and the woman in red had been standing in a line directly behind him.

There was something eerie and uncannily threatening in the way they spread out on either side of him, without making a sound.

'What . . . ?' began Cat.

'He's Magua,' said Victor. 'And so are they.'

Behind the three of them the longer line of Indians and pirates began to move forward to join their leaders.

Whatever they were, one thing was sure: they outnumbered Cat and Victor and Silver and Alan at least three to one.

'It's for you,' said Magua, turning the thing in his hand so it faced her.

And as she saw it she realized the familiar/unfamiliar noise was her ringtone and as she saw the illuminated glow of the touchscreen on her smart-phone she flashed a memory-hit of Magua the first time she had seen him, running into the riverside meadow, crossing her tracks and swooping low without stopping, to pocket something, and she now knew what it had been

He held the screen towards her: it was too far away for her to read the words but she knew the photo that she'd assigned the caller: it was her mum and dad and Joe in a picture that she had, at some stage, enclosed in a cheesy digital heart-shaped mat, and the caller ID below it read HOME.

'Give me the book, I give you this, you go home,' said Magua.

She looked round at Victor.

'They will not help you,' shouted Magua. 'Look at them. They have reached their happy hunting ground. If they step across the bar they lose it and have to wander the world trying to find it again.'

The woman in red pointed at them.

'If they cross the bar, they will be old and hurt and have no guarantee that they will find another way back there,' she said with a triumphant smile. 'You are on your own, my child . . .'

'Aye,' said Flint, drawing his cutlass. 'And we, girlie, we are many.'

'What they say is true,' said the woman. 'This is the end of it: you are truly alone.'

The line of Huron and pirates closing in behind them sniggered nastily.

Then stopped.

Cat felt a hand on her neck.

'The hell she is,' said Victor. She looked round.

He had stepped over the line.

His head was cut and crusted with dried blood once more. He looked older again too, but the fire in his eyes was as bright as the sword in his hand.

'Not by a long chalk,' said another voice, and she saw a crutch tip plant itself decisively by her left foot. She turned. Silver rested a hand on her shoulder. She couldn't speak.

'Well. I'm used to one leg now,' he said without meeting her eyes as he stared Magua down. 'I'm a simple man. Two of them'd just confuse me at this stage.'

Chingachgook stepped up next to Silver and braced a hand firmly on Cat's back.

'This girl is a great-heart and a Human Being,' he said. 'I will not let carrion like you feed on her.'

She felt the fourth hand on her other shoulder and saw Alan's foot step on to wet sand beside her.

'Which is to say, if you're of a mind to harm this lass who we're proud to call friend, you'll take your last dance with our steel first.'

She saw blood from the wound in his shoulder splash into the sand, and knew he was wounded again and that they had all forsaken their peace and well-being to stand with her on this lonely beach at the end of the world.

She wanted to cry, but was damned if she'd let Magua see her do anything so weak, so she gutted it out and swallowed the lump in her throat.

And anyway. It all made her so very angry. She could use that.

'Four against me?'

Magua nodded to his line of warriors.

'Against all of me?'

He laughed.

'Nothing changes. We are many. You are few. We are Magua, and all fear us, all run from us. But we always catch them in the end.'

He did look like a rooster crowing on a dunghill, Cat decided. Her voice came out lumpy and hoarse, but it strengthened as she spoke.

'You know why you're the Magua?'

Magua looked momentarily confused. Cat answered for him.

'Because people run away from you.'

'Exactly . . .'

'And you always catch up.'

'Always.'

He said it with relish, like he was licking the word and liking the way it tasted.

'So running away from you doesn't work.'

'Never. So give me the book.'

He held up the phone. It was still taunting her with its bright screen and painfully familiar ringtone.

'Cat,' said Victor.

She stuck the book back in her jeans.

'Come and get it.'

Magua laughed, pocketed the phone inside his red jacket, and hefted his tomahawk.

'Then run away, little girl. For my axe is thirsty . . .'

He kicked into a sprint, running right at her.

'Sure,' she said.

And before Alan or Silver or Chingachgook could stop her she yanked Billy Bones's sword from the ground and ran.

Not away.

Right at him.

On the run she dipped and scooped up Chingachgook's tomahawk without breaking step.

That felt right.

That felt like she had somewhere to put her anger and her fear and her grief – because of course she knew what Victor staying here while she left meant.

Her feet pistoned sand as she ran with tomahawk in one hand and sword in the other.

She didn't feel scared.

Or powerless.

Or lost.

She felt balanced.

She felt in the zone.

Magua's eyes opened wide in surprise, and she knew in that instant he was vulnerable, that this was her edge and she had to act now in the fraction of time before he adjusted.

Her wrist was cocked and thinking for itself, and she threw

the tomahawk with all her strength, sending it spinning ahead of her across the rapidly narrowing gap between them.

The steel hatchet blade flew straight and true, whirling at Magua's head.

He had no time to dodge it.

But just enough time to get over his surprise and sweep his own hawk upwards and parry the throw. The handles of the axes clattered into each other as the force of his block took his arm high over his head, sending Cat's axe flying harmlessly into the air behind him.

Cat threw herself into a low sliding tackle, the kind that would have got her sent off any soccer pitch in the world. She hit his ankles feet first, studs up, taking his legs out from under him as she slid past, her body parallel with the sand, her sword arm stretched high above her head, blade at right angles to the beach.

Magua snarled and scythed his tomahawk back down at her as she passed beneath him, slicing cleanly through the shoulder of her buckskin shirt and leaving a stinging cut across her upper arm as he went down like a felled tree.

She felt the impact as he hit the sand, and her momentum ripped her hand off the suddenly anchored handle of her sword. She didn't stop to look back but tumbled back up to her feet and ran to retrieve her axe from where it had landed in a thin pool of water.

Only then, with a weapon back in her fist, did she turn and prepare to stand her ground against Magua's counter-attack.

'Come on!' she shouted as she spun, voice ragged with adrenaline. 'COME ON . . . !!'

Magua wasn't coming.

Nor was he going anywhere. He was lying sideways on the sand, kebabed on her sword.

He looked more surprised than hurt, but the blade had passed through his chest from side to side where he had fallen on it.

He was trying to push up, but not getting very far.

'But,' he spat in disbelief. 'But . . . this is . . . wrong! You're just a—'

Cat didn't feel elated. Or relieved. She just felt very tired all of a sudden.

'I know,' she said. ' I mean, I know you're a big strong man and I should run away and wait for another big strong man to come and rescue me, but you know what I never get?'

She looked back at Victor.

'Why do the guys get to do all the rescuing? I mean I loved all the stories you gave me and read me, but one thing: where were the real girls? Half the books, they weren't there at all, and the other half they're wimped-out girly-girls getting all weepy and falling in love with the mysterious complicated dude or waiting for the right guy to save them.'

Magua coughed at her feet. His eyes were draining away as he rolled them up to look at her in confusion.

'You're just a girl . . .' he snarled weakly.

'Just little old me,' she agreed.

And then she leant down, gripped the sword handle decisively and gave a sharp tug, yanking it free and dropping him back to the sand. Magua's eyes flared up at her as if he was about to retort.

Then they fluttered. And were still.

'But then, that's all it takes,' said Cat. 'Real girls rescue themselves.'

47

Paradise Lost

The line of pirates and Huron stared at Cat and the fallen Magua. Cat bent and retrieved her phone from his coat.

Flint took a step forward, but the woman in the scarlet dress held up a hand and seemed to say something to him, as if she was now in charge.

Cat looked down at the ringing phone in her hand, at her family smiling back out of the screen. Victor stepped up behind her.

'Answer it, Cat. You earned it.'

She shook her head and looked beyond his shoulder and saw with a lurch that Fiddler's Green or Far Rockaway or whatever the welcoming island had been was gone, and just a strand of wet sand and a flat gunmetal sea beyond was all that remained.

'But . . . I never made it to Far Rockaway.'

'The point wasn't arriving,' he said. 'That was never really it. It was the journey. Answer the phone.'

'But we were meant to make it together!'

She was mortified to find that she was crying. Tears blurred her vision as she reached out a hand and linked her fingers through Victor's as he reached back in return.

Alan and Silver and Chingachgook loomed in behind him, and added their hands to Victor's and hers. And just for a moment it seemed as if they all came together and coalesced into his one figure – just as Magua's silhouette had fanned out into Flint and the scarlet woman, but in reverse.

'I don't know, Cat. Maybe we did make it together after all.'

And he winked. And as her vision unblurred and she saw the other three fan back out behind him more clearly, she realized in that instant that all her helpers along the way had perhaps had more than a little bit of Victor in each of them all the time, only she hadn't been smart enough to notice.

'But I still have to help you!' she said.

'You have,' he replied. 'You faced your Magua and won. I think we have to defeat ours. Maybe that's how we start to find our way back to the island.'

'But how . . .' she began.

'Don't know,' he smiled. 'That's another story.'

'But I can help!'

He nodded at the three men at his back.

'With this crew? I think I'll be fine.'

The phone was ringing louder it seemed, vibrating in her hand. He pointed to it.

'Those are the people who need you now, Cat.'

Her vision began to blur up.

'I can't leave you here—'

He laughed.

'At the beginning of an adventure? Cat. I can't think of a better place to leave me.'

The phone seemed to be getting hotter and hotter in her hand. She wanted to turn it off.

'You have to answer that now, Cat. Before that lot attack.'

'But I don't want to leave you,' she said very quietly.

'I know,' he said. 'But you have to. You must tell them how much I love them and how proud I am of them. Then I can go on my way with a light heart.'

'I can't go home,' she whispered.

'You can *never* go home!' shouted the woman from the centre of the line of Magua's followers. Cat didn't know how she could have heard what she had just whispered to Victor, nor did she like the way she now held a sword in her hand. Like she knew how to use it, and liked what she knew.

'Who is she?' said Cat.

'Just a different kind of Magua,' said Victor. 'She's Milady.'

'Who . . . ?' began Cat, and then remembered the unopened novel in her flight bag.

'Read the book,' said Victor with a forgiving smile. 'Read *The Three Musketeers*. She's treacherous and dangerous, and a duplicitous mistress of disguise and murder – but she's one strong, interesting woman.'

'No one goes home. Ever!' shrieked Milady, and it sounded like a battle cry as all her followers yelled and stamped their feet in response.

Victor laughed, his eyes on the shifting line of pirates and Huron who were beginning to look like they were about to charge . . .

'Of course she's a liar too. And that's the biggest lie in the world. Know why? Because if your family raise you with love and let you go, you carry that home inside you always, right here in your heart.'

And he took her hand, the one not holding the phone, and placed it in the centre of his chest and held it there for a long, long beat. And then he smiled deep into her eyes.

'And so you can *always* go home: all you have to do is open your heart and listen to its call . . .'

There was a loud shout, and Magua's followers charged.

She saw Alan and Chingachgook run to meet them, followed by Silver, and then before she could do anything Victor's other hand closed over the hand she held the phone in, and he folded her into a fast, tight hug and whispered one last thing in her ear.

'. . . and then answer it,' he breathed. 'Safe home, my roaring girl.'

Then he squeezed her thumb down on to the button on the screen.

And the ringing,

and the shouting,

and the clash of steel

        stopped dead

                and

                the

                world

                went

        white.

48

Nobody lives forever

Death did not come for Victor.

Death doesn't *come* for anyone.

People who write stories try to put a face on it by saying it does, but if you've ever been lucky enough to be there when someone dies, you know the truth: nothing *comes*, there's no Grim Reaper, no scythes, no terror. There's neither flutter of black wings nor rush of shadows nor any melodramatic falling swirl of violins or indeed any suddenly approaching spot of pure light coming to swallow you up.

You just go.

It's as simple and undramatic as walking out of the room. It's not freaky or frightening, and perhaps the most surprising thing is that it turns out to be the most ordinary thing in the world. And why wouldn't it be?

Everybody does it.

And so did he.

Victor stepped quietly out of the room of life, and though all the machines around him bleeped and wailed their sudden warnings, the actual going of the man was gentle, almost unremarkable.

And Sam saw it all.

He was surprised to both recognize it for what it was and know that, though the wave of grief that would hit him was now on the way, he was not frightened by what he had seen. It was natural and curiously unthreatening.

And he knew what to do.

He simply leant in and kissed Victor and squeezed his hand one last time, feeling the final fugitive warmth of his father's life on his own skin, and filing the memory of it away for later years.

And then he backed quietly away and watched the sudden posse of doctors and nurses worry in around the bed, knowing that his father had just gone away and that they were only so busy and urgent because they didn't know that yet, nor the other thing he knew: that he was not coming back.

Since they were all crowded round Victor looking down and working on him, one other thing none of them knew was that Sam looked up over their heads, smiling through the unbidden tears that were the forerunners of that inbound wave of sadness, and not a one of them heard him gently say goodbye.

Or that he loved him.

And that he always would.

410

Death did not come for Cat either, nor did she step out of the room of life.

She may have hovered in the doorway for a few hours, but she didn't leave. Instead she rallied. The repair in her torn meningeal artery held and – in time – scarred and was stronger than before. The fever stayed away and the intracranial pressure remained absolutely normal. And when she came round, two and a half days later, on Christmas morning in fact, all her family were in the room. She stared at them for a long beat and then smiled.

'Grandpa's OK,' was the first thing she said.

Sam looked at Annie. Joe put a hand on Cat's shoulder.

'Cat—' he began. 'Grandpa—'

'I know,' she said. 'He's gone. I know. But he wanted me to tell you, especially you, Dad: he's OK.'

They all looked at her.

'Cat,' said Sam. 'That doesn't make sense.'

'Well,' she said, shrugging. 'What do you expect? I got hit in the head by a truck.'

49

The clock at the end
of the world

It was, as it turned out, a Sunday subway that took them to Far Rockaway, which Victor, the lover of words and poetry, would have appreciated. His instructions, laid out in a simple will, had been quite precise. But he left it up to them to choose which route they took getting there. Cat decided there was no choice.

They went via Jamaica.

They stayed on the train until the end of the line, not talking much, enjoying the journey, noticing things Victor might have commented on, and remembering stories about him.

Cat was quietest of all, sitting with her hood up, to protect her cold shaven head, Victor's cane resting on the seat next to her, her lower leg heavy with a plaster cast as she cradled the urn in her lap.

Because of course Victor got his way in the end, and he –

or at least his ashes – went with them.

She had stopped telling them about her adventures because they all – except Joe, most of the time – made it clear that it was a dream she'd had whilst in her coma. Sam got especially distressed somehow when she tried to tell him it was real, as if she was making up a fairy tale to make him feel better.

So she had a double reason to keep quiet as they headed towards the sea.

The first part of the route was underground, but they emerged from the tunnels into the late afternoon light and low winter sun lit the last section of their journey. The train clanked and rumbled along the elevated railtrack leaving the high-rises behind as the buildings around them became lower and more scattered as the city ran out of energy as it reached for the lip of the Atlantic Ocean.

They walked out of the station, past the Last Stop Deli, and headed across the concrete cycleway, past the rusting chain-link flapping in the offshore breeze, and headed for the grey sand and the pale ocean beyond. They didn't walk fast because Cat still needed the cane.

They headed towards a lonely-looking piece of Victorian cast iron sticking out of the edge of the beach, like an ornate lamp-post with a four-faced clock mounted on top of it.

'There it is,' said Cat. 'Just like he said it was.'

'Yup,' said Joe, resting his arm across her shoulders. 'The clock at the end of the world.'

He'd cut his hair and looked much younger, Cat thought.

She also liked the fact he was only wearing one earring these days, and that was a silver eagle feather that she'd bought him.

He didn't look like just any old Joe in some dark-thrash-metal band now. He looked like his own man, but he also looked like her own Joe again. And the long green tweed coat that Victor loved and which he now wore looked, to her eyes, much cooler than the skanky leather jackets he used to wear.

Annie walked round the stand, looking at the clock faces.

'These clocks are all different,' she said, checking her watch. 'And all wrong.'

'No,' said Cat, smiling with the memory of the clock on a distant and very different shore. 'They're all right. Just not here. They're all right somewhere else. Come on.'

She led them across the sand to the very edge of the water, and they stood looking out at the Atlantic.

Sam cleared his throat.

'I don't know what to say,' he said.

'Yeah you do,' said Cat. 'He wrote it in the book.'

She reached into her pocket and pulled out a small oilskin notebook. It had been in an envelope on Victor's desk, amongst his papers, and the envelope had had her name on it. The book was blank except for one page of writing at the front.

'This is for us,' she said, and read the first line. 'Keep your face always toward the sunshine – and shadows will fall behind you.'

She pointed to the second block of writing and held

it out for Sam to read.

'And this is for him,' she said. He looked at it, and nodded, taking a moment.

'It was his favourite,' he said.

'So read it,' said Cat simply.

Sam cleared his throat again and began.

'Sunset and evening star,
And one clear call for me!
And may there be no moaning of the bar
When I put out to sea . . .'

His voice gained strength as he read the next three short verses, and as he got to the final hopeful lines, Cat stepped across the line between dry and wet sand, opened the urn and shook the ashes up into the sunset.

'Safe home,' she said softly. 'I hope I'm doing this right.'

A sudden skirl of evening breeze took the ashes and twisted them high into the sky, and as they all turned and watched the cloud winnow upwards against the rose gold of the sinking sun, it seemed to Cat for a moment that the cloud took shape, and that shape was of four men, one in a long flapping coat, one with a mohawk and long rifle, a man with a sword, and his hand on the shoulder of the fourth man, who had only one leg.

And then, just before the wind dispelled the illusion, she was sure that the man in the flapping coat murmured something as he raised a hand and waved back at them, and despite herself she answered, and then he seemed to reply before turning and joining his companions as they walked up into the light.

She felt the tears on her cheeks as the wind cooled them, but they weren't only tears of sorrow, though she was sad that only she would have seen what she'd just glimpsed, and only she would understand and take comfort from it.

She turned and looked at her silent family.

They all looked dumbstruck with amazement.

Her heart stuttered.

'That was—' she began to explain.

Sam just reached out and hugged her to him, his face shining with wonder.

'I know who they were, Cat. He read me the same books too.'

Cat didn't know how it was possible to feel sad yet have her heart soar so high at the same time.

'What did he say?' said Joe. 'I'm sure he said something.'

'I thought it was the wind . . .' said Annie, hesitantly.

'He said "I'll be seeing you",' said Cat. 'And I said "When?"'

She took a deep breath and felt the clean sea air fill her lungs and buoy her up.

'And he said: "Once upon a time . . ."'

Acknowledgements

I fell in love with swashbuckling adventure stories at a very early age, and for that (and a great deal else) I thank my parents who first read to me, and then pointed me at the right books (and films) to keep the fire burning.

When I was half way through this book and definitely needing to recharge my batteries for the final push, Nick Barley of the Edinburgh Book Festival allowed me to curate a one-day micro-fest called 'Story Machines'. One of the many pleasures of this was to compère a conversation between William Nicholson and Alan Moore who might seem very different writers but are equally and extraordinarily open-handed and inspiring, huge in both talent and heart. The talk became such a generous and passionate discussion about creativity that sitting between them was like being stuck between the shiny globes of a giant Van de Graaff generator as bolts of pure energy sparked from one to the other: there may be better ways to recharge ones batteries, but I can't think of one more enjoyable or exhilarating:

I'd like to thank them both for that, and Nick for the opportunity.

By no coincidence, I know the 'story space' that Cat falls into in this book is a terrain absolutely contiguous with Alan's 'Idea Space', and what Victor says about it is so heavily influenced by Alan's perceptions that it leads me to believe Victor must have heard him talk about it, maybe once upon a time in Northampton . . .

And speaking of inspiration, thanks as always to Domenica, and to all the other inspiring girls, especially the ones who swim the bracing waters off North Uist with us every August: Rose, Molly and Hannah. Here's to first in, last out: Barnaby, you're not a girl, but thanks for being a fellow walrus.

I owe a serious debt of gratitude to two doctors – Jacques Kerr of the Borders General Hospital for taking time out of a very busy schedule to talk me through the intricacies of Emergency Medicine in general, and the scary world of head injuries in particular, and to his colleague Victoria Dobie for introducing me to him in the first place. Any technical inaccuracies are absolutely mine and not his.

I also owe both the unsinkable Winnie Brook-Young on Skye and the extraordinarily gifted Gaelic singer Paul McCallum from North Glendale, South Uist for helping me come up with what I hope are still suitably atmospheric and correct Gaelic place names: *Mòran taing, agus slàinte mhòr agad.*

Finally, this book is also dedicated to the very lovely

and much-missed Katie Pearson, who knew a thing or two about guts and real girls rescuing themselves. See you further along up the road, my friend. Don't worry. We'll find you by the sound of your laughter . . .

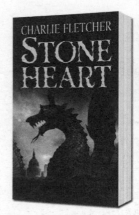

MIST

The last shred of the mist swirled and drew back, and she saw where she was. She was very, very far from home.

Midnight: a mist-haunted wood with a bad reputation. A sweet sixteen party, and thirteen-year-old Nell is trying to keep her sister, spoilt birthday-girl Gwen, out of trouble. No chance. Trouble finds Gwen and drags her through the mist.

Only Nell guesses who's behind the kidnap - the boy she hoped was her friend, the gorgeous but mysterious Evan River.

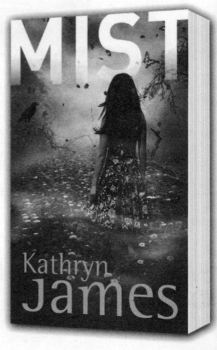

Kathryn James

Available as eBook

www.kathrynjames.co.uk
www.hodderchildrens.co.uk

Hodder Children's Books